DeepStorm OutTack

George S Boughton

First published 2012
Published by GBP GB Publishing.org 2013

Copyright © 2012 George S Boughton
All rights reserved.
ISBN: 978-0-9572970-8-1

A catalogue record of this book is available from the British Library

Cover design ©2013 GBP

terms * in the Glossary Copyright © 2012 George S Boughton

GB Publishing.org
www.gbpublishing.org

For Natasha

Acknowledgement
Grateful thanks for their constant support and encouragement
through the years to Brenda Marsh and Carolyn and David Andrew

Contents

Commander's Log   Boxing Day (26 Dec) 2067

Mankind has the potential to be what we abhor most – devourer of worlds – having come perilously close to wrecking our own planet. Yet we still have the chance, on the very verge of leaving *home*, leaving *Mother Earth*, to instead join in redefining ourselves as master builders in the cosmos.

Right now, nature seems to be challenging that resolve to the limit. Ever since the relentless quakes, tsunamis and floods early this century – in Indonesia, Pakistan, Haiti, Japan, New Zealand, China, Egypt, USA and elsewhere – we have had to create ever more Construction Exclusion Zones (in areas most at risk of disaster) whilst also coping with exploding population densities.

The devastation has been horrendous, with no let-up in sight. Some even fear the Earth's surface breaking up – as catastrophically, possibly, as when the dinosaurs went extinct.

And yet our extraterrestrial migrations, now underway, will take decades before they even begin to mitigate the risks to mankind.

We have to move fast. *We* have to understand what's going on with nature, before it's too late for billions of people on the ground.

That is *our mission.*

Destiny

1

The unsuspecting inductee under my gaze stood marvellously entranced in the same verdant landscape of grassless seed ferns as when desolation choked and leached out plains, glades and moors stretching from sunrise to sunset around the globe.

In the garden modelled on that ancient time, Mei's clear eyes gleamed with the awe of a small child – no doubt imagining the brilliant flash eclipsing the sun, the deafening shockwave coursing from noxious fallout, cinders falling onto the fanned-out leaves of lakeshore ginkgo trees, acid raindrops splashing on rocks dappled with lichen and moss, dark shadows drawing over estuary dunes and marshes, fires raging in giant conifer forests. Throughout the lands, smouldering as if supervolcanoes had spewed out globally, she would scan seashells piled up on shorelines amongst the carcasses of giant plesiosaurs and mosasaurs, and tree branches draped with rotting pterosaurs, while prehistoric opossums and iguanas burrowed to safety beneath ash and dust. Signs of carnage would pervade everywhere, dinosaurs reel and gasp their last breaths with just a few – cormorants, flamingos, parrots, penguins and, oddly, even flightless ostriches – somehow managing to flee or hide.

The ardent young observer had always marvelled at this dramatic depiction, despite knowing it was NOT reality. For that, to see the real effect of the impact, she would reflect solely on coastal waters wafting with the death-throes of invertebrate clams, snails, slugs and such. As in present times, the blue waters everywhere else simply teemed with fish without the presence of marine reptiles and pterosaurs, whilst birds overflew plains eerily devoid of giant dinosaur herds.

I could just see her stepping back to reflect on the entire living planet, known as the entity *Gaia*, at one moment having a distinctly reptilian semblance and the next looking, well, more modern with no clue whatsoever as to what had happened in between to all the reptiles. Extinctions as selective as that were hard to come by and even harder to explain. And then wham, right at the end, life in the shallow seas was annihilated.

In Paleorama, a study of Earth's paleogeography through time, Mei would have seen attempts to explain other weird bouts such as that. She'd first come to my attention as a fresh young zoology and subsequently palaeontology undergraduate at Beijing University, China – when she was engaged in the *Late-Cretaceous* chapters of that ambitious project. I'd checked out her work, with a hunch I had on whether the planet could somehow have been slammed into Natural Selection on steroids! If true, then this might have been a good bet for what was again happening to our world.

I felt so strongly about this that I was set on fully researching it and, though I had to await clearance, I expected Mei's specialist knowledge to make a stellar contribution in doing just that 'upside' [a phrase used by World War II fighter pilots, now understood everywhere as extraterrestrial]. There was a directive of 'UNSDO' [UN Strategy Development Organisation] – a permanent agency of the Security Council – for a number of research agencies, ours included, to relocate to the *Near Earth Territories*. Such initiatives were expected to kick off the greatest land rush and skills drain of the 21st Century.

Of course, I hadn't expected any of our inductees to have a problem with that. Most girls laughed at the reluctance of some grandmothers to leave terra firma. Except, of course, for the serious minded Dr Mei Sai Ling, who had a pain in the ass predisposition to stay grounded right there! "If God had intended us to be space dwellers," I'd once heard her chide, "we'd be made of what – carbon nanotubes?" No lack of confidence in her. And yet, she was not far off the mark. Our guys were made differently from others, to ensure they could go.

No matter, she simply had to be brought round. There was no question, in my mind, that mankind had to get up there, and I was envious as hell of our lot's abilities to do just that. It was the crowning moment of the incredible line of vertebrates – having mastered swimming in the seas, braved crawling onto the land and taken boldly to the skies – that we'd now spawned colonists for the microgravity-ocean of space. After all, what we'd always been about was to adapt. And not just to 'terraform' [make habitable] anywhere

6

as parochial as the Moon or Mars. Not when there was the great expanse of the cosmos itself to wander endlessly through, and master. No, these guys were meant to grasp that opportunity as earth-spacelings.

Ah, but coming back to Mei. What had struck me as awkward was that she'd ensconced herself far from loved ones, in a paleobotanical garden on Moloka'i, Hawaii, where she'd immersed herself in field research so passionately. Naturally I was okay with that, I had to be, before events would soon overtake us all. Yet, as our programme's Chief Scientist, what vexed my mind was pulling her, along with all the others, from wherever they were. I knew what we'd be doing to their personal lives, and I didn't relish doing that to them. But then... outweighing everything was saving the planet.

For now it was simply gratifying to see that Mei had adjusted, to being an outdoor type, when she'd grown up only knowing the clamour of city life. And I imagined her to be at least pleased that her Shanghai pallor, a legacy of life in that city of perpetual smog, had brightened with the clear air and splendid nutrition of this place.

Images of her continued to flow into my head – her fine hands now propping a slender neck as she lay there, peacefully and serene upon the pungent earth – her every move transmitted via the cellphone 'biombot' [bionic communications nanobot], an implant all of us in the programme had. Specifically switched on for me, I was receiving and enjoying 3-D images of her from park optics.

Just then, my focus was diverted. "Professor Mark Madison wanted in Block 3." I moved on as directed, whilst my mind conjured up Mei's thoughts on the asteroid impact massively wiping out life. Having come to know her love of music, I envisaged her accompanying the global melt down with Mussorgsky's demonic 'Night on Bald Mountain' and the recovery with Beethoven's 'Spring Sonata'. And with that recovery she would muse over breaks in the pall opening, the strong enriching sunlight seeping across lands and waters and fresh mists and greenery suffusing all.

Her rice-white lids closing, she'd then undoubtedly go over what was really known about Gaia's bizarre rebirth – while marine life populated shallow seas anew, sharks still chased large prey about blue waters and large crocodiles still cruised up murky rivers in search of the 'dawn' creatures (beaver, horse, deer, hippopotamus, elephant, primate, marten, armadillo) of today's fabulous biodiversity on continents. Whilst all that remained of the once mighty dinosaurs were birds and fossilising bones, their beings having already slipped into ghostly silence.

I watched Mei rise, her glossy black ponytail swishing beneath a rhino-horn topknot. Atypically, for I'd noticed she was a tad vain about her looks, her forehead creased. Advances in g-cosmetics – the salons now awash with such runaway genetic products dwarfing the recreational drugs trade – ensured she could rough it glamorously out there.

Not that this vanity distracted her scientific focus, as I'd witnessed in the argument to which she always returned, "So what's the answer to that dramatically weird transformation? How come clams and sharks met with such different fates, and crocodiles, horses and dinosaurs too? Coincidence? Different forces at work? Rubbish!" I so liked that icy directness of hers, swivelling on her heals to get mean with her subject. "Poop! Coincidence! No such thing! Some bastard phenomenon must have radically altered the matrix of life, thrown the Natural Selection of reptiles upside down, so much more clinically than mere fire and brimstone could have done. But what? What was that?"

That question had hounded Mei through her highly imaginative childhood, and had later inspired her to write copious notes for that hitherto patchy chapter in Paleorama. And all the while her gut instinct had her wondering about any of that primeval past recurring. I suspected she was right. That, in all probability, something of the sort was behind the escalation in natural disasters witnessed this millennium.

On her journey home, blissfully unaware of her partially activated biombot transmitting anything she said, Mei quipped aloud, "Solving this is as hard as locating spit on the summit of Everest." This was for her a sad reflection that several of her earlier premonitions had merely remained fragile theories. "Just as you think you've got it, you find only snow and ice."

Arriving home – a translucent 'terra-sphere' [a habitable and self-contained space life-raft] perched high on a canopy walkway – Mei glanced at the crystal paperweight-like server on her desk. Everything passed on by her biombot today would be in there, ready for her continuing work on her Master's paper.

Before settling down to it Mei tidied her hair in a mirror and chose to spend time with Twing, a playful robot so named because he was 'twee' and of no particular animal order. "You're just my *thing*," she reminded it fondly, patting his head while at the same time popping a button to set a cocoa-tea brewing. This in hand, she skirted around her sofa-bed touching and talking to flourishing pot plants, but sparing no words for the remarkably 'alive' plant holograms. "They okay, you reckon?" she playfully asked Twing, whose ears twitched in response. "Hmm mm, delicious those hologram scents!" she added and watched his nose now twitching, too.

For *'The Balance of Nature in Terraforming the Planet'* – Mei's paper sponsored by 'WOMB' [World Organisation for Maintaining the Biosphere] – plant specimens were not all she studied. "You'd think, maybe," she said wryly, "I hadn't tinkered enough – you know, to turn this place into Natural Selection *hell* for reptiles. Then we should have ended up with some idea about their Mass Extinction sixty-five million years ago, right?" She regarded the plants again, now with mock dismay, "Yeah, well, okay! A tintsy bit too healthy looking for that."

With no additional evidential lead from the plant life, Mei scratched the tip of her nose and then, after adding some finishing touches to her paper, declared, "Damned planetary cancer. *That's* what doomed the dinosaurs."

Still observing her via the Biombot, I did not then imagine how insightful her seemingly flippant sentiment would prove to be. For now, her look and tone were contrite. "That's it then! No closure for any reptile ghosts out there," she said apologetically, but then added, "Anyhow, what could I alone possibly have contributed?"

That cheerful modesty was something I sought for my teams, as much as her cheek in inviting everyone with the words, "Come see *my* authentic garden," when they all knew it to be the University of Hawaii's *Cretaceous* Park, designed thanks to the collaboration of international universities and museums.

One impromptu tour she'd give was through a *Mid-Cretaceous* glade, stocked only with conifers, ferns and cycads, by the seashore. It was there that Mei had ended the day taking around a professor of marine biology named Rad – to whom she'd uncharacteristically directed a passing remark when he was sitting at a nearby beach-bar, which had led to him chatting her up.

I noticed she'd taken far more elation and pride in casually showing this amenable looking guy around than when escorting others. Certainly she looked alluring in a black one-piece swimsuit with burgundy blouse floating about her trim frame and a gentle breeze vitalising her sleek hair. Nonetheless, the girl's expression betrayed only her more characteristically august feelings for the area. "What do you make of it? Strange, huh?" she asked him, dimples creasing just a little to encourage his response, "See? No palm trees on this tropical shoreline. That's how it was, at that time, no flowering plants."

Noticing Rad's gaze fixed not on the landscape but on her, Mei blushed and turned to lead him along the shore towards the exit.

The next morning the biombot transmitted to me Mei's lean frame, clad in the swimsuit. She was strolling along, her bony feet progressing through wavelets that lapped on the sand. What struck me most in that moment was her fiery gaze. I was taking stock of her and all our candidates for recruitment, strictly in the international interest, with notes that were passed on to me by an 'AI' [Artificial Intelligence]. These included, most intimately and delicately, what Mei was just then diarising in the biombot, "Not at all like me – to meet a guy in a bar!" She kicked off with her usual reserve but then came more girly intimations (and certainly she had no idea I was eavesdropping): "No matter, these whiffs of sea air are rekindling my mood today... Rad's eyes, hmm, honey sweet... that rugged body... hmmm, tousled ginger hair less irresistible perhaps... his Aussie quips were fun though... rugby tops football! His head-spinning cocktails certainly got me into those arms... Wow! Lips... that kiss!

"Yikes! Eighteen years my senior! Yeah? But he's strong, engaging, spontaneous. Okay, more is, we really have things in common – extinctions, overpopulation, reviving wildernesses, Climate Change..."

I found it hard to believe that this particular girl had connected so quickly with this guy. Of course, I could have enlightened her some on the present climate, with signs of an end to sea levels rising. For now though what was so extraordinary, and what I wanted, was

Mei's single-mindedness. For even on what had turned out to be an intimate and even passionate evening, she had still got onto her pet subjects, with unrelenting seriousness! Given the serious goals we had to achieve, this was great news for me.

"He mentioned he'd be studying kelp reforestation, funded by ecotourism. That'd be massive, contributing to biosphere maintenance the same as in the *Cretaceous* period! Except," she suddenly crossed her arms and dug her painted fingernails into them, "in nearby seas? He'd mentioned doing it in nearby seas! I told him the new appointment, for research out there, was mine! I wanted it, but yes, I remember now – he chuckled!" Her mind spun, her expression one of disbelief, "Huh! What a fool I was! He didn't care!" This was more like her, detached and now antsy.

It was hardly fair, I felt. Her new study into deep cold-water corals would have thrown fresh light on paleoclimatology. But my overriding concern was how she was going to deal with the let-down. Ominous files on Mei revealed a vicious prep school temper that had earned her the nickname RaptorMei, after her unusual interest in *Cretaceous* velacoraptors. "Seen her open a carton?" classmates had cruelly taunted, making claw-like ripping motions with their index fingers.

As it happened, she was remarkably in control, which was fortuitous. For, where she was destined to go, such qualities would prove vital and anything short of it would have failed her.

Calmly averting her gaze seaward, Mei waded out and slipped under the tranquil surface. Immersed there, motionlessly she whiled away time, apparently enjoying the sensual caress of currents that could perhaps soothe her ire.

I knew differently – something extraordinary was taking place. Along with her muscles firming to bring a special agility – something I'd watched develop in her over the years – they also now enforced a fearless relaxation. Deep down this must have told her something about who and what she was, despite the hard time she'd had growing up with it. Yet, all she'd ever wanted was to be ordinary. I'd related to that and just wished I could have consoled her with how she was to fit in to our upside programme.

Flexing muscles in her superbly graceful limbs Mei leapt from the water and, raptor-fast, slender feet scarcely touching down, pounded from surf and sand to flagstone path. Further along, she disappeared purposely into the trees to crouch out of sight. This caution sprang from the secrecy she'd pledged to her father – not to display the ability growing within her, which would ultimately render her so very different from her peers.

Whereas the changes had been subtle from birth, they now increasingly kept her apart. She was forbidden from telling anyone of this, even though Mei was not a solitary child. She had a sibling, a brother, but she'd not been able to confide even in him about her changing condition. Little by little, perhaps out of fear of harming someone, she had shied away from gregariousness and become quite introverted. "Oh hell, what it'd be to be free!" she sometimes diarised, "To know what it is to let up! Really let up, with *someone!*"

To me the isolation, which in part kept her on Earth, brought maturity beyond her years but also rendered her socially fragile, as in now not wanting to be left out. "Rad, wanna be my soul mate? My confidant?" After all, in company we all seek some mirroring of ourselves, to know ourselves by. "But, oh no! Amazing as it was, you had to go and trash it, didn't you?"

Grunting dismissively she took off again, her slight form flitting wraith-like through the forest. On reaching her rope ladder she flew up to where, alone in her own domain, she could release the surge of power and rekindle contact with her cheerier more accessible self. Except... "Shit! It was fun last night! A pleasant relief!" She broke, then, pouting and looking around dolefully as if for a reassuring embrace. "Dad?" Mei whispered, "Dad?" And there it came, his bass tone entering her mind, prompting her about a dive trip she'd taken bookings for that morning, "Duty before self", and then adding in reference to her predicament, "Tackle crisis before emotion".

His was a tough line and noble, too. Mindful that it was the middle of the night in Shanghai, Mei didn't call. "Huh! You'd bloody well lose your cool too, dad," she murmured, looking beyond the window at nothing in particular, "Over what? Some guy? What a waste!"

The tipping point I was still looking out for was Mei losing her temper. Her private life was of interest to me only in whatever might aid or impair our teamwork. We had to know them all, that well, to be one hundred percent sure of them. So I was relieved to see her take her edginess into the therapeutic storm-shower and reappear soothed and toned, albeit looking dripping mad from the heat.

Happily, Twing sprang into action, landing heavily on the sofa-back to hand her a silky robe, his peculiar face offering a daft disarming smile. "You dumb jerk," she levelled, her look purposely disapproving, though suppressing laughter.

Calmed and assuming a professional manner Mei called the Dean, who confirmed that the university position had indeed been taken. He denied having misled her, apologised if that was how she saw it, and expressed regret that he could divulge nothing more. Except, finally, worn by her gentle persistence, the now tired man let slip that the fellowship had gone to a professor, one Rad Traker.

"That's it!" Mei grimaced, prompting Twing to return another daft smile. "The fellowship is really, really, gone! Fuck!" Twing, having no archived reference for her current expression or mood, resorted to offering a meow and purr. Mei's fury rose higher. "He's got it!"

A moment later she became doubly fraught, "Shit – and crap! I've passed up Cambridge University, England, the only other place I wanted!"

I could not tell, but maybe it was then that it crossed her mind that she was jealous. However, when Twing, determined in his be-a-cat pursuit, curled his genetically cultured fur into a silver ball and snuggled comfortingly into her lap, Mei's expression changed. Some weight appeared to lift from her. Slowly she stretched her arms high, pushed out her lithe legs and, truly cat-like, exclaimed, "Heck. What the hell?"

Did I pity this studious wisp of a girl? Sure. But then, I'd seen so many of our candidates with emotions shoved into hyper-drive by hormones raging in their highly tuned bodies.

As it turned out, however, Mei's angst was by no means over. Wearing an elegant white bathing suit, linen jacket and sailor's cap, she'd have made her dad proud, more so by her spirit now composed. Thus she arrived, the embodiment of efficiency at the dive boat she skippered part-time. With one foot on the boat step, and about to board, catching sight of Rad made her head turn so sharply that her ponytail swished like the tail of an irritated stallion.

Casually attired in shorts and top, he was stashing gear into a big powerboat. Although her body stood motionless, her expression flashed from clear admiration to a searing scowl – and with it her muscles kicked in, taking her full steam towards the guy in her sights.

Rad, squatting on his broad bare feet, felt the timber-decked pier reverberate and, seeing Mei approach, rose with a smile and open arms. But his pleasure was instantly dashed by the look of burning dry ice on the girl's face. "G'day," he greeted, voice warm, still hoping for a better response than could be predicted.

The boat listed as her feet landed on the stern. "Oops," he gibed, a tad stilted. "Want to sink us?"

Mei wasted no time. "You've won the place in Manoa?" She was not curt, clearly benefitting from the persistent redressing of her sibling in childhood. Nonetheless, her brows were knit and eyes tightened when she added, "The one paleo-marine place going?" Rad merely looked bemused and then confused her all the more. He shrugged. Mei was stupefied. There was no fight. "Pity," her tone levelled out, "I was after that."

"Oh," he wasn't about to be drawn, "The fellowship, huh?" His firm tone conveyed he would not be drawn into troubled waters.

Mei broke. Ponytail whipping round, she grabbed at the remote control on the dashboard, eyes sparkling, her index finger caressing the button and scanning his face for a reaction. Gaining no response, she shrugged and clicked. "Whoops," she taunted, now expecting a reaction.

As the powerful engine roared into life, Rad only returned a resolute grin. That did it. Her second click released all lines. "Whoops, again," she declared.

While glancing around to check for any hazards, Rad was also anticipating her next possible move. His look now appeared to encourage her to take the boat out. Her resolve grew. Eyes dancing, she yelled, "Wait for it!" And, without a wait, her hand thrust the throttle wide open.

The cannonball lurch whisked Rad off his feet and felled him onto the stern. "Oomph!" he protested, as the powerful jet-keel rode seaward. "Is this part of the grand tour?" he taunted.

Mei was oblivious. "Wow!" she whispered to herself, clearly thrilled by the awesome power at her fingertips, the broad flat wake behind them, and even Rad's unflappability, all of which she had not anticipated. "Heck!" For all her lashing out, the guy could not be dented. "How good natured is this hunk?" she murmured, eyeing him carefully.

It was then that she also noticed where novices were approaching the dive school and, further along the coast, where a film crew was in a sandy cove. "I guess you won't be working today, stuntman," she shouted, alluding to some part-time work he had mentioned when they met yesterday.

"Fuck 'em," although with a professorial grant affording him few luxuries, he was already regretting the loss of a day's pay, "I'll dazzle 'em later."

As the craft sped along and the shoreline slipped by, Rad sank into his own thoughts, leaving the boat and direction entirely in her hands.

Finally, when the boat eased up and stopped in the lee of an islet, he rose fully resolved to comfort her for the loss of the job she clearly had wanted very badly. To his amazement, however, Mei had gone. In the brief instant of stopping, she'd flown to the bow, thrown in the anchor and was now kneeling to watch it settle at the reef edge.

Judging by his consternation, I knew he had never seen anyone move so fast. "Oh, no," she whispered, instantly looking up at the disbelief in his eyes, a thinly apologetic smile overtaking her dread of putting him off. That damned unwanted agility had frightened others off. Strangely enough, the fellowship issue seemed to shrivel in importance now. She smiled at him disarmingly and, relieved to receive her sweeter approach, Rad felt it appropriate to tease her a little. "So, all this because of my fellowship, huh?"

"Hah! *My* fellowship!" Mei snapped, quite enjoying the spark between them. "I'd won it," she added, under her breath. Strangely this link appeared to be bonding them again, although both looked a little awkward. Grasping for more common ground, Mei spoke hesitantly, "Dinosaurs. I have to discover what happened to them." He raised an eyebrow, responding, "Whatever it was, it was devastating beyond belief." Her eyes searched his, "Really. Can you imagine dominant creatures wiped clean from the planet like that? Just imagine it happening again – to us?"

Eagerly he added an angle, "Hailstorms." He braced himself for her to go with him on this. "You know – a gigantic cosmic jet-stream, millions of tonnes of it stretched out over millions of

kilometres, intermittently hitting the atmosphere with hailstorms...
Vaporising on entry, those would have what?"

"Heated higher layers on entry, and then cooled the atmosphere,"
delighting in finishing his words she was now dancing with them,
"by blanketing it with more cloud cover..."

"Exactly," he cut in. "In some ways having the same effect as..."

"A millennium long flood basalt eruption. Climate Change!
Like in the world having no summers through that time..."

They debated the idea, then both shrugged, having no clue
whatsoever as to what the ultimate impact on the climate would be.
What they did recognise was a rapport that felt electric and inspiring.
They had twirled out their concepts as if a natural duo, bringing Rad
to a tangible conclusion. "Hey! Do you reckon the Dean would go
for a joint study?"

Mei, still caught up in their cataclysmic concepts, was rapidly
shifting on, "Massive eruptions like that occurred through the three-
million year decline of the dinosaurs, forming the Deccan Traps in
India," she was eagerly seeking his attention to this point. "Huge
walls of lava, a thousand kilometres long, generated millennia long
mega-storms..." She stopped abruptly, his last question registering.

"Hell! The two of us, working together?" her puckish smile said
it all, "You feel it too? We're a team now? Dino hunters, huh?"
With zeal she could no longer contain, her fingers shot alarmingly to
the handrail next to him.

Noting its speed, nonetheless he reached to hold her hand and
fondly inspected the brilliant genetically sculptured moles that
shaped a green Chinese dragon across the knuckles of her left hand
and a red across those of her right. Their vividness absorbed him,
until suddenly his attention was diverted to the sea around them.

Quickly reaching for ping-pong ball size probes, he was floating
them on the water when he noticed the temperature reading on his
wristband and dipped his fingers in while swishing his hand around.
"Jesus! Hot enough for a sudsy soak – and rising!"

"Diversionary tactics?" Mei teased. "You want to play-act with
this poor cheated postgrad?"

Determined not to freak her out Rad rose and drew her close, his
voice low, "Look!" He pointed to the water, "There's a feeding
frenzy coming our way." True, beyond the stern the formerly

tranquil surface was breaking up, pierced by fins and agitated by wild thrashings.

Mei, obliviously ignoring the water, was arching her back in response to his closeness and lifting her face to his in expectation. "Feeding frenzy! Funny way to describe feelings, but that's okay," she murmured, aching to bury herself within his being.

Rad snapped. Drawing to his full height he gripped her shoulders, "Look!" Compelled by his tone, Mei stared around them.

Shoals of fish leapt up from the water. Dead fish floated by. "Think zoology. Think animal behaviour. Your specialisation, yeah?" Exasperated at her lack of immediate comprehension, Rad shook her, "The water's near scalding. Heat dulls inhibition, releasing aggressive tendencies." Anxiety increasing, his pitch rose. "For Christ's sake!" He turned her head, as shapes longer than the boat streaked past, "See! Even docile reef sharks have gone fucking psychopathic. They're attacking each other. What the fuck's going on?"

A bump to the hull and the boat lurched sideways. He struggled to keep their balance, recognising that Mei was at last alert to the dangers increasing around them.

Any other time the girl might have marvelled that even bigger sharks had survived the *End Cretaceous Mass Extinction,* but now she could only gape at them in horror.

Rad grasped for control. "Let's hope those are getting the hell out of here – as we must!" He raced to haul in the anchor. Mei reacted instantly, reaching to fire up the engine, but then it came – a deafening blast that hurled her over the windscreen onto the bow, where she lay mildly concussed, blood trickling from her lips.

I watched in admiration as Mei's eyes flashed open, her raptor transformation taking hold. Adrenaline coursed through veins, her body rapidly transforming as the fight-or-flight instinct surged and the girl rose into a fierce crouch.

Holding this stance she glanced around for Rad. He was no longer on board. In seconds she located him over the bow, splashing in the simmering sea, blood releasing from a gash on his terror-filled face. Hands lunging into the hot water she aimed to pull him amidships where it could be easier to pull him over the gunwale. "Get up here, now! Now, Rad!"

It was her super-agility that had built over the years, not the strength to save this man now. Momentarily weakened, Mei sank to the deck, chastising herself, "Dumb ... so dumb of me. Why did I bring us out here!"

Again she rose, arms descending over the gunwale, fingernails ripping on Rad's T-shirt, hot salt water splashing and stinging her skin and eyes, seeing through the blur his burning tear-streaked face mirroring her horror.

As their eyes locked in mutual helplessness the blackened palm trees on the islet, suddenly silhouetted against a fountain of red lava, disappeared into billowing ash that ripped across at them with a fiery blast.

~*~

2

Summer 2063

After two decades of preparations the occasion was there – a UN Security Council Summit on the Near Earth Territories – for me to present my report on candidates and seek UNSDO approval for phase II funding. Our guys had come of age. It was time to get on with their recruitment and training, and formally go public with the programme.

However, though I'd prepared to speak confidently in my UK English, and my command of the sciences was never in doubt, we'd been gagged. All we heard, apart from mention of American and British intelligence somehow connected with sabotage of the Territories, was that our work was now classified. None of this made sense. We were scientists. Who would do this to us?

The timing for all of this was awful. While still mourning Mei, I had to let go, shut everything out, to concentrate on the other candidates. What made that hard was keeping my distance and not letting anyone else become as precious to me. On reflection I did really well, considering being in my sixties, by presenting a firm detached officer's face, living the lie – though, I'd rather have been regarded as a father image to these youngsters.

Thankfully a distraction arrived. Zeta station, at anchor off the Moon, gained my attention with a report on a discovery up there. So remarkable was it that I had to seize the initiative and schedule a hasty visit, ostensibly to organise the site's transfer to authorities. When in reality, envisaging the scientific community stampeding to the place, I had to get in quick to safeguard our mission's prior access to the findings. I had a UN 'D-Notice' [Disclosure Notice, or gag rule] slapped on it.

In the two days it took to reach the station, with the Moon to one side and three very distinctive Galahad hulls to the other, our view of them from the shuttle grew and grew. The Galahad hulls, mere skeletons at that time – each with outer walls of reinforcing steel forming a huge cage-like pipe one and a half kilometres in diameter and just as long – were the very impressive beginnings of the Near Earth Territories. Hanging there so magnificently, lights moved within as construction craft and workers whizzed about and welding arcs flashed. The teams were fixing laminated plates of carbon nanotubes to form concentric terraces and walls within the void. Other crews were busily pouring concrete into the hull walls and weaving pipes and cabling throughout. The whole venture was made viable with materials – volcanic ash, rock, water, iron, copper – mined and refined on the Moon and very economically 'blown' to the site in a tight tornado-like vortex.

With a footprint as big as a city district, and accommodating 150 stories within, each vessel would be by far the biggest structure, let alone biggest craft, there'd ever been. Even though I was fully conversant with their designs the sheer size of the operation stunned me every time I went up there.

It was another day before I alighted on the Moon's surface and thus my excitement had mounted about seeing the reported object first hand. Initially, we had to agree on procedures for the dig and prepare the equipment. I also had to debrief the survey team who'd come across it.

Once out there in the pitch black of the Moon's dark side, and with one-sixth my normal weight in 'MoonG' [Moon gravity], each bounce I cautiously took when stepping from the landing craft was agonisingly slow. My heart burned with anticipation until, amongst searchlight lit footprints in the drab dust, I saw the yellow marker planted next to a shallow crater.

Recording our progress, the cameraman at my side zoomed in on something protruding from the dusty crater wall. It was just as I'd seen in the images taken by the surveyors who'd found it strange enough to report to us. My alarm bells sounded. The elongated shape before me seemed so out of place amongst the irregularly shaped moon rocks in the vicinity. Containing my excitement, I leant over to study the object more closely in the camera's monitor.

Finally, with the camera still rolling, another guy slowly brushed away the dust to reveal a dull charcoal-like surface.

Astounded, and impatient to see more, I signalled the crew to use a hand-held scanner as well. "Christ! Is that...?" My heart thumped. My hand reached out as if to touch what appeared on the monitor. "What... a grainy texture? No!" Flabbergasted, I remained silent for a while, before whispering, "That's *not* what I think."

I rapidly signalled to the crew and on cue they gently introduced the nozzle of a vacuum pump to draw debris little by little off the object. As it appeared, everyone must have known or felt something was wholly 'wrong' here. My mind raced through the possibilities, most of all disturbed by the absurdity of what now looked like a palaeontological dig in outer space.

Reality prevailed. What looked like a tibia, or certainly something man-made that looked like bone, could have survived there from an early-day Moon-lander vehicle or from equipment in use today. This would be more plausible. My flash idea that it came from an animal faded. This 'bone' was far too big even for an elephant – and, its discovery couldn't have been a prank. The only tracks out there were left by its discoverers, added to now by us.

At last, the freed object was handled with surgical gloves and sealed in a canister. My final order was to have the site cordoned off, so that institutions could conduct further studies and for the UN to debate the claims and rights of member states to this as yet unidentified and extraordinary find.

We were in for a huge surprise. Back at the Zeta station lab examination of the vacuumed material revealed more than the bone-like fragment. The sudden commotion in the lab was but a faint precursor to what was about to break out in the media.

Charred organic material surrounding the specimen was positively identified as fallout debris from Earth! Incredibly, this ejecta had been preserved for eternity on the airless, weather-free, surface of the Moon. "Scientists will have a field day," I predicted. "Here comes the holy grail of palaeontology, especially if there are clues to identify whether the ejecta had been thrown up by a massive bolide – asteroid, meteoroid, comet or planetesimal – or from a supervolcano."

Meanwhile radiocarbon dating was already putting the age of the material, from different depths in the dig, at around the *Close* of the *Cretaceous* period.

The real surprise was when samples taken from the cleaned up specimen revealed it to be actual bone! "Unbelievable! We have bone – not a rock fossil." Words spilling, I was almost trembling in delight. "My God, is it possible? Could it really be from a dinosaur?" On closer inspection I even entertained another conjecture – the bone had belonged to a triceratops!

The possibilities were immense – a big enough sweep of the Moon and Mars might bag a sizeable cache of prehistoric bone and wood. Such specimens, perchance with some DNA intact, would have greatly enriched the paleobiogeography we hitherto had from the fossil record. Key to opening that up, as soon as this site could be substantially investigated and the findings published, I aimed to push for palaeontologists to have free rein upside. Hopefully we'd then gain some insight into what happened so long ago, and how we might best protect ourselves this time round.

~*~

3

Summer 2063

I used satellite-views to locate a candidate of ours, Sashia Dubchek, in the outskirts of Motyklejka. She was easy to spot where she'd stopped on the dazzlingly white Sea of Okhotsk, Siberia. I then received close-ups of her, in white snow-gear, sitting astride a battered pink snowmobile.

A white hare dived headlong into a snowdrift near her and over the windscreen she spied the humps of a white Bactrian camel. Smiling, she swung her machine up the slope in its direction and over the top spied her favourite uncle, also head to toe in white snow-gear.

Pulling up sharply, she swung ungainly legs off the saddle and lunged towards him for a welcome hug. Then, standing solidly in her thick leather thigh boots, topped with fur, she pushed closer to him purposely to share his view of the wide river stretching before them, a view defining his preparedness to venture out alone and then go upside soon after returning from the wilderness.

I watched her there, in the everlasting daylight of 'white nights', looking at the wide horizon he was sure to miss. I was sure she'd have thought about all the beautiful old cities she wanted to visit and so, naturally, I empathised with her wanting to stay put, here on Earth, although it was also easy to imagine her feeling left behind when he'd gone.

Her expression read, "This is so like you," while his glance at her legs betrayed thoughts of her physical disability – that were ended, abruptly when she tapped an index finger on his lips and then hit him with a stream of descriptions of classmates at the graphic design college from which she'd recently graduated. Sashia rambled on, though now to divert him from the can of oil she was taking from her haversack and how she was then draining her engine sump onto the snow. She didn't dare look back at him as the black slick trickled over the snow towards the gently flowing waters.

He remained silent. "What?" Sashia's laugh did not convince. "Some Green GDP officials might come by? Way out here?"

Task completed, she joined him at the campfire and chattered about keeping in touch with her former Singapore boarding school friends. Lobbing another log on the fire, sparks flying up, he noted her milky white face and brow, with deep-set eyes modestly shaded in her grandmother's tradition by a pink and mauve tribal scarf. Gently he reached over to slip it back and reveal the clear silver-blue of her eyes, her pretty Russian features, a face artificially enhanced only by purple eyeliner, a brushing of rouge on the cheeks and, above, Sashia's creamy blonde hair styled into a double Mohican.

Although I'd long been touched by that delightful caricature face of hers, and by her sweet nature, I was far more moved by how wounded she had been – by us.

"I was so privileged," she sparkled on about her school days, "having that experience of the world, I mean." She became a little wistful then. "Maybe I should have told my dad that? Do you think then he wouldn't have gone to work in structural engineering upside – I mean if I'd said that?"

Although she showed disinterest in space, I knew she had none of Mei's aversion to travelling up there. Sashia had spent most of her exeats with her Chinese nana – her actress mother working in the city of Magadan – and that's all she'd ever known, Earth-bound stuff. But, she was inquisitive, "So what was it that took him out there?"

"Double the pay. Big tax cuts." Her uncle's voice was comforting, "Spacious living – who could pass that up?" Although not trying to influence her, he still wanted to do a little more to defend her dad's and his own actions to be away in space, "It's not half bad. There are liners as big as many down here, with shopping malls and leisure facilities. It's a far cry from the cramped quarters of early space exploration." He didn't mind her mocked yawn. "As you walk around nowadays you feel your normal weight with 'EarthG' [Earth gravity]." He looked at her in a more cheery way. "Except *you* would also enjoy the relief of floating weightlessly, whenever you want."

Sashia had been the only casualty of our programme, with a condition that had long baffled physicians. From early childhood a complication in her vertebra had progressively impaired motor neurons in the lower portion of her central nervous system. Now she hardly had the use of her legs, other than for directing how she wanted to move.

Her 'smart' thigh boots were actually more like waders. Stiffened enough to take her full weight while flexible enough for fluid mobility, they 'carried' her almost as gracefully as others, though tragically not fully, and noticeably more powerfully.

Technology was advancing as never before. I had to reflect on how the land rush to the Territories was set to become as meteoric a growth industry as air travel, communications and media had once been. Public perceptions had changed. People no longer saw it as a leap of fantasy with limited possibilities. It had become a reality – as reflected in a recent media article, "If there's a snowdome in the desert of Dubai, why not up there?"

Bringing him down to Earth, Sashia changed subjects, "I just wish my momma had kept on at me to continue with my music. I did try dancing, when I was still able to. Anyhow I might take up an instrument again, in Hong Kong maybe. One of the girls has suggested," she continued brightly, never seeing herself as a victim, "that I look for work in a 'bomb ass' overcrowded metropolis like that."

He chuckled, full of admiration, and meant well quipping, "There are two guys, to every girl upside." Sashia feigned a flirtatious shrug. For her, bagging herself a 'hottie' was far more challenging than he could have imagined.

I shared his look of admiration. He would always be there for her and give her encouragement. Sadly, I had the unenviable task of judging her 'fit and able' for recruitment and training – and I was not about to do that for her sake alone, even though I knew all she wanted was to make it in the world on Earth. Nor would my decision be made out of guilt or sympathy. Simply, there was no room for stragglers where we were headed. Oddly, the very metal that made her fight despite her plight was what I needed in our teams. On the down side, she was among the least qualified professionally and not overly ambitious either.

On balance, considering solely what we were up against, I'd already marked her file *Marginal Prospect* – a shame because, despite all odds, Sashia was just as lively and had the same gregarious spirit as her nana. And certainly I'd been amazed at her tenacity, in the face of slowly losing leg muscles while gaining a super agility in her upper body. Of course she had lapses, moments when she felt horribly alone and different from others, especially now.

Naturally enough, she wasn't alone. Most of the other candidates had felt similarly isolated at times. So while parents had been given the opportunity for one child to have the enhancement, which for many was all the family they had anyway, we'd arranged for all to benefit from an overseas education with others in the programme. The plan was to have a richly mixed community, of backgrounds and aspirations, in the Near Earth Territories.

Eventually Sashia tired of chatting and, snuggling in to her sleeping bag, was soon falling asleep albeit with an odd sense of unrequited expectation.

She woke with a jolt to a whooshing sound. His dark purple snowmobile was revving up. Rapidly unzipping the sleeping bag, she leapt to bury her face in the shoulder of his jacket and give a huge hug to remember her by.

Some time later a patrol boat came to a stop and two green-uniformed guards alighted. Reaching Sashia, while one politely pulled her upright the other brought the can she'd discarded, still dripping oil. Not at all intimidated by the confrontation, she knew not to resist as they courteously but firmly escorted her to their craft to give her a fine. That done, they left.

Unperturbed, Sashia scanned the horizon and picked out her uncle now a long way off across the great gleaming expanse of white, and she smiled to see him and his Bactrian camel moving so slowly it was hard to tell if they were progressing anywhere at all.

Finally she looked up to the ever-blue sky, clearly appreciating its radiance and the hugeness of space. I also imagined her inwardly celebrating her freedom, feeling alive, and exuberant in her decision to head for Hong Kong. In the passion for music I knew she shared with Mei, I enjoyed thinking that perhaps she was matching her mood by summoning up 'Venus the Bringer of Peace' from Holst's 'The Planets'.

~*~

4

Summer 2063

In the metallic grey room with heavily framed doors, high walls and thick grated floor, a square-set mulatto, in his thirties, stood in matching grey suit, shirt and tie. Brandishing a wildly raked aerial hairstyle, one that shifted dynamically in sync with his passion, he also wore a crystal skull at the centre of a grey-green carnation buttonhole.

Stars twinkling in the blackness of space filled all portholes, the only movement there came when a second figure materialised. A smart navy-uniformed officer, in his twenties, he approached Vice President Duardo Contrea, with nerves that turned to ice even though he was not physically here but on 'holoe' [videophone hologram], "Sir."

Expecting the officer's call, and sensing rather than seeing his need for attention, the courteous VP returned a stare set in iron. Dispassion obvious, he focused on the scene behind the clean-cut young man – a forest clearing at dusk. "Everything's arranged?"

The VP scrutinised the scene as, on the grassy runway, limousines pulled up at the red-carpeted steps of an immaculately reconditioned Cessna Citation.

Out they came then, a bevy of heavy-set suits, all high-powered businessmen, departing with smiles to their liveried chauffeurs and greetings towards the primly attractive flight attendants.

"Yes, Sir," the officer responded smartly, barely daring anything further, "All directors are present. The crew is ready."

"Angela?" he holoed a boyish looking ruby red lipped aide and re-checked every planned detail with her. Finally, with one last question, "Press release uploaded?" he observed her confidently raised eyebrow, tilt of the head and betrayed hope for the barest hint of approval in his steely eyes.

Satisfied, holding the Cessna in his sights, he awaited its jets to fire up. Of rugged Incan ancestry Contrea had devoted his life to a tough, challenging clamber up the Manax Corporation ladder. He was brash about building Brazil's biggest timber business up to become a worldwide empire, whilst covertly – and very much for his own ends – aiming to redress imbalances in ethnic power. Now he was rubbing his hands. This flight would mark a new phase for both his endeavours.

As the executive jet taxied down the field, he saw the aluminium wings glisten as it rose into the evening sunlight to soar out over the ridge. With a powerful roar the jet banked and levelled, glare from the cockpit window blurring his view. Then the plane appeared to hold still and silent in the air.

Contrea's square fists clenched tightly and he gave out a strange little gasp, an equally odd glint in his eyes as they followed the slow spiralling nosedive that ended in a fireball explosion in the jungle foliage below.

In the ensuing hush, his cold eyes were fixed on the burning jungle. Then he strode away from the holoe, rasping, "How very unfortunate" and commanding the aide to, "Wait, with the breaking news on this most tragic of accidents. Let traffic control raise the alarm. Contact them now." Complicity hung there, in their eyes, before she disappeared. Soon, as President, he would appoint his own people to the Board.

He dismissed the holoed officer and, shoes resounding on the metal floor, was about to leave when another, more battle hardened officer, materialised in the room, "Sir. Classified information of ISWA's." The information he was passing had been gleaned from the International Spaceways Authority. Although the officer received an unwelcoming glare for daring to intrude on this the Vice-President's glorious moment, he remained unflinching. "We've located a reference in their database to 'threats of mass destruction'. It's now established that those are natural threats to the entire 'World' [Earth plus upside colonies]."

The VP remained disengaged allowing nothing to chip away his sense of accomplishment. At last he pivoted slowly in the officer's direction, attentive now and waving encouragement for more information.

The officer moved aside to bring on holoe of a frightened-looking man in cardigan and jeans. "What are those threats?" he demanded of the man, who shook his head wretchedly. Dispassionately the officer turned to Contrea. "He'll talk. We have his son. So far what we have is that this is by far the greatest risk from 'NEOs' [Near-Earth Objects] yet discovered." He qualified this for emphasis, "It's *not* just one. A whole spate of them is headed this way."

"NEOs? A spate, you say?" the VP's lids lowered. "Headed for Earth?" Suddenly he broke into laughter. "Hell! Double hell!" Elated, he stepped forward to observe Earth through a porthole. "What fun! What a show! Northern lights on steroids, coming to cinemas near you. Right *on* you, literally. Hah!

"What are the chances of that?" He grinned broadly. "This news arriving now? Today of all days!" The Presidency of his corporation, even of Brazil, fizzled out by comparison. "Huh? Bombardment after bombardment! Pulverising populations! Toppling economies and governments! Opening up territories." He paused, rubbed his hands with glee, and concluded, "For us! Huh? Ripe pickings – for *us!*" The full magnitude of the news now fully hit home. "We must hurry. It's so sudden."

Scarcely considering the gravity of his next order, before he dismissed the officer he ordered, "Learn all you can, then clean up." The ISWA captives were to be disposed of. As the officer saluted, making to leave, the VP stopped him and calmly drew him to view a screen on which, with the Moon as a backdrop, hung an enormous pipe. "*That* is Galahad, or rather, the start of it. The new world." Clearly in admiration, he also attempted to conceal his awe. "Spaceliners with complements of three and four hundred people ply close to Earth and the Moon. Every two years one goes to Mars. But *this* is altogether different. When finished," he waved his hands at the onscreen pipe, "this will be practically invincible. More armour plating is being added to withstand BoBo bombardments." The officer already knew that BoBos, as ISWA pilots referred to them, were boulder-bolides as small as coconuts and as big as vans.

"*This* is it," Contrea expounded excitedly, "the start of the massive Near Earth Territories. Others, hundreds and thousands of them, all loosely clustered together, will mushroom into a superpower colony as big as North America or even Greater Europe." The powerful vision gripped him. "It'll be like a second moon growing and shining out there as a beacon for the mass population of space. Except," he murmured, eyes narrowing, "it won't be peopled by the likes of us. Not by regular humans. They'll be young ZeroGs, a whole new 'ZeroG' [zero gravity or microgravity] tolerant breed. And the UN Security Council is planning to headquarter all of its permanent agencies there – UNSDO, 'UNNDC' [UN Natural Defences Committee], and 'UNRO' [UN Rapprochement

Organisation (successor in the same role as NATO) coordinating armed forces of Security Council members] – along with the UN Peacekeeping HQ, as defenders of the World, protectors of all mankind. UNNDC task forces will be out to stop threats like the NEOs. Stop our windfall BoBo storm! Stop *us*!"

Fury ebbed slowly from his eyes as he observed the dark hull against the silver Moon, "It's stupendous. Magnificent." Then, he spat out, "And it's toast! It can never be! We'll incinerate it, with everyone aboard!"

He turned to the officer, explaining, "There's a tiresomely meddling organisation behind this, in one or other of the Security Council agencies." His voice rose, his look manic, eyes burning and fixed on those of the officer, "with their loathsome candidates of *NEW BREEDS! I've issued the order – Find them! Find them all – and DESTROY THEM!*

~*~

5

Spring 2066

I knew Sashia would 'rock' in Hong Kong, Asia's World City, where the workplace 24/7 was anywhere 'connected' (and not in any communications dead-spot). This was just fine by her. Young and fresh to city life, she happily took to the open life of the streets – as a communal living room – where everyone lived, worked, mingled and shopped among café-bars, bistros and galleries, whatever the time of day or night. And as everyone else did she augmented her meagre income, from a job as a junior graphic designer, by waiting on tables or whatever else came her way – simply to pay her *Lifestyle* membership.

One of many such centres, Lifestyle provided large lockers for personal possessions, along with most of life's comforts – fitness facilities, changing rooms, domestic services, padded divans for lounging and sleeping on, first class airline style single and double bunks for privacy, crèches for kids, recreation areas, gardens and business rooms. Even schools were now connected with the centres, with open membership to sports grounds and other amenities. Since the explosion of 'highly developed' people in the 2020s to 30s, with prosperity, health and longevity now shared by all, apartment living – where privilege anyway bought little more joy than sharing three or more to a room – became a faded memory to all but the truly privileged or those keen to raise a family the old way, despite crippling costs.

This city life, globalised for most of the planet's population capped at ten billion – an incredible ten-fold increase in the one billion highly developed people (out of seven billion) at the start of the millennium – meant 'having it all' simply wasn't possible, that is not without the outbreak of wars! To accommodate everyone to the same standard as the western half of the European Union in the 2010s, would have necessitated an *impossibly huge* increase in the planet's usable land of 100 to 150 million square kilometres (subject to the progress we were actually making in terraforming deserts), between Antarctica and the frozen taiga belt in the north.

According to Sashia's file, her zest for living, which still had her precariously clinging in my Marginal Prospect list, had shot this girl onto a new level, particularly when Fayez came along a couple of years back. This laid-back cockney of Eritrean Muslim ancestry, barely filling a worn beige pullover and frayed medium-size jeans, had enraptured her with his zany jazz.

Not long afterwards, a small firm of consultants, impressed by her creativity, had placed her in a team handling promotions for a mega development project. At last, Sashia worked among professionals – with an actual office to work in. The difference was invigorating. The Docks, an intra-modal transport hub, featured a man-made atoll with an eco-friendly island of wharfs in the centre.

A real spur to her enthusiasm came when the media heralded the concept as 'a visionary alternative to the proliferation of global-warming seawalls everywhere'. Seeing the respect she gained from this made me wonder whether she was, after all, just a late starter.

Developments on this scale, driving Hong Kong's free-trade economy, with its banking institutions keeping it in the World's financial hub – alongside London and New York – secured indefinite autonomy with its Special Administrative Region charter within China. For Beijing, that role model was ideal for the super power's new colonies upside, the first of which was in the international Moon base Ecstasy.

HK's grace was epitomised by the Wan Zai district (using its Cantonese name, or Wan Chai in English). There, textured streets, which splendidly offset gleaming glass tower blocks, were brought alive by podcasts billowing about them and traditional red lamps still illuminating roadside stalls in the market area at dusk. While, in stark contrast, the all-familiar night scenes of Lok Hat Do (Lockhart Road in English) were of open-fronted bars, babes, buskers and bluster.

Twenty storeys up, appearing as a head and shoulders hologram, the crowd-stopping Sævrama Channel newscaster Jude Nade was telling all how things were in the World. Drivers, battling heavy traffic on translucent flyovers, hung happily on the New Yorker's straight-talk, *"...around Earth everything's coming up rosy again this spring, with lots of blue, blue sky. Strange as that's been – but hey, go with the feng shui. Get bullish with those stocks. And party, party, party!"* It was all in the voice, soothing, uplifting, topping the weather bill 24/7, up, down, and around the latitudes. For now, she was iconic tonic to Lok Hat Do night-lifers.

32

Sashia, elegantly attired in a smart black jacket with thin red stripes and a matching full-length coat, stood on a pavement clutching a faded green beret. Her 'striders', as she called her indispensible thigh boots, were now glowing red. Half turning, she glanced up at the newscast as the refrain of bar-top-stomping Aussie AstBelters in cowboy hats floated through an open door. The singers – girls famed for their vitality, slim blonde looks and shallow, bombed out tastes – had done the tour of upside bars. They'd even entertained the Mars-based crews of robotic mining equipment on AstBelt, as the Asteroid Belt was colloquially termed.

I watched Sashia quietly absorb every sight and scene around her, including two little grey-haired Hakka ladies in oversized straw hats pushing over-laden trolleys.

Such scenes were reminders to me that time was running out for her, as it was for all our candidates. Naturally, I felt for her impending misery at being wrenched from Fayez – and upside scenes, conjured up by those AstBelters, would further aggravate that loss.

A year back, when the HK branch of the UN F-Academy had begun its worldwide enrolments, Sashia learnt from her grandma that it was a precondition of her genetic enhancement to join. All that the Academy divulged was that she, along with all the others, would train for active duty abroad. The time had now come for them to prepare for their departure.

Wistfully, she looked at the beret, Fayez's, doubtless reminiscing what a spectacle she'd made of herself at their first meeting. For fun, she had gyrated into a packed Lok Hat Do bar, where she'd immediately drawn attention to her 'hot' skin-tight plum-red top by instantly lengthening the heels of her then burgundy striders – no mere prosthetic appendages, but ultra-smart ones, the kind of fashion accessories girls envied for their changing colour, texture and shape, all at her whim. The pianist, Fayez, was full on her, and just slammed the electric keys. "Are you real?" he'd let slip, noting a barely discernable robotic hesitancy in her movements, and then corrected, "Are you fire?"

"Fire? Hah!" Arms stretched out to him, Sashia spun and wove her body provocatively, "Take this fire!" The now capricious girl was aching, just this once, to run with it, throw out inhibitions, go totally out of control.

"Hah, godsome!" he'd shouted, standing to hit out a rhythm so body pulsing that it sent the girl vaulting, chin out, arms high, over his wild, screaming fans. Eyes alight, with astonishing grace and agility mid air, Sashia had completed the somersault, heart pounding from excitement, by springing straight into a double back-flip and landing right at his side. From that day on, the two were inseparable.

On seeing this in her file, and imagining that zeal and pluck in my teams, I began to formulate a different view of this notable nymph. And a nymph she surely was, to look at!

More recently she'd been made-over as a suit, for a spate of business functions. Accessorising her maturing Russian sophistication were leopard-like locks and an earlobe-piercing white rock. Her nana's crimson tribal scarf added mystique by shadowing her eyes.

She was meeting up with Fayez outside of the HK Conference Centre to attend a landmark reception. In black-tie dress, actually the more popular metallic silver-black, Fayez offered her his arm and they proceeded through the glass terrapin shaped building to view the dazzling lights of HK's Victoria Harbour.

Along with a splendidly colourful mix of Hong Kongers and other international guests, they were in plenty of time to watch Hu Ma, Premier of China, arrive and then receive King William and Queen Catherine of Great Britain and the Commonwealth of Nations. Following this, and perfectly timed, Admiral of the United States Sixth Fleet Connell Althorpe disembarked from his pristine grey launch to top an auspicious occasion the World had anticipated with optimism and about which the people of China and HK were overjoyed.

However, as the Admiral's craft began to depart, a junk fishing-boat that had arrived inconspicuously enough, now noticeably manoeuvred around it, Greenpeace banner unfurled from the mast and, hanging below, a white sheet bearing the large red rubric, 'SAVE OUR PINK DOLPHINS'. To unified gasps from the Admiral's group, a heavily laden net then swung out to dump a large catch of dead fish on the ferry quay.

A crowd rushed forward. Immediately agitated, Sashia was soothed by Fayez, neither recognising Jude Nade near the plate-glass window overlooking the spectacle.

Recognising her big chance the presenter coolly went into action. "Quick!" she instructed her cameraman, as she smoothed her trademark sleek blonde chignon. "Direct optic 1 at the pile of fish. Optic 2, at the flowing banners. Optic 3, aim there." Her index finger targeted protestors on the junk's deck as police boats converged on them, "Cover that."

"Hi babe," Jude's chief was there. A little nervously she adjusted the heads-up-display of him in her glasses. Having outgrown her two-minute weather slot she had been imploring Sævrama bosses to try her out as a reporter covering ceremonies such as this. She was not exactly career driven. She simply loved the business. It also filled an emptiness she felt in her marriage since her son had grown and flown. Life had become dull. She'd become dull.

This Greenpeace protest was turning an important ceremonial event into something more newsworthy. "What have we got there?" her chief encouraged, while news reporters were racing to grab the tails of the evolving story. "Is this a cut above the usual stunts from those guys?" Without an answer, Jude shrugged, knowing the backup team were hurriedly seeking archived information to feed to her.

The chief was making contact from his NY apartoffice, which was as busy as press offices of past generations. An accomplished man in his mid-thirties, he was clearly not out to make a fashion statement in his white singlet, black braces, unconcealed balding crown and wire-brush hair. Nevertheless he was the epitome of global market success. Surrounding him were ambitious girls with wild animal hairstyles – which made Jude appear marginally prim – and equally ambitious guys with wildly raked aerial styles.

"Another junk!" Jude suddenly yelled at her cameraman. Although betraying none of Sashia's girly excitement, the presenter was just as awed and puzzled "Swing optic 1 there now!"

The first junk had pulled away, chased by harbour police. Meeting mid-channel with the incoming junk, spider-like arms as tall as masts slowly extended to the sides to float fan-like white nets across the water. The converging police boats immediately hit difficulties, though possibly they were disengaged awaiting orders.

Sashia heard as Jude called out again, "Optic 2 over there." Straight away onscreen, Premier Hu Ma, William and Catherine and Althorpe could be seen unruffled and even bemused. Jude then introduced a young woman with vivid red and green dragons on her fingers. Along with these, Sashia noticed a nasty scar on the right side of the girl's pretty face.

Having clocked in to observe Sashia's behaviour at a high prestige event, I too observed the young woman with interest that led to a considerable shock.

With welcoming smile Jude introduced, *"Doctor Mei Sai Ling, of the University of Hawaii. Dr Ling is a zoology consultant to the AFCD – that's the Hong Kong Agriculture, Fisheries and Conservation Department. I'll let her tell us what all this is about."*

Mei was not only alive but out and about, her scarring sufficiently healed for public appearances! We never discovered where she might have been taken, probably by the same intelligence body that officially cloaked our entire operation at that time.

"Thank you," Mei said, her thin smile betraying tension. *"I'm here to review impact studies commissioned for The Docks."* An ashen emptiness, easily mistaken for jetlag, in eyes that once sparkled, clouded a memory so violent that, as I later discovered, counselling was still unable to bring it back to her. *"We're looking into the habitats of Chinese white dolphins, affectionately known here as pink dolphins and globally as Indo-Pacific humpback dolphins. I'm a scientist. I have to study all the facts impartially, objectively."*

Both reporter and interviewee looked uncomfortable, Jude's composure probably waning faced with the doctor's right cheek twitching a little and Mei showing some embarrassment at this unexpected exposure.

I also learned later that Mei was distraught at having been taken from her research by the Hawaii branch of the F-Academy. Sadly I had to await UNNDC clearance to involve her in research coming out of the Moon digs.

"That said, I'm concerned for the dolphins," Mei continued onscreen. *"Everyone in the scientific community deplores the plundering of environments seen this millennium."*

"That sentiment has been repeated over and over again in the past decades," Jude's eyes lit up. *"Isn't it beginning to be a cliché?"*

"What!" Mei's look was one of disdain. *"You know, there was a reason,"* the station was getting the spark it needed, *"for the high level of extinctions that regularly took place on Mid-Cretaceous*

continental shelves – violent geological activity – and I mean really violent."

Thrown by unexpected fury from someone talking like a radical environmentalist, Jude was now bowled over by the doctor's switch to prehistoric times, about which the presenter knew nothing and therefore incapable of sharp questioning.

"When that eased masses of organisms in the soil, sea and air, finally got the balance of nature right and terraforming really got going. Regular extinctions plummeted from around seventeen to eight percent, by the Close of the Cretaceous and got right down to two percent in recent time, until that stability – hundreds of millions of years in the making – was unbalanced by Mankind!"

Mei's quivering ponytail was a dead giveaway of irritability. *"In just a few generations, we'd slammed extinctions right back to pre-Cretaceous levels – before eventually coming to our senses and tried to protect our wildernesses."*

She was speaking of how winners and losers, as they were called, slowly evolved by Darwinian Natural Selection, while at times suddenly torn apart by what we'd termed a 'Natural Correction'. That's where my research came in – to connect the extinction of dinosaurs with intelligence on a catastrophe, or Natural Correction, now heading our way.

"Anyway, enough said," Mei's brows cleared. *"What I'm here for are the pink dolphins."*

On safer ground, Jude responded, *"We've got things under control though? WOMB collaborates with departments round the world, like the AFCD?"* Mei's nodded response obviously pleased her. *"They're as concerned about damage to the environment, aren't they, as the World Health Organisation is about pandemics?"*

"Right. It took something as big as AIDS before WHO got the muscle to manage the mass risk of pandemics such as SARS, the Asian bird flu and so on. And it took the wider impacts of overpopulation, on Climate Change and also species losses of over 50 percent in recent decades to jolt the UN into forming WOMB."

Just then Jude's team alerted her to a commanding-looking man, aboard the first junk. "There! Zoom in!" she commanded, taking in the youth's epic style jet-black-shot-with-red 'snaketex', a lightweight snakeskin-like material that moved and flexed realistically. Once online his features became clear – stubble on his longish face, slick black aerial hair dishevelled by roughing it at sea and euphoria in his eyes. *"We're now looking at the Greenpeace group's leader, whom I'm told is Dr Steve Nord,"* she announced, watching him take two supremely fluid strides to leap from deck to gunwale to pilothouse roof.

In an explosion of fireworks a rocket shot from the mast-top, pulling out a length of green cloth that instantly inflated into a hot air balloon. As suddenly as a dolphin shot up from the water passing right over the junk, Steve Nord grabbed its tail and rose, higher, higher, until he could jump gracefully into the balloon's ascending basket. There, on an egocentric high, he waved at a cheering crowd as the dolphin holoe splashed into a podcast on the balloon's surface of real dolphins swimming in the vicinity.

"Gorgeous Nord – but watch out! This guy's a woman-eater!" a female journalist had headlined. As one of my possible team contenders, I'd taken that as a glib observation of Steve, certainly expecting more from him than that.

Now accompanied musically by Holst's 'Mercury the Winged Messenger', Internet media were presenting aerial shots of the two junks, nets outstretched amid an entourage of police craft and other harbour vessels, the pair resembling huge white butterflies whirling flat on the water below the optics in the basket.

Steve looked and sounded pretty delirious over the impressive show. *"So, what's all the fuss about?"* came that Liverpudlian lilt, his tone not unlike that of a snide circus ringmaster. *"Just can The Docks. Let the dolphies be."* Leaning out he motioned to the dolphin podcasts. *"Those poor beauts aren't bothering you, are they? Course not! But they've put up with decades of your pollution – and now you want to stir up muck, build something more for us? Us! Taking up more of the planet? That's greed, pure and simple!"*

What I saw in this candidate, a geologist conversant with fossil fuel bearing formations underground, was a logical match to complement Mei's specialist knowledge on the *Cretaceous* period. But gee – what a clash in personalities! His temerity, which had become evident in his fight to resist conscription by us, couldn't be more at odds with her not getting on with her peers. I reeled at the prospect of managing this pair.

As ever more people rushed to the Conference Centre windows, cameras recording the spectacle and the charismatic snaketex man addressing them, the moment was building. *"Now there's a protest,"* said Jude the rookie reporter adjusting to being in the news spotlight and now remarkably relaxed. *"It seems the atoll scheme – pitched as, 'a boon for marine life as well as tourism' – has angered environmentalists."* The feed kept coming in from her office, *"They say the construction work will displace HK's famed pink dolphins. The site, right next to Chek Lap Kok Spaceport, is stirring up memories of when the old airport was built there in the home waters of that species."*

She bit her lower lip. *"Apparently there's a real scarcity of viable alternatives to this deepwater site."* Jude instinctively paused to read something in Mei's eyes, *"It's not fully resolved, is it – the environment?"*

Mei hesitated for a second, *"Sadly, yes. Wildlife losses can't be reinstated using seed banks, gene banks or even zoo specimens. Not when intricate balances, involving complex symbiosis, are severely disrupted. That's how badly the last few decades messed up the natural world. And we'll never get it back. That Humpty Dumpty can't be put together again."*

"It's lost, forever?" Jude's keenness to nudge on was now tempered by dismay.

"That's right. With re-terraforming we can put life back in the wild but not bring the wild back to life." Bewildered eyes now faced Mei. *"It's never as it was. Our techniques are far too crude. Sure we've restored lost hedgerows and waterways, hundreds of years in the making, in England (UK) – forests and meadows too. But we've got no hope of restoring the likes of the Serengeti or the full extent of the Amazon."*

"Yes but surely we can build anew even if it's not the same?"

"Well, we've had our failures – with invasions of alien species, bungles in terraforming arid areas and even mismanaging terraspheres on Mars. So much for us assuming nature's time honed magic – Gaia's magic! And yet everywhere from the pre-2030s era is managed for forestry, recreation, eco-tourism and whatever else. None of that is left to evolve naturally, not when farmers use breeding stock to replenish parks, lakes and even game reserves. That's the importance of the new strategic wildernesses – our only hope for the planet to heal itself with its own balances.

"It's hardly big news," Mei added. "Civilisations through time risked overwhelming environments and often did so into collapse."

"And the underlying cause is?"

"Basically?" Mei shifted her weight looking a little uncomfortable, "Babies. The basic human right to have them – unbridled. China, despite worldwide condemnation, was the first to do something about it. Admittedly, their initial crudely managed implementation led to widespread suffering. But there'd have been even greater poverty, suffering and strife if they hadn't tried."

"Since 2047," Jude threw in, "we've been capping populations with licensing births outside of the Near Earth Territories, where it will be more relaxed? Right?"

"Thankfully, yes. But that's another story," Mei steered the subject back on track for the presenter, "Returning to the issue here, we'll ensure that our findings gain support for the dolphins. Doubtless the whole scientific community's support if there proves to be genuine concern. We can't afford to lose any more species."

I empathised with Jude as she took a cue and closed the interview with a relieved sigh. Her first news reporting assignment was over. Covering more weighty issues and unexpected happenings had clearly surpassed merely reporting on the ceremonial event. Gratifyingly she received an approving wink from her chief.

The harbour spectacle continued to anchor onlookers at windows while others mingled in the main hall listening to speeches. Both events needed coverage and Jude again directed her cameraman.

Still in the hall, Sashia was looking displeased that The Docks had come under attack and this at least told me she had pride in the project. Apparently this late starter was capable of commitment – even though she'd brusquely swept aside a leopard lock protruding from her crimson scarf and muttered, "Bloody dolphins..."

Embarrassed, Fayez tugged at her elbow. "Hey hush up! Peace!"

Her voice tailed off to a whisper, "They'll get by somehow, or move on maybe. Anyway, so what if that's the price of progress?"

Fayez cast his eyes skyward in mock despair.

I noticed Mei had overheard them and had shaken her head disparagingly. With little chance of getting her and Sashia together, I was now in no doubt – of the two, Mei was by far the more valuable.

Jude, fortuitously out of earshot was seeking out a drink when she became aware of the Admiral close to her arm. "Sir, could I..."

"What?" The superbly smart authority figure awaiting her words with the engaging eyes of a seasoned biker added, "Hear what I have to say about dolphins? Or docks?" His tone appeared to be in keeping with his years of rank-induced solitude. "You can put what I know about either of those subjects on a single pixel." Her chuckle and return of his amused look, doubtless acknowledged the huge amounts of data a pixel could in fact hold. "Perhaps you would be more interested in seeing the Sixth Fleet?"

Jude offered a disarming smile that also expressed regret that his offer could not be taken up. The admiral was undeterred. "Well, come on over anytime. I'd be glad to welcome you aboard for a tour."

A mutually pleasing moment seemed to have presented itself. And turning away, to signal her cameraman to leave them, she elicited a grateful smile from the Admiral. They were off camera now. No need to interview him, not just yet. "So," she continued softly, while eyeing the sprightly fifty year old, "at least you'll remember this visit to HK."

"Oh yes, I certainly will."

"The Greenpeace guy, Steve Nord," she offered as a conversation piece, "looked pretty determined."

"Him? He's a peril, doctorate or not," he responded firmly but pleasantly, while nodding and smiling toward Mei wending her way in their direction. Clearly Jude had not picked up on Steve's track record in the media, no doubt from being too focused on her new role. "The man's notorious for recklessly interfering in offshore oilfield operations. That's been his main activity, targeting the oil industry as if it's some plague to society. And each time he does that he risks lives. He's an arrogant menace, often enough apprehended by one navy or the other."

"Off the record? I agree." Mei, comfortable with joining mature company, welcomed the Admiral's courteous gesture. "And his girl, Carla Drew, is right now in the Antarctic. Where she's spectacularly churning up the high seas to wage war on Japanese whalers. Not that I don't admire her for that. The cruelty inflicted on those mammals should have been curtailed decades ago." The biologist then turned to respectfully enlighten the reporter, "They're a high profile couple, ice-board champions actually, both of whom mean well and on

41

balance do a lot of good. It's just that they're apt to draw the public's attention sensationally rather than reasoned-through scientifically. I'd say." There it was, sparks flying. I made a note to, regrettably, place her and Steve in separate teams.

"He's got balls, though," gravitating into their sphere Sashia impulsively braved an opinion of her own, before immediately cowering in their highly professional company. That insecurity of hers was again disappointing, I felt. Except I was surprised to see the Admiral shift his gaze, from her leathery boots – those remarkable striders – and admire her pluck.

Fayez eased her protectively away, while speaking to her softly, "No need for blood. The protestor can fight his own fights." I felt so bad, as the pair slinked off. For I understood how much was going wrong in Sashia's life, draining her to zero tolerance, and how that was affecting Fayez too. Yet I couldn't intervene, with not knowing myself how things would turn out about keeping her or letting her go.

I reflected on Sashia's defence of Steve, when his protest was so blatantly aimed at her precious project. Though maybe, with his having demonstrated a fluid agility she'd ache for, I shouldn't have been so surprised for her to be drawn to him. And in glancing back, Sashia's jaw dropped at seeing him on screen with a distinctive button on his collar. It was an emerald enamelled flying horse – a merit earned by somersaulting with outstretched arms from one galloping stallion to another, at dusk, all the way through HK's extensive nature reserve wetlands. Mei caught sight of it too, as a fellow equestrian, before the girls' eyes then connected fleetingly.

Out in the harbour the police had finally managed to stop the junks. And, coming to, they clambered aboard. In usual HK manner they courteously gestured for Steve to descend and accompany them quietly. They also pulled on the balloon's tether to bring it down. He twirled flamboyantly, whilst returning their courtesy with a polite bow. Then, facing the crowd, he boomed out a last disparaging word, *"What'll happen is the dolphins will get pissed off. They'll hike off someplace else. Where they'll swallow oil dumped from a ship. Or they'll just get depressed at what we're doing to the planet, and beach themselves mysteriously as hundreds have in the past. Then Hong Kong will have seen the last of them. Maybe we all will. Along with so many other species that have disappeared."*

~*~

42

6

Spring 2066
(Autumn in Southern Hemisphere)

Having passed muster in Hong Kong, Jude Nade's chief had given her an even bigger break and here she was, standing atop the Andes in Peru marvelling at the precisely joined stone-block ruins whilst preparing to present a Climate Change angle on the news. Fresh and professionally smart in a cream outfit that matched her blonde upswept hair, she angled herself to face one of three cam-optics. *"Once more we have a beautiful morning, with blue, blue skies over this simply stunning location. Just along the ridge from this ancient site,"* she gestured eastwards, *"the UN Security Council is convening in the resort bearing its name – Machu Picchu."*

She led off in that direction, cameramen bustling to follow. *"What isn't apparent,"* for this wasn't convened at UN Headquarters or a major city of any of the Council members, *"is what this Summit is really about."* Easing into the assembling crowd with the same reticence as slipping into a cold pool she actually had little time to reflect on what anything was about. Heart thumping, she scanned the scene then fixed firmly on a cam-optic. *"I'm Jude Nade, Sævrama Channel. I must report that press officers for this Machu Picchu gathering are avoiding the climate issue – in fact they're actually dodging it. But what's significant is the number of WOMB executives I see here, as well as the high number of leading scientists.* She turned to another cam-optic... *"It's not about the gloriously clear skies we're having,"* she gestured skyward, *"but the long winters.* She moved in those delegates direction, confident of her research on weather systems and climates. *"You've all heard about the Little Ice Age of the seventeenth and eighteenth centuries,"* she continued, stopping on the conference hall steps, "rivers *as far south as the Thames in London England and the Hudson in New York USA froze over and crop failures and famine were widespread in Europe."*

Jude strode on into the entrance lobby, continuing... *"It's never been resolved how that came about, whether from arctic melt-water slowing the warm Gulf Stream or from reduced sunspot activity or whatever else."*

Locating her position on a press balcony she absorbed the generally upbeat mood on the floor below. Celebrated dignitaries

43

and their entourages were filing along rows of seats, while aides busily acquainted Council members and delegates with the consoles they'd use. Once seated, holoes of ambassadors for non-Council member states appeared on seats reserved for them.

At last all eyes were drawn to a small figure in a colourful flowing sari, mounting the dais. Jude directed her cameraman to zoom in. *"There we have UN Secretary General Sustra Matri, radiant and poised as ever, she is a remarkable stateswoman."*

The sprightly sixty-two year old calmly took a sip of water and began, *"Friends. On this day we can look back with satisfaction and pride at some great United Nations accomplishments. We have peace on Earth, at last. With all people having a say at home and in the international courts, backed up by UNRO should the need arise. And in the Near Earth Territories programme we're collaborating to ensure that that peace will endure with us – even as we set out, doubtless unilaterally, to the outer reaches of space."* She motioned to acknowledge the hands of delegates either side of her in this. Resounding applause followed, with all present unequivocally in support. *"Key in that success was the role of International Private Public Partnerships, using established Build Operate and Transfer frameworks to revolutionise and transform the economies of developing countries into highly developed nations.*

"What we also had to do was save the biosphere from all that prosperity – from us material beings destroying it! 'Ah,' it's been said, 'just balance people with nature. Reserve some areas for nature and others for people – sufficient to grow things and to maintain the atmosphere and the climate.' Simple, huh?" She gave her knowledgeable audience time to chuckle over this naivety.

"Right, well, the problem there is that the most effective driving forces in the biosphere are wildernesses, and they're much too vast, complex and fragile, also," she looked relieved, *"too little understood to get under control. As we see with the archaeological graveyards of collapsed civilisations everywhere, rotting in the wildernesses they dared to control. And why try? When nature does the job so much more efficiently and sustainably.*

"There are no true wildernesses anymore? Wrong. Taking urgent action, strategic wildernesses were identified for re-terraforming naturally – the vast mountain ranges of the world, the steppes of Siberia, kelp forests, tropical reefs, and so on. That's

where we're at last making progress, letting nature heal itself. Most spectacularly there are the true forests – ones that, unlike Eurasia's valuable temperate forests, are random, chaotic, and wholly unmanageable for forestry. And in that you've invested heavily in policing the borders of the Amazon rainforest, the Burmese jungle, and parks now joined up across Africa. Without those controls, covered by international carbon credits and tourism, wildernesses would have become wholly reliant on man's Lilliputian efforts to survive before inevitably dying out."

Having given their full support over the years, none of this was news to the members. The Secretary General's following report became more riveting.

"That brings me to the Near Earth Territories, the new frontier," she said. *"There we can have growth and expansion that is virtually unlimited and well beyond the prospects on planets and moons. Trainees for that programme are being inducted at this very moment. With their genetic enhancement they'll enjoy unrestricted movement on 6,000 hectares of low gravity industrial terraces, 20,000 hectares of medium gravity terraces with farming and parks, and 700 hectares of EarthG in built-up areas at the rim. That land will be sufficiently sustainable for a complement of some 50,000 to live very comfortably in each vessel. Just 20 of the ships will accommodate a population of a million people – and 200 ships will constitute a fair sized city state."*

While members had been advised about the trainees, nothing about them had as yet been made public. *"We'll get into that in our next sessions."*

I'd been an advisor to the design panel for the Territories, which were marvellously far reaching in concept. Completely free to drift, immune from all of nature's geological and climatic hazards as well as from NEOs and radiation, the whole colony was to eventually roam to Neptune and mine the resources of trillions of bolides out there.

Matri continued to touch on the urbanisation or industrialisation of land. While she managed to skirt around the other extremely unpopular issue amongst electorates, despite the clear need for it, of controlling Earth's populations, *"Meanwhile we've made great strides down here, with compromises we've had to make. Every corner of the planet is precariously vital. This is exemplified by The*

Docks project right now in Hong Kong. I understand a recommendation of the Hong Kong University, now being looked at with the University of Hawaii, is to move the project into deeper water.

"As that shows, for all the pitfalls, the scientific community has risen to the challenges brilliantly. With making many a distinguished career, including some high flyers among us today."

With this, she extended her arms, motioning to the assembled crowd, "The thanks of the UN and all peoples of the World go to Council members, UN member states, as well as to the many organisations and spiritual orders that have helped and also to corporations and masses of ordinary individuals who have made this all possible. The list is legion, commemorated for posterity on smart-plaques in hillside parks surrounding this ancient site.

"The day after tomorrow, in Cuzco, we'll turn our attention to having fun. Speeches will give way to a week-long celebration of the arts, with parades, theatre, concerts and an extravaganza of fireworks. Thank you."

In a gradual surge of applause the assembly rose to its feet to solemnise the occasion, but there was among them a disquiet that reflected the discord of their citizens. Poverty and political tension were in the past and Gaia's wildernesses were saved. But the price – family planning for the privileged few – was high. The Near Earth Territories had been planned far too late. Even the most optimistic prognosis put the real build-up – when they would begin to alleviate overcrowding – was well into the next century.

~*~

7

Spring 2066

When each of our candidates received what was to them an unexpected summons from the UNNDC to attend an *F-Academy*, none could discover in advance quite what an F-Academy was and most assumed it was some sort of fitness centre and part of the current public fitness drive.

One week after the dolphin protest, our candidates learned the truth about the F-Academy – and themselves. They were being enrolled in a college for *fimans*. Why? This is what they were, the various deans explained. In line with their parents' agreement to have their babies genetically enhanced at birth, each of these extraordinarily agile young people had gained those abilities – and that name – from genecrafting [genetic modification].

Horror sheared over the faces of thousands attending F-Academies around the World – including Hong Kong Sashia Dubchek, London Steve Nord and Hawaii Mei Sai Ling – as it sunk in that their human form had been 'scientifically evolved' to make them the world's first known hominini breed to appear this side of the ice age. They were all fimans!

"A *New Breed*!?" Sashia's protest echoed the chorus of fimans everywhere. "How dared they!" she raged at their use of her, at the perceived betrayal and let down by her parents, "Why? What *for?*"

"For endurance upside. You'll be told more on a need-to-know basis," came the voice of an instructor.

"Fuck! Upside!" The news understandably appalled Sashia, who after all had greater physical reason to be fearful than the others. She had other grievances, too. "I'll have to quit The Docks! And hellbytes, what about Fayez and me – what'll it do to us?"

Until that day she'd got away with telling him very little, just that she'd been enlisted in an extreme events programme. It was, after all, just about everything she knew – if not all she feared. The college documents they'd received were thin on information and even now she had no idea where their 'training' aimed to lead them. Except, covert as it all was, it would mean leaving everything behind.

I hated all the secrecy. It made for far more tension than was necessary. Deep down, what got to her was that she was being made to do what she'd vowed never to do – leave her partner Fayez to go upside, as her dad had done to her. Reliving that sense of abandonment over again Sashia fought her tears.

"On top of dealing with this," she slapped at her legs, "I'm now not even a human. It seems I've never belonged anywhere. Apart from being paraplegic, what am I? A sick-assed alien?"

"Shit! Shit! Shit!" Mei's worst fear – now realised – was that her dinosaur quest would have to be abandoned. This was tough. In character, anger beamed from her eyes and projected from her knotted brow. Her lower lip also trembled, nerves aggravated by nightmare images of tortured hands engulfed in fire, images that still haunted and drained her being. Fury erupted, "*Me*? A bloody space being! An evolutionary marvel, oh, marvellous, engineered to walk off Earth just like that prick of a fish that walked out of the sea half a billion years ago! Terrific! But why me? Why in hell's name *me*!?"

"*Damn*!" boomed Steve Nord to no one in particular. "Well, at least Carla Drew's a fiman, so my partner's coming, like it or not. But, damn, we've put so much effort into our campaigns and spent months organising an elaborate campaign against oil exploitation in Antarctica. With Worldwide coverage we're finally getting massive support."

The UN was in the closing stages of reviewing sovereign claims to Antarctica and, after decades of prevarications, various governments were now braced to award exploration licenses for strategic resources there, including fossil fuels. All the major oil companies and mining operators were primed to get started.

"It's all building, coming to a head,' Steve was telling a now interested female fiman. "Soon the invasion will begin, as it did in the Arctic when our organisation fought hard in the 2010s to 20s – and this time Greenpeace must succeed in stopping it. The devastation from oil spills, including in areas of natural beauty, has been horrendous. We've been in the forefront in protesting that – often protesting the exploiters being there and always protesting their failing to protect environments. They're a menace and must be stopped – and now I'm being dragged off the case! For What!?" He paused, looking momentarily confused. "That's it! It's a conspiracy to get me away? What could be so crapping important that I have to go – and even Carla?"

The fimans' sentiments ran high for days, each reacting in his or her individual way, some bottling up, most simply sickened by their loss of independence. Finally there was nothing left but to cope, move on and accept that their lives as ordinary humans were shattered.

Their schedules were also gruelling and they'd arrive home pushed to the extreme.

On this particular day off, Fayez was tugging at Sashia's plum-red sleeve to coax her through Wan Zai's crowded market lanes – a familiar and much enjoyed haunt of theirs. There, immersed in a 'jamble' of vibrant Hong Kongers and visitors, their senses were treated to a fusion of sights, smells and sounds. Except this time Sashia petulantly snatched away her arm. Over her tragic eye injury, received three days earlier, she wore a decorative patch. The damage had compounded their woes. On top of her stiff gait she was temporarily one-eyed, condemned to leave home and job and unable to share her concerns with Fayez. She was certainly unhappy and the last thing she felt was sexy.

He was trying to deal with those pressures, along with her absences most evenings. Observing her stress, he coped by giving her space and not complicating anything or asking too much. Nonetheless she'd retort angrily, "Okay, it's all right by you, but what about a bit of angst or jealousy or something?"

Her gripe to herself was, "He actually wants to go upside! What's that all about?"

Today she was grudgingly following his lead between market stalls and stopped alongside him to take in a window running fascinating ads for lens replacements. "Is this it?" he prompted with forced cheeriness. Ignoring her doleful nod he drew her on to enter the shop and, melting a little, Sashia caught at his arm while squeezing it apologetically. His smile was a blessing.

"You got an eye for my friend?" Fayez began. "Hello – anyone home?"

Surveying the dismal little shop did nothing to lift their spirits. On the left, a stark white counter was backed by white display cabinets and clinically white walls and, to the right, some posters and leaflets added the only colour.

Long strands of black hair slicked down on a sweaty balding scalp slowly rose above the countertop, to reveal bulging baggy eyes set in the round glowering face of an obese Chinese trader. Finally, his grin revealed gaping red gums stuffed with blotchy crooked teeth, "Wah? Wah you wan? You wan eye?"

Fayez straightened up, tall and thin, squaring to face the man before turning to look questioningly at Sashia. Eyes large, she shrugged and simply returned a quizzical look. "Okay," she ventured, "perhaps the Academy is testing my reactions by sending me here. Or maybe they're just making the technology more widely available – in out-of-the-way places like this. How weird is this?"

Fayez let that ride. He lifted her crimson scarf and pointed to the patch. "Pissing off Triads again, my Starburst?" he teased using a striking name to bolster her confidence. But when she slid onto the stool, her composure dissolved and she grimaced the instant the trader's broken nails and gnarled fingers touched her pale cheek, his rough skin snagging in a few fine strands of her leopard patterned hair. Slipping off her patch, to expose Sashia's black and bloodied bruise, the man moved a handheld pen-scanner to each of her silver-blue eyes oblivious of her resignedly staring up at the ceiling.

The file we had on her injury was spine chilling. On a training exercise the bow of her kayak had plunged into thrashing white-water at the entrance of a narrow crevasse. Waves churned, tumble-washing her and buffeting enough to upend the girl against a rock ledge, where a jagged rock had smashed into her eye.

"Mustah buy leplacement," the trader cut in, dropping his studious gaze to reach for a transparent pack of lenses. "These goodah, high-res."

All too glad to get on with it, Sashia dolefully slipped a $pendant from her gold bracelet, her universal credit card cum driving licence and smart ID received from the Academy. It tickled her to see the trader smarten up at the UN insignia on the token, and she shared that moment with a sideways glance at Fayez. Briskly the man produced another tube. "This more betta, hundled time zoom."

Fayez was bemused. "How? That's got to be Special Issue?" He referred to UNRO Special Forces, "What's up here?"

50

Sashia studied them both, a little wary of the trader's sudden overt attention. "You fit?" her eyes flashed impatiently, fixing the man's gaze for signs of faltering. At the same time, with taking in Fayez's reaction, something about the operation dawned on her. "It's so I have the acuity to work with dim and distant objects, in space," she whispered, avoiding his attempt to hear her. A look of finality overtook her and a tear ran from her good eye. And yet, tougher now after the long weeks of rigorous services training, her spine straightened like a rod.

"No ploblem."

"Okay," she swivelled round to the trader, "How much?"

"This, 2,000 dolla." The trader poked the first tube away. "This," he nudged the other towards her, studiously fixing her gaze, "15,000."

"What!" Fayez was ready to bargain.

The trader, his move, used a penlight to shine $13,000 on the counter. Sashia's brow knitted. Impatiently she waived her hand. "Hang the cost. You fit." Her eyes moistened as she looked longingly at Fayez, acknowledging now that she was really destined to go, his face the one she was preparing to leave. Theirs was the life she loved – the life she could no longer have.

Fayez held her gaze in an agony of suppressed questions. Then he simply winked to show his admiration at her dealing with the trader and her bravery at the fitting. His parents would have respected as much – true desert tradition was to be as straight as the path that goes from horizon to horizon in the bare sand.

Sashia's anxiety over his enforced involvement in this could be read in her uplifted brow.

Just then the trader whispered in her ear. "This include night vision."

The smart lens was energised by a transductor, which fed cyborg fashion on the body's electrochemical energy. Sashia glimpsed him drawing the new lens into a syringe before the expert's firm hands tilted her head back. Vision blurring, she purposely drew on flashbacks of the past weeks of training.

In one, her group had crossed a misty bog, cut through a chain-link fence and had crawled under a pitch-black platform when suddenly they'd tumbled head-over-heels, becoming nauseous as they'd bounced bizarrely off the underside. They'd later found that the platform was made of immensely dense teutronium, electron-stripped neutron material, with its colossal gravitational attraction, which was used extensively in spacecraft floorings and upside structures. The exercise was for coping with the disorientation of sudden weightlessness.

The lens expert had made a minute incision in her cornea, retaining the fluid aqueous humour behind, and using one syringe he now sucked out the old lens, while simultaneously using the prepared syringe to inject in the new lens. Finally, he closed and resealed the cornea. "See? Quick!" he said, clearly delighted by his own skills.

Warily, Sashia opened her eyes to look in the mirror she was handed, and then up, to check the acuity of her new sight by focusing on the counter and around the shop. She then sought something more discerning as a test. Her biombot relayed to me the movement she perceived, through a hairline crack in a rear door. Zooming in, in sharp contrast to the apparently dishevelled shop, she spied white-coated technicians preparing lenses under laboratory conditions. Zooming more, she found she could meander through the moonscape pores in faces. When she looked again at the lens man Sashia was beaming ecstatically over her newfound ability. "Jumpin' Jaisus! This is fantastic! Thank you!" She shook the man's hand and he returned his still terrible smile.

When she turned to kiss Fayez's fingers, she whispered, "Thanks for coming with me. It's incredible!" He was so delighted, to see her elation and feel her fondly pinch his butt as she brushed past to look through the shop window, that he encouraged, "Try it long distance. Compare new with old." And he began to whistle, notes shaping into chords in his head, chords he would shape into a symphony just for Sashia.

His thoughts were soon interrupted by her excited voice coming from the corner of the lane and Lok Hat Do.

"Fayez! I can read Jude Nade's text-stream!" She was actually glad to see the presenter's familiar face back in her slot, reading her cues "...*over the years we've seen a lengthening of winters, along with changes in skiing venues. It's a recurring theme these past decades, with reports of snow and ice building in places. We'll have more on those developments in a special feature coming up soon...*"

In this respect, Sashia had her nana's home in Motyklejka to worry about, although since learning of the genecrafting her feelings were mixed when she thought of home. "They make me so mad," she muttered, reflecting on her mother's and nana's betrayal in not explaining the roots of her disability. "I suppose they meant well – deep down," she argued, now, of all times, determined to love them unequivocally – another sign that she was nearer to accepting her impending and unavoidable journey.

"Where?" Fayez asked, seeking the hologram they'd passed earlier and finally spotting it, small as a matchbox a couple of blocks away. "Oh yeah? You can really see that?" he exclaimed, observing her light up with excitement. Although he felt this mood would be short-lived and their recent tensions would return, he yearned to hold her and not restrain his devotion. Their rich individuality brought much to the relationship and the mere thought of losing it brought a dry lump to his throat.

"Uh uh. But that's not all. I can see Jude's eyes," Sashia's voice trailed off – something was wrong, very wrong, in those eyes. Some inkling of the gravity of the situation was registered there. Sashia sensed real danger. She turned anxiously to Fayez, her look desperate. But behind him she noticed the trader tapping his penlight on the shop window and signalling her to return for the second eye op.

"Did you read this, by the way?" Fayez was pointing at a backlit flyer on a wall and she turned to where he was pointing. *Astound your friends. See more with Silverworm,* the advertisement read. Further down it said that the nanobots carried molecular-level imprints along the optic nerve to the brain's temporal lobe and then dissolved. The imprints selectively activated neuron pairs. *This new brand, delivered non-invasively, not only enhances the acuity of sight but also short-term memory. Tenfold!*

"Even more goodah," the unfazed trader added, quite unprompted shining $1,000 on the counter. Perceiving a glimmer of interest, he immediately brought up a flyer for a *hundred-fold* enhancer while shining $5,000 before Sashia. "This special plice."

Fayez bowed his head in consternation while she cheekily winked at him and plumped back onto the stool, "Okay, you fit." She'd done with bargaining, wanted this over. Fayez shook his head admiringly and handed on to her the thick metal tumbler of water offered by the trader.

Face tilted back to receive the second lens to be injected, Sashia stared transfixed at the trader. Holding up a plastic sachet, he was probing the aquamarine fluid within, using fine tweezers, at last carefully withdrawing a writhing translucent thread no thicker than a human hair. Colour drained from Fayez's face. With a twist of the trader's wrist the creature glistened and writhed into Sashia's exposed pupil. "What's happening now?" she demanded, eyes wide yet blurred. Mustering composure, muscles taut, she flinched when something strange occurred behind her eye. The tumbler crumbled in her hand. "Whoops. That's clenched it."

"Going along optic nerve to blain," the lens trader explained. Fayez glowered at him protectively, while also betraying consternation over his lover's apparently newfound iron grip.

Procedure completed, the trader also glanced at the crushed tumbler before gently wiping her cheeks and covering both eyes with a black visor. "Mustah check no have ploblem." A faint buzz, followed momentarily by an ominous silence, preceded the man carrying on undeterred, "Goodah." Removing the visor, he prompted a reaction, "Yes? Goodah?"

She shook her head vigorously, pupils strained behind eyelids that flickered at the bright psychedelic starbursts slamming inside her head. "Honey?" Fayez coaxed, "You okay?" Sensing her disorientation he steadied to prevent her falling from the stool and, waiting for a nod from the trader before leading Sashia to the shop door, he watched her squint at bright lights before following the vague direction in which he was pointing and focusing on a craft hovering over rooftop traffic. At first blinking, at a glare and fog of shapes, she soon made out a commuter shuttle and gradually could see inside. The sensation uplifted her. "Stupendous! I can see people... and, yes, even what they're reading! Would you believe that? I can see the words. Fantastic, so *goodah*! Oh sweet, sweet worm!"

Surprisingly even the trader laughed. "You goodah!" and he ended there, "Goodah. Goodahbya."

Paying with the $pendant, they took their leave.

Two days later, they received shattering news. Orders had been issued. Fimans were to prepare for their imminent departure. All that was disclosed was that they were going on a training exercise as highly classified trainee 'reconneers', reconnoitring scientists. Sashia's tears said it all for Fayez. She was no longer a free spirit.

She was being fashioned into some strange adventurer. She kept her own thoughts to herself, "Leave Fayez for where – to become what? And to come back – when!?"

~*~

8

Spring 2066
(Autumn in Southern Hemisphere)

Chairing the meeting, UN Secretary General Sustra Matri remained on the dais, her expression severe as she awaited a lull among her Machu Picchu audience. At last impatient to continue, she raised her arms. *"There's something more we must attend to here. Costa DelMonte, President of the United States of America, will speak as Chairman of UNNDC."*

"This is interesting." Jude Nade pounced on the announcement, *"Council members are not due to speak until open sessions tomorrow. What we have now is, well, a departure from that schedule.*

"It would possibly be relevant to recall when in 2025 Senator Eduardo DelMonte, Costa's grandfather, furthered Abraham Lincoln's classless society by taking on America's powerful gun lobby. He took on board the international agreement for the Near Earth Territories and other upside colonies, actually like the rest of the industrialised World, to be gun free. He withdrew the right of US citizens to bear arms. That message finally dashed the all-pervasive ideology that 'might is right'.

"In the same year the United Kingdom reversed a related influence from across the Atlantic, that had just a few police bearing arms in public. They returned to that only ever being an emergency response. Also, quite incidentally, the Governor of the Bank of England, Senator DelMonte's friend, left city investors to find other arguments to raise their 'tax' on money – when he drove a super tanker through the myth that interest rates in any way controlled inflation."

DelMonte, a stocky fifty-one-year-old comfortable in his own skin and quite able to stand out even in crowds of gorgeous gene-treated people, looked sombre as he changed places with Matri on the dais. Nonetheless his presence held charisma. With a significant glint in his eyes he addressed the hall, *"The UN charter and international courts have given us the means to protect the World from what threatens us most. Ourselves. We have awesome power* over peoples and lands. *As we thankfully just heard, conflict is over, people everywhere are prosperous and the biosphere is safe.*

"Regrettably, there are dangers we have no power over. From 2004/5, 2010/11, 2017 and right up to this day, the world has been rocked by disasters of epic proportions." Many in the audience now began to shift uncomfortably at this changing theme. *"Tsunamis flattened coastal districts around the Indian Ocean and in Japan it also triggered one of the worst nuclear accidents on record. Quakes demolished hillside towns from Pakistan to Iran. Floods swept away whole communities in China and Pakistan. Hurricanes and tornadoes battered communities in North America. And, in the most devastating volcanic eruption, Vesuvius buried whole districts. Altogether millions were killed and tens of millions were displaced. We can all agree it's been a savage century of wholly natural catastrophes.*

"Sure, our excesses – fossil fuel emissions and also the depleting of wildernesses with expansive building and agricultural programmes – and our deficiencies – in building standards and zoning – compounded extreme weather systems and their effects as well as the effects of surface upheavals."

DelMonte paused to run his eyes sternly around the hall. *"That's all in the past. We did much better when we finally learnt to tread softly and make our presence on Earth far less onerous. It came down to accepting that Earth is not a man-made world – never was. It's a natural world, where our power is limited. We can't stop the forces of nature, our oldest of adversaries.*

"What we now aim to say – safely say – is that at least we're on top of the situation," he raised his hands resignedly. *"And it's precisely for that reason that the UN Security Council formed UNNDC, and tasked us with anticipating events and mitigating effects – primarily in the areas of early warning systems, Construction Exclusion Zones, rapid evacuation, aid and temporary shelter, and reconstruction – in essence Worldwide disaster management in the broadest context.*

"The key to succeeding is to anticipate what's coming up. And then, it's all down to Prevention. That's what we'll turn our attention to next in this Summit – Prevention. Thank you."

Jude Nade quickly commented, *"Well, perhaps something is at last being done about the plight of people – hopefully worldwide.*

Given the lengthening winters and closing down of power stations, which I've found myself increasingly reporting, the signs of Climate Change are certainly here, even in migratory patterns across the Arctic – think, for example, about caribou roaming southwards from their routes of late and thus encroaching on farmlands. So, we'll be following that lead closely – with more features for you."

Off the air Jude mulled over DelMonte's statements and particularly his final word, "Prevention." She cocked her head. Could this relate to the increasingly challenging aspects of the change in climate? "A bit *too* slow!" she threw out, off air.

The general assembly, traditionally open to the public via a press presence, adjourned. Closed-door sessions would resume after the break. Remaining on the press balcony Jude scanned faces in the audience as they shuffled along the aisles heading for the lobby and refreshments. There had to be someone among them – a Council member, press officer, agency administrator or scientist, anyone – who might give her a clue as to what this Summit was truly about. The weather girl was surely turning serious reporter. This was real, and big, and the excitement had her hopping. "Come on, which of you is really in the know – and with no empty political line?

"There," Jude spotted him – an eminent and reasonably self-assured expert on the environment. She signalled her cameraman to focus on the man in a paisley jacket and, hurrying down the stairway, pushed past media crowding around the leaders.

And here she was, at my side. *"Professor Madison, a word please?"* I turned to give her a cool, business-like look, which she bulldozed aside, introducing, *"Jude Nade, Sævrama Channel. We've been documenting some significant climate swings. Would you care to comment?"* My dismissively raised eyebrow in no way deterred her – indeed she appeared to be reading my face like a news sheet and was undoubtedly being fed information by the anchor team back at the Channel.

"It's rumoured that ISWA's Chief is just now seeking an increase in funding of 20 percent." I was not about to comment on that. *"While WOMB's Chief is after 23 percent."* Debating what to say, an involuntary cock of my head might have indicated too much.

I glanced quickly behind her and just as fast she'd picked up the object of my attention. DelMonte, part way up the stairs, was solemnly shaking his head. In that instant she'd lost me. I simply looked at her kindly. "I have to go, I'm afraid." Interview over.

Nevertheless, although hearing nothing, Jude now 'knew' something. She was astute, and undoubtedly had caught some suggestion of unfinished business between DelMonte and myself. And that's what she related to her chief. "Jack, some serious shit," adding a sweet rider, "from this reputedly upstanding Englishman."

"I saw." Jack frowned in serious concentration, oblivious of a loud young Glaswegian girl trying to gain their attention.

"Worldly important shit," Jude could see he was with her.

The Glaswegian persisted. "Your bright summer look and that blond topknot. Not a good mix." The girl wrinkled her nose and shook her head, asserting her role as wardrobe mistress. "The Prof had it over you with his flashy jacket." Her voice rose, half apologetically, "Lose the outfit – or ditch the topknot!"

Jude looked deadpan from the girl back to Jack, who grinned and winked before dismissing the girl with a smile and wave. "Okay. Important stuff is about to break when they go into closed-door sessions." Jude was feeling her way. He was giving her some slack. "All I can tell you is that whatever is up, it's in Professor Mark Madison's court – and right now he has the attention of none other than the head of UNNDC, also the President of the US of A!"

"What's your take on the reaction to what DelMonte said about prevention?" If Jack had any reservations about elevating his weather girl to reporter these had clearly dissolved.

"Not big, neither confusion nor surprise." Jude knew he wanted more guidance as to where her thoughts were leading. "What's next? Right... I haven't the foggiest. More volcanic eruptions? Like the one that formed Ni'moloka'i a few years back? But that wasn't that extraordinary. Eruptions occur all the time. I'm damned if I know if any of that, or whatever else for that matter, could influence the climate shifts we're experiencing."

"Yeah, right." He could see her weather knowledge coming in handy. "Then again, some scientific articles have reported a trebling of continental plate movements over the last thousand years or so. Where's this taking us babe? Can anything tie this in? Anything be corroborated?" He had turned cautious. "We had a hell of a time with that feature last month – the one that said upside colonies are endangering planetary balances by moving mined ore across space.

Hot mess! Nothing substantiated." That feature had come from another reporter, he just needed to stress the pitfalls.

"Absolutely not my style.". Jude sounded confident and assertive, concealing well any nervousness. "I'll get everything corroborated."

An overhead voice prompted everyone to begin their return to the hall, giving Council members a few more minutes of discreet sociability. UN Secretary General Matri was conversing with a lean man some 20 years her junior, the Premier of China – Hu Ma, "…So! China merely took its time to get elected assemblies in the provinces? Apace with maturing economies, cultures, and electorates?"

"Huh, Old Man China! That old walnut – so hard to crack," Ma chuckled good-naturedly, "But, sure," he smiled at his friend, "even more challenging was deciding on statesmen, of impeccable standing and vision."

"For your *all appointed* upper house. Modelled after the United Kingdom's House of Lords and Canada's Senate?" Matri winked congenially at her friend, "The 'Branada' pack influence?"

"Admittedly so. We've followed their path of principle-based government, as opposed to the heavy regulation of the federated EU and USA, in our case starting with a constitutional politburo."

"That's been our guiding light, in the Commonwealth of Nations. Which you're associated with through Hong Kong joining." Matri welcomed receiving all this direct, "For the tough challenges this millennium, democracy needs strong and stable bodies at the head."

"Yes! Even with liberalism devolving ever more powers to the provinces or states, as happened in the UK and USA."

"That's been natural, the same in India too. Now the tide will turn again, with those same states reinventing borders with us in the *infinitely* bigger Territories initiatives."

"Fascinating, how humankind keeps evolving. It's certainly been healthy, for World peace."

At the dais, getting *closed-door* Security Council sessions underway, DelMonte was visibly grave. "Friends, I said earlier that, powerful as we are, we're still powerless to stop natural events.

"What's on everyone's mind today is whether the Icehouse Climate, which we are advised is coming, could in fact deepen."

Apprehension hanging in the air, he had no choice but to disappoint. "Well with no precedent in modern times, no way to predict developments, the likelihood was always there for that to happen someday." This news was met with deadly silence. "And with the information we'll come to later, we believe that a return to ice age conditions – affecting the whole of 'Ameurasia' [geographically encompassing North America, Europe and Asia] – cannot be ruled out. What is uncertain is the time scale. With the expectation of it taking several decades, we stand a chance to prepare. Should it turn out to be quicker – we cannot." Initially uncertainty registered in their faces, then their expressions blanked at the realisation that a bomb had been delivered and was about to explode.

"Thankfully," DelMonte cleared his throat, "we have some measures to buy us time – such as destroying moorland and peatland that were cultivated in the 2020s to lower greenhouse carbon dioxide levels. Or, we can open out the Ra Sun screen, the belt of NEOs that mining companies arrested and put in geo-blocking orbit in the 30s."

DelMonte held his hands up. "That was this morning's breaking news." He braced himself to spill out the worst, "The reason we can be so certain about the ice age threat," he twisted his heels, imagining billions of faces soon filled with as much foreboding as those about to change in this room, "is that something else has come up." Throat and mouth drying, the President sipped some water and drew his tongue over his lips.

"UNNDC scientists have discovered a phenomenon, codenamed DeepStorm, of such magnitude that it's impact will be felt by everyone, everywhere – on Earth and upside."

Wishing he could offer even a titbit of better news, and having none, he introduced, "Our Chief Scientist will present the findings to you," and gestured towards me, "Professor Mark Madison." Not a sound was uttered as we traded places at the dais.

"Thank you, Mr Chairman." I heard my native English accent cut through the room clearly, though regrettably with a faintly doleful edge. Fearful of raising a sword of Damocles I took a deep breath, resisted looking at my notes and began in modulated tone.

"Einstein predicted the existence of 'gravitational-waves' in space. Gwaves, as they've come to be called, are the pulsing gravity produced by giant stellar entities twirling about each other." I expected that spectre to seem remote enough, benign enough even, not to be alarming. "Then early this millennium the NASA-ESA mission Lisa used three craft, spaced five million kilometres apart in orbit around the Sun, to detect faint Gwaves."

My acid responsibility was to deliver pure objective science, regardless of the sword lifting. "Four years ago the NASA-ESA mission Sun-rider reached far beyond our Solar System, with the fastest craft ever, and we were initially delighted when a sizeable Gwave was detected, at a distance of 100 AU [Astronomical Units] from Earth. However, to our horror, instead of Sun-rider speeding quickly over the wave, as we'd imagined it would, it continued to pass over it," I swallowed, dry mouthed, "and continued over it for a very long way. Measurements of its force got stronger and stronger." The sword now hung there. Tongues were as if gagged. "This was no mean wave. It was a tsunami of a Gwave – in space."

"Its top, the crest, was put at 215 AU from Earth. Two months ago – nearly four years later – that Gwave was 145 AU away. It's coming at us that fast." I felt tension tighten my brow, as I foresaw everyone envisioning gravity forces slamming at Earth.

"Sun-rider had done its job and sped on, unequipped to receive new instructions at those distances. However, data from it is producing startling insights. For starters, we see from the wave profile that the base stretches all the way to the Oort Cloud at the opposite side of the Solar System. What does it mean? We are in the wave right now! And, possibly have been since the last ice age!

On cue a large hologram appeared, with the Solar System superimposed on the Gwave. "This model shows what we're dealing with." I moved from the dais to the projection. "This perfect wave form," I could never resist admiring the graceful symmetry, "is crossing the Solar System's orbit, in the Milky Way Galaxy, at an acute angle."

I'd presented them with DeepStorm – now I had to convey what it might do. Worse, I had to ensure they understood what precious little time we had to prepare. "As to its impact on Earth? It'll grow and grow, with the greatest pull on the Earth being when the steep wave crest passes through.

"An early effect, we've considered, would be to pull the Earth's orbit out. And that could mean, as in the Milankovitch cycle, our re-entering an ice age climate. We even wonder if that's not already begun to happen, as we alluded to at the start of this session.

Another effect would be to nudge the Earth enough to reduce its 'obliquity' [or tilt in rotation], and eliminate the seasons on Earth.

"Those are dire possibilities. More practically we'll use measurements – which we've begun to take – to predict the changing times and movements of ocean tides as the crest approaches. We already anticipate its pull, when closest to Earth, not to exceed that of our Moon. Though that means yet again reinforcing seawall defences, for a *doubling* of present day tide heights and storm surges!

"We're also working on gauging the tidal movement of continental plates, to aid in the predictive analyses of quakes, tsunamis and volcanic eruptions. The Yellowstone and Toba supervolcanoes are flagged for the threat they pose – globally." In no way an unemotional being, I felt my audience's fears, but all I could do was maintain a calm tone. "We will do our utmost to update projections concerning extreme weather.

"On other fronts we're initiating a programme of tagging and tracking NEOs and 'BoStorms' [storms of BoBos] nudged our way – with the expectation of them taking ten years and three years, respectively, to get here from the Kuiper Belt and AstBelt. We'll deploy mining operators to deflect, arrest, or destroy all those tagged. It'll take millennia for anything from the Oort Cloud, 50 'KAU' [Kilo-AU] out, to reach here.

"And, in our monitoring of Solar flares, we're already looking out for extreme CMEs [Coronal Mass Ejections]. Preparations will be made to identify and shut down threatened power grids and communications as well as to warn citizens to stay indoors."

I gave way to silence for a moment. Lame mutterings in the audience swept in like rustling leaves on autumnal trees. I had to move in fast, raising my voice a tad, "There is cause for concern, of course. But, as I've said, UNNDC is sparing no effort in strengthening early warning systems and defences.

"On a final note, this is a totally new development – unknown to science. What's important is to be calm and get as much early warning as we can. And, when the time comes to make this public, everyone must know that it *is* manageable. We are *not* facing a global catastrophe.

"Thank you."

DelMonte returned to the dais to sum up, motioning for me to remain there. The outburst we'd both expected did not arrive. The rustling leaves were immobilised, by shock.

"Now is when the decades of our concerted work will show dividends, as amply demonstrated in the rebuilding of our economies in the strong EU-Arabian alliance, 'UNASUR' [Union of South American Nations] and 'ASEAN' [Association of Southeast Asian Nations]. Applying the same will and determination, we can fight this thing."

The leaves stirred. Believing they'd heard all, the leaders shifted from stupor to begin a chant for more information – objectives, funding, public announcements, emergency measures, evacuation plans, shelters and whatever else UNNDC needed to deliver. They were demanding answers.

DelMonte stiffened and held his hands high to beg silence, finally resorting to shouting above the din. "Our first priority was to brief you all regarding this threat at the earliest opportunity – as we've now done. Copies of our report on the phenomenon are now being circulated among you." The distracted crowd of heads peered into screens, to ensure receiving the report.

"Tomorrow, the Professor will go into more detail with you, to fully impart as much as is known at this time. The intent is to work through this *with* you, fully evaluating the situation with a view to formulating strategies before doing anything about declaring a state of emergency."

Outbursts became more heated. The President of UNASUR spoke loudly, "Do we have time? Shouldn't we disband to prepare our populations?"

"Certainly. But before announcing anything so alarming to the whole World, with upside colonies affected too, we must understand just what we are about to face and must prepare for." DelMonte was now admirably in control. "We will not be withholding anything from you. Quite to the contrary, we're putting together a scientific task force assigned specifically to explore this DeepStorm threat. This we propose to undertake jointly with you."

Hu Ma rose imperiously and DelMonte pointed to him for his views. "From what the Chief Scientist has just divulged it would seem that the greatest threat is presented by the steep Gwave crest," China's leader recapped. "And that, as he indicated, is still some considerable distance away. You'll presumably send more probes out there. But is there time to collate and analyse the data? Communicating at distances like that would slow down the whole research effort intolerably."

"That's a major difficulty," DelMonte agreed. "We're battling time and can ill afford those delays." He paused, judging the moment to proceed with full effect. "We propose to send manned craft – now in preparation – to analyse close-hand what's happening out there."

"Manned craft? So far out? A round trip out there to meet that thing even half way will take what – a few years – and, with time for research, even longer? The crew's lives will be at risk," the President of the European Union countered, as the assembly quietened to listen. "It was firmly established back in the 2020s – recognising the limitations of human physiology – that travel was to be strictly restricted to those areas of space within 'GEM' [Great Earth-Mars divide] that have spaceports with terrestrial conditions."

This had meant full terra-sphere style infrastructures with docking bays, overhaul hangers, provisions warehousing, medical units, rehab facilities for colonists and, most essentially, simulated EarthG.

"Only robotic exploration and mining has been sanctioned further out – in 'GAM' [Great AstBelt-Mars divide]," the EU President pointed out.

"True, there are risks." DelMonte was unflinching. "There are alternatives."

Matri picked up on this. "Space-breeds? Fimans? You're referring to the young citizens intended for the Near Earth Territories?"

"They're now of age." DelMonte measured the general surprise and had more to come. "Fortuitously, we've already initiated their induction and training."

Matri was clearly thrown. "But can their training be enough now? And is there enough known about how their physiologies will react?" She could see he stood firm and added faintly. "They'll be at risk?"

"There's only time to be highly selective, test them rigorously and pick the best of the best. They'll get full training once they're underway. And yes, they'll be at risk. It's not an easy call – but it's them, or the lives of countless millions."

~*~

Legacy

9

Spring 2066

In bright leather-look armour for external construction work, a building crew made its way deep within Ice Mine II on the Moon, where they had half their Earth weight in the 'EcstasyG' [Ecstasy gravity] of the teutronium-paved tunnels.

They passed guys in mining they'd never met and never would. And they were happy to keep it that way, keep to their own company. Their routines were so totally different, their lives so different. The miners drove big machines under a roof of rock over 100 metres thick, where they were safe from the thousands of tiny BoBos that hit the surface daily. The construction crew, on the other hand, quipped light heartedly about dodging BoBos out in open space. Where they were okay with the occupational hazards of their precision tasks – which had them dubbed 'space jockeys' – although, in the back of their minds, were the handful of accidents reported every month.

On reaching the cargo bay they went straight to a shuttle bound for cruise liner Lascaux, one of three Galahad vessels destined for the Near Earth Territories and presently at anchor a short distance from the surface. Each knew the drill – *Once aboard, stow gear before taking a seat and make yourself comfortable for takeoff.*

One of them, a woman with a broad Kansas accent, looked through a portal, casually remarking on a uniformed man on the ground, "Fancy calling them flyers. He's rooted on his ass within that flight-deck down there."

"Our pilot? Yeah, those guys don't fly with us anymore," the big Texan next to her, returned. "Now they fly these things remotely, and mostly on auto."

"You don't say! Well, he can come with me any time. He's a doll!" She sent the flyer a saucy wink. Having fretfully watched her family grow up, her husband included, Kansas felt free to go out and get some prime-life fun.

"Looking to play, eh? Heck, he might be there when you get back," the Texan, a good deal older, could scarcely appear more disinterested.

The airlock doors opened, followed by a loud hum, before the shuttle shot along a long launch track for the two-hour journey through space. The pilot watched that virtually and tracked its progress on his instruments. Once out there, he often observed passengers mingling, semi-weightless, sociable as they were, rather than sitting and watching entertainment. Around then he would carefully go through a checklist of readings before switching his attention to a football game.

Kansas chatted with another woman, from Maine, whose daughter planned to marry the following year. Kansas, unluckily as it happened, congratulated her. Maine frowned, looking a trifle distraught. "I can't stand the creep. I'm doing all I can to get her to dump him."

"Oh," Kansas returned, not welcoming chitchat about unruly youths and keen to change the subject. "You fixing on having a break anytime soon?"

"Sure," Maine rolled her eyes. "Boy! Not that I'm looking forward to having more of the slouch to deal with. He's everywhere. Except at work, or anywhere productive."

"I've got an idea. Why not come over to my place? Sounds like you could do with a change of scene." Kansas added within herself, "So long as we can talk about other things." She spoke out loud again, "My club isn't as cosy as we have up here, but comfortable enough. We can go skiing from there – in Utah – and have grand grumple stew, a favourite recipe of my grandma's."

Some ninety minutes later the two Territories vessels Lascaux and Avebury were clearly in view. So magnificently elegant and pristine, hanging there in space, with no windows, portholes or superstructures whatever, their uniquely stark appearance made them quite the talk of the base.

Through the tube-like structures' open ends, construction crews within could be seen working on the immensely strong graphene hull walls, whilst those in the Sun outside were finishing a classified outer-shield of five-metre thick reinforced concrete. On the dark side a mist resembling a short beard tailed off over half the hull lengths, where crews were fixing five-metre thick ice tiles onto the already set concrete. The slick ice shield was designed to withstand the bombardment of BoBos, the surface automatically replenishing after impacts and also providing stealth protection. The sheer size of the operation commanded full attention from all passing shuttle passengers.

A highly audible buzz alerted the remote pilot to an object onscreen, with its trajectory initially to one side of the shuttle's and then overlapping it. Messages read OBJECT – SMALL BoBo. RISK OF COLLISION – 57%. RESPONSE – 'BoCracker' [BoBo laser defence system] ACTIVATED. Crosshairs zeroed in as the shuttle BoCracker automatically prepared to destroy the boulder. A countdown message read FIRING IN – 5, 4, 3... At that the pilot, who'd gauged the effect that changing trajectories would have, switched the controls to manual and made a one-degree course correction. The vessel veered slightly.

"Yahoo, it's fireworks time," Texas screamed in delight. The guys on board saw the BoBo glint in the sunlight and crammed to the windows smiling, little boy or girl still inside them to the fore. BoCrackers pulverised small rocks all the time out there, with a short starburst that was fun to watch – but also a reminder of dangers.

"Whoopee!" Kansas, in the mood for fun, yelled, eyes alight at the sight of the cracker flashing silently in the vacuum of space, hitting home with the tip of a faint conical light. It was surgical – operating much like a giant hospital cyber knife. Convention ruled out laser bolts in peacetime military as well as civilian use, because of the danger to spaceways, in travelling endlessly and perhaps even being slingshot back by planetary gravitational forces.

The passengers retained their broad smiles and were cheering when Texas gasped, "No!" Happy faces turned to horror. Out of the exploding cloud of dust a big fragment of rock was shooting straight at them. "No!"

"Pilot! Something's wrong!" Maine piped up weakly, "The laser missed!"

"I see it," their pilot responded reassuringly. "Don't know how that happened. I'm checking." Instead, however, he ran a finger over the trajectories on screen to gauge how much to veer the craft – for a *direct hit*. The corner of his mouth lifted sardonically.

"Sure!" Texas insisted. "Get us the fuck out of here!"

"Do something!" Kansas was getting angry.

"I am locking on to fire again, and I'm changing the course of your craft. Hold tight onto something," The pilot maintained a calm reassuring tone.

The construction workers scrambled, none reaching seats in the time they had before the craft veered sharply.

"Hey! This baby is still coming!" Texas managed to regain some composure and take a view again, beads of sweat decorating his terrified face. "It's close! Fuck! Fire the goddamn laser!"

Others joined in, "Fire!"

"For Christ sake fire!" Maine pleaded.

"Hit it! Hit it hard!" Kansas ordered.

"Okay, firing." The laser's flash was wide of the rock, narrowly missing the craft, they were that close together. "No good! Quick, get to your seats. Brace yourselves in the crash position," his tone remained firmly confident.

"Wah? No! Fire again!" Maine pleaded.

"Fire damn it!" Texas and Kansas shrieked in unison.

"Remain calm. I'm activating emergency procedures. A rescue craft will be with you shortly. All will be well. Don't worry. We'll have you out of there in no time." He punched the emergency button. Whereupon the stricken craft's full disposition was streamed to the rescue centre. Meanwhile, the pilot simply folded his arms, sat back in his chair and watched the show.

"No, oh shit!" Texas was now resigned to his fate.

"Help!" Maine yipped hopelessly.

The pilot listened with satisfaction for the loud dull crunch of the rock punching clean through the hull. He heard that clearly, over the vessel's 'coms' [communications] channel. He leant forward again to watch petrified passengers being thrown out of their seats by the impact. A loud rush of expelling air depressurised the cabin. Loose objects and bodies were sucked to two gaping holes in opposite sides of the hull, where they were ejected like trash. Everyone, that could, clung onto something and quickly snatched down oxygen masks gasping desperately.

"Aaah!" Texas gave out, losing his grip, his body flipping about as helplessly as a rag doll in a wind tunnel.

"Please God, no!" Kansas let go to drift feebly in the craft, the last rush of air already expelled with Texas.

The pilot heard all of their terrified screams, their harsh frantic wheezing. One by one he watched their uplifted eyes bulge lifelessly, including Maine and Kansas. Before him the craft's pressurising 'HVAC' [heating, ventilation and air conditioning] instruments merely indicated: Unit Inoperative. He knew all too well that the rock had gone right through, rupturing it.

72

"Rescue, this is flight control for construction shuttle 038. Are you en route?"

"We are," the response was immediate, "We have 038's position. Our nearest unit is locked in and making way. Estimated arrival time thirty minutes."

Without compassion, the pilot turned and, with a gloved hand, signed in to the neighbouring console as a maintenance administrator. There he accessed the log to record a failure in the automatic guidance system and the BoCracker. And then, in the audit trail, he wiped out the manual override he'd performed.

Just as he completed this, the rescuers arrived at the shuttle and he watched as they boarded. Each remaining body was checked in the hope of survivors. Of the 50 souls who'd set out on the trip, none lived on.

~*~

10

Spring 2066

Social networking, the main artery of information, was beginning to bleed out news of the World under siege to a point where Sævrama and other media channels tapped in to source alarms about localised natural disasters. While UNNDC scientists, concerned about the absence of any real public awareness on DeepStorm, injected their own blogs on Climate Change.

Keen to stay on top, Jude Nade boned up on a whole range of weather topics – from snowdrifts to avalanches, electric storms and wildfires, storms battering coasts, monsoon level rains and flooding, and even lahars [mud slides], as well as rescue and recovery operations.

Naturally each of the F-Academies were fully abreast of developments. They could have instructed their AIs to filter out all DeepStorm content wherever fimans and their contacts had access to the Net, but they had decided against this. The distraction, however harrowing for loved-ones and their communities, was just that – and it also came with a bonus. Through it the new breeds were seeing their roles in perspective. They set aside their angers at conscription to reflect on their opportunity to save lives – they felt this their duty.

On a clear moonlit night, Sashia and Fayez were in a state of numbness as their cab moved past busy throngs, zanily decorated trams and melodious buskers on HK Central streets. Very soon to be separated, they wore stony-faced resignation.

Nonetheless Fayez strove to lift Sashia's spirits. Noticing her eyeing buildings through their taxi window, the novelty of her new eagle-like ability still fresh, he challenged her to discover new visual oddities or secrets. Obligingly, she immediately pointed. "There, can you see? First floor up, a metallic blue ceiling with reflections of harbour lights and a westerner face-up having an Indian scalp-massage."

He squinted to make out anything more than a window. "I can zoom in on his eyes and, hell-bytes, there's a *mirror* reflected in them." She zoomed in more, "It's fantastic! In the mirror I can clearly see a pretty Chinese face, fine soft lips, large Mongolian eyes – and trendy eyelashes just like mine! Her stylist is lightly stroking at his creation – a zebra-striped mane on top and a tail smooth and sweet down her bare back. She's getting up to go... giving him a tip... Oh, her hand! Its got a red dragon sculpted into the fingers – and the other one.... There's a green sculpted one. I remember her! Yes!" Sashia's memory hadn't been the sharpest, yet this woman she recalled vividly. "Sin-bugs – at the Conference Centre. Jude Nade was interviewing that biologist, Dr Mei Sai Ling. She was there about saving the pink dolphins!"

Sashia beamed. "Yikes! I can remember everything and in incredible detail! The whole dolphin protest... how they trashed The Docks... lots more."

As the cab mounted a flyover, a very excited Sashia shrieked on sighting a Sævrama hologram. "Let me hear that!" Startled, the driver quickly tuned in to the channel.

Jude Nade was transmitting live from Machu Picchu. *"As forecast, most places have been sunny this year, though once again temperatures are generally down on previous years. It's certainly been a long winter in northern latitudes, only now ending. This is quite without precedence – although good news for ski resorts.*

"On another note," her tone altered, "you'll be aware of some gloom-and-doom on the social nets.

"If you're in farming, manufacturing or power generation, either in high latitudes or high altitudes, you're sure to be aware of changes below snowlines over the years. Snowmelt, for example, has not been filling river systems and reservoirs as it used to do. Authorities in such areas, concerned about maintaining supplies of power and water to households, have been setting aside contingency funds to deal with any worsening of the situation. They're also mindful that jobs might be at risk, in industries that are reliant on those supplies."

Sashia wasn't having any of it, not gloom-and-doom, not tonight. She commanded the cab driver to stop and leaped out momentarily teetering on the pavement, her extraordinary striders shaped and repositioned for a glamorous night out. As soon as Fayez had paid, she pulled his arm around her. "Let's go... this way," motioning to boisterous crowds overfilling arty bistros and bars in popular Soho. However, as they reached the party-mad mêlée, everything caught up again. "It's so strange," she whispered, her mind all over the place. "Last night was my last sight of Lok Hat Do, the bar, the girls, the crowd. They were so sweet saying goodbye." He nodded, stonewalling her, while trying to conceal his own damage. It was all too surreal, even her stopping abruptly so he'd bump into her, and her then being able to nuzzle her bot into his groin and give him that throaty giggle. "Miss me?"

Fayez' smile meant everything. It told her the bar and his *keys* were all going to be miserable without her. He ached to know why she had to go or even know whether she herself knew, which she did not. "Okay. Change of scene... got something to show you."

Sashia just nodded and followed where he led, down the outdoor escalator and through more revellers in adjoining Lang Kwai Fong's cobbled alleys, there to grab a quick bite before sauntering to the Peak Tram.

From the steeply climbing car, it was all too poignant watching the familiar buildings fall away beneath them and seeing HK's glittering harbour open up at their feet.

At the top they strolled to a favourite viewing spot of theirs and stood under the stars, pointing out sights she considered her home along Aberdeen Harbour – floating restaurants, boatyards, marinas – even the small houseboat they finally called home. Everywhere offered up their personal memories, she was already missing, though still here.

They wandered to the Peak Lookout, the old rickshaw stables tastefully converted and decorated colonial style, from parquet floors to wooden ceiling fans and the deep mahogany panelled bar. HK was not particularly known for preserving its heritage architecture. This precious exception had only recently been restored (a second time).

Fayez continued to take the lead, ushering her on to the tiled terrace with its vine-entwined trellises and little fireplaces brought in winter to the tables. He skirted around the balustrade to where the terrace had been extended and stopped at a half-covered bar area where dinner tables and a dance floor were arranged half-circling a piano, to which he pointed and smiled.

"Ho-hum." Sashia's pleasure was evident. "So this is *your secret* – your mission while I've been preparing for mine." He nodded, knowing she'd guessed his new workplace. "Goodah, no cocktail waitresses here! Oh, Fayez, I like it!"

"Yeah, and I can compose what I like." Lightly, he fingered the piano keys. "Think of me here, my Starburst – thinking of you when it opens – and ever after. They're naming this area Fayez Dachet's Bar or **FDB,** after me."

Making a conscious effort to forget everything else, she held his face in her palms and softly kissed his lips. "I will. I will, my love." Lingering, glad to have the place to themselves, they sipped beers, and he played for her and she swayed to his melancholy notes, her eyes hardly leaving his, all too aware of time passing too swiftly. Ironically, in these hours before division, they were more at one with each other than in the previous weeks of terrible tension.

Thoughts of the exercises pushed in again, now particularly of a high altitude exercise. The craft's captain had given the all clear, "...all systems are GO, wind shear 60 kilometres per hour north easterly." The task co-ordinator had called the orders. "All systems READY. We have: Team one – GREEN. Team two – GREEN. Team three – GREEN..."

Time up, her pod had shot with a jolt into space. Stern faced she'd concentrated on her astronaut training, noting her heads-up instrumentation – temperature, speed, trajectory over maps. As quickly, the thrill of weightlessness had overridden her tense breathlessness until she'd observed the curvature of the Earth stretched stupendously before her.

Falling alternately through clear skies and cloud she'd imagined herself a she-shaman, soaring as an eagle to her sky's boundaries.

And even after spying the white cross of the drop zone, her chute opening to land her with a gentle bump, she'd reeled at her newfound skills and clarity of thinking. Here, now, she shivered thinking about the adrenaline high and freedom of floating that had robbed her of ever wanting to stay on the ground – those moments, although fleeting, had proved life altering.

Noting her reflective state, Fayez felt locked out and helpless, until her eyes returned to him, clearly held only in thoughts of him and the daybreak that could not be held back for them.

When it arrived, they all too soon found themselves in the harbour, staring silently into waters that slipped serenely under their aquataxi, and soon they were traversing vast spaces under the sail-like canopy of Chek Lap Kok Spaceport, which echoed the huge emptiness of the occasion. They had said all that could be said. They walked in a state of surrealism.

Sashia focused momentarily on a far off screen switched to the Sævrama Channel and something heard during training came back to her about these newscasts. She'd been standing among hundreds of young Asians and Oceanians, casually dressed guys and girls from all social sets, when the F-Academy principal had concluded his term-end address rather ominously. "You've always known that you're different. And, yes, you're already very special. The training you're receiving is essential to fulfil your destiny, to complete who you are. You will all be able to live, work, and stand alone anywhere upside. That's when you will be able to serve your World – in its hour of greatest need. More on that in due course."

Throughout the principal's address there'd been concerned looks among them, and some dissenting voices among those more bitter at being torn from their home lives. "Meanwhile," he continued, "keep up with events in the media – such as on the Sævrama Channel. That's where you'll see what's happening worldwide and why you are needed in the fight to save it."

At the waiting craft Sashia yielded to one last lingering kiss before boarding and, conscious of her steel-edged will melting, she jestingly wiped a tear, headed towards the craft and signalled back that she'd holoe him on the flight.

Her aches for Fayez and home were exacerbated by the craft's dull droning as well as her growing dread of soon being among perfect strangers. During takeoff Sashia's tears became real.

As promised she holoed and found him seated at the piano and guiding the optic with her eyes she scanned for familiar things – the rubber plant she'd nurtured, a brass lamp she'd found years ago, an ornamental elephant she'd given him and a picture of a sailboat they'd been on in the Mediterranean. This was *their* houseboat, *their* shared home. Tears flowed again. Had the choice been hers alone, she acknowledged she would never have left.

"Fayez? I'll tell you one day what this is all about," she promised silently.

"Wah!" she yelped as he reappeared mockingly wearing a scarf. "What are you doing?" He cocked his head cheekily. "You look ridiculous. I want to see you!" He only raised an eyebrow, point made. Choosing to ignore his antics, she continued, "One day all this will make sense. I promise you. Meanwhile, trust me... and if it gets difficult to make contact, just remember it'll always be for a reason – not because I don't want to talk. Just remember that, *please*, 'cause I love you."

~*~

11

Spring 2066
(Autumn in Southern Hemisphere)

The following morning at the UN Security Council Summit in Machu Picchu, the Sævrama Channel crew gathered with other media members, only to be informed by the Council press officers that open sessions were being rescheduled. Only *closed sessions* would resume now. Among an inevitable barrage of questions, Jude Nade's probing as to whether Climate Change was on the agenda received no response.

"Jack. Jack, you there?" Jude's tone was terse. Waiting for his holoe she bit her lip.

"Yaaah?" Roused from sleep, Jack was groggy.

"Something's up," impatience in her tone, "Closed-door sessions went on into the night – and they're resuming now."

"Uh, you said something about that on the air. The strongest indication... Something *really* amiss with the climate..." Jack rolled off his bed, to sit on the floor.

"Yeah." Rolling her eyes at the sight of him, "Not a pretty sight."

"Then you said something to me, about Ni'moloka'i?" He held his forehead in his palm, shaking his head to clear his thoughts, "Christ! Are we facing another Indian Ocean tsunami? Another Haiti – or what?"

She cringed, "Maybe. Or worse – if that's even possible. That's what I don't know. I'll keep you posted. But just have crew on stand-by if things hot up." She half grinned at giving *him* an order. "He's okay," she murmured to herself, shrugging. This is a *big* scoop."

He was coming round, focusing, and finally awake was in the kitchen pouring a glass of milk and advising, "Hold on. I'll get hold of McGuire." A click on his wristband, he pulled down a pane with his appointments diary and dragged the reporter's profile to attach a note to him. "He can get there from London. By evening I guess."

She froze, caught off guard, murmuring, "Of course he'd want a celebrated presenter to take over, give my story more weight." Her frown was deep.

Jack noted it. "You stick with it, your story," he confirmed. "Just let him in on summing up tomorrow. Then he can follow through in Washington. Okay?"

Opening the closed session, Matri set the mood in her own composed, measured manner, "We've heard UNNDC findings and concerns over DeepStorm – and," she addressed me, "Professor Madison, you've heard the concerns of the hall. This is an informal session in which we'd ask you to speak freely. In effect, conjecture for us whatever our outside chances are, and, answer any questions frankly." I nodded as she waved me up to the dais.

I'd given them the breaking news, now I had to deliver the grisly details about an accident billions of people had little chance of avoiding. Nothing in my long professional career had prepared me for this. Yet, accustomed to delivering weighty issues calmly, I too was direct, "How else will DeepStorm affect us?

I hesitated before answering my own question, prepared for a question from the members, which came on the direction that UNNDC research would take. Answering, I was relieved to have positive dialogue. "First we'll focus on bodies that are closest to the wave crest. We'll catalogue their changes in orbit, obliquity and spin. On the surface of rocky moons we'll record tidal movements and surface upheavals. In the Kuiper Belt we'll log collisions between planetesimals, for their potential to become NEOs." I paused for the display on the dais to indicate that the answer was acceptable. It was.

"That data will be invaluable for benchmarking what we can expect to happen here. Except what will be missing, is the combination of atmosphere, protective magnetosphere, oceans and continental plates that is so unique to Earth. That combination, found nowhere else, underpins life as we know it. Underpins our biosphere. Everything we need to forecast – tides, earth movements and weather – relates to that. In short, the behaviour we absolutely must model – is Earth itself impacted by a DeepStorm wave crest." I expected no answer when I then asked, "And where in hell can we get that, ahead of time?"

I paused briefly, scanned their faces. "Which begs the question. Nothing like this has happened before?" Again I cast around for a response. "My view? With luck, it quite possibly has." Conscious of stepping outside of UNNDC views, I refrained from being assertive. "Quite possibly some answers are on the Moon as well as elsewhere upside! Beyond all expectations, it has been discovered that fossils as well as dinosaur bone fragments were scattered there as ejecta from asteroid impacts and volcanic eruptions on Earth. Importantly, palaeontologists just recently unearthed a forerunner of the cormorant. And researchers have even succeeded in extracting some DNA.

"What needs to be answered is whether something similar to the DeepStorm Gwave – if not the same as – was ever as destructive in prehistory. A prime candidate for investigation would be the relatively quiet geological time, just preceding the famed Chicxulub catastrophe. That's when over 160 million years of dinosaur evolution – that's longer than most creatures ever lived, with surviving the most violent quakes, impacts and eruptions there have ever been on this planet – came to an end.

"There's a lot of speculation about this but with nothing much, if anything, substantiated. Yet what happened, what really happened, might well give us the model we need for DeepStorm's full force today."

That appeared to go down okay. Except then, DelMonte challenged me. And his more placid manner, reserved for public viewing, slipped away in the knowledge that he was not on air. He was curt. "You're saying that a Gwave *was* involved back then?"

"No." My notion had no support from the scientific community, let alone from UNNDC. "There's no evidence of that." My feelings edged on the desperate. I would not have another shot at this, not in a summit. DeepStorm was my discovery, my baby. All my instincts were shouting – yes, DeepStorm had also visited the *Cretaceous* world. And, if that was right, we *had* to learn from it. It would be a travesty not to. But, I couldn't come out with it, unsupported as I was. My only recourse was to tease it out in some scientific manner.

"As a start, we'd have to locate a source. Some cosmic system close enough to have transmitted Gwaves across the Milky Way, over the whole span of time to now."

"And are there any such candidates?"

"No, none." A welter of frustration and anger had me poised to pounce. "Yet, the source of the present Gwave is not known either. We'd have anticipated it otherwise." There was deathly quiet, my hands clenched on the dais as the moment slipped away. "But then, little is known about dark systems all around us."

"But there's nothing definite?"

"That is correct. At this juncture no large system, whether comprised of twin stars or black holes, or whatever else, has been catalogued anywhere close enough to influence Earth with super Gwaves."

I would have said more but for the President of Europe, perhaps led by DelMonte's negative tone, taking things on from there. "What other avenues are you pursuing?" I couldn't conceal dismay. He was moving the session's agenda forward.

That was it, my cue to drop the *Cretaceous* quest. Although gutted at losing this chance, I had no choice but to keep calm and carry on. "UNNDC will take a central role in coordinating preventative activities internationally. And we're already looking at erecting protective terra-spheres over cities most at risk of a BoStorm, or the fallout from a supervolcano eruption." Council members held their copies of the UNNDC report to refer to details. "BoCrackers will also be deployed in geostationary orbit over cities, such as on thermoports."

The high altitude spaceports, located over ground spaceports, were designed for the new generation of lightweight shuttles moving about space. Tough 'LTA' [Lighter-Than-Air] graphene nanotubes were used in constructing the floating platforms, 120 kilometres up in the thermosphere, where solar-collector steam columns towered kilometres up, to feed the thermoelectric power plant for cities on the ground. "Many of those have been enlarged as living-tower greenhouses, to cultivate the first breeds of space crops as well as sphagnum moss (for controlling greenhouse gases). As a last resort, those giant platforms can be moved in the path of BoStorms."

The hall was ominously silent, with members holding their breaths in the hope of a reprieve from all this.

DelMonte signalled for me to remain while he, with a confident tone, summed up the UNNDC's view. "We're at the earliest stage of formulating strategies, which will be kept dynamic and open to you all while new information flows in.

"What we must do, is get the facts," his tone sotto voce now, a trick he used to make his point firmly, "urgently, with just over three years before the wave crest gets here."

His tone rose again, "So going back to what I said yesterday, it's vitally important that we get a mission of trained fimans out there – as quickly as we can." He addressed everyone there as much as Commander in Chief for the American people as he was head of UNNDC, and was speaking of the fimans as troops going into battle. "Which sadly means, regardless of the risks to them," he added reverentially.

While previously such talk would have struck a negative chord, those present now appeared to accept his announcement as a dire necessity.

He signalled for me to resume, which I did. "Fimans are being trained at purpose built academies round the world. They'll soon be on exercise at Mount Hengshan, Kathmandu, Zurich, Machu Picchu and Whistler."

There was no escaping what I had to impart next, which arose from intelligence on sabotage attempts. One such was a truck with radioactive material that crashed through perimeter fencing at ESA's Bahamas Spaceport, disrupting supplies to the Moon. "The fiman training is basically scientific in nature. However, once underway, zero tolerance will apply to crew losses. Which means, the mission must fend for itself. And also defend itself." The words felt acidic in my mouth. "For that, we aim to select Best of Breed fimans and give them Special Forces training. It's war." Not a sound came in response.

Eventually the Council members shuffled away, faces ashen. As I followed, DelMonte caught up with me. As we walked, strictly matter-of-fact, he asked, "What's our stat? I heard you and read the reports, but you tell me – and straight. Are we going to be hit hard by this thing?"

I aimed to be equally dispassionate, burying my disappointment over his dowsing my *Cretaceous* angle. Anyhow, on reflection I'd half expected it and should have been better prepared. "It's bad, really bad." He gave a quizzical look, urging more. "Many densely populated areas are at risk. Everything I said we'll do, but what do you think? Can we really deliver that – with resources already stretched to the limit?"

I was sure he knew as much, but not about what I added next, "For all we know, even the stability of the Earth's crust is at risk!" I stared at him. "And then what, if it starts to break up? Will World peace hold up? Will civilisation?" He watched me frown testily, I was that angry about the *Cretaceous* angle.

The man had a way, a public knack, of throwing out scraps to collect a big response. His respecting me, even liking me I thought, had no place in this. With these stakes, it was strictly business. "How soon?"

My brief retort matched his, "It's already started – the Earth's crust is already under stress and getting more active. Disasters are mounting – have been in recent millennia." In return for his astonished look I formed an icy resolve that had my own head humming.

His face froze. "What'll it take?" And he drew up, Commander in Chief role surging forth. "Any ideas, on beating it?"

"Reconneering." I watched him contemplate that association, "Rapid reconnaissance and research. Measure, model and project all effects, on the ground here and upside. We have to get out there." On this I could be emphatic, having full UNNDC support.

"Sure, just as was said in the sessions," his tone eased. His support of me on this was never in doubt. He knew I was good for it, professionally. His irritation was in not being able to go with my gut instincts too, "What do you need, what resources?"

"I figure the basic requirement to be a flight crew of eight top rated fiman reconneers rotating on duty, 24 in total. A two-year tour on a long haul research ship with artificial EarthG, supported by 24 mission project-control crew and 48 ancillary staff of cooks, nurses, technicians and such."

The arrival of a DelMonte aide, middle-aged, lean and seriously lifeless looking unsettled me some. This man also called over Admiral Connell Althorpe, who'd been acting in an advisory capacity to UNSDO. With a nod, DelMonte left us to continue without him. We needed no introductions. I had met the aide a couple of times earlier and seen the Admiral during the HK dolphin protest. The aide picked up the dialogue, "So, a complement of around 100."

"The Security Council strategy is to make the mission fully independent of Earth's fate," the Admiral declared pointedly. "In effect, to survive Earth's fate – survive DeepStorm. And for that the entire NASA-ESA style mission control is to go up." Here was a whole new ball game. "The US President will at all times be within minutes of boarding Airforce One, en route to the thermoport Airforce Two. Up there, he and his staff will be safely off the surface and above *all* upheavals." His emphatic stare drilled into me. "Likewise your people have to stay on their own out in space, the whole crew sustainably self reliant, for as long as it takes to keep Earth warned of dangers – and well beyond that, if it comes to it."

"And we're not expecting crew quarters as on a warship, or on the old International Space Station, but the regular housing of a thermoport, or billeting of a military base. *Terraccommodate* them, long-term, your term." The aide was alluding to one of my published works on terraforming.

"Right," I gritted my teeth, not so much at the large-scale facility inferred, of which there'd anyway been talk, but the grim prospect of a protracted stay isolated in space. "Okay. Long-term means what? Five years? Ten? Twenty?" In the ensuing silence my emotions sank with thoughts of banishment. "Fine, a regular research facility on indefinite tour, in space, with *no* external support whatever. No crew relief, no re-provisioning, nothing," I stifled exasperation over the impact there'd be on everyone aboard and took the continued silence as affirmation from the two men. Looking from one to the other, I saw nothing more was forthcoming, except I had the weird sense that I'd been given *ownership* of this.

I became more assertive. "At the very least we'll need a Territories style vessel, with EarthG quarters, along with its crew *and* a major refit – with workshops, hospital, farm – as well as provisions of livestock and crops. Plus, we'll need the staff to operate those."

Although this could have been met with iron-like coldness, instead they let me continue. "Altogether, with 'redundancy' [inbuilt backup], I'd put the full complement of crew at closer to 500 or possibly upwards of that."

Althorpe had advices on mission control numbers, to add to his considerable experience of the complement on aircraft carriers. "Noted, upwards of that. Not to mention radiation and BoBo shields, in the refit, and an incredibly big budget."

The aide, who appeared a little out of his depth, interceded, "Wait one." He was receiving instructions and now addressed me again. "President DelMonte is going with advices from UNSDO that there isn't a lot of choice when it comes to suitable vessels. The first ships built for the Near Earth Territories, both to the Galahad design, are liners Lascaux and Avebury. These can easily be refitted as they're still with their fabricators, at anchor off the Moon."

To my surprise, he seemed to want an answer there and then. And naturally, considering that the Galahad design had more space than a city district, I had no difficulty in concurring, "Sure! Either would be good. With ample space for terraforming." Heartened, though now also apprehensive, I looked quizzically at Althorpe.

He imparted no surprise whatsoever at the scale now being contemplated. "Fine. We wanted to hear it from you, directly." He raised the corner of his mouth, and then gave a satisfied smile to the aide before relaxing his stance with me. "I'll support you with whatever you need. Can you cope with the space, even if we hike the complement to 2,000 for good measure?"

I was now thinking of the whole exercise having taken on the magnitude of a town planning exercise – as if giving birth to the Territories after all. Nevertheless, glad of reaching an accord, I gave a very relieved reply, "Sure."

For all the aide's blandness, his eagerness was positive. "On advisement you get both liners, each a complete replica of the other as a back-up, with the full complement of crew discussed." At this my eyebrows involuntarily shot up. I'd anticipated a significant scaling up, but nothing like this. The realisation that things were actually progressing thawed my discomfort with the man. "We're already talking about a sizeable task force out there." I had to admit to myself I was impressed – overwhelmed even.

"But, on military advisement, you also get a navy escort, a battle-carrier with a crew of 6,500." Althorpe leant toward me, lowering his voice, "Don't tell anyone but the US Navy actually requisitioned the very first Galahad to build that, extending and renaming it the Bering." Straightening, he had just one more, burning, question for me. "How long? How long do you need to draw up terraccommodating plans for the refits?" He looked from me to the aide. "And to complete the work?"

"Several months," I hesitated, too aware of the stakes, "Six, nine months at the outside."

"Twenty months starting from now, in parallel with the design work." The aide had already done his sums on the construction effort involved.

DelMonte returned on that cue, having eavesdropped via a secure coms line. He had his answer. "You've both got fourteen, tops." With that he signalled his aide to withdraw and addressed me. "You appreciate that'll be the largest task force – of any kind – to be assembled upside?" There lay much of the reason behind his tension. So much was now at stake. And he certainly didn't want any new tack, such as my *Cretaceous* pitch, to derail the plan.

I rolled my eyes affirmatively, while fully aware of the responsibility I was taking on. Rather than dwelling on that though, I simply had to follow through on what was eating me up and, come what may, open up the issue. Lowering my tone, almost beseechingly now, I waded right in. "When I say civilisation is at stake," I swallowed, expecting a hiding for bringing this up again so soon, "I have to think of when else was that big. And that has to be the *End Cretaceous* Mass Extinction. That's all we have to go on." I waited anxiously.

DelMonte raised an eyebrow, attentive but impatient as he dismissed the Admiral with an informal salute. He turned to me again. "It was an asteroid impact, a NEO, right?" The man was immovable, engaging me alone now. "Which we'll guard against? Your job?"

I shook my head hopelessly, yet continued with as much assertiveness as I could muster. "Sure we'll monitor NEOs. But if you're concerned about collateral damage, major losses, it wasn't with the impact. May I?" In my gesture to my bracelet-coms he could see that I wanted to contact someone.

Mei's face was quickly on the video screen. I was already comfortable with how authoritatively the biologist could speak on this subject. And, although we'd never met in person, she knew of me in connection with the University of Hawaii. At my request, she immediately quoted species losses, at the *Close* of the *Cretaceous*, "Stats from the fossil record are – 85% throughout the last age of the *Late-Cretaceous* epoch, 15% with the Chicxulub impact."

That was it. I'd made my pitch. I closed the coms. Now it was up to DelMonte. The numbers had to tell. I concluded, "So, what's the strategy to be? Guard against impacts? No problem, it'll be worked out. Or guard against whatever was *bigger*? Because, as it stands, we've absolutely no idea what that was."

The man looked to be in a quandary. My reasoning was convincing, but just so out of sync with everything on the table. "You said we're to expect large continental plate movements, quakes, eruptions and such, which you'll monitor and anticipate, right?"

"That'll happen. We'll take care of it."

"You've come up with this now, at this time?" I nodded, while hardly daring to purse my lips defiantly. "You want task force resources to go in search of dinosaur clues, on top of tackling the real and present menace out there? Is that in the UNNDC report?" He knew it was not.

"No."

"Your own initiative then?" I nodded again, though fully aware of how this might have blown my credibility.

He shuffled irritably. "That's it? Nothing more?" I nodded. DelMonte had backed me all the way as an eminent scientist, and I knew he keenly wanted to now. "You know where those clues are upside?" I shook my head. "Hell," he shook his too, "Don't hold your breath. Your plans have moved too far, too near to closure to make changes now. I'll have to get back to you on this."

I felt he wanted to relax and smile, show me solid support, but not this time. "You planning on going up?" The resigned shrug I gave, was confirmation enough.

"Good, keep me posted."

~*~

12

The DelMonte confrontation only heightened my resolve, and the dig on the Moon fortuitously served up more ejecta, while what we needed was to step up the effort. Palaeontologists, amateurs among them, even a group of smart school kids from Edinburgh (Scotland, UK) and another from Denver (Colorado, USA) were scouring the Moon. Although sifting down through dust was like looking for the proverbial 'golf ball in AstBelt', they were getting results.

However, we had to widen the search to gain a far more detailed picture. Only how? The round trip to Mars was well beyond the pockets of regular travellers. The Moon was accessible, thanks to the Upside Elevator Corporation (USEC) network, which connected ground spaceports with thermoports. Bubble shaped upside-elevator cars rose, hot air balloon fashion, to a height of 15 kilometres. From there they continued up a 'mag-cable' [magnetic cable] trailing from the thermoport. With abundant thermal energy from the thermosphere, costs were comparable to commuter subways on Earth.

But we had to have a lot more finds. I racked my brain for where organic ejecta might have been spared the ravages of decomposition, and weathering, and not crushed underground or fossilised. On Earth whole seas, plains and mountain ranges had come and gone since the *Cretaceous* period. And that's when the snow-capped peaks of the Transantarctic Mountain Range, running for over 3,500 kilometres and poking to a height of over 4.5 kilometres, came to mind.

Drilled from deep within glaciers, ice cores had long been examined – for entrained greenhouse gases like carbon dioxide and methane, as well as volcanic gases, soot and even windblown organisms – bacteria, algae, spores, pollen and such – largely in studies of Global Warming. The cores were read like tree rings, aided by magnetic field analyses and radiocarbon dating, in building detailed climatology timelines. Mineral profiling and even DNA analysis were used to pinpoint the sources of volcanic soot and organic material, for instance. The overall picture was as old as the glaciers, which was through the whole Ice Age. Russia's Vostok research station even brought up ice cores with a time span up to 30 million years old – in drilling down to a prehistoric lake there.

But, to find *Cretaceous* specimens 60 to 100 million years old, which had not been subjected to high pressure, we needed to find some extremely slow moving ice that was hardly buried at all. And that, I reckoned, had to be in a cave.

We were lucky. Incredibly lucky. Ground penetrating radar found caverns, high up in peaks that up to sixty-five million years ago were mere hills with permafrost. ESA used a precision rig named 'BlueLightning' to cleanly punch lightning bolts through ice and sedimentary rock, a super fast technique pioneered by it in the 2020s. The operation was completed when a probe, lowered to the cave floor, roamed over millions of years of thinly accumulated sediments. And, finally, a drill retrieved pencil-sized ice cores.

ESA researchers were ecstatic. As with the earlier ice cores, at last they could begin building detailed timelines – except now for *Cretaceous* paleoclimatology.

I was hugely encouraged. At the same time researchers rushed to examine large ejecta, with flora and fauna from around the world found on the Moon. All told, what they were piecing together varied little region to region – just from temperate to temperate-subtropical to tropical vegetation, of course with arid areas and wetlands – nothing more extreme than that. Greenhouse gas levels were much higher than today while sunshine was around one percent weaker. And though there were no ice sheets, the tropics weren't any warmer than today.

No surprises there, from what had been deduced from the fossil record. Nevertheless, a low energy climate system like that – characterised by gentle temperature gradients over all lands and through all seasons – was completely foreign to us. How could it have been? And yet, aside from extreme storms and even hypercanes, there had to have been millions of years of slight to steady prevailing winds and calm Tethys Sea conditions – for algal blooms profuse enough to have deposited the vast hillsides of chalk and 'kerogen' [from which oil came] found today.

We were getting a clearer picture of that ancient world but also more questions. And that made me anxious to get the fiman reconneer training over with and get our DeepStorm programme underway, fast.

~*~

13

In the months since leaving Fayez, Sashia had endured extreme training in gusty canyons, icy crevices, dank potholes, deep-sea torrents and stormy seas. All of which left her little time for reminiscences, especially with having to finish each event engrossed in studies. I was witness to it all, in overseeing the gruelling fiman curricula.

So it was that, in dusk's fading sunlight, high on the Flying Mountain (Mount Hengshan), Hunan, China, members of a training detail were mere shadows dancing from rock to rock like black flickering flames on murky monochrome slopes. Having come through everything with the stealth, wit and grit to survive anything, they were now there to hone those skills on this beautiful rugged mountain.

Sashia rubbed her gloved hands to stimulate her circulation in the icy dry air. "All here for the same thing," she'd have mused as she ran hands down her strider legs. While her nerves quivered in the enveloping darkness, her brow tightened in a headache. Yet, torturing her mind would have been visions of the jagged chasm walls, hidden beneath the ledge on which her kayak was perched. Over the edge, chilling spray wafted from the black void, where the quiet was shattered by water crashing hollowly. She flinched, doubtless at the thought of her earlier eye injury in less treacherous waters and in daylight. "To bloody well prove we've got what it takes." Her jaw was tight. "Well, throw it at us mother." Perhaps she was also thinking of the number of casualties there'd been. Only the very best would get through.

Poised to pull herself over, she tucked a loose strand of hair under her tight-fitting thermal scarf and helmet, "You want a superman army? Okay, give us your worst." Glancing around she took in the grave expressions of her fellow recruits and a defined hostility in the eyes of her opponent who also tucked in her scarf and donned night-vision goggles.

"Class VIII rapids reengineered for the 2052 Olympics," she recalled their tutor saying, "Master these, and you'll truly find yourself."

A beep sounded in Sashia's earpiece, prompting a warm adrenaline flush to surge through her body. Shivers instantly dispelled. The pair yanked forward in unison, plunging through air and mist. With a swish narrow aerofoil deployed from the sides, both competitors instinctively leaned this way and that to trim their flight. With the far side of the chasm abruptly ahead they expanded paddles into fans to push at the air and bank away. Honed muscles worked, supple fiman spines twisted, bent and rolled with the acrobatics of songbirds. No longer disadvantaged, Sashia banked expertly and, with the other kayak now directly before her, flipped into a backward somersault to narrowly avert a collision. Each peered in the gloom just in time to veer from protruding rocks flashing into near view. Corkscrewing over each other, plummeting fast, their confidence grew.

Nearing splashdown they retracted all extensions just in time to slam into boiling waters before surfacing and skimming across. Momentum dissipated, caught stolidly in icy swirling surf, deafened by the roar and disorientated by cold spray, squinting to see anything, they cleaved numbly with the fear of being sucked uncontrollably sideways and rolled under.

Five arduous kilometres later and they faced infinity where the river became a waterfall. Judging it well, both competitors went over steadily in the flow. Having dived the five-metre drop and bulleted deep into a chilling pool they both bobbed up in close proximity, only to be immediately drawn by relentless currents and having to work to control their pace. Sashia, now midstream, was gaining speed again. Then came another drop, and then another, and another. Kilometre after kilometre was the same, riding the Da Oh Ling cataracts. Both now experienced exhaustion, bodies beginning to tremble, endurance fading, confidence ebbing.

Lower down, the river funnelled into a cave. A wall of turbulent white water foamed in its mouth. "Fuck, what's this?" Sashia paddled frantically in line with the opening – but then held back. The other girl's bow nosed ahead, shooting in at an awkward angle. An instant after, Sashia slammed into the thrashing waves and corkscrewed sickeningly, hitting something underwater. Flipped over, head under, her Silverworm mentally aiding reconstruction, she peered through the murk and located a ledge she narrowly managed to dodge. Off to one side of it her super sight delivered the vicious contact of a helmet crunched into a rock. The other contestant!

Sashia broke surface, forced herself upright and frantically fought for control, simultaneously turning her head this way and that to find the other fiman. When at last she sighted the upturned contestant, strong waters were spewing them both out of the cave and over expansive bedrock. Striking out, Sashia grabbed at the drifting kayak, managed to flip it upright and there she was, the fiman, torn and slumped inside.

"*Jaisus!*" Instinctively, Sashia snapped a short line onto the bow, winced in pain as the bow was yanked from her hand, but quickly snapped the other end of the line to her own stern. Then she cleaved at the water as if pursued by a demon – before the lifeless tow could drag her sideways and under. Adrenaline coursing, she strained to think, knowing she had to make headway to gain control. She had to take up slack and pick up speed. Suddenly the line snapped taut, her forward movement abruptly checked. Her worst fears rose. She felt the deadly pull of the other kayak hauling her sideways into another current. Reassessing the situation, redoubling her fiman efforts, she swiftly turned about and headed fast past the girl. Again jolted, the dead weight checked her progress. Teeth clenched, eyes wide, face strained, she yelled in exertion, fighting, fighting. "Aaah!" Her very soul fought, muscles tearing, screaming with pain. At last making headway, she dragged her tow in line downstream still maintaining speed to keep control. Seconds counted. She had to get out of there fast, to resuscitate the contestant.

Sashia scoured the dim riverbank for an exit point, keen night vision making out the silhouette of a large rock. She slewed round to head there. Waves buffeted, the midstream current pulling elsewhere. A narrow gap between solid granite boulders brought hope. So very narrow for the swift flow, her only chance was a direct stab at the upstream face.

She aimed at the rock. The distance shortened, her speed remained high. With the rock dead ahead she whacked straight at it, praying she'd timed it right. Instantly her bow was onto the rough gleaming wall, the current taking her. Bang, she grazed past and slammed up a pebble beach. On impact, she recoiled with a back-flip twisting motion that sent her flying striders first through the air. Landing hard in the shallows, right by the towline, she steadied herself mechanically while grabbing hold. In desperation, oblivious of having banged her side on a rock, she heaved to bring the slumped body in before the second kayak could be swept past the gap.

Once there, with her and freed from the kayak, Sashia laid her out, bent over and whipped off gloves to feel for a pulse. Faint but enough. Swiping off the helmet, goggles and scarf she stroked away wet zebra hair from the girl's cheeks, gripped nose and chin, opened the lips, so blue with cold and, sucking in air, pressed her own quivering lips to them, forcing air into the girl's lungs.

When red and green dragons twitched on the girl's fingers, Sashia disengaged and leant back as the girl's mouth spluttered and she coughed up a substantial watery vomit. The girl wheezed, gasped for air and opened her eyes. "Gotcha!" exclaimed Sashia, excited as a kid landing her first fish. "You're all right, really okay," she reassured, looking into the girl's frightened eyes, almond shaped eyes, eyes that brought a flashback – Dr Mei Sai Ling!

Breathing more evenly, Mei's eyes closed. Touched by her vulnerability, Sashia reached to hold her hands and was strangely saddened to see the once glamorous fingernails now so dulled and broken. Nor did the diamonds sparkle from her ears, all jewellery gone, like Sashia's own, given up for this their new life.

The sky filled with droning, a paramedic dropped beside them, the injured girl was swiftly on a stretcher and taken up through the floor of the rescue craft.

Left alone, Sashia resigned herself to launching back into the waters to complete the event. To keep the cold from her mind, she reflected on satellites and their 'LNs' [LifeNotes]. "Are we to be tracked like pawns in a deadly competition?" The molecular level health monitoring LN implants, powered by a transductor, emitted the fiman's life signs, disposition, location and DNA-ID. Albeit disquieting, it was comforting that such information was tracked from space to aid search and rescue. "Is this *really* about competing? Or is it more to do with getting one another through? Hand picked to face whatever – together?"

~*~

95

14

Winter 2066

Dowsed by warm water in the safety of her shower, Sashia peered through mist to write on her mirror *Da Oh Ling* and then she added *White-waters... kayaks awash...* She was staring at the words and through the haze at herself, hollow eyes a betrayal of shock. "We made it!" she whispered.

Slowly her focus roamed over her powerful arms as she pressed her naked body up from the handrails and absent-mindedly ran her soaped hands over her newly developed, compact, life-saving form. "This is," she shook her head approvingly, "me, now." Indulging this discovery, the darker memories of her escapade were temporarily stashed away. She eased herself up onto a bathroom chair, leant back with eyes closed, her body at first lifeless, then active again as she stroked her feeble legs as if to comfort an ailing friend.

Next, her fingers ran over her flexible-high-impact striders – thankfully finding just one small dent in one leg. Gently she eased her deformed limbs into them and rose in them to her full height feeling again strong and even powerful.

"Phew." Eyes wide, she moved to a full-length mirror to explore her entire body – the now tight curves, firm shoulders, slender neck. "The new me – Sashia – and not just in top form," smile shaping, her tone lifted, "some kind of extra top form." She willed the height of her heels slightly taller and changed their colour to a pretty feminine peach. "Hmm, hmm. Wait till you see this, Fayez – I can't wait to watch your eyes when you see me – all of me!" The intensity of her longing for him had accelerated since the schedule limited any time to holoe.

Swathed in a cream bathrobe, Sashia adjusted the holoe optic to call him. "Hey," Fayez breathed softly, eyes brightening, "look at you my Starburst!" Laying on her pièce de résistance, Sashia dropped the robe and watched his jaw also drop. "Phew. Don't do that to me!" he responded huskily.

Her voice came light as silk, pleased with her effect. "Huh? So, what do you reckon? Wanna tangle with this body, buddy?"

He stepped back to check her out, realised the reason behind her euphoria, and felt delicious stirrings. She was the bait for his distanced yearnings. In a silent entwining of their senses, they released their pent up passions, steeped in virtual satisfaction, reunited as if never parted. And yet, aching in the reality that this could not be physically real, they resigned themselves to exchanging reassuring smiles. Fayez resorted to being his comfortable laid-back self, "Hmm, well, you'll do," he teased, simply loving the girl he knew to be his. Yet, her melancholia did not go unnoticed.

"You know, it wasn't classified experiences that hurt me to keep from you," her expression was pained. There was so much more she wanted to share with him. "You know, feelings?" She ached for more, to regain their stolen lives and fill the terrible emptiness she felt whenever alone in her space.

"I know," he said softly, knowing only how to be there for her when most needed – and sensing it to be now for this trainee reconneer, or not, and with a separate life, or not. "I've missed you too, Starburst. Hey, check this out..." He struck some provoking notes on his piano keys coaxing for a response, and respond she did with titillating movements, her magic still there for him, despite the signs that his lover was outgrowing the woman she'd been.

Moving slowly along the clinic's corridor, Sashia nonchalantly glanced at Jude Nade on Sævrama. The weather girl's chance at bigger news breaking had unfortunately turned into such a big scoop that it was handed over to McGuire. Here she was, back in her familiar slot, though outwardly radiant and cheerful as ever. *"The Sun certainly seems to be here to stay. This hasn't done much for water shortages. Despite that, again temperatures have been generally down on previous years. Confusing? Sure, skiers are having it all their way, plenty of snow, sun and longer winters. Indications are next winter will drag on some."*

Further along, the trainee reconneer stopped at a sign outside an open doorway and then awkwardly entered. On the bed, dragon patterned fingers were impulsively smoothing down a top sheet. The girl stopped and looked up dispassionately, then hardly registering anything awkward about the approaching girl's movements she became impressed by, what looked like, her stunning thigh boots.

"You okay? No complications?" Sashia prompted cheerfully, hoping in a way for a spark of recognition, "The last I saw, you were taking the easy way out." Undeterred by the patient's abject disinterest, she ventured on, "with getting a lift in a rescue craft."

Mei's surprise at mention of her rescue couldn't be concealed. "*You* rescued me?" The thought then occurred that this girl, her rescuer, was not walking easily and must have sustained severe leg injuries on account of her. Almost immediately apologetic, her eyes glistened with sympathy as well as gratitude.

"Ah ha," encouraged by this palpable sincerity and warmth, despite the hugely felt competitiveness at the start of their race, Sashia floundered about either discussing their chilling scrape with death or even their set-to over The Docks. "Na," she mouthed, finding neither uplifting. "So, you're rested? They treating you well?" She let the patient nod before giving her name, whilst also gesturing to a chair for approval to sit. Mei's apparent changeover to welcoming gradually encouraged Sashia to dispense with caution. "We met, remember? Hong Kong, The Docks versus dolphins?"

"Ah," Mei's gaze was overtly fixed on Sashia's boot-like striders. "I was trying to place you. What happened to you?"

"Oh, it's nothing. Just a bruise," quick on the uptake, Sashia pointed to her side and waved aside any further chat on that subject. Time for that later.

"You've an incredible memory, considering all we've been through." Slowly coming back to her was the first impression she'd formed, in HK, of Sashia having a strong will but not the confidence of a graduate. And here Mei was now, squirming with humility at how incredibly tough she had to have been to survive their training and, then, topping that off by saving her life. Although losing energy and tiring, she demonstrated her respect for this fellow fiman. "I remember," she said, her voice kind, "your angle was in promoting The Docks project."

"Right." Sashia's chuckle aimed at lifting the mood further, "The one everyone was set on trashing."

"No!" Mei rightfully assumed the high ground, "You've got that wrong. Agric and Fisheries were trying to find a compromise, some way to let the project go ahead while still protecting the dolphins. That's why I was there." Her words tailed off, eyelids drooping due to the effort of explaining, and agitated that she couldn't continue.

Later that day Mei was perturbed by what she gleaned from nurses. The paramedics had found her rescuer's dice with death incredible in the pitch darkness of that white-water, and had simply commented on arrival at the hospital, "Some heroics!"

"Oh, no!" Straining to remember the near disastrous contest Mei bit her lower lip at the recollection of her earlier near-death misadventure. Distractedly she touched the scar across her cheek and thought of Rad, guilt resurfacing like an irritating neighbour, ever ready to haunt her space. When the nurses also commented on Sashia's permanent disability, Mei was again sickened with remorse. Happily, the sight of Sashia returning cheerily, flowers in hand, blew it all away. "Jo san," Mei humbly greeted *good morning* with her sparse Cantonese picked up in HK, where English and Mandarin were common enough to get you by. Still with that spirit she reached out to the girl. "I owe you a massive debt – for my still being here."

"Hm, let's hope that's the last pickle we get into." Ah, Sashia the realist, ever out to live life to the full – she would spare no time for accolades or regrets. "Ley ho mah?" she followed up, asking after Mei's health with a better grasp of the language. Their look of uncertainty and weariness was now mutual. "This is not us," she added quietly, "We're not soldiers!"

"Gay ho ah," Mei shrugged, saying she was okay, while feeling a surge of empathy for the girl who, despite her acts of cheerfulness, looked forlorn. "How can we now be who we were?" she responded about their condition. And along with that feeling came an overwhelming urge, so out of character but understandable after Moloka'i and now the Da Oh Ling cataracts, to open her arms for a hug.

"Bruised, but I'm strong," she furthered, with the softness of Sashia in her arms and feeling her shiver almost imperceptibly, "but you, you're even stronger." Sashia allowed Mei to hold her with the warmth of a sister, filling the emptiness of her missing Fayez, and listened as the scientist now expressed anger at herself. "What's odd is that I'd failed and should be pulled from the programme. Instead, I got a pass," inquisitive eyes latched onto Sashia's, for answers, "*Someone's* doing – anyone you know?"

"Oh, not mine." Sashia, nestled in that warmth, now felt goose bumps tingle, as they'd done when they were perched to dive into the unknown – into the cataracts. Sensing something, she pulled back to look Mei in the face. "Must be to do with your qualifications."

"Hm," Mei studied Sashia's face. "I've been given terabytes of data to study," her brow wrinkled, perplexed, "all about the evolution of terraforming processes in the biosphere."

"You know," Sashia looked away, but at nothing in particular, "I haven't a clue what we're training for."

"Me neither," the girl hung onto the promise of complicity and trust surfacing between them, "I've heard nothing." None of the trainees had. "Well," she searched about awkwardly, in anticipation, "maybe it has something to do with how a hotchpotch of living organisms, on a quietening rocky surface, took hundreds of millions of years to get sorted and terraform the biosphere. It was all so haphazard, experimental even, conflicts were bound to flare into serious setbacks. Catastrophes even."

"*Mass Extinction*?" Alarm simmered in Sashia, "*My* extinction!" as her thoughts turned to Fayez. Quickly she slammed the door on anything other than the here and now, overlooked thoughts of the gruelling exercises of late, and coolly strained to recollect morsels from paleobotanical lectures she'd been attending, "Like when the dinosaurs disappeared?" She slid back to the bedside chair, mind racing to instruct herself, "I will stay calm and connect on the same level – *her professional* level." Her own study subjects, however, were more to do with manoeuvres in ZeroG, where her keen eyesight was considered a powerful asset.

Having dropped her usual cool, professional stance in their shared vulnerability, and the discomfort of someone penetrating her natural defences, Mei was not smoothing down her crumpled sheets again. Rather, with a friendly smile, she turned to Sashia and spoke without aggrandisement. "Well, yeah. My research, which is all about that, has moved in an interesting direction. I'm looking for something, a disorder in the biosphere really, that kills."

It had heartened Mei that she'd the chance to pick up that research again, since she'd given up hope of doing so, "Maybe some ultra acquisitive organism – plant, animal or bug – ran amuck in overpopulating the planet toward the *Close* of the *Cretaceous* period – and, with a domino effect, collapsed food chains and crippled the biosphere." She was also trying, while judging Sashia's look, to make a subtle point, "It's beyond comprehension, huh? You'd think so. But what about one extremely *smart* organism, which very recently came close to doing just that? Mankind? We came close to overrunning everything."

Sashia's eyebrows lifted as Mei continued, "So, a *dumb* organism doing that in the past shouldn't sound all that absurd. Wouldn't you say? And then the big question is – could whatever *that* was, happen again? Indeed, is it happening again?"

~*~

15

May 2067

Longing for warmth, the fimans were dismayed. "It's ridiculous," Sashia complained to Fayez, on holoe from the F-Academy library, "Six weeks into spring and it's still cold."

"Yeah, we've got the fires at tables still – it's a pretty scene, with good views and my music. But people are getting fed up here, too." He paused in the hope of eliciting more warmth from her. "I miss you here... our cuddles..."

"Hey Fayez," Mei chided cheekily as she wafted by. "Drop the dumb scarf," and added, referring to Sashia, *"We're* going to the tropics!"

Fayez looked flat, sensing perhaps a wedge driving between them, although Sashia had explained how she and Mei had become like oddly matched sisters, and he was glad she had made a friend. "Hey! Respect!" Sashia gibed, about her tribal scarf, before clarifying for him what Mei had just announced. "Remember I mentioned the international competition at the end of this training? The 'InviHundred'? Well that's it. Thousands of us around the World will be taking part in the four-day events."

"It's a race," Mei elucidated, butting in again, "between 25 four-man teams, making 100 competitors in each venue – hence the InviHundred label."

Sashia was excited by this latest snippet. "Yeah, the tropics! It's supposed to be classified, destination undisclosed, all hush-hush," and with that turned apologetically to Fayez, "even with holoe silence – sorry, hunk."

"Yeah, but we still don't really know where," Mei informed them, her fingers momentarily feigning a grab at Sashia's scarf before she mockingly stuck her tongue out at him. He was trying to decide whether this was an insult or a tease, when she flung in, "Seriously – if we fail this, we're out! Gone from the mission! Which sounds great, yeah?" Her eyes went skyward and she placed her dragon decorated hands in mock prayer, before giving him a genuinely unapologetic grimace, "Except, sorry! You see? We're committed now!"

"Yeah," Sashia could do no more than regard him wistfully.

Ill at ease with how things were going and how strangely Mei was behaving, and possibly growing jealous of her, Fayez simply shrugged and commented on how tough the obstacles they'd face sounded. "Four days? Chris' that'd be Special Forces stuff!"

"Endure that and we'll for sure have what it takes, apparently," Sashia searched Mei's expression for support. "What did the Prof say, 'Overcome failing the InviHundred, and you'll never in your life face failing again'?" She so wanted to share these things with Fayez. "Sorry. We're okay with this, all trained up to fight. If we blow it, we'll never know what difference either of us could have made – for the World, and especially for those we love. You too love."

"We'd never be able to face anyone again – not families, friends, everyone," Mei backed her up.

In accord, the girls clearly wanted him to understand and believe in them, particularly Sashia. "The F-Academy hasn't told us much. What we do know, or have known, is that our training has something to do with what you're seeing in the news." Here was Sashia's chance to break more to him. "We've no idea how tough the field exercises will be. We just know that mostly we'll be carrying out field research into what's behind the news items, what's causing all the eruptions and stuff."

As if to underline her words, across the room a Sævrama feature showed snowdrifts and avalanches that had brought highways and railways in several valleys to a standstill as well as isolating livestock and wildlife. Reservoirs were also so deeply frozen over that their outflows were reduced to a fraction of normal volumes. However, what moved Sashia was Jude Nade's unusually sombre look and tone. *"Weather conditions are certainly cramping parts of Europe, much of Canada, also the Rockies, Andes and Himalayas. There's no let up in the severity of this year's winter storms, continuing now well into May in northern latitudes.*

"Snowlines have advanced and, as you see, are beginning to encroach on outlying districts. A number of power stations are on reduced output, as are factories in remote mountainous regions.

"As gloom-and-doom sites on the internet, collectively referred to by some as the 'DoomNet', have been predicting – there's no question now that, while every effort is being made to maintain essential supplies and services to households, jobs are at risk. The question is, how many?"

Were it not for the suffering involved, Jude would have been elated at having this weather-related scoop. *"It's too early to say but this reporter is going on record now. Beyond mere weather, what looks like a change in climate looks set to power down whole economies. The World situation is now very grave."*

All three stood transfixed at hearing such suspicions now broadcast so publicly. For Fayez it also brought home the real gravitas of Sashia's life and training. Whilst he had died a little as their bond had grown, now he felt for them as he observed their serious faces. When eventually signing off, the holoe, his well wishing presented absolute sincerity.

"Okay, since the going's getting tough," Sashia threw out, "let's do what sensible gals do…"

"Go shopping!" Mei's tone echoed her friend's, as she drew her into a lively step, "Sure, dazzle me with space gems!"

"Okay, that one!" Sashia urged as they stared through the window of a jeweller's window glittering with a special exhibition of rare stones and fantasy designs. "Hmm, impressive!"

"Apparently they're drilled from the ground," Mei pointed to what appeared to be a large diamond with a sapphire fused into the centre, with brilliant blue-white washing imperceptibly inward to fiery red. The label described it as a *Star Luna: A Rare Variety Of Tourmaline Found Only In Peaks Of The Moon.*

Next to this was a transparent blue topaz like gem, described as *Iopaz: A Rare Stone Forged On An Airless Surface By The Immense Heat Of A Meteoroid Impact, Such As The Specimens First Found On Io Where It Was Named.*

Sashia ogled the price tags. "Eeyaah, imagine the loan interest!" they chuckled lamely, not really in the mood to play, "for such a tiny bit of real estate."

As they were about to leave, I sauntered along. With, "Ah, you've discovered my little treasure-trove," I was sure of getting their attention. The trainees were naturally taken aback. Here was a total stranger greeting them and claiming a fortune in precious stones. Then they recognised me, but only from recent lecture podcasts they'd seen.

Mei was as comfortable as ever in mature company, but Sashia, held back, probably repressed by my professional standing.

Nervously, she struggled to appear cool. "There are some beautiful stones in there."

I made a conscious effort to avoid visually examining her striders, which had fascinated me in views I'd had of her. "Those are," I agreed, waving dismissively at the display cabinet where they stood and then teasingly walking straight past them to another containing jade-like stones, "however, *these* are my special interest." Neither of them looked impressed by these dull, uncut stones, even though Mei would have been ecstatic had she any idea what they were, sharing with me, as she did, a burning desire for prehistoric knowledge.

Greater than with all the digs there'd ever been – on Earth, the Moon and even mountains in Antarctica – that knowledge was right in front of them now.

"Hm," Mei peered disparagingly from the gemstones to Sashia, both now with a 'Who'd wear those?' expression.

"Imagine glimpsing conifers," it was such a treat for me, having this moment with these two and seeing their bewilderment first hand, "and ferns with brightly coloured flowers and birds – and barely a dinosaur in sight."

Mei was initially confused by my 'esteemed' self, standing there spouting such apparent nonsense. "Well, that's quite a picture," although condescending, she was now squinting for closer examination, or perhaps so to concentrate harder, "of the *Close* of the *Cretaceous* period?"

"Sure. What would you give, for such a rare peek?" I looked to see a sparkle at that mention but also consternation at the crude featureless stones lying there. It would have been enough to leave it at that, judging it too soon to let them into the secret, except that another thought formed. "Sashia, with your keen eyesight I'm sure you'll see far more." Gratifyingly this hit the mark, with the impressionable young trainee sorely wishing to be counted among the professionals here. The late starter was advancing again.

On that note I let them get on with their day, and left.

Some weeks later, with their training coming to an end, I was packing up my quarters when I invited the pair to visit. Looking mildly inquisitive they followed me to a partially wrapped wooden desk, which though handsome was a tad gnarled. "It's my favourite piece of furniture," I informed them, "Thought I'd share that with you."

I noted the due respect in their faces at that gesture – doubtless with raised expectations of being selected. So, when I then laid a dull uncut gemstone on the desk, much like those in the jewellery displays, they tried hard not to look underwhelmed. That tickled me. Playing with them, I let their anticipation build. Finally, I ended the tease by placing before them a cut and polished stone. Although knowing it could never have become the prettiest gem they'd ever beheld, I couldn't resist being smug when gesturing for Sashia to pick it up.

Fingers delicately around it, she turned its coal-black face uppermost and her eyes were instantly drawn to what resembled tiny specks. Except, Sashia made them out to be white dots. And then, as she zoomed in, more and more white dots appeared. "It's nice. The night sky?" Urged on by my non-committed but steady gaze she zoomed further. "I can see planets. This one," her super keen eyesight slowly drawing her in, "is, yes, definitely like Saturn with its rings." Ambling over to the window, her striders fascinating me, she zoomed in more. "Wow, moons and asteroids in the rings! It's so clear! But, hmm, I can't relate to anything else. No recognisable constellations." With that she cupped the stone in her palm, guarding it preciously as if sensing its significance, while I could see her mind race for answers.

To her relief I brought the intrigue to a halt. "You're right. It is the night sky – but not the sky you know. There's a lot more to it. Anyway," I opened the centre drawer and took out a box, "I've got this small collection, all cut, that I'd like you to go through. They're valuable and highly classified, so you'll have to examine them here. None of them are to leave this office." Aware that they'd need help, I added, "You'll store the images you find in the stones, digitally, with our AI, FayWell, who'll work with you to enhance them."

Admittedly, I enjoyed their puzzled looks. "Okay, are they important? Yes." I looked pointedly at the stone in Sashia's hand, "I'll come to that. Firstly, I had FayWell use her smart image recognition to find a match, from any angle in the Solar System, and *she* came up with nothing even remotely like it out there."

I stared purposefully into their now gleaming eyes, and lowered my voice. "I had to stretch my mind, to not just think *where* they're from." I backed off a little to let this sink in and then, watching their questioning looks, added more pointedly, "That's right. Not just *where*, but *when*.

"For the mission to succeed, we must visit the catastrophes of our past. We must *go back in time*. Images in these stones are absolutely the key to that – you'll see."

~*~

16

June 2067
(Northern Hemisphere)

To get things moving, I arranged for Mei and Sashia to visit Vijay Singh, Head of Research at a leading research centre for the analysis of ejecta found on the Moon as well as ice cores from Antarctica. For this, the girls had to take a USEC upside-elevator from Rajaspore Spaceport, seven kilometres up the Himalayas, to Rajaspore Thermoport. Both operated jointly by 'ISRO' [Indian Space Research Organisation] and 'CNSA' [China National Space Administration] these were among the World's biggest. All the while – in making their way within bustling terminal buildings, along a passenger bridge to an upside-elevator pad, and even through an unobtrusive immigration gateway for India, China and ISWA upside domains combined – the girls were visibly taken aback, having been absented from crowds for so long, by how glum everyone was. Nonetheless, they marvelled at the incredible river valleys and snow capped peaks all about them. Finally, they stopped excitedly at a porthole to watch bubble shaped upside-elevators rise up on broad blue and amber laser beams stretching skywards.

Hearing their breath catch, a fellow passenger – a journalist – enquired, "First upside-elevator you ever saw up close?"

"What?" Turning, stiffly as usual, Sashia could see she didn't know the guy.

"Look! See it?" he pointed skyward, while taking in some rigidity in her legs and certainly her ever-present scarf, "That's where we're headed. Rajaspore Thermoport, anchored 120 kilometres above us." He let her look quietly before cutting in, the three of them observing a bright dot directly overhead, "And one of these is going to take us there." He motioned to an upside-elevator. "It rides up the beam well into the stratosphere, then up a mag-cable – really weird. You'll see."

"Uhuh," Sashia was all ears. Her training, her aroused taste for learning and indeed hunger for it, lit up her eyes.

"It's quite quick, takes just three hours."

"You've done this before?" Mei joined in cautiously. He nodded. Passengers were visible through the clear canopies of vehicles that rose and landed right across the spaceport apron.

"They're all going to the Moon?" Sashia kept the chat going, while also coaxing Mei out of her reticence with strangers.

"Well," the journalist chuckled, "many will be rotating, to or from somewhere upside, so they're just there in transit. Although, in the past hoards of tourists were drawn to bathe and sleep semi-weightless there. It's great, so close to the stars you can imagine reaching up to touch them and so well served with telescopes your eyes can swim even closer. Add to that the best in fine cuisine while zooming in to see continents on Earth and, of course, there are the famous Steam Tower Sports..."

"Sport? Up there?"

"Yeahh! Golf in a hot house surrounded by black space, with abseiling (or rappelling) semi-weightless between greens... there's nothing like it! You must try it sometime!

"There've been a long list of dignitaries and celebrities too. King William and Queen Catherine celebrated their fiftieth wedding anniversary in accommodation they have reserved for themselves! But right now," he could see Sashia was confused, and also noticed Mei ease closer to her, "they're mostly scientists and journalists, like me, preoccupied with what's going on in the World. Among the things we're currently covering is a look at how some climate refugees are being given work there."

"They're moving there?"

"No. Work assignments upside, including the Rajaspore Thermoport, come with short-stay health insurance cover. Everyone has to be on rotation from an EarthG place, which means from the ground on Earth or soon from the Near Earth Territories. Those on tour of duty to Mars have to make short visits to the surface's 'MarsG' [Mars gravity], rotating from Leo."

He was referring to a Territories prototype in orbit around the planet, of course lacking the knowledge that these two girls, with their freedom as fimans, could move about space at will.

Once on board the pilotless craft, the passengers sat strapped three abreast, in four rows of seats. Looking around them the girls were quick to notice press-passes on the others before becoming more interested in other sights all about them. Slowly the pad and spaceport, falling away beneath them, was becoming minuscule and veiled in haze before being fully clouded from view.

And so it was that they rose through endlessly clear air, shifting over the wondrously majestic Himalayas.

Later, when one of the journalists coaxed them to while away the time with a few rounds of 'wigi-pic', Sashia joined in, watching each download personal pictures and then stack them one on the other. And she laughed, a little apprehensively, at the spooky looking composite holoe that came alive. Mei, a little put out, typically abstained, choosing to peer, entranced, as more and more of India and then China came into view.

Finally, when the gentle movement stopped, a recorded message advised, "Please keep your seatbelts fastened while the USEC upside-elevator connects to the Rajaspore Thermoport mag-cable. We'll be on our way shortly."

In no time, they were climbing rapidly and marvelling as India and China shaped serenely in their view and other sights gripped them – the incredible aurora borealis, eyes of huge storms, and much else of mystery, until slowly the Earth resembled its depiction as a perfect study-room globe, but all centred on the Himalayas.

Suddenly they had ascended through the floor of the port and on stopping were being greeted by a pleasant toned male 'AA' [Artificial Attendant] standing outside the opening door. There he was, smarter than smart in his human male uniform. "Welcome. Please follow the signs to the arrivals hall, where you'll find a USEC reception desk."

Alighting semi-weightless on the teutronium walkway, Sashia burst out laughing at seeing Mei – apparently as legless as her for a change. "So, wow! Whizical you, eh?" Sashia propped her up just as Mei helplessly grabbed around her waist. "And wow, look at me," Sashia pirouetted, marvelling at the fluidity of her movements. "I love it up here, already."

In high spirits they made their way past sweetly scented walls, where yellow and white sycamores and pink and purple mountain laurels were planted in niches, and passed through a crowd vibrant in beautiful multi-printed sarees and sherwanis. Alas again, here was a continuing sign of the times – everyone looked sombre.

A highlight for all visitors was the physical greeting by real AAs (not their holoes). Now another was handing the girls complimentary sarees. Microgravity robotics had developed to produce a whole range of fun models – big hat elves, long footed goblins, lifelike humanoids, gigolos, carmen electras and so on. But the AA ushering them to gawk at the Earth and Moon from a glass lift had the face of a young boy but, in place of hair and ears, he owned the delicate petals of a grey orchid.

The lift opened directly into Singh's eighth floor office where the 'boy', Agnos, left them. The girls barely noticed me – though I was there, briefly, on holoe, to go over what I'd arranged. They simply continued to gawk at space views all around the glass walled room. Their host and I allowed them that respite, in deference to their recent gruelling training. Then came the introductions. Singh was to bring the girls into the research, being conducted along with ESA and NASA, so that the pair could be kept up to date when studying my gemstones.

From their vantage point at the port, Singh's researchers had undertaken the most extensive studies ever of the Deccan Traps. And Singh, with his correct yet engaging manner and wearing a handsome kurta top in deep purple, zoomed right in to that feature's triangular shape on screen. "For millennia at a time, this huge two kilometres high plateau," he pointed to where it covered much of western India, "was aflame with some of the greatest eruptions in the whole of the geological record. From some three million years before the famed Chicxulub asteroid impact," he looked specifically at Mei, "right through the dusk years of reptilian orders, and possibly for five million years after, it intermittently dominated weather systems the world over." Suddenly and surprisingly, Singh became sweetly beguiling, "As you well know," he said softly, and then corrected himself again, "and your boss knows even better."

The girls settled down, Sashia apparently entranced by his charisma whilst Mei was by his words. "Which is why," a vague recollection of having touched on this, in Moloka'i, flashed through Mei's mind, "some in the scientific community see the massive sulphur dioxide clouds, which long emanated from this, as the real cause of the *End Cretaceous Mass Extinction*."

"Ah," he wagged a finger at the hint of coquettishness in Sashia's smile, "our research has moved a long way from that extreme position," which elicited an irked look from Mei, whom he more seriously addressed with, "That was a highly complex time, in the geology of the Indian Ocean Basin in particular but also globally, with many different factors coming into play. Not many of which are understood even now."

"Yes, pretty inconclusive," sensing his rising interest in her friend, Mei stiffened, "in what's been presented with *Late-Cretaceous* paleoclimatology models."

What worried me was what I had gleaned about those mood swings in Mei's file notes. She now appeared distracted by her feelings for Sashia, when I needed her to push her peers to pursue new leads.

"Right," with a twinkle in his eye he stole another glimpse at Sashia before, mindful of my gravitas on the DeepStorm threat, he cleared his throat. "Big claims aside," he continued a little abashed by Mei's cool gaze, "in very realistic models of ours, we have easterlies blowing a band of warm dry sulphurous air from India right across central Africa and even across South America. This didn't last long, just decades or centuries at a time. But, like aiming a blowtorch there, verdant plains and dense forests quickly shrivelled up and went from sparse to scarce." The screen refreshed to show that changing geography.

"What the...? It's so striking!" Mei's amazement reigned in other feelings. "How? You've got the Climate Change of mere decades or centuries – your data is that fine?"

"Absolutely!" Singh was clearly encouraged by her renewed interest. "Thanks to invaluable new data from the Moon, and also fine timeline data from Antarctica."

"Incredible! Big herds couldn't possibly have survived that aridity, certainly not for that long, not without the conservation activities we have today!" Mei was clearly thrilled. But, before accepting anything so conclusive, she had to cover all angles. "That topography, the hills and valleys, is unchanged from the old paleogeographical models?" Singh nodded. "Africa had nowhere for them to escape to, flat and isolated as it was, neither into high mountain ranges nor over land bridges!" His look urged her on. "So that with Natural Selection herd animals, trapped in sparse pockets of land, must have downsized anatomically as well as in numbers or otherwise failed altogether."

"Except?" Singh again prompted, knowing she knew.

"Except, all considered," she ventured quietly, "species did disappear, only for some to make a come back in some form or other." He lifted his hands, palms uppermost, drawing her on again. "Possibly by downsizing in the interim? Or escaping somehow?"

"Yes. A continents-wide Natural Correction, as your boss would have it, somehow reversed. Which, alas, is hardly conclusive. There's so much more to this, which we've yet to uncover. Come, something to show you."

Impressed with Mei's enthusiasm and knowledge, Singh wanted to give the newcomers a tour of the port. As he led the way at speed, down a corridor and towards a stairway, Sashia hung back needing to put something to Mei. "Back then, there weren't any arctic ice sheets anywhere, like we have today, were there? Maybe you should ask him if the Earth's obliquity was somehow reduced then?" From basic prehistory studies, she had picked up how that would have made the seasons less pronounced.

"Ah! You mean if the Earth had less of a gyroscopically stabilised, tilt?" Mei responded, while speeding to catch up with Singh. "With the poles having year round twilight?" She shook her head, "Sorry, but in fossil tree rings we see 'white nights' summers long and nothing but dark days winters long. Just like now."

"Oh," approaching Singh, where he had stopped, Sashia was anxious as a teenager to correct with Mei any misunderstanding concerning her earlier playfulness with him. All she'd wanted was to get Singh to open up a little and kindle his interest in her friend. Her whispered questions came quickly, to now spark her interest in him. "He's a real dish, right? Do you like him?"

Mei just stood there, in shock, and watched that same sensation spread over Sashia's face – as they gaped at clouds and mountains they were standing directly above, beneath a wide glass floor with no supporting ribs or girders they'd walked onto. In that view, India stretched to all borders and beyond. For Mei a nervous convulsion of giggles began as she watched Sashia shrink back, eyes widening like the horizon, her striders rapidly lowering to flat, and turning to charcoal black as the girl's instincts kicked in to combat mode. Then, realising their apparent safety, they both laughed, steadied one another and looked to Singh for an explanation.

"So, there they are," he offered, not quite sure how to take these two, "the Deccan Traps!" That feature lay at their feet and just ahead a bit, with the Himalaya mountain range right beneath them. Behind lay China, and to the left Nepal, Bhutan, Bangladesh and then

Myanmar. Country names and borders, lit white on the floor, completing the zoomed in picture just like a satellite map. It was surreal and yet the real Earth!

"Ah, but what about this?" Singh was now relishing their awe at fountains of lava slowly ripping beneath them across much of central India. The relayed roar and crackle was deafening, the sensation of quakes coursing up their legs while flames and smoke licked towards them high above the ground. The girls' eyes now reflected an enormous cloud of ash stretching across the Arabian Sea in the direction of Africa. Shortly after, a cyclone system formed and grew over the whole sea, before moving threateningly over the African coast. Another followed and then another.

The floor moved that way too, crossing over the ocean to lock over Somalia, Kenya and Ethiopia, from which violent electrical storms now blasted their ears. And then, in time-lapse scenes, tropical forests turned into thinly wooded savannah and fire-ravaged scrub. Here and there big herds dwindled, leaving only small family-sized groups. And finally, much of it turned to desert conditions bordered by scrublands.

Singh watched them closely. "Impressive, huh? The fallout triggered an endless stream of mega-storms, with a footprint on the land thousands of times bigger than any eruptions in recent times and lasting massively longer. Imagine the effect of that – happening again and again for millions of years, in the southern hemisphere!"

As he spoke the skies opened for powerfully bleaching sunlight to beam down, and they watched everywhere slowly cloak over with sedges, along with lightly wooded rivers and coastal plains, until gradually areas in between started to carpet over with verdant savannah and luxuriant forests, again painting the continents green.

With heads still abuzz with the death and rebirth of the Earth, so spectacularly witnessed, the girls did not speak though they appeared keen to leave the glass floor.

Singh stayed them with upheld hands. "Turn around and you'll see a desert area just north of the Himalayas – which you're now back over." Turning gingerly, they watched the area flood and finally sink under blue waves. But then, it slowly resurfaced. "That was the other great event in our shared Sino-Indian prehistory – when the continents crashed and crumpled in the Himalayas, and lifted two ancient Tethys Sea basins to become the Taklamakan and Gobi Deserts."

"Oh! Anglo-Sino oil companies have made big new finds there," Sashia rebounding, was, to Mei's relief, at last contributing more seriously.

For my part, I was pleased that the girls had come face to face with that most real reconstruction and at last got a head start for our mission. Certainly their emotions were all over the place, given all that we were putting them through. But despite, or because of, everything that we had flung at them, they were blossoming into the reconneers we wanted. They were holding out physically *and* mentally, each in their own way. All I now hoped was that they'd bear up in the harrowing tests still ahead of them. Meanwhile, what was burning me up was my struggle to get UNNDC clearance for the *Cretaceous* research to carry on once we got underway.

For the second of the girls' three-day tour, I'd arranged a holoe session in one of the famed microgravity gardens up there. Singh's teams had created a wonderful *Cretaceous* theme to celebrate the fabulous prehistoric heritage of both India and China.

We approached the place to the echoing accompaniment of a corridor busker, whose jazz, so reminiscent of Fayez on piano, brought Sashia almost to an ungainly standstill. Oddly enough, Mei wasn't unsympathetic, gently touching her hand to coax her onward until the haunting notes, as well as the chatter of a dozen or so eight to ten-year-old school children, were abruptly shut out in a silence as marked as the black of space surrounding us.

The thick glass door had closed behind us. We stood on a steamy floor in one of the towers, bigger than a football stadium, where a brook, within a glade of fern trees, was surrounded by a forest of giant conifers. The kids, who had vocalised their excitement before leaving, now simply stared back, doubtless storing some memories of the marvellously big, luxuriant plants. Without a doubt, theirs would be the last of such visits from Earth.

The conditions, constantly moist with temperature and pressure low, were not unlike the calm before a big storm and very representative of this prehistoric theme. And what I wanted my two girls to take away, was a memory of those microgravity plants – which were growing faster and bigger than any on Earth today. A comparison of tree rings showed how much they'd been fattened by the high absorption of water and also carbon dioxide there.

While those thoughts were uppermost in my mind, I also noticed that Sashia's eyes looked moist, so I immediately brought out the gemstones I'd shown in our previous meeting, "Did you get anywhere with the first of these?"

"Sure." Shaking off reminiscences, Sashia's response was fast. "FayWell, bring up the sequences?" The AI slowly became visible moving in the bark of a huge redwood tree, with eyes hidden behind wild straw-coloured hair and sunbeams in raindrops glistening freshly on cheeks, until her uncanny sparkle was there in the eyes of the girls, who sighed as they had done when they'd worked with her earlier. That's how she was, always was, moving within living material – wherever plants and living walls were associated with the UNNDC… Now she blew a kiss to materialise a transparent pane.

Touched by the AI's intangible softness, Sashia let her voice float on the still air, "I looked but, as before, found nothing recognisable on the surfaces of any planets or moons – except this one looked a bit familiar. I had FayWell store the image for you to see." With a sideways glance from her, and another misty kiss from FayWell, the pane refreshed to show a globe.

"It's a virtual, Earth-like, world. Right?" Mei's voice was also silkier than usual, but then strengthened. "Oh! But wait!" She studied my look, aware of its deadly seriousness. "These stones have images?"

"Yeah well, wherever it is, it has miserable looking weather. All over wet and overcast! Look at all that cloud!" Sashia was also shifting to a higher note, keen to contribute from her keen memory. "You said," she turned to me, "Go back in time!"

"Well," Mei peered intently at a stone, "your average low pressure system, except it's everywhere." She then caught glimpses of land. "Hm, the outline of continents looks interesting. Yes, I see." she stood back, satisfied with her observation. "It's a reconstruction of the Earth in the *Cretaceous* period. Not bad too, but for all that cloud! That's over-the-top."

"But," Sashia's eyes questioned mine. She groped for the right words. "There's more, isn't there? We've got to look closer?"

"Yes closer, get much closer," I smiled encouragingly, "Go figure – and ignore the cloud." I was goading them to hopefully fashion a new direction with the other stones, as if getting them to swim for the very first time, they had to trust in my guidance. "This could just be our secret weapon – against DeepStorm. But, supposing it is a *Cretaceous* view, what will you look for? How will you get to its catastrophic Mass Extinction? *And,* how will that help us to avoid the same happening again – *now*?"

I knew Mei would develop her thoughts from this, having much the same outlook as mine on the subject. Sashia, on the other hand, had little to go on. She simply took a stab at something, "The Chicxulub asteroid impact," she searched my face for some acknowledgement, "coming on top of the Deccan Traps devastation that we just saw. Wouldn't that have resulted in a global catastrophe?"

"Good. That's a start," I contributed, "Environments altered globally, by two colossally powerful Natural Corrections, for life to then reshape by Darwinian Natural Selection."

"So we're looking for anything that changed the land, like earth movements or volcanic eruptions," Sashia said, desperate to keep up, "as Natural Corrections?"

"Right." I turned to talk directly to Mei, "But I'm not so concerned about asteroid impacts. We have means to deal with NEOs."

She immediately engaged with this, wondering at the direction I wanted them to go in, "Then, we're looking for something more? Like whether a DeepStorm Gwave was involved? That sort of Natural Correction?"

I shrugged. "Well, if that was involved you'll certainly see its effects. But, for now, concentrate on what Singh showed you. That's what we really have to worry about." There was so much we needed to address. "Something turned that scene catastrophic. Powerfully complex terraforming forces deposited whole countrysides full of chalk and such. What else happened? Were there any huge environmental imbalances?"

I studied the two fimans as they left, eager to know if they'd make the grade. Oddly, FayWell hung around. "Yes?" I prompted, for her to say what was on her mind.

"It's not always *lucid* – I mean, what's said or meant?" This ever-friendly AI, with her Aussie inflection, wasn't so much puzzled or seeking answers. I was stunned at such a non-mechanical observation. Of course I'd been impressed by her neurocomputer self-learning logic, especially her ability to follow and even anticipate in helping researchers with their observations and studies. But her 'cybsilorg' creation was a marvel – self-propagating nanobots sewed logic into the siliceous tissue of certain plants, for her to grow physically, in tune with her thought processes developing complexly. This lady lived in plants! And as this was so organic and totally unpredictable, I had to always think about what she'd put to me – and why – because it was the only way I had of knowing what she now was.

"People aren't?" she shared, without expression, leaving me to wonder whether I'd ever see her eyes. "And that's their mystique?" What the hell was she on about? "The Earth, or Gaia, cloaked in her surroundings, has that. Something that's not lucid." It was beyond me where she was going with this. "Her shroud of mist constantly fusing, dispersing, and wafting makes it impossible to fully read her. Even I cannot fully fathom cloud, not precisely."

"Ah, she's referring to the *Cretaceous* image. Interesting." I was indeed taken aback.

Later that summer I invited the two girls to come up again, and this time, on returning to Singh's *Cretaceous* garden, Mei gently touched arrays of laurel with purple berries and whispered to blooms of yellow witch hazel, pink magnolia, greenish-yellow sycamore and light blue cigar bush. Eyes closed she inhaled their fragrance. This fresh young fiman was in ecstasy, so at home was she in the company of plants. And yet, she had only the vaguest recollection of how her time ended so disastrously in Moloka'i.

"Of course the origin of everything in this corner of the garden was in Ameurasian *Mid-Cretaceous* landscapes. While white pachysandra was in 'Antarctralasia' [encompassing Antarctica, Patagonia and Australasia]." Singh studied Mei, seeking a spark of recognition. "Ah, but," he teased, "it turns out now, that all those plants, in fact everything you see here, was far more abundant than previously realised, and what we're picturing are herbaceous or bushy varieties in heathland areas – where they had sunny well-drained slopes, brisk breezes, seasonal bacteria-killing frost, seed regenerating termite mounds and even brush fires.

"Ideal places for this would have been in highlands remote from the fern meadows and savannah, of big herds, where things were more readily fossilised in bogs and alluvial plains. In essence the two, herbaceous heathland versus fern meadowland, were worlds apart. And hitherto we only really knew about the latter."

"And these?" Mei stroked at some grasses growing in front of groups of birch, beech, sequoia, willow, elm, oak, walnut, yew, maple, grape and pixie moss.

"Ah, those arrived as bushes in Ameurasian *Late-Cretaceous* heathland. And over there are Antarctralasian varieties that came in then," he motioned to bushy spreads of soapberry, spurge, citrus, myrtle, hazel, banksias, winteraceae, restionaceae, macadamia, ilex, oak and Australian almond. "The sedges," he pointed to them, "filled new meadows of wildfire ecologies in South America."

"Hell, we've had some idea of the flowering plants that got started in the *Late-Cretaceous*. And we knew that heathland was in the migratory trails of dinosaurs, from grass 'phytoliths' [mineral secretions of plants] in their dung," Mei was loving this, "But, wow! All of this is so modern looking! And if it was as extensive as you say, then it puts a whole new perspective on that world's climate as well as the ranges that were available to creatures."

That afternoon we resumed privately, and without Singh. I dived in. "Okay, tell me! I'm dying to know! What's in the first gemstone I gave you?"

I could see Sashia shared my eagerness and indeed my urgency. But first, she tilted her head to elicit a friendly nod from Mei, to kick off what was in essence her subject. I was then truly surprised at Sashia's rapport with our AI, who had appeared in a tree. "FayWell, show the globe and say what we found."

Hair as usual veiling her eyes and somehow adding to her ever-intangible air, the AI's information proved riveting. "I filtered out cloud from the globe we had, using infrared imaging – as one does!" Her voice skipped along, characteristically a little squeakily but cheery. "And, what did we get?" As the screen near us refreshed my surprisingly elated AI continued, "Why, this! Which, yes, indeed, looks like a very pretty paleogeographical model of the planet – the Earth roughly a hundred million years ago – at the *close* of the *Mid-Cretaceous* period!"

"We could scarcely believe it." Initially chuckling at the commentary, Sashia now more seriously expressed their scepticism. "You've repeatedly said *'Go back in time'*." She received an encouraging wave from Mei. "But! The thing is, FayWell, you've found nothing like this on record? Right?"

"One hundred percent!" FayWell was almost congratulatory, "Nothing's been published – not a paleogeographical model or paper or anything – that's precisely like this!"

"It looks right." Mei gave me a sideways look, that I read as partly curious though also somewhat impish. But I guess it was only natural for the serious minded girl to wonder at her Chief Scientist's, indeed her boss's take on the AI's frivolity. "From what we've known of that time, all continents were inundated with inland seas and tidal wetland just like this," a frivolity I chose to shrug off, "with no ice sheets and Ameurasia cut off from the southern hemisphere by the warm circum-global Tethys Sea..."

"Ah, except!" FayWell wagged a finger, her tone deepening, "What's wrong? Huh? Well, of course, in this the Atlantic wasn't as wide as has been postulated for that time! The island continents of India and Madagascar appear to have been much nearer to their present positions! *And* the vegetation in some high ground areas, as Singh's teams have only *now* discovered, were beginning to have a more modern look than had been thought!"

"You're sure?" I chuckled. "Great! Nobody should ever have imagined they'd got it all exactly as it was, in their models!" Oh what fun their looks of incredulity were! "Yes! This is *exactly* as it was! As in a photo! And, yes, that is what it is – a *photo* from space!" Mei, jaw dropping, was about to speak when I held up my hands. "Time, to break for lunch."

Giving them no chance to protest I signalled the boy, Agnos, to roll in the trolley and watched their faces fill with joy at seeing him lift off silver plated covers to reveal grilled trout and snapdragon asparagus, prepared from an old Blumenthal recipe, and then pour glasses of a chilled Sauvignon Blanc.

It certainly tickled Sashia, "I know, all specially couriered from Ye Olde England?" She winked cheekily.

"Not actually." Mei looked at me, her seasoned English boss, with fresh eyes. "The asparagus is grown here?"

"Well, actually, everything is 'grown' here." I found it more than a pleasure, with these young and diligent trainee reconneers, to relax with them and let them know they counted. "There's a trout farm and an award winning vineyard, too." And, yes, my ego was also nicely lifted by their youthful attentions. "Everything is growing superbly up here, extra superbly even." When we'd chatted sufficiently about the port and such, both girls looked pleadingly for a return to our subject and I motioned for them to ask away.

"That's..." Mei was pointing to the screen whilst simultaneously placing her hand over Sashia's mouth, to get in first, and giggling to encourage forgiveness. "That's a photo? A *millions* of years old photo?"

"Okay." The time had come to put full trust in these two. "You must swear to secrecy on everything. Speechless, they were forced to nod to hear more. "Get serious. Say it, in full."

Fascinated, and with deadly serious expression, Sashia dived in first. "Present company excepted, I swear not to divulge anything said or yet to be said to anyone." Mei followed, repeating much the same.

"Okay," I pulled forward a silver tie clip I wore, with its image of a half-Moon, "this is our Moon. Right?" They looked closely and nodded, which made me chuckle. "Well – not actually. This might look like a gemstone but it's really a very special volcanic glass, denser than regular obsidian. *And* it solidified long ago, with a light-stopping refractive index. Freezing this *ancient* image of the Moon! The other 'gemstones', just the same, have ancient images – but of Earth!"

Sashia carefully examined one of the specimens. "Photos – in volcanic glass? Like what's on Ni'moloka'i?"

"Well, possibly. But this is much denser than regular volcanic glass." Their excitement was palpable now. They were seeing what no one else had ever seen, except through me. "Anyhow, never mind that. As you see, the resolution is exquisite. Fine enough to zoom as close as that..." I pointed to the screen.

Mei was dumbfounded, "Yow! Seeing planets, so far back in time!"

"Well more than that. All the stones, those found so far that is, are from the Moon. The one you've examined was formed there, so has a view of Earth from space. But *this* stone," I teased them with another cut stone, placing it before them, "like my tie clip, with its image of the moon, was in ejecta from Earth. Except – *it* appears to have images on the *ground from Earth*!"

"Yowie!" In their unison, the girls were transfixed.

"It gets better," I was beginning to feel like Santa, "At the very moment of solidifying, images piled up in these. Whole sequences of images froze, as in ice. Hence my name for them – *icegems*."

"It's as if we've got movie clips?" Mei pressed on, "of creatures moving around?"

"Absolutely. Just cut the stones – into fine slivers – and you'll have each frame in a sequence." In their dazed expressions was all the commitment I needed. They were pulled in, hooked and primed to research the past with obsessive thoroughness. "Store them digitally, join them together, and you'll have a movie. Just here, is the slicing equipment you'll need." I pulled a box from the trolley and handed it to Sashia. "You also have your Silverworm, which FayWell can tap into to see where you're looking.

"The icegems are a highly guarded secret, not only valued by powerful collectors but by mystical orders," I really projected my seriousness now, "and so extremely hard to come by that I had to lend them to the jewellery store – where you first saw them – with tags for FayWell to track wherever they went."

The responsibility for what she alone could do now fell on Sashia. Glancing apprehensively at Mei and then FayWell, to ensure they would follow her focus, she took up the first stone and zoomed right in, while FayWell kept refreshing the screen. First came a coastline. Mei's eyes scanned for detail while commentating almost in a whisper. "That's the southern coast of Eurasia." Next they were seeing a large bay, and closer in, rivers meandering below the dappled green of treetops.

"This is so amazing!" Sashia's eyesight was not only astonishing them all, but handing her a new sense of importance.

"No! Look! A forest!" Mei's words faltered in her excitement. "It's an enormous expanse of greenery. Many shallows. Wide sandbanks. And those, are what?" Sashia zoomed in. "Yes! Monkey-puzzle trees! Hell! Can you believe this? We're actually looking, at a *Cretaceous* landscape! The land of dinosaurs!"

~*~

122

17

Levelling off in the upper stratosphere, the captain of a military shuttle came on air. Voice clear and authoritative, he addressed passengers in their assigned capacities. "Trainees, 15 minutes to drop zone. On schedule. Crew to exit doors. Unlatch rear door." Throughout the passenger cabin fimans, clad in grey-green lightweight suits with side stripes of fluorescent orange, stared ahead apprehensively. All minds were on plunging into the InviHundred, their rendezvous with destiny.

During the flight, Sashia and Mei had busied themselves with checking gear alongside their Red Robin teammates. These two young blokes, both with aerial hairdos, were Guillermo Sanchez (Guille for short) who possessed a tennis-pro build, hairy blonde chest and quiet unobtrusive manner, and Bryn Griffiths, owner of a rugged rugby stature, who fussed over just about everything.

In a forward area they had the opportunity to study a hologram of the extreme InviHundred terrain – a black mountain peaking in cloud, foothills terraformed with forests, and volcanic slopes crisscrossed with lava streams and white-water all the way down to the sea. The drop zone was football-field size, atop black cliffs. The finishing post was on an atoll islet, some 10 kilometres out to sea.

Bryn voiced their concerns. "Guys. It's active." There was some debate about that but, in the end, they had to put their faith in the F-Academy. He did persist once more. "This is Ni'moloka'i, right? Didn't it erupt, violently, just recently?" No one could argue there but nor could they do anything about it. Instead they had to find the safest, quickest way down, and out of there. All eyes fell on Sashia, the team aware that her eyesight was their greatest asset – they also knew what this girl was made of – the guts and determination that had driven her to overcome all obstacles, evidenced by the legs that could never hold her back.

Putting all her energies into seeing routes, when Sashia eventually left the hologram she was surprised to find Mei absent and could find her nowhere. Seeing her concern, Bryn joined her in looking around. Guille had also noticed her separation and feared she might be struck from the programme.

They found the biologist squeezed between two seats, staring blankly ahead. For Mei that hologram of the volcano was as horrendously terrifying as her continuing nightmares. Only on this shuttle, after seeing that volcano, she had visualised a vaguely familiar face, Rad's face, drowning in water. Tears were streaked down her cheek, making the scar on one shine. She was mumbling. Sashia leaned in to her. "It's all so unfair. With my strength now, I could have heaved him out – so easily. It was *my* fault!"

Sashia held and soothed her, stroking her hair and gesturing for the others to leave them alone. And so they remained silently locked together for some time.

Finally, anxious that time was running out, Sashia reminded Mei about their planned descent and all that it implied. "Once we drop, there'll be no turning back," she whispered, concerned as to whether her friend was up to it. "You okay with that? You could stay on board, you know." Mei indicated she needed a helping hand, to extricate herself from the space she got wedged into. Once out, she straightened up, smiled and, with an affirmative nod, moved aft beside Sashia, acknowledging the relief on the faces of their teammates with an equally confident smile. 'I'm fine now, thanks. We're fine – great together!"

All four fell into line, Sashia eyeing the other three with certain pride.

"All systems READY. We have: Team one – GREEN. Team two – GREEN. Team three…" It was time, for the drop. The craft dipping at the top of a parabolic path rendered them all *weightless*. The Red Robin team pulled themselves floating to the exit area, each with a chute pack as well as a backpack crammed with 20 kilograms of superbly engineered gear. There were provisions for camping, survival, first aid, climbing, as well as rations, kayak and, essentially, sections of a white-water raft.

More than anyone, Sashia truly revelled in the floating sensation, again briefly free of relying on her trusty striders, before thinking to ensure that Mei had rechecked her gear. But, to her relief, Guille was already doing that. "Hm," she reflected about those two together, "that looks promising." They were soon donned in silver over-suits and helmets, Sashia checking that her scarf was secure over her hair and lower jaw. Finally, they slipped on their packs.

Team eight – GREEN. Braced for action the team pulled to the open doorway and went straight out, into free-fall. Initial altimeter readings at 30 kilometres were dropping fast. Their sealed suits, pressurised at three kilometres, protected them from biting cold. Transductors, attached to their bodies, powered displays of speed, temperature, maps and such, which appeared heads-up in their visors.

"All systems, *check*," Sashia reported and received the same from each of the others. Helmet coms switched on, bracelet-coms off, they were instantly babbling, high on adrenaline. Her commentary was of Silverworm enhanced glimpses of the ground, while the others saw merely cloud. At 15 kilometres she could make out specific features. "Hell-bytes, it's so…"

"What? What is it?" Bryn sounded apprehensive.

"…hostile. Steam coming off bare, black rock. Just the green of the jungle looks at all bearable."

"Yeah, depending on what's in there!" he added cautiously.

"It'll be a complete ecosystem." Guille was grinning.

"The whole food chain!" Bryn took the bait.

"Sure, with predators." Guille, a cool Basque, spoke plainly, with a twist. "What? You think it was made just for us?"

At 10 kilometres Sashia banked round on sighting the drop zone. The others followed. And there they were, incredibly, one hundred skydivers soaring majestically to their team targets – looming large on the ground – and she filling her eyes with their Red Robin bull's eye. Just then, her concern became Mei. She'd heard not a word from her since their coms check, not even with the thrill of skydiving from this great height. "Mei, you okay?"

However, her concentration had to shift quickly to the cliff, to pick out the best routes down, as quickly as possible, and also note where ledges and footholds were.

Mei was staring wide-eyed at a tranquil blue sea, with Ni'moloka'i centremost, watching the island erupt with lava and smoke in all directions. From far off she heard a voice, Sashia shouting, "Mei, your chute! Mei! Open your chute! Your Goddamn chute, Mei!" Startled into the present, her straps jarred. The chute had been automatically opened by her altimeter emergency release, while steadfast Guille was tugging at a strap to steer her away from the cliff edge and onto target. The ground rose fast. Bracing herself as best she could, Mei hit dirt and rolled hard.

They had made it – landed together, and other teams were landing about them in rapid succession.

Guille helped Mei up, with Bryn at hand, too. Fimans ran about them in all directions. "Where the fuck are you, Mei?" Sashia shouted tersely, nursing leg muscles jarred by landing. All she knew was to get away fast, as a team – and she knew the way, "You okay?"

"Okay! With you."

"Yeah, only 'cause you're a fucking fiman." Exasperation marked Sashia's tone. She had to lead. She knew the way. Back on her striders after so briefly having been weightless, remorse and regret at her handicap slammed into her.

"It's okay," Mei soothed, coming near and angry with herself for causing added anxiety to her friend.

"I'm with you," in a flash Guille, firm and gentle, confirmed his backing to both girls.

They all threw off their backpacks, pressurised suits and helmets. "Okay," Sashia told herself, "snap out of it!"

Pressing forward all four were buffeted by hot gusts of wind that instantly had them sweating. "Follow the drill!" As they pressed forward they were re-donning backpacks and climbing helmets with coms, and finally exchanged nods of readiness. "Ready over?" Sashia yelled above the wind, checking over her shoulder that Mei in particular was there, Guille and Bryn beside her, and then they rushed straight to the cliff edge. "Christ," Sashia muttered. "How could I have doubted her. She's the pro. They all are. I'm just a graphic designer, me. So, one of *them* ought to lead."

"Ready!" the team responded.

When Sashia stepped onto lava rock, gleaming with sharp black obsidian that crunched underfoot, her confidence had returned. She stooped stiffly to jam a power cam into a crack as her anchor, and in one continuous movement she clipped and yanked a thin red line there, swivelled round mechanically, stepped out, and fell face down body flat. The line zinged out from a winch at the back of her belt. Raptor fast, a small back-kite keeping her feet pounding on the sheer cliff face, she abseiled down. Adrenaline high, spine arched, eyes wide – and weeping with the draught – she sped super fit and in ecstasy while venting weeks of pent up stress in a great shout,

"Yeooowee!" She was following the rocky way as if running upright. "This is *great*!!"

Dead ahead, over a kilometre away, was a wall of green treetops. Nearer, she focused on a rock ledge spied earlier, 50 metres down. There she pulled in and stopped.

Now on cue from Sashia, Guille stooped to clip his line to the cam and switch hers to the front of his belt. Without hesitation he swivelled around and went over, his line zinging out while hers steered him down. "Eeyaah!" he howled joyfully, running powerfully, muscles bulging, before landing on the narrow shelf next to her – the two slapping hands at their success.

Rugby-built Bryn now clipped and switched lines before his stocky frame pounded down the cliff face like a primitive ape. At the same time Sashia dropped down to the next level, beautifully coordinated. All along the cliff a hundred fimans were doing likewise – without a hitch.

Mei had clipped and switched lines on cue but stepped unsteadily to the edge, and there she froze, again seeing the face in her nightmares, washed in water. Voices shouted through her coms, the wind buffeted her body. Feeling tears streak her face, she stepped out – and fell. Lives were at stake. Professional to the core she would not let them down. The rush of air sharpened her resolve. Cold sweat on her neck, adrenaline pumping, feet pounding, she snapped back to the here and now.

Reaching Bryn on the ledge, it was barely wide enough for their feet, twisted precariously sideways. "You okay?" he asked discreetly, muting his coms. Her nod wasn't too convincing. In the split seconds before Sashia would continue down, one of them having to follow, Mei acceded to switching lines with him and instead make Bryn the anchor man. They were doing this, first hammering a cam in the rock face and clipping Guille's line there, and Mei's to Bryn, when, as he also began to clip his on the cam, the entire cliff face shook, jerking his feet off the ledge. Falling in apparent slow motion, Bryn waved his line to alert her that the two of them were not anchored.

Horrified, Mei lunged to grab his sleeve, his arm, anything. "No! Not again!" In that moment his petrified face transformed into another's, the terror filled eyes swirling in water, her words echoing, "Pull with me! Pull with me!" And up came the face, clamped in

127

the jaws of a *great white*, gleaming teeth so close to her that she could have touched them with a blink of her eyelashes. Petrified she watched it fall away again, a tooth slicing her hand as if making a parting mark, before crimson waters washed away Rad's agonised face. That was the conclusion unrevealed in her nightmares, her mind blocking that final image. Now, it was released.

Wind slammed her tear-smudged face against the rock, snapping her back to reality in time to see her line zinging out. Mei grabbed hold with gloved hand, slowing Bryn's fall, whilst also grabbing hold of Guille's anchored line. Just then, her belt yanked painfully down on her hips, jarring her forward and perilously buckling one leg, as the dead-man-brake in her back-winch arrested the fiman. Desperately straightening, she let go of her line to him and clipped a safety line from her belt to the cam. Relief instant, Mei quickly hauled the fiman up and, giving him a reassuring smile, received no protest to switching back to anchor man.

Once firmly on the ground, all four high on danger and excitement, talk was all about the earth tremor. Bryn shrugged off, "No problem," they were okay. They had coped. He received a nod on that from Mei. Their real concern was what the F-Academy was making of the quake.

Mei rubbed her hands to conceal their trembling, her face nonetheless flushed with some measure of closure over Rad and the exuberance of being a life-saving team player. What was remarkable was the speed of the incident on the cliff, with her reflexes so tuned that only Bryn was even vaguely aware of her momentary hesitation up there. Except, yes, Guille was perceptive, quietly reading her body language, yet saying nothing.

Nearing nightfall now, they decided to tackle the forest ahead of them at dawn. Quickly setting up camp was more urgent. Short distances away, along the cliff base, they could hear other teams doing much the same.

All their time-out, along with their course progress, was recorded by the 'SPS' [Space Positioning System, extension to global navigation systems 'GPS', 'GLONASS' and 'Galileo'] they each had. After eating, the four sat near the campfire recapping the plan they'd worked out in-flight. They knew the white-water they wanted to head for, aiming to end up facing the atoll, and where they could join it at the far side of the forest. They had no idea of the terrain in between, to get there.

"Hm," Mei, her old Moloka'i vitality back at last, looked at the forest canopy engulfing them, "coniferous." To their blank faces she explained, "It's not a jungle."

"You're sure?" Guille's tone expressed the relief they all showed at seeing her so alive now, as much as what she said.

"Yep, rainforests were not common in *Cretaceous* landscapes. And, they're not your favourite to create or maintain in reforestation today." Mei also looked at Guille, and Bryn, in relief as well as amazement, that her usual reserve with peers had evaporated. It was as if, just as in bonding with Sashia in that earlier life-threatening experience, she had now also bonded with these two since their near disaster – they were now inside her defences. "Huh," Mei gave an inner smile before carrying on, "and a *Cretaceous* park, most commonly woodland within extensive fern plains, is what this looks like to me. This is good – you wouldn't want to fight your way through thick black anoxic coal-forming bog. Not in a race!"

Their minds turned to wondering what race officials were saying about the tremors – and they weren't let down. A voice of authority began to communicate to all competitors, "Volcanologists, here, do not consider an alert is warranted. But with a hundred of you down there, they're being ultra cautious. That means – you are all to be vigilant, make haste to complete the course and leave the island."

All eyes were wide open, no one yielding to sleep just yet. Despite the uncomfortable silence that ensued, Mei announced, "Going for a pee," and set off in the dark.

Guille's eyes followed her movement, compassionately, and Sashia, sensing a need to accompany her for a girly let up, rose quickly, "Me, too." Making their way by torchlight, in an open space Sashia concertedly unzipped her suit and squatted a short distance from Mei, as if to demonstrate her ability to do so, despite her disability. The torch beam lit steam rising about the girls as they relieved themselves. "Hey, hot stuff. Huh?" Sashia laughed, gaining a reserved but happy grin from Mei that at last broke into laughter.

"Hah! Guess it would be bad to tip backwards onto these rocks." Mei laughed again.

"Hah? Yeah!" Quickly Sashia plunged at Mei to stop her losing her balance as she shook in uncontrolled laughter. "Bum sears? Real bad bum searing!"

Sashia scoured the girl's face in the hope of understanding what had so unnerved her on the flight. Whatever – there was no hint of that now, but she feared for Mei that it might return. In silence, they began to return to the others. Then, just out of earshot of the camp Mei swung round, brow furrowing, "I can't tell you Sashia. I can't say." Since Rad, she had never longed so much to open up fully. Self consciously, she gazed at a scar on her hand and fingered the one on her cheek. "Nightmares – to do with this place – this place changed my life..."

"No, wait! Not *now!*" Fighting overwhelming compassion, Sashia urged, "I want you to tell me what's troubling you, but, *another time*. Tomorrow we'll be in some serious shit, possibly life-or-death shit. You can't afford to have anything else on your mind – none of us can. Okay? For now just clear it out of your head, right out, and instead concentrate on getting us through."

Mei stared at her, thinking of how this disabled girl had so stoically ridden the Flying Mountain's Class VIII rapids. In self remorse but renewed confidence, Mei stretched out her hand. "Okay. Believe me, I'll not let anyone down."

"Hey, what's up?" a short girl with a Latin lilt strolled past casually. Coming from another team, she was doubtless sizing up the competition. Sashia gave the newcomer a warning shake of her head, but the fiman homed in regardless, as was her Mexican way, to sweetly express her concern. "I'm Tixa Gomez." Her short Arctic hare hairdo framed a dainty and pretty face. "If there's anything I can do, let me know – okay? See you later."

Prompted by Sashia, the girls said nothing and turned to move away. As they approached the camp, feeling marvellously alert, Mei opened up, "You know, the *Mid-Cretaceous* clips from the icegems? So much cloud, wintertime, over both polar regions?" She was openly mulling over what they'd since found by zooming in, FayWell's immense computing power having helped to splice the images so quickly. "Clearly it was constantly wafting there, after forming over warm sea currents and so many more active volcanoes than in relatively modern times," just for an instant Mei shuddered as she glanced up to the smoking peak of Ni'moloka'i, "as well as more expansive hotspots than under our Galapagos and Hawaiian Islands volcanoes."

The clips had also confirmed that there were no big mountain ranges or winds to dissipate clouds over, nor any ocean currents to prevent warmth reaching the Arctic and Antarctic.

"Okay!" Sashia, who saw this rather as a distraction from getting off this mountain from hell, nevertheless got the point and attempted jocularity. "El-Niño gone global – and on steroids!"

"Hm! Hardly any wind chill or continuous permafrost anywhere. And so," Mei concluded, palms upturned, "nowhere frigid, with ice sheets. Just permafrost on the Transantarctic Hills."

"Ah, right. I noted what you and the Prof came up with, in revisiting the notion of Global Warming." Sashia sounded impressed. "You reckoned *'Polar Warming'* drew dinosaur migrations summertime to sunny polar meadows, which in winter had not frozen over thickly in the warm, still air caused by all that cloud cover then."

I'd contributed to this with NASA records of wintertime cloud extensively covering both poles, early this century – which it followed, had to be the product of increased geological activity in recent millennia. While the records showed that, over the bulk of the ice in Greenland and Antarctica, there'd hardly been any summertime cloud. Polar Warming, though as yet not as severe as before, was nevertheless back as a major component of Climate Change today! The risk, of any further developments there, was sure to put greater pressure on international efforts to manage green house emissions from human activity.

"I still can't believe what we saw everywhere else," indeed Sashia had been smitten by the images they found, "whole panoramas, continent after continent, millennium upon millennium, of beautiful heathland." Though she'd rather they didn't concentrate on it right here and now. "Much as Singh's teams have envisaged, just so much *more!*"

"Hm. Slopes of grasses, bushes and herbaceous plants, bathed in sunshine with intermittent cloud." The more Mei reflected on it, the more seriously engrossed she became. "Breathtaking, above tree lines, with springtime and summertime blooms. To me they looked like Scottish highlands, loftily overlooking still and misty lowlands."

"Frustrating, isn't it? The training exercise keeping us from that research?" Excitement was growing in their voices, yet, discernable in Sashia's was fear. She moved in dread of failing to lead them to safety and would have preferred to dump the prehistoric subject for now.

"The thing is, those landscapes were pretty," Mei's fear was more to do with failing to anticipate the worst from DeepStorm, "but not perfectly balanced. We know extinctions took place quite regularly, peaking on occasion, and became more marked since the Deccan eruptions started. What was it Singh said about that?" Mei found resorting to Sashia's fine-tuned memory far more congenial than conversing with a machine – which, they now had to remind themselves, despite her super friendly manner that's what FayWell was. Besides, right now she couldn't contact her anyway.

"Uh, just how the southern hemisphere was destroyed by fallout and mega-cyclones," Sashia was hiding impatience to leave this. "You know. Wildlife millennially hit by droughts, flash floods and wildfires. He said they'd worked on something else too." What tore at her was the desire to prove she was up to Mei's level if not her professional qualifications. "They've found mineral traces in some nursery ground down, as a clue to where those might've been."

"What? Oh that." Unfortunately, Mei was rather dismissive.

"As in ejecta, found in Moon digs! From known eruptions and impacts around Earth!" Sashia's voice rose a few notes. "And they're piecing together some migratory trails! Like those of emperor penguins in Antarctralasia."

"What? Of course! Their migrations in early spring." Mei reflected on how, still today, penguins headed inland across the ice deserts of Antarctica blinded by shifting icescapes, clouded skies, blizzards and even total darkness. "And there're much longer migrations that birds, marine turtles too, have determinedly stuck to."

"No matter how onerous the journey," Sashia encouraged now, "or how tempting the distractions?"

"Yes, wow! Routes locked in their genes, not just over millennia but millions of years ... perhaps from as far back as *Late-Cretaceous* times? It's staggering! I've long imagined some invisible landmarks, indelibly printed on the land. But what could those have been? Nothing's that constant. Surface features change and star constellations move over time. Also the Earth's magnetic field shifts about, waxes and wanes – and even reverses.

"But, what the heck! It's great! We can help in mapping some dinosaurs trails – and if we find one abandoned, that would suggest where a Natural Correction had occurred! That rocks!"

"And you'd mentioned the absence of ancestral dung beetles, in South America." Whilst appreciating the importance of all of this, Sashia's tension remained and she hoped to end their talk. "In recycling mounds of dinosaur pooh." This had Mei chuckling. "You said they're a characteristic of modern savannahs. And, that's why there weren't likely to have been really big herds on that continent."

"True," Mei considered this for a moment, "but not so for western Antarctralasia, where there were very large herds in Patagonia at least."

This was great stuff, a very healthy dialogue. I'd hoped to see into the past, using those icegems, but the pictures emerging were already more vivid and the discussions more enlightening than I'd ever dared dream.

At last, sleeping bags zipped, Mei chose to fall asleep with chat rather than nightmares. Sashia spoke of missing Fayez and Mei countered with a tale about a guy named Jacques, in Shanghai, who never got back to her after she moved to HK.

In the dark, Sashia reflected over this very confident professional, who it seemed had long lost her spunk and now was hopefully ready to contribute - meaningfully. "I've had to cope for both of us – in a race!" Sashia mentally noted to her diary, "Requiring competitive drive. Enough! That's not me, my nature. Thank God for Guille, with that quiet inner strength and observation, he really helps out."

Eyelids heavy, Mei sought positive closure. "By the way, how the hell did you find me in the Da Oh Ling cataracts, underwater, in the dark?"

"Ah you've a worm to thank, for that."

"Really?" Mei's respect for Sashia, despite her not being highly qualified, continued to grow. "Ah, not a common or garden worm?"

"Oh-oh, no. Mine was a robotic one, going by the trade name Silverworm." Under the cover Sashia grinned. "So everything good now is *wormy* or *goodah*, just like the trader said, when he let me in on this powerful classified beauty. *Goodah*."

~*~

133

18

October 2067

A snow-white Machu Picchu greeted the heavy coated and winter booted UN Security Council members arriving for further closed-door sessions. UN Secretary General Matri commenced proceedings with a very direct opening brief. "Friends, at last year's meeting we were presented with scientific findings that we've precariously managed to hide from the World. Now that the predictions, which we also heard, are clearly coming about," she waved vaguely at the window, "and icecaps advancing in polar and mountainous regions are being shown all over the media, I propose that we have no option but to go public and release the full extent of the DeepStorm dilemma."

As members were showing their unanimous ascent, an aide drew Matri's attention to the Sævrama Channel on view in the hall, and Matri indicated she'd be along presently. "I'll now make the interim statement agreed upon. Excuse me."

The aide led Matri out to where the press awaited them, along with ambassadors for other UN member states brought in on holoe. On screen, Jude's seriousness reflected the occasion. She'd convinced her chief to let her cover this event alone, leaving McGuire to cover the Washington end, *"...We've just heard that UN Security Council members are here and at this moment meeting behind closed doors. So far, there have been no press briefings. Ah, here they come – UN Secretary General Sustra Matri."*

Jude's image faded into a scene at the resort terrace, where Matri was facing a crowd of cam-optics to deliver her statement. *"Good morning. Recent climatic developments have become of growing concern to the United Nations and general public. Under the codename DeepStorm, UNNDC has been studying the underlying causes, and long-range effects, as a matter of the highest priority.*

"While our immediate concern goes to families and businesses in affected areas, we ask everyone not to hinder relief operations in those zones and to co-operate in whatever way they are or will be requested to do. That's all we can tell you at this time. We will keep you informed as and when more information becomes available. Thank you."

Jude came back on air, her presence bright, despite concerns for the public rising. *"Well, what we've been witnessing is now viewed as a global phenomenon of some sort – maybe like a storm that's NOT expected to blow over, hence the name DeepStorm? Speculations about another Little Ice Age might not be wholly unfounded after all. However, I'm not suggesting a connection. We'll keep you advised when there's a fuller explanation for that DeepStorm label – and of course all other developments."*

"Jude," Jack tussled to conceal nervousness.

"Hi Jack," she snapped, equally tense.

"We should get a profile on this guy – Madison." Jack's experience told him she needed direction. He didn't want Jude to miss any openings. "He's there?" Simultaneously Jack was pushing his team to get Madison's info and then guide her on questions to ask.

"Sure, he's on the list." Now off camera her anguish, reflecting all the suffering she was mindful of, unnerved him too.

"Haven't seen him yet – and I didn't get anywhere with him the last time, if you remember...." She broke off, seeing the little Glaswegian waltzing distractingly around Jack. Suddenly Jude couldn't resist taking her frustration out on her. "No choice words today about my outfit – from the office ornament? Don't tell me I've got that priority right after all?" She watched the girl shrink back, and deep down understood why Jack empathised with her. Yet, he motioned her aside. "Sorry, it's a bit tense here."

Putting him on edge was the viewing ratings, not to mention the growing concerns of an alarmed public. So much rested on the reporting of his fledgling news girl to bring the news truthfully in.

Back in the hall, before resuming at the dais, Matri glanced over to the Sævrama Channel. "We must now resolve whether to follow up with declaring an International State of Emergency."

DelMonte rose, unusually grave and somewhat haggard, musing over a metaphor to focus all attention. "Real grief is never deeper than with the loss of a child, your child," he intoned, looking about and noting general apprehension. "Our populations, our children, are what DeepStorm threatens." He paused. "To protect them, UNNDC scientific task forces, assigned to DeepStorm, have been increased to give uninterrupted support for all your efforts, 24/7, round the globe and upside.

"Their findings will be relayed to you. For now, we'll get straight to our report on how the DeepStorm threat is progressing." He motioned to me.

Despite the tension of the previous session fresh in my mind, I was nevertheless calm when going over the same Solar System hologram. "The crest is still a long way off, far from reaching the Kuiper belt," I could not prevent a frown as I pointed to the far right, "but with no sign (or hope) of it slowing down.

"The status across Ameurasia is that UNNDC is awaiting our decision on the International State of Emergency before their meteorological office advises affected states to make effective – a *Little Ice Age Warning* and an *Ice Age Alert*. Failing this, the office will issue the advice, regardless, within seventy-two hours. Hence this urgent meeting.

"Northern regions are expected to cool year-on-year and the advice, to local authorities, is without delay to draw up contingency plans. Measures aimed at retarding the cooling have not been as effective as we'd hoped."

The air in the hall was drained, like a whale had taken its last breath. As they became more conscious of the PNR (the Point of No Return) reached, I had a chilling prognosis for them, "In the next decade or so some states will face spiralling costs to maintain infrastructures, coupled with year-on-year downturns in GDP. International financial crises will lead to recession. Job losses will drive Ameurasian climate refugees southward, to camp in neighbouring states."

"What's fundamental..." DelMonte came in to, thankfully, bring a more positive edge to the situation, "is that we manage these developments concertedly and collaboratively – providing solid research and knowledge into how the Earth and Solar System function, and will function differently as the DeepStorm gravity advances. We can and must find solutions – together."

Glancing at me, DelMonte also indicated to Matri that we had finished.

She got straight to business. "Are we then resolved to declare an International State of Emergency?"

The Council members cast their votes via their own consoles, influenced in part by the total count they were privy to. When no more changes were forthcoming, Matri announced the consensus. "We are agreed. I'd like to reiterate that we've shown, in the past, the fortitude to win through in severe adversity. We've done it before. Let us be steadfast and do it again.

"Our next task is to resolve whether to send a manned mission deep into interplanetary space."

DelMonte prompted me to resume at the dais, and I felt huge relief to switch from talk of the dangers, to our positive plans. "As the UNNDC Chairman proposed to you over a year ago, our imperative for finding answers was to get a task force manned by fimans far out into space. To that end, we now propose to officially form the DeepStorm Questor mission.

"Right now we're evaluating the readiness of our candidates, several thousands of whom have been undergoing training around the World. We're getting very promising results. Top performers are physically superb specimens, more advanced in skills and endurance than was hitherto thought possible.

"Their fiman development was an evolutionary leap," I was only too pleased to impart that news, knowing that this was history in the making, "brought about by a breakthrough in science – the development of a *new gene*. They are not quite human, they are fiman."

The impact of this revelation froze the hall. All genecrafting to date had been by introduction of the genes of existent species, naturally generated, into subjects. No one had contemplated developing entirely new genes for new species. This was as revolutionary as it was daunting, with prospects of a future plagued by monsters.

"The complex procedure involves propagation through the foetus of specially designed nanobots. They tend to the new gene's developmental effects, from the time it starts to introduce carbon-kevlar-fibre (in place of calcium) in the metabolising process of bones. By late teens the calcium is virtually all replaced, except for teeth and nails. Once complete the fimans are impervious to osteoporosis, or bone loss suffered by human space travellers. Additionally, their 'xo-type blood' [refined plasma] inhibits corpuscle deformation, muscle attrition and the effects of radiation, as well as having other properties.

"Their development was authorised by the UN's Bio-Diversity Council – which sets standards and norms for the administrations of member states to follow, in the genecrafting of animal and plant species, with great success in thermoports, Ecstasy on the Moon and Martian terra-spheres.

"Quite exceptionally, the Council has endorsed our training of fimans to superhuman levels. Qualifying groups, all top ranked in a range of disciplines, are right now being pitted in the InviHundred – the ultimate challenge to select *Best of Breed.*"

Enough said about fimans, I had to reach the matter in hand. "What's proposed is a task force several thousand strong, terraccommodated in fully self-sufficient vessels, as a research colony in the Near Earth Territories spirit. Full details are appended to the report you have before you.

"We recommend that the mission is formed and despatched as quickly as possible, and charged with getting immediate results." Leaving the dais, I involuntarily gave an almost imperceptible bow, not for the hall, but for all those young reconneers for whom I felt so very responsible.

Matri looked unusually grave. "You'll recall the much publicised spate of disasters involving earlier trials in AstBelt mining, the only other attempt there's been to adapt humans for space operations of long duration. Those were exofimans. I'm assured fimans do not have the same neurological vulnerability. There is, I quote, 'a 98% certainty that fimans will be neurologically and psychologically stable in all theatres of operation'." She received a nod from me. "I submit that, in the circumstances, we consider this as a quasi-military operation and, as such, not debate the risks to individuals. Accordingly, all that is required is to agree on forming the mission. Are we so agreed?"

The President of Europe spoke up. "Why the need for a new breed, when the full complement of personnel will have EarthG quarters. And, as I see in the report, there'll be radiation shields too?"

I'd anticipated this. "As ZeroGs, they'll routinely attend to duties everywhere within and without the task force vessels, not just in EarthG quarters," I explained. "They'll also function unperturbed in the unlikely event of a vessel's simulated gravity failing. The human complement, just executive officers, will have to be transhipped in such emergencies." I could have left it there but decided to be a little more informative. "That's not to say that some microgravity disorders won't surface. It's too early to say."

Seeing that the Commissioner was satisfied with the reply, and that no other questions were forthcoming, Matri again asked for agreement, and at last announced, "We are agreed, to form the mission."

Before the break, there was a response to, 'Any other business'. Duardo Contrea, acting for the President of UNASUR, commented, "A matter of concern, which I believe the Council should review, is what, in social networking, is dubbed the DoomNet Syndrome. The concern is of gloom, about DeepStorm right now, critically dispiriting netizens and incapacitating communities. It's been suggested that we prepare emergency restrictions, such as in areas of the Web outside of government, commerce and essential public services..."

A clamour of angry voices drowned him out. No one appeared to welcome further controls on the web – beyond protecting privacy. The same outcry would have come from the public.

Matri firmly responded to the clamour ahead of everyone rising from their seats. "We'll take the short break now, and resume to discuss DeepStorm defences."

~*~

19

October 2067

The Red Robin team broke camp at first light, took course bearings, and set off downhill to find the going bright while dry underfoot with little undergrowth to press through. The sweet scent of pine needles even induced smiles. With everyone keeping eyes peeled for hazardous sinkholes, thermal vents and snakes, Sashia swivelled on her striders to check that Guille was able to watch out for Mei.

At noon, they slipped off backpacks to take a bite, and Sashia noticed Mei gently resting a hand on mosses coating tree roots and rocks. Looking up, she said, "So soft! Have you noticed, how verdant it is?" Eyes roaming, she then murmured, "So much like Moloka'i, except with Sashia and these two men it's good now. Fancy me thinking that!" Pleased, she suddenly announced, "A *Mid-Cretaceous* forest, as I'd expected."

"So, this was it," Guille kept her going, "all of that world, pretty much like this?"

"Of course not, vast fern savannahs and lightly wooded valleys too. Also open marshland. And overlooking it all, from on high, we now know that heathland stretched all the way to the poles."

"There are clues everywhere, right?" Sashia chipped in, wanting inclusion in support of Mei. "Petrified tree trunks. Leaf litter impressions in travertine and coal. Trackways. And so on." She looked to her friend for an answer.

"Then wham! It was all gone, right?" Bryn grinned.

"Well," Mei nodded and teased with her response, "maybe. But, look all around us... so much of this had its roots in *Late-Cretaceous* terrains. Like this chap, from South America," she pointed to an opossum curled up on a tree branch. "There was already a dispersion of birds," she shook her head to dispel their bemused looks, "with the break up of landmasses around that time. Mammals also differed – with the forebears of kangaroos in Australia, hippopotami in Africa, horses in North America (up to the Ice Age). While, the ranges of penguins and 'ratites' – they're the running birds – came into being in the southern hemisphere. In fact much of the rich biodiversity we see today, continent to continent, came down to us in some form or other from *Cretaceous* times."

"Ah, except, not a single dinosaur." Guille knew that much.

"Precisely. None survived anywhere, whether as colossal as a whale or as tiny as a sparrow, apart from the birds. Strange, huh? The dinosaurs arrived, just about as soon as there was sufficient vegetation on the land for them, and went on to fill and dominate just about every niche going in ecosystems," with a light-hearted chuckle she opened her palms to invite ideas, "and then," she clicked her fingers, "they'd *gone* – from absolutely everywhere – gone. So what was that? Bird-flu got the dinosaurs? WHO has had tens of millions of birds destroyed, present day, to contain avian pandemics. Or was it extreme hay fever that got 'em? Perhaps a comet delivered a fatal alien bug?"

"What about a cosmic jet stream – that the Earth might have intermittently swung into, ahead of the asteroid?" Sashia piped up, remembering from the news that a huge stream of gas and dust had just been classified as a highly hazardous NEO.

"Sure. Either hothouse or icehouse spikes from that, depending on the energy dissipated and the screening effect in the atmosphere, could have thinned out the reptiles," Mei frowned, now lamenting how right Rad might have been after all. There were many possibilities.

"So, it's still a mystery?" Mei gave Guille an affirmative nod.

Bryn waxed lyrical, "Ah, but there be dragons… that lived on. So ancient and medieval bards have told."

Crack! A nerve jolting sound, harsh as a rifle shot, was followed by a thunderous beating noise as a large waterfowl flew out of a bush. Taking that as their cue the team set off again, conscious of the animals both seen and unseen around them. "Plenty of game," Guille quipped, "and predators," taunting a bothered Bryn.

After a while Bryn remarked on their bad luck. "So where's all the water for us to ride? In the hologram model it was streaming out of the forest."

"Possibly, underground," Guille studied the forest for any signs of that.

"Oh well, at least it won't be boggy." Shortly after, pushing through thickening undergrowth, Bryn disappeared. "Yiiiipes!" his yell brought the others to a slippery mud bank, verging on a lake of green algae where he was stuck knee deep.

"You okay?" Mei yelled.

Stony faced, he regarded the stinking slime. "Yeah. I'm okay," he said disconsolately. Their teasing grins preceded them making sure of their own footings as well as holding fast to branches, to haul his slipping, sliding body up the slope.

"We'll have to find another way." Guille took in the bare tree trunks reaching high into the canopy. "I'll go up and have a look."

"Why hide it?" Mei dared a wink. "You're actually Spiderman."

Returning her wink, Guille drew out an extremely powerful hunting bow and shot an arrow through a branch as thick as his arm atop the nearest tree. With a nod from Sashia confirming that the arrowhead had gone through square and true, he winched himself up and called, "The swamp is too wide to get round quickly. It'd be best to go across."

"So, raft across?" Bryn offered.

"There are too many submerged branches. Kayaks will get through better."

Back on the ground the skilled woodsman scrolled through images on his wristband. "Something wasn't right with this lot," he pointed to birds on the far side, "taking off and landing – they're agitated."

"More tremors? They can sense them?" Mei worried.

Cutting to the chase, they got on with extending and inflating poles into kayaks and paddles. "No splashing," Guille warned. "Can't tell what's in there." Unsettled, they pushed off barely forming a ripple.

Distance to shore soon lengthened until, with just twenty metres to go, something brought them to an abrupt halt. Sashia peered through the murky water. "It's a tangle of submerged branches." With one nod from Guille she rolled under, ever keen to plunge into water. She had slipped out into algae up to her shoulders and, just momentarily, let herself float there weightless.

He grinned and then quickly explained to the others, "There's just a couple of hours, before nightfall. We'll only make it in time if we drag our kayaks and gear over this mess."

After trudging blindly through the murky water for some time, and finally with daylight fading fast, they clambered up a bank straight into thick undergrowth. Bryn hacked at it with a machete, not really caring that Mei recognised it as *Late-Cretaceous* foliage. It had flowering creepers that snagged their tough lightweight suits.

142

In time, they were drawn to an open spot by the sweet scent of pine needles, and there they stripped to burn off leeches and tend to minor cuts.

A deer scampered past, so close it almost knocked Bryn over. Nearby, bushes rustled with the scurrying of other animals. The group tensely exchanged glances, Sashia noticing goose bumps on Mei's arms and her frightened stare. "What is it?" she whispered gently, squeezing Mei's hand hard to bring her round. She received no immediate answer.

At last, Mei nodded, understanding her friend's anxiety. "Okay. I'm okay." She was just wishing to be left alone, but turned to join the others and make camp warily glancing around every now and then. Her vision was of fish leaping frantically out of water – the prelude to Ni'moloka'i erupting. Shivers began to run down her spine. She dared not look towards the smoking peak.

A warm meal, glowing campfire, togetherness, it all calmed nerves. To ease things further, Sashia cheerily directed their gaze back to the water, "Crocs got through," she said lightly, tilting her head quizzically and to encourage Mei's input. "And others, too, like monitor lizards, snakes and turtles? Not a lot though? Out of the age of reptiles, huh?"

"That's the point," Mei's gratitude for the diversion brought sparkle to her eyes. "So, what magic did the other reptiles lack?"

"Well," Guille threw in softly, enjoying the camaraderie between these sisterly fimans, "something else happened, right?"

"Yes," Mei hesitated before returning his look, to share what she knew. His features, lit by the fire, displayed both appealing candour as well as inner strength. "Huge eruptions were not uncommon, nor were hits by massive bolides," she responded, and smiled at him, encouraged by Sashia's brightening face. "When peace was shattered it was *big*! Hugely bigger than anything in recent times – even the eruptions of supervolcano Toba in Indonesia."

"Then one or more bolides, or super eruptions, finished off the dinosaurs?"

"Possibly – and possibly, something else," Mei flashed a friendly grin at him, and then taking her cue from Sashia nodding toward the woods she offered to her. "Why don't we take a walk and have a *real* chat."

"Off for a pee, you mean?" Sashia rose with her to stroll together along the shoreline.

"Our clips of termites, ants, bees, wasps and placental mammals abounding in the *Late-Cretaceous* heathlands, would thrill Singh," Mei began.

"Yes, as we heard he's placed them there, with theropods, crocodiles, snakes and turtles, but with no idea of how *profuse* it all was," Sashia did find it a treat learning from those two – Mei and Singh – and, while choosing a log to sit on and rest her legs, hoped that in some small measure her memory was helping Mei to move ideas on, especially if it kept her mind off repressed fears. "Hm, right, we were talking 'down'. Especially down covering heathland theropods, big and small."

"Right, down. Like the flocks of running dromaeosaurus we saw, down was their protection." The trek through the woods had hardly been gruelling and, wanting to regain her earlier train of thoughts, Mei remained standing. "In the exposed, scarcely wooded, highlands they had wind burn and wind chill as well as cold seasons and nights to contend with. The crocs, snakes and turtles relied rather on burrowing or submerging in water for protection."

"You identified the 'T-Rex' [tyrannosaur] packs we saw in the icegems, in the highlands of Arizona and again in Colorado, as territorial – as predators generally are. You went on to report from those scenes how they stayed up there, in their cave lairs. From that vantage they descended, wolf pack fashion, on herds of grazers and browsers lumbering through thinly wooded river plains below. Those beasts were up from the protection of cloudy lowlands, on their way north to Montana and then the luxuriant 'Beringia' – the land bridge between Alaska and Siberia. We saw similar herds making their way there, too, all the way from the Tethys Sea shores of the Taklamakan and Gobi basins in China.

"At other times the T-Rex packs preyed on dromaeosaurus flocks and crocs as well as other small reptiles that abounded in the hills," Having seen all this in the icegems and then in the movie clips they'd laboured to compile, Sashia was getting all of Mei's insights as fast as she was developing them, "and, occasionally, the young of hadrosaurs, ceratopsians and iguanodons that strayed in the valleys. They also caught nocturnal mammals, out from their caves and burrows at dusk and at dawn."

144

"Yeah! They only used those tiny forearms of theirs for grooming, and sex!" Mei's eyes glinted with mischief. "But, getting back to it, I want to see closer images of their windswept down. It's tempting to think of that, especially on the small theropods, giving the experience of *lift*? Perhaps that's how flight feathers came about."

"Asymmetrical feathers, as you said?"

"Right. That highly specialised evolution had so much more to do with *lift* – rather than some chance gliding of theropods. In some *Late-Cretaceous* clips, we saw migrating birds return to the highlands but better yet... much better... some sequences we worked on, and left with FayWell to finish off, certainly appeared to show how they got into the air in the first place. As soon as we can, let's see if those are ready. Can't wait to see how they turned out. Okay?"

In the twilight of the next morning Sashia was away making a comfort stop, when she leaned against a tree to check her striders and then became caught in wonderment at Spanish moss. It hung high up in the branches, and trailed fine as lace in the faint breathless light, with mist rising up to it like a wizard's fine white web cloak. It was then that a sensation so strange came over her that she diarised it all even as it was happening.

She stared and stared at an agelessly wise face take shape, with a beard completely covering the lower part. Although with no mouth visible, he seemed to be saying, "You wonder at me. Is it my countenance? My stature? My nature, perhaps? Yet what can you know? I'm closed to you, am I not?" He brushed his beard, "Why is that? Am I afraid of you?" Sashia blinked involuntarily and averted her gaze. Looking again she found him gone. Half turning, above her striders, she sought him everywhere, and then he was back. "My maker." He corrected himself, pointedly motioning to her, "*Our* maker, has said I insult him. Made in his image I should be proud – and not hide. What do you say? For you are the same, shrouded by your scarf." She blinked again – and once more he was gone. This time she spun around, looked and looked, but now he was nowhere to be seen.

Deciding on another twirl before giving up, she moved faster – and he was back again. Except – now his beard was gone and he was strong, handsome and vibrant with understanding. And, more so, he exuded joy. Brilliant joy. "Well," he chuckled, "no prizes for guessing what you're thinking. I'm proud of my maker's image and that of all of my brothers and sisters, also my sons and daughters, around the World. Above all earthly considerations! See?" He gestured to her, but all she could do was watch, as dawn spirited the vision away.

She had been so mesmerised that, beyond notice, her traditionally worn Siberian scarf had come loose and she felt her cheeks caressed by nature's fresh clean air and the Sun's warm rays. The cloth she was hardly ever seen without, slipped softly to the ground. Eyes closed, an incredible sense of fulfilment overwhelmed her, and she remained there, still and lost to time.

The others had finished breakfast and were breaking camp when she returned, scarf-less and notably radiant. She was giving Fayez his wish at last, thought Mei. Passing her, Sashia whispered softly, "Go lle ah – just don't ask. Okay? When you're ready, after this is all over, we'll talk."

Mei looked intrigued. "Okay, we left off," she nudged for Sashia to join her along the shore, "talking about the evolution of flight. You've got access to files, through FayWell. Let's see if you can summon her to give us the one of a river delta, with brachiosaur cows in a wood."

"What! You're kidding?" Seeing Mei hold fast, in disbelief at the request in the middle of nowhere and with coms silence imposed with the outside world, Sashia mockingly aimed her wristband at the surface of the water. "Okay, here's to nothing." Nothing it was not. When FayWell did in fact appear beneath the surface, Sashia turned open mouthed to Mei, who'd suspected correctly that I'd be eavesdropping and would make her appearance happen. These girls were on a roll and that was paramount for me. Pointing her finger up through the water, hair floating around like wet string and water entering and leaving her mouth, the mute AI obediently produced the necessary image large and clear on its calm surface.

"Hah! Super, FayWell, thanks! You can dry off now," Sashia joked.

"Great, you've got it!" Mei ignored her fun, too thrilled at seeing a steamy storm shower in a forest clearing, where twelve giant beasts trundled through a quagmire of runoff water. "Wonderful! What a mess!"

146

The bulky long-tailed adults snaked their long necks to reach young shoots at the tops of tall trees, over twice the height this century's giraffe could reach, and lingered a while as their young rolled and played about them in the mud. When they eventually strolled out, shifting their massive bodies of mottled grey and green across open ground, they arrived at an expansive riverside beach. "Look at that nursery, alive with scores of herbivore dinosaurs!" Half the length of those giants, but nonetheless jostling with each other walrus fashion for where to roost, ceratopsians brandished their beak, horns and head shield, while iguanodons reared up.

But, "Ouch!" suddenly their ears were blasted, "All that noise! Where'd that come from?" The cows were grunting and barking. Some brachiosaur calls were shrill. Sashia almost shrieked, "FayWell, what the ... what have you done? Turn it down!"

I allowed FayWell to answer, "Oh, okay... Wild, huh?" Appearing now within a tree, hair dried silky straight and in a prim bun, though haphazard pieces fringed over her eyes, the AI – now number one ace show-off – was toying with her appearance. "It's for real! Sort of." She fully expected their raised eyebrows, of course. "I found the sounds in your clips."

"But how?" Mei almost giggled with amazement.

"Zing! There it all was... Billions of my archived lightning clips have flickers of ultraviolet and claps of thunder, covering the full audible range of sound. Movements in your clips have UV undertones too. I guess I got caught up in the art of matching all that up. It's not perfect. But effective, yes?" She pouted prettily, head cocked to one side, begging approval. I smiled at how endearing this man-made creature could be, not wondering for a second that she had the computing power and the self-learning capability. But, yes, I did wonder where on Earth she got the inclination! For an art form!

"Anyway," Mei shook her head in consternation before pushing the conversation back on track, "this is what I want to see." She pointed to pterosaurs small as blackbirds with dull green-brown colouring and distinctive yellow markings on their snouts. They were pecking on the backs of cows. "It's not merely their ancestral nesting ground that these cows were fixed on returning to seasonally. This was their *cleaner station*! They'd have returned downstream millennia earlier, or even millions of years before, to *cleaner fish*." Mei had done some neat figuring. "But they had shifted away from the horrendous hypercane tidal surges – because the Moon was closer then – and then along came these *cleaner flyers*." At the same time her attention moved to even smaller creatures on cow backs. "And look here, at these other fellows…"

"Cute, like oxpeckers," Sashia referred to the starlings Mei had introduced her to, which pecked for parasites on present day African savannah game.

"What about these? What shall we call them? Raptors, for short?" Mei continued to study the tiny sparrow sized dromaeosaurids, "They've got feathered arms and legs."

"Rather cat-like, you said last time," Sashia chuckled at their antics as they leapt and, hands over feet, clawed up undergrowth and even worked on the legs of cows. "As you said, with each leap and twist mid-air to land on those beasts' backs – they glided part way. But look! Mostly they hit low and then they flapped frantically with sinornithosaurus-like shoulders. They were getting *lift*, to get up there and clamber on!"

"*Flight feathers* in the making!" But, even more riveting, Mei pointed to where one of the dromaeosaurids, on an iguanodon, was defending its ground from a challenging pterosaur. "Remember this? It's stupendous!"

The challenger advanced, hissing, shuffling on all fours, and accentuated its advantage in size by threateningly opening its wings. Arching its slender neck it lunged at the raptor with gnashing teeth. The alarmed defender squawked and ducked, weaved and stabbed with its distinctive oviraptor-like red beak. The pterosaur, pressing on with the attack, pounced full weight as the raptor rolled defensively onto its back. "Look! Just like a cat, it lashed upside down with hind claws! Except, this little guy had a mean microraptor-like sickle claw, now used to slash at the delicate skin membrane of the pterosaur's wings. It was reptile pterosaur with wings it had to manoeuvre out of reach, versus dinosaur raptor with feathers it could shed."

The reptile hissed ferociously as it leapt off and super fast turned to face off for the furious rounds of attack that ensued. While the little raptor rose up on its hind feet to hop and flap for stability, with arms free. "The little guy's on the offensive now. Hear that sharp cat-like hiss it spat out?" The rolls reversed. And there it was, one of Nature's pre-historic shows, all ended when the pterosaur suddenly dived off into the undergrowth.

"Ooh, I bet that beastie was hurting." Sashia grinned. "I'd put my money on those wiry little raptors winning every time – so fast and agile! You reckon?"

"Yeah!" Mei was smiling too. "It's *our* discovery, Sashia. Shall we call it 'mundussaur', for cleaner dinosaur?"

"Not too unlike archaeopteryx to look at," Sashia recalled the much earlier flyers from FayWell's files, "So what was it, the forerunner of modern birds?"

"Hm, yes I'd say so. It had true bird-like attributes – able to search out bugs and parasites standing tall, with binocular vision, and dig them out with a sharp beak specialised for that. Big advantages over pterosaurs and bats." Mei was marvelling at the little peckers, "And look! One is clinging acrobatically to a tail while pecking at the cow's ass! It's got just enough flapping lift to do that. All around, whether on beasts or in trees, though not yet flyers these little guys were already serious contenders."

I was delighted, already recognising the huge importance of these discoveries – about the vast heathlands and now about flight.

Conscious of time loss, the girls joined the others and got right down to business with Bryn bringing them up to speed. "Guille reckons we should head south-east, straight to the gorge we have to cross."

Sashia jumped at this, squaring to face Guille. "Sure, lead on woodsman."

"We've been watching flocks of birds overhead," Bryn observed casually, "and lots more wildlife activity all of a sudden."

"Yeah." A sombre note had overtaken them suddenly. "Did that commotion in the night wake you?" Mei asked edgily.

"There's agitation, like the birds I observed from the tree." Guille, almost as much as Sashia, was sensing Mei's unease. Unexpressed, among them, was whether the volcano's magma chamber was rumbling and they couldn't hear it.

They pushed on through thick undergrowth. By noon, they had reached a rise that afforded a view through the trees to open ground at the end of the forest.

Sashia smacked her striders, invigorated by their progress as well as her legs holding up. She strode ahead – then disappeared with an

"Aaah!" Rushing forward, dropping backpacks, the others gaped into a hole in the centre of a small crater.

Guille was quickest to react. "Sashia, can you hear me?" No reply. Seeing nothing but blackness he tried his coms. "Sashia? Sashia? Are you okay?" Just then dry black shingle moved under their weight. "Mei, Bryn, move back! You'll go down too."

Mei snapped into action, disregarding Guille's advice, and knelt to lower a grapnel. Her heart sinking, she felt it run down a slope and stop some five metres down, "I'm going in." Bristling with confidence now, 'assertive she' was ready to take charge. Guille looked startled at this new persona. "If she survived that fall she won't be conscious, or in any state to get out." As Guille made to go in he was stayed by Mei's vice like grip on his arm, "I'm going! Fasten my lifeline!" There was no argument. He ran to a tree to do just that.

Helmet on, light and coms on, she slid into pitch black that had her coughing and donning a gauze mask – to no avail against foul sulphurous gases and carbon dioxide.

She groped for Sashia, calling to Guille, "Send down rebreathers!" Struggling for a foothold and holding her breath, her foot touched an object that flopped pitifully under it. Sashia lay like a rag doll on a dry shingled ledge, which was shifting. Rebreathers quickly donned, she held the girl close and put her own winch brake on – horrified to sense them slipping. "Got her. Wait one!"

Mind racing, she immediately checked her out. "She's unconscious but okay... Breathing faintly... No serious injuries evident." Without hesitation she snapped the rebreather line to Sashia's belt and released her backpack. "Okay, pull up! Send down another line!" The other line quickly there, she attached the backpack to it and tugged. "Pull that up."

Mei's eyes rapidly enlarged. A deep rumbling had begun, far below them, "*Pull*! It's going to blow!" The rumbling got louder. The ground shook.

"It's a vent hole!" Guille bellowed, hauling Sashia up. "Get out, quick!" He turned to Bryn, who'd pulled up the backpack, "Go, go, go! Get the gear away!" Bryn laid out a stretcher for Sashia before sprinting to the top of the crater carrying and dragging everything else. Dumping it all in a kayak, he dragged it, running downhill away from the impending danger.

Using her winch, Mei caught up with the ascending girl, angled Sashia to go through the hole first and shrieked, "Pull!" The roar grew louder, a waft of air rushed past her. "It's about to blow!"

Guille drew on his full fiman strength, wrenching Sashia out, laid her on the stretcher and, without stopping, dragged her sprinting up the crater wall. Still racing, he glanced back.

"Go!" Mei commanded, head and shoulders out of the hole. Guille sped over the top and down to Bryn, some thirty metres off, just as a blast of hot steam screeched deafeningly behind them.

"Jaisus." Bryn was awestruck.

"Leave the gear. Get Sashia clear of this," Guille ordered.

As he himself flew back over the crater, excruciating pain built in his ears. Steam was jetting out of the hole. Mei was not there. He found her doubled up behind a tree, and began to go to her, but she pulled herself up, gripping at her ears, and leapt towards him as another scorching jet threatened. "Okay? You're okay?" he inquired, uselessly. She shook her head, pointing to her ears. Arm under hers he pulled her into a sprint and led the way to where Bryn had left the kayak.

They caught up with him on the bank of a brook, well clear of the screeching. He had removed Sashia's torn suit, brought her round, and was sponging her abrasions clean. Guille led Mei to sit beside her, while he looked about at other jets venting around them. "Jesus!" he shouted, "This does *not* look good!"

"Anything serious?" Mei's shouting was addressed to Bryn, who pointed to her foot. Aware that something was wrong with their hearing, he couldn't yet relay to Mei or Guille that the alert was still on Amber. The vents, like those in Yellowstone, were not considered to be from the main magma chamber.

"My bum hurts," Sashia uttered crossly. "Apart from bloody bruised and sore, there's my ankle." She pointed. Having heard from Bryn how Mei had saved her, now she whispered in her ear, "Touché, baby, touché and quits." The biologist she'd saved had, most bravely, repaid her. "What a turn of events. Now you're in control."

Mei, not having heard a word, was carefully pulling off Sashia's precious striders, as she'd come to know them. She then began to cleanse and spray-dress her leg wounds with no hint of hesitancy, despite the sadness of seeing her friend's emaciated legs, no thicker than her wrists. Now, even more, she could scarcely believe everything this girl had done. "Does this hurt?" With extreme caution she moved the ball of Sashia's foot up and down.

"Yow! Watch it!" Sashia's excruciated grimace threw her.

"And this?" Now physician Mei had to be objective that the pained look on this fiman with non-brittle bones but a rare condition signalled nothing to warrant her being pulled from the race. It was a weighty call, one that would have her friend struck from our programme. "My dear, you've sustained a wrench to your ligaments... it's what you might think of as a sprain!"

Mei had no realisation that her voice was greatly raised as she re-dressed Sashia and gingerly pulled on one leg of her striders. "Is this okay," she held Sashia's injured foot, "if I build a strong cast? I mean, will your striders still support you?" Reassured by Sashia nodding, Mei made sure in setting the cast that she could still get the other strider leg on, challenging her when done, "Can you sit up?"

"Sure." Sashia was gritting her teeth, determined not to let this mishap let her down. This was a trial from hell, but she'd pull her weight or bust! Getting up, aided by Mei she managed to balance on the one strider leg.

"You have to help me here! For starters, are you good on this leg?" Mei was still shouting.

"Yeah, sure, see? It's good." Sashia then reached to touch down with the cast. "Bloody well hurts, though. That's all." Though aware that Mei was still awaiting answers it did not register to Sashia about the girl's hearing. "My striders support my hips, though I could probably do with a cane too." She had to chuckle at the absurdity of it all. "Okay, there's also sort of a bum-perch in those and I just drive with my feet, taking no weight on them... It'll be fine, so forget about counting me out... Hell, you're not getting rid of me that easily!"

Then came the realisation, motioning to their ears to express it, "Hey, you can't hear a bloody word, can you?" Mei shook her head crest fallen and Sashia surveyed her torn, scorched suit, pained expression, dirty face and wide eyes brightly set there. *"You're* in more need of attention..." She foolishly went to take a step, faltered and Mei caught her.

"It's dusk!" came more shouting. "Have to stop here for the night!" Mei wasn't up to assertion, energies ebbing fast, but having regained her composure, and being among friends with whom she felt comfortable, she could be outspoken. Right now she also had zero tolerance for indecision.

The men were getting a fire going and setting up camp. They helped get Sashia into the other leg of her strider and bedded in her sleeping bag. "I'm going to give you a sedative!" Mei shouted, and tilted her head to shine a pen-laser pulse-beam into her pupil. The girl was ready to sleep in seconds.

Guille and Bryn offered the tired physician food now and sat beside her to eat, in silence, though their occasional glances in her direction imparted their admiration in her acts, and amazement at her huge show of confidence. For her part, Mei could only motion to her ears and rather than shout, bow to impart her thanks. One eye open again, Sashia caught the act and smiled before sleep swept in.

Meal quickly over, Guille noticed Mei's eyes moisten again. Clearly she was in pain and perhaps even fearsome for their progress. He pointed to her prepared bed and watched her settle there, struggling to get out of her suit. "Ayah…Ah!" When he shifted to her side to assist, she made no objection. Guille followed with more… cleansing and spray dressing her surprisingly few wounds and sponging her cuts and scalded areas before spraying them with antiseptic painkiller.

Emulating the gentleness he had bestowed, Mei drew his face closer to sooth the pain in his ears, using a pen-ultrasound, and she indicated he might do the same for her. Relief immediate, they slept in their bags, which he had drawn close together. Guille had decided to watch over her at least until light.

~*~

Vision

20

October 2067

Sven Hadder paid no attention to panoramic harbour views from his Stockholm penthouse, not recollecting those once there nor seeing the sea of ice that had gradually overtaken them.

Tall, in his forties, with smooth blond hair, he hardly seemed to fill the charcoal jacket and open necked shirt that he wore. What held his dispassionate attention were the climate refugees driven there by chilling blizzards. Half turning he addressed a grey-suited man sporting a distinctive crystal skull set in the centre of a grey-green carnation in his buttonhole. Duardo Contrea, was speaking on holoe. "It's happening – or soon will be. The exodus of Scandinavian-Baltic States will disrupt traffic right across Europe. Then negotiations will have to get underway in Paris, Madrid, Rome, Athens, Bucharest, Ankara and Rabat to take the displaced. The same will happen right along the Canadian border with America.

"Our factions in Pakistan, Azerbaijan and Iran are organising to ferment more chaos and unrest."

Hadder smirked. "Huh, don't you just love it. It'll be the same scene with the Andes-Patagonian exodus. Our rebels in Colombia and Chile will create more mayhem. They're already hijacking relief supplies to rural areas. There's plenty to go around. Venezuela is such a soft target, after decades of isolation, we'll topple that government easily, when we're ready. For now, we'll just keep a low profile."

"While the North Koreans build alliances for us in Bulgaria, South Africa and Nigeria," Contrea continued his own update, "and everywhere sub-Ameurasia will be in our sights just as DeepStorm hits. Then – we'll really have some fun."

A naval officer joined them on holoe. "You asked about our coms. Security agencies, notably the CIA and MI5, are using web ferrets to pick out key phrases in conversations as well as the distinct tone of everyone making calls online. They can track what's planned and by whom – right across the World. So, we're routing all your calls through the few remaining subscriber lines, where we're able to switch about and lose them – so far with success. And we're using old telex machines for text."

The two men looked reassured. "It's time, to call Nodus," Contrea instructed the officer,

"Ah, Nodus," Hadder rubbed his hands, "Mr Exofiman. I can't wait to see his lot in action when they take the chaos upside. UNRO won't expect it, thinking as they do that they have the supremacy to hit anywhere and anytime from there – especially with the British LTA craft-carriers cruising the globe 75 kilometres up."

He activated the home entertainment wall and switched to Jude Nade on the Sævrama Channel. *"Arctic weather is hitting Canada and northern EU countries. Winter ice gripping southern Chile, Argentina and Australasia is just now easing as summer approaches those latitudes. The good news – there's no mention, yet, of an impending return of the kilometres thick icecaps that once covered much of Ameurasia."*

Just then the naval officer ushered in the holoe of a lean, bald headed figure in coal green cloak and matching armoured suit, who addressed them immediately in a low, rasping voice. "Is the World in a teeny bit of bother?" His dry, dead look was enough to make even Hadder uneasy, had they been on opposing sides.

"Hah! Perceptive!" Hadder hailed Nodus boisterously, dismissing the officer. "You ready?"

"Do eagles have talons?" Nodus' tone was markedly calm, soothingly strong even, exuding an aura of invincibility. "Are you?"

"Brewing! Everywhere's brewing," Hadder confirmed.

"But, not quite yet," Contrea reined in their zeal. "Not quite. Soon the World will be on its knees. *That*, is when we will strike."

"Yeah, at they're weakest." Hadder glanced out again at the struggling refugees. "Meanwhile, we'll get you primed and ready with all you need."

"We're being patient," Nodus beamed, following Hadder's gaze and producing a slow, thin grin, "We've nothing to lose now. The tables will certainly turn – and that's when we'll get *rich*!"

~*~

158

21

Waking with the memory of the apparition in the Spanish Moss, Sashia felt as liberated as a bird on a breeze. Sure, there was pain, the sharpest one in her ankle. Sitting up, she grimaced at the number of geysers steaming behind the team's camp. "How odd. It's so quiet – just the hissing of those jets."

Bryn frowned up at the forest canopy. "Yeah, the sky is empty. Yesterday it was full of birds." There was, he assured, no word of the alert having changed from Amber.

Guille was sitting on his bed watching Mei stir and anticipating her flinching with pain soon. He motioned that he'd do the ultrasound for her ears, if okay. She nodded. This done, he prompted her to turn so that anaesthetic spray could be re-applied to her burns.

She squeezed his hand in gratitude, and produced a pen-laser she'd worked on before dawn, when all the others slept. Motioning for him to watch, Mei went over to Sashia and flicked the icy blue light into her pupil, saying, with a reassuring wink, but still loudly, "This blocks pain messages in your nervous system, in this case from your ankle! I'm resetting it for me, for my back and so on ... Would you do it for me?" Sashia's pain relief was again immediate and she was soon helping her friend, wordlessly. "It remains active until cancelled with this!" Mei imparted, her words and actions taken as a reassurance to all that her confident involvement was there to stay.

Bryn had brewed them an energising tea, and gone off scouting. His return brought hope. "Hey! We're out of here! Done with the forest – We're right on target! The gorge is there, just through the trees!"

Excited, they followed him through the woodland for a view, Sashia extra-cautiously making it with the help of a makeshift cane fashioned by Guille.

On closer inspection, far from being happy, however, they froze at the sight of an intense heat haze over a river of red and black rock flowing down below. "Okay," Bryn shrugged, "What's plan B?" suggesting by gesture that they proceed on this side.

"No good!" Mei reminded loudly, wiggling her index finger, "The islet is across – over there!" Sashia eyed her friend,

159

recognising the biologist's readiness to take the lead, but knowing the hopelessness of that, given her deaf state.

"Yeah, right," Bryn eyed each of them in turn. "My merry band, my band of brothers!" He summed them up and laughed without malice – laughed at their dressings, the cast, scorched and torn suits, two of them pretty deaf. *"We're* taking that lava flow on? Us?"

The four jolted as a repeating text stream began on their bracelet-coms. *"Alert RED • Teams haste off island • We have your LNs • Rescue craft en route • Will assist those in need • Do not panic • This is a precaution • Eruption not imminent."* There'd been some debate among officials on how that message might be sent to the Red Robin team. Safest for them, would have been to activate their biombots for receiving coms. That would also have helped Sashia and Bryn in communicating with Guille and Mei. But apparently even these circumstances didn't warrant disclosing that particular attribute, reserved only for those who in the end were selected.

The Red Robin team members read and reread the message, before busting out of their freaked out states and concentrating on breaking camp.

In full agreement and subsequent silence they returned to the gorge where Guille excelled at shooting a line across to a tree and also securing it on this side.

Free of injuries, Bryn clipped on for the trickiest crossing – with Guille the anchor man on lifelines and Sashia on coms to guide him swinging hand-over-hand. He only faltered a couple of times, when glancing quickly down at the searing lava. Wanting nothing else in his head, he concentrated on Sashia coaxing him on. Once over, he secured his lifeline to the tree so that the others had a hand-line to clip onto as well as a tightrope.

As they each privately diarised in their crossings, sweat trickling down brows, hearts pounding, Mei said – "Under this Nemesis of mine, the Ni'moloka'i peak, I implore dragon fingers dedicated to my father to give me inner strength."

Sashia – "I see Fayez, his hands on the keys pumping up my confidence with strong strident chords."

Mei, again – "Sashia's progress is too slow. She's putting her weight on the hand-line, anxious about her injured ankle. But we're not props for each other, we're allies."

Guille, who followed after all the gear had been hauled safely across, recorded – "I can feed on Sashia's confidence. She's someone I'd always want in my corner."

Once over, rather than setting off downhill they first skirted the tree line to scour the lay of the land to the distant sea. It would perhaps prove their last chance to catch breath and psyche themselves up before sprinting ahead. The view was discouraging – a bleak desolate landscape of black volcanic rock, with jets of steam venting to clouds cloaking the ground.

Worse was seeing Sashia's horrified expression. Peering far into the mist her view, straight out of prehistory, was of a mesh of white-water crisscrossing rivers of lava. "Jaisus," she whispered, but loud enough for close by Bryn to hear, "The water's boiling over there." Sashia knew snap decisions had to be made and only she could pilot them through. Lacking confidence in her present state, she whispered, "How can I do this? I'm not prepared." Lips tight, she regarded each of them in turn, her look apologetic. All they returned was understanding and trust in her abilities. She couldn't let them down. Temples aching with strain she used her eyes to scan closer to their location, and the stream they needed to ride first. "Oh, that's better – it's actually placid!"

Not able to get the big picture in the same visual way as Sashia, Mei was nonetheless shocked and shouting, "Incredible – it's so barren it looks like the aftermath of a supervolcano eruption – or a massive impact. Those braided streams, like rain on a windowpane, or lahars and logjams, crashing and thundering to plug and bust rivers."

"Shit!" came a voice from somewhere near. "This is the hell of dinosaurs when an asteroid stopped them in their tracks for good!" Bryn judged the newcomer to be a rough Liverpudlian, and sighted him through the trees, impressive in jet-black-shot-with-red snaketex his hair slick black and aerial, his face smooth as he coolly surveyed the scene. Steve's team had gathered close on Red Robin's heels.

"Ah, but..." his eyes twinkled, "was it *all* down to the impact? *All* buried and dusted, under fallout peppered with the asteroid's iridium, at the *Close* of the *Late-Cretaceous*. Case closed? Right? Yeah? Well, not exactly. Broadly speaking," he began lecturing his team and all else, "those deposits are heaviest in the ancient Tethys Sea basin – stretching from ground zero, west to the mid-Pacific and east into the Mediterranean." Braced for a stress-relieving argument, Steve was unaware that Mei and Guille appeared to be ignoring his taunts. "So how come everywhere else was devastated?" Still surprised that no one picked up the challenge, he shrugged. "No matter. It's confirmed now. The impact really was planet blasting."

Mei, deafness rendering her oblivious to his address, was shouting again, "Soon this area will be overgrown with ferns! That always happens – though I'd never imagined actually seeing this!"

Sashia swivelled awkwardly to face Steve, "Ah, dolphin man," her memory of him from The Docks protest crystal clear. Although seeing him up close, unshaven and dishevelled, she murmured other thoughts about his manner, "A tad opinionated – and oh so rough!"

"What?" he cocked his head in her direction, certain he had neither seen her nor any of her team before. "Anyway the *Armstrong Effect*" (named after the discoverer's great-grandfather), has finally wrapped up what happened."

Delighted to discern an audience of at least one, Steve obsessively carried on. "Dinosaurs lived through millions of years of the Earth's rotation slowing that caused imperceptibly small redistributions of atmosphere and oceans to polar regions. The vast ocean under continental plates, the mantle, moved more spasmodically and violently, and where that happened it wrinkled and stretched the plates with powerful tidal tugs from the closer Moon. What we now think is that – every now and then – *bang*! The whole crust gave way in an explosive reshaping – a mega '*geoshift*'." He waved his hands at the devastating scene lying before them and Sashia winced at the thought of what he described happening again – now.

"The asteroid that 65.5 million years ago blasted out the Chicxulub crater in Mexico's Yucatan Peninsula," Steve was off and running, "also triggered a geoshift! *And* oops, as the Peninsula is a keystone at the apex of the North American, South American and Caribbean continental plates…"

Mei followed the direction of Sashia's stare. "Ah," came her shout, "Greenpeace man! Pulled off any big stunts lately?"

"The shockwave triggered colossal quakes, tsunamis and eruptions," Steve was bent on finishing, "They went all the way along the Rockies and Western Interior Seaway of North America to the Chinese eastern seaboard and down the Andes to the

Transantarctic Mountain Range. What a double whammy! It shook the whole crust! Case closed! A combined Natural Correction confirmed – of the impact and the geoshift!" His smug expression said all. There was nothing more to be said.

"Yep, cocky!" Sashia reflected, although intrigued. Empathising with Mei's condition, she enlightened Steve, feeling a slight delight that he'd wasted his 'lecture' on a deaf expert. "You'll have to go over all of that again – some other time. Her hearing," she pointed at Mei, "was deadened in a crater blast back there. Anyhow, now's not the time for a tussle... Dinosaurs are really *her* thing."

A fair aerial headed guy was so busy eyeing Mei up, that he almost bumped into Sashia, who managed to impede his advance by tripping him with her cane, though the effort to twist around caused her a stab of ankle pain.

Within Steve's team, the Mexican girl they'd met earlier, Tixa, was also admonishing the youth, wagging her finger negatively in his direction. "Torf, naughty!"

"I don't think he meant anything!" boomed Mei.

Mumbling apologies to her, which went unheard, Torf shuffled back to his group, hurt by the lack of response.

The awkward silence that followed was broken by a sweep of urgency throughout both teams.

The Red Robins headed downhill, intent on making it to the islet while there was still daylight.

To their joy they arrived at a flat rock banking the stream. There they pushed together yellow sections from their backpacks, to assemble a SharkTex mat. Made of that smart material, the mat was programmed to form a rugged circular raft when subjected to an abrupt temperature change – as in this chill river. Sashia sat and helped to stow gear, a twinge of hysteria reflecting what lay ahead. "Madness." It just slipped out.

The raft fully assembled they took up stations, paddling midstream away from the rocky shallows. There the fast but tranquil flow had a soothing effect on all four and gave them time to shape their private thoughts.

Mei, paddling firmly and in tune with Sashia and Guille either side of her, had gained something. As a lifesaver twice over, she had shifted a little further from the bloody visions and impotent defeat that haunted her.

Guille, pensive as ever, motioned to the sky in the direction they'd left and, for Mei's benefit, locked his thumbs and flapped his fingers while shaking his head. Bryn, caught on, "Yup, it's empty. Not a dickey bird, not even in the tree tops."

I learnt of these concerns, from Bryn's and Sashia's aurally active biombots, and straight away checked whether the officials' instruments had detected what troubled the birds. There was nothing.

Paddles slicing the surface, ripples lapping at the front, all danced on their nerves. For distraction, Sashia mulled over Steve's words, "Earth's rotation slowed…" She rummaged over what she'd heard in palaeontology forums. "That can be seen in the daily growth of corals in fossils, just as annual growth is seen in tree rings. Wow! They had a *nine-hour day* three billion years ago. An *eighteen-hour day* nine hundred million years ago. And, phew, a *twenty-three-hour day* at the start of the Mesozoic era of dinosaurs."

All too quickly her thoughts were drawn to the here and now – as the silence surrounding them became permeated by the thunder of white-water up ahead. She shuddered involuntarily. It was too much… Fearing weakness, Sashia sought a distraction from her now nerve-racking anticipation. "Bryn, sing for me," she implored. Voice ringing out obligingly, he encouraged her to join in and soon they heard other teams join in the choruses – helpfully revealing their positions upstream.

By mid-afternoon Sashia and Bryn were exchanging knowing nods. Rounding the next bend the rumble they'd heard deepened and at the next curve they were met with a thunderous roar. Although Bryn sang louder and louder, his song was soon drowned out and singing became a futile pastime.

The raft was speeding up. Mei and Guille, other senses heightened through deafness, sat on high alert. As the team rolled their paddles like warriors readying cudgels for battle, a wall of mist and steam hit their faces. Breaths uneven, each cast around to gauge their position and chances, the Red Robin team all bandaged, partly deaf and already war wounded. It was then that Sashia laughed, and this incongruously grew, shaking her frame and squeezing tears from her eyes. Seeing her, and initially astonished, the others caught the infection and began to laugh. Then she was up, standing and grinning, an expression of defiance lighting her face. Paddle in hand, she looked at each in turn before releasing a shrill eagle-like yell, "Eeeeeh...yaaah!"   And they all rallied.   Like warriors, they shrieked, their defiance carried in the mist, echoing on the enclosing rocks with Viking vigour.

A quick rocking motion heralded the onset of the newly dreaded challenge. Taking up positions, minds set on battle, they watched Sashia quickly gesturing – oral exchanges now out, sign language in. They would have to rely on as much rote action and instinctive synergy as a wolf pack, she reflected. In response, the team gestured to confirm what their tasks would be – Guille would keep them headlong into waves, Bryn would keep the stern straight, Mei would read the currents, Sashia's focus would be on reading the rocks above and below water. Fully resolved, their paddles cleaved to make headway midstream.

In momentarily thinned mist, distance to white-water shortening, they heaved over a half-metre standing wave that slewed them off course. Paddle in one hand, rope handle in the other, they bucked up and bolted down, slicing their only tools frantically into the rolling surface. Sliding over a one-metre fall, the plunge into surf jarred their bodies, drenched by a chilling bow wave. Soaked to their skins, their hair clung.

Peering through hair that clung like wet string over their eyes, in intermittent visibility they made out turbulent waters in narrows dead ahead. Funnelled into a foam filled ravine, hooking off to the left, they could just about make out the confluence of another stream joining theirs, and found themselves running the gauntlet of boiling waters that buffeted and corkscrewed the raft, sweeping it under a waterfall the force of which thumped at their heads and jarred their spines.

Out again, the raft wallowed like a dead hippo. Desperately they strained to make headway, hoping the self-bailers would work.

Too soon the stream split again. Sashia signalled to take the right fork and they heaved in unison to swing the raft sluggishly around.

Visibility mostly nil, they narrowly missed rocks until suddenly one side lurched upwards, pitching headlong onto a two-metre wall of water – though fortuitously spilling water from within. Still heavy in the current, they now slewed fast towards sheer rocks.

Calling on all reserves, Mei swivelled her butt onto the raft's side to land her feet on the rock face and ran madly along it, rising up with the raft as it spilled water. With a mighty heave she headed the craft back into the stream and the others back paddled to make use of the current. Now lightened of water, the raft began to respond better.

Mei lunged at it as it slipped away, only managing to grab rope handles. The rest of her vanished in the surf. Gasping for air and assessing the next down swing of the hull, she summoned even more strength to haul and lurch herself head first onto the side and upward. A slither inward, a splutter of water and she was grinning, shaking a fist at the cliffs and shouting triumphantly, "Not yet, you pile of useless shite! You've not got us yet!"

Entering thick fog, they were now barely visible to one another as they were being bumped and heaved about. Sashia strained her eyes and glimpsed a rock ledge in time for them to duck. Ominous red flashed beneath. Muscles strained to switch this way or that, cleave here or there. Stomachs heaved. Nerves screamed. Cold hands switched between gripped rope handles and paddles. Boots and striders slid on swamped floor ridges.

Blinded and disorientated as skiers in a whiteout without sense of up, down, or wherever, sans sight and sound their other senses kicked in sharper. Sashia sensed a switch in the river's direction, riding up and over a succession of one-metre waves, while bow waves poured in repeatedly. A terrifying shriek filled the air. Bryn turned, expecting to find Sashia overboard, but she was there, shrieking, "Left... left... left...!"

"Christ, she's bloody echo locating!" Bryn cried out. He tapped Guille and Mei to watch her strokes. Paddles cleaved port, starboard and back again. "Left... right... right... right...!" Sashia's screeches punctuated their frantic state.

Rocks shaved past. Cold spray stung faces. Bow spray scalded too. In patches of visibility Sashia pointed out flashes of vivid red lava running along the riverbed, beneath steam and bright white foam.

They'd hardly registered the danger when a shockwave knocked them sideways and the raft slammed into a rock wall. Upended, they slid down the raft floor to the stern so awash that Bryn and Mei had to swim and scramble back into position. Guille and Sashia moved and slipped to the near side, to push off with paddles and feet, in the effort Sashia feeling her cast tear and loosen in her striders. Back paddling, the other two got the stern around and suddenly they were free, swirling in the flow, and cleaving hard to bring the bow round.

Horrified they watched how, in stark contrast to the white shroud all about them, delicate shades of yellow and orange burst in the mists overhead. Red fountains appeared, punctuated by bright red starbursts. Their hearts sank as they registered the diffused aura of the volcano erupting. A sonic boom ripped into their ears, shaking the raft. Mei's face crumpled and she doubled up, shuddering and whispering, "No! Not again!"

The team was off balance. Lurching up a three-metre standing wave they again lost control and the raft skewed around. Bryn was hurled up, breaking his grip. He toppled over the uplifted stern and was disappearing when Guille grabbed at his lifeline, one handed, only to slip and slide down the slick floor as the bow lurched up.

Still screeching, Sashia single-handedly strove to bring the wildly spinning vessel around and away from rocks. She felt her cast shred in pushing on the deck. Mei, looking horrified, was thrown sideways, white knuckles showing beneath the two dragons now frozen over the raft handles. That fear registered in her, disgusted her alongside the stoical Sashia, and snapped her out of shock to a fierce anger. With a hateful look at the erupting mountain, she scrambled for her paddle and chopped furiously at the water with her friend.

Guille had his boot on the stern wall, heaving on the lifeline with both hands, until with another lurch a body appeared. Grabbing at Bryn's belt he hauled the songster aboard and secured his lifeless form to the raft. His shoulder was stripped to the bone, flesh charred black. The raft heaved and crashed against rocks, dumping them all to the floor alongside Bryn, while wrenched arms held fast to handles, then managing to reach their positions, and padding madly, they were suddenly off the rocks.

Sashia took the chance to break coms silence. Voice breathless but calm, "Base. We see eruptions! Bryn Griffiths seriously injured!"

Relieved, there was a response. She heard a general call go out accompanied by a text stream for Guille and Mei. "All teams. These eruptions were *not* anticipated. Continue on course! Repeat, continue on course! *Do not* attempt to abort! Get right clear of the island, right to the end, with all speed! Acknowledge!" Sashia duly acknowledged, hoping for a direct message. She was not disappointed. "Red Robin. We have a fix and medical status from Bryn's and all your LNs. Will take it from here. He's okay for now. Carry on and get out from the mist fast. A rescue craft is tracking you and will be with you when you get clear."

Once again Sashia was reminded of their LNs giving away where and how they were. "Comforting and yet how like pawns we are, in a game we know for sure is deadly now."

Then someone else was on her coms, tone and face firm – mine, "You're doing well. Hang in there. Get the team through. You can do it, Sashia."

It was her call, hers alone. I'd not included a text stream. I now saw what guts and steadfastness this kid had, and I resolved to show her how to put that to valuable use in research. The little reassurances I'd tried to give her before now, to make her feel included, had been dwarfed by events.

"Sir," Sashia's tone was positive, strong even, she switched off just as a large fireball exploded on rocks to starboard. Cinders showered over them. Another streaked down somewhere up ahead. "Lava bombs!" she shrieked – for no one to hear. The hell they were in had intensified.

Mei recoiled enraged again and brushing a red-hot cinder from her hair. Again she shook a fist at the mountain, "You fucking heap of shit, lay off us!"

Guille was also shaking cinders from his clothing as his feet kicked at bright embers on the raft floor, and his hands brushed at those on the helpless Bryn. Now bow waves came in handier, helping to quench the smallest of them. Their hell ride raged on.

When next the mist cleared, the turbulence below suddenly flattened out and the roar of water diminished. Still pelted with ash and smaller cinders, they had slipped into a flat calm estuary, trembling hands gradually releasing iron grips on the ropes.

Quickly they swept embers away as Guille placed his reassuring hands, one on each girl. Then he nudged Mei and gestured a sign of victory at the mountain, taking her fingers to do the same and watching her face crease into a smile. Behind which her thoughts ran, questioningly, "He's that strong? To be gentle, in this?"

Sashia pointed out a mess of lava hissing steam along the shore – the end of the flow. Looking back, they saw a huge plume of smoke pouring up and out of the mountain peak. They dared stop not a moment more. They paddled furiously, their target now the deep blue sea ahead.

There was still no room for complacency, however. The port side heaved violently again, a shower of water dowsing them as a red lava bomb dived through the water under the raft.

A few strokes more, just a few strokes more... They were clear! Yet they could not bring themselves to slow until well out to sea.

Guille was checking the raft now, while Sashia and Mei dived to Bryn, relieved to find him unconscious but breathing.

Head spinning, Sashia had not noticed a droning noise until the rescue craft was bang overhead and a paramedic was almost down with them. Both girls helped to raise Bryn onto a stretcher. Sashia hiding her hurt from the ankle wound as their rescuer took in their wretched states, questioning with a look if they too needed help. They shook their heads, almost in unison and accepting this, the paramedic was about to lift off with his charge, when he scanned their supplies. "Need anything?" he shouted above the din. Sashia managed a cheeky grin, "You got a jet pack up there for this tub?" The guy laughed and waved.

Slumping back, Sashia contemplated her own limp foot within the tattered cast and went to Mei to do what she could expediently. That done, and her strider leg back on, Sashia raised her hand to indicate that Guille, who was paddling rapidly again, had a gash on his neck. She gestured for Mei to tend to him, and made Guille sit before resuming the paddling herself. They had to get out of there, end this ordeal.

Eyeing this fine-honed dynamo who had not let up once throughout their ordeal, as a mark of admiration, Mei diarised, "A firestorm must be driving li'l 'ol *torch eyes* here."

Guille was also diarising, "She's some *velocity maiden*."

Having cleansed Guille's wound followed by spraying on a bandage, Mei allowed herself a look at her nightmare volcano, and somehow felt a closure of the past. Her visions of Rad had become fainter, replaced by those of Sashia, Guille and Bryn, fighting on – and winning against the mountainous odds.

169

Guille the woodsman had added to his diary his reasons for admiring these two fimans and was now checking his SPS. "Hey! We're drifting off course!" He pointed in a northerly direction, and joined Sashia to pull quickly across the current.

Now all three paddled madly despite sapped energies. Even as fimans, the InviHundred had tested them to destruction.

Reaching deep water, rising up mounting waves, they sighted other craft emerging from the estuary. More wounded were being airlifted out. Two rafts were escorted away by navy vessels. They heard later they'd thrown in the towel. The rest were struggling to close the gap to Red Robin.

By dusk, after skirting round the broad southern edge of the atoll's reef, they landed on the narrower northwest quadrant. Sashia had spotted this area when dropping from the shuttle. Moving with great difficulty, they stepped out, onto the sharp coral. Guille and Mei raised overhead the tattered craft, laden with their remaining gear, but stumbling under the heavy weight they dropped it. Exchanging glances of agreement, they shrugged and dumped everything but paddles, line and anchor.

Cut, bruised, enfeebled, they dragged their craft, feebly picking their way over the razor sharp surface. Repeatedly they missed their footing, steadying one another before they could fall and score their bodies.

Sashia struggled helplessly. "Fucking useless painkiller!" she sobbed and stumbled again, her stick more of a hindrance than help, jamming in crevices. Away it went, hurled in an angry gesture. Splash! "Aaah! Fuck! Fuck it all!" she screamed standing stock still to vent her misery. "This bloody stupid event!"

Guille and Mei secured the vessel in the lagoon and returned to her, each taking an arm to prop her, and help her to the craft and to board it.

In dwindling light, all three made slow headway, eventually running the raft on to the beach, where Guille and Mei shuffled up the fine sands either side of Sashia, safe at last. The symbolic gong up ahead, that they should beat to signify their race was run, was of little interest to them – and yet, "What the heck," yelled Mei, haring up the beach towards it, perhaps for Bryn or to assuage their losses of sanity and strength. Boom, the sound resonated for effect only, for the electronic signalling of their success was already relayed.

Collapsing and rolling on their backs, the grins they managed looked squiffed and (understandably) inane.

As the last rays of light faded, a highly impressed camp cook appeared with a special pick-me-up, and Sashia offered up a toast. "Well! Huh, fancy that!" The three looked a bit teary now, yet somehow they smiled at one another.

The moment was cut by an official text stream on their coms, "We regret to inform the Red Robin team that your colleague, Bryn Griffiths, passed away peacefully."

Their faces turned to granite, eyes enlarged in shock and grief. "Considering your exemplary work as a team he will be awarded a posthumous medal of honour, to be forwarded to his family."

"We were four," Sashia rasped, "Four of us battled supremely and four should be here now." The trio wept openly, arms around one another. But, as other teams arrived, they dispersed to silently guard their own thoughts.

Some while later the others noticed Mei standing alone, staring at that volcano, her expression unreadable. Coming to her side, Sashia and Guille simply held her again.

~*~

22

October 2067

UN Security Council members streamed over the impeccable Machu Picchu lawns, as military craft hovered and landed and media crews, encamped there, gathered around. The scene was as significant veiled by snow flurries as by the D-Notice covering the ad hoc UN meeting.

Jude Nade was there, with the Sævrama Channel team. "You've got top billing on this," Jack, appearing in the heads-up display of her glasses, was quick to encourage.

"Hi Jack," she bit her upper lip, with a gravitas that pervaded the whole press corp, "It'll be interesting – with the D-Notice keeping *us* out."

"True, but even though you're not in the conference yourself, they're showing your sequences live in there. Powerfully influential stuff. You're on to something big with this. Keep it up."

"Crunchy. Thanks boss," Sharpening her thoughts, Jude couldn't resist having a muffled dig about the wardrobe mistress, "Just don't let the office ornament chew on my outfit."

With no further delay, readying herself for the take, she nodded for her cameraman to roll, *"What's the latest on global events, that DeepStorm is attributed with? Well, as you've seen, deep snow is reaching the outskirts of many towns and cities – as glaciers inch relentlessly down valleys.*

"All this was forecast up in the sky. Remember those clear sunny days, that we've all enjoyed these past decades? Well it now seems, they were heralding a return of the Little Ice Age of just twenty decades ago. The chill is biting hardest along the north-eastern seaboard of the Atlantic, where the Gulf Stream's warmth is fading."

Behind closed doors, Sustra Matri's opening address to Council members was again grave, "Friends in the past months there's been no let-up in DeepStorm – with disasters mounting, human suffering increasing. We must work ahead of those developments. To that end we have a whole range of programmes to discuss – from protecting cities as well as trade routes and communications, to safeguarding international security as well as political and social unity.

"The plight of our populations is our main priority. While the sheer scale of counter measures, that will have to be drafted into our budgets, is quite frankly staggering, we will have to take steps for that not to overwhelm some states and thus lose the balance in Gross World Product the UN has worked so hard to achieve.

"Most essentially, however, we must, with all haste, complete preparations for the DeepStorm Questor mission. The purpose of this session is to update you on progress there, and to finalise arrangements for their speedy departure."

Admiral Connell Althorpe, in attendance as a candidate for commanding the mission task force, was instead absorbed with watching Jude Nade's Sævrama report, silent, subtitled and relayed to an end wall of the conference hall, *"...there are grave concerns about the severity of the weather we're experiencing. Experts are predicting widespread damage, although less violent than the monsoon floods of the 2020s to 30s.*

"A disturbing side effect, featured on this channel, is DoomNet. It's feared that the gloom-and-doom prevalent there could produce mass depression among netizens. Whole communities could be traumatised and vital services paralysed. Already, restrictions are being considered on the material that the media and other sources can make available to the public..."

Unmoved by that last content, Althorpe instead listened to what DelMonte was now saying, "...there's no doubting that DeepStorm is a gigantic threat, yet one that we should take the opportunity to research first hand – for future generations to be better prepared. For now though, I'll hand over to Professor Madison."

Meanwhile Jude's subtitles rolled on, *"...the situation is deepening, with reports of isolated incidents in a number of populated areas. Yet even though the incidents might seem to be occurring disparately, and even different in nature, we understand they might not actually be unconnected. That they might all, somehow, be part of the continuing and increasing DeepStorm event..."*

More scenes followed. Dazed survivors were clambering from wrecked vehicles on an isolated section of expressway, pulling out the injured and dying in the aftermath of serious tremors in Los Angeles. Stampeding sports fans were trampled to death in a collapsing football stadium, as tremors also hit Beirut. There was no shortage of news.

"Deteriorating conditions are wreaking havoc in many areas of the globe, causing widespread shortages of food, power and water and crippling drainage and refuse services. Concerns over the spread of disease are also heightening – while global job losses, now thought to be well into the tens of millions, are liable to impact the World economy."

All eyes were now trained on me, waving to our hologram of the Solar System. Prominent were orbits of Earth, Mars and AstBelt. A nearby screen presented images of three vessels at anchor off the Moon. "We're aiming to assign these ships to the DeepStorm Questor task force," I pointed out each of these, "liners Lascaux and Avebury, right now being requisitioned from the Saturn Shipping Line, and the US Navy battle-carrier Bering. Refitting is scheduled for completion later this year – and, the mobilisation of several thousand fimans is well underway. Top candidates are undergoing final selection as we speak."

Matri took the floor again. "We have a dilemma – new breeds. Big advertising campaigns have created social acceptance of ZeroGs, for populating terraformed Near Earth Territories. However, the mere mention of them going on long haul journeys – into deep space – will have the media sighting the highly sensationalised AstBelt exofimans."

Duardo Contrea's input was terse. "Well, where's the choice?" He actually looked sincere! "They'd come down on us even harder, if we'd mentioned humans going." Unable to resist, he stirred the pot. "Or perhaps, we should reconsider – and send robots instead?"

Unfazed by the snide edge in his tone, years in office having conditioned Matri to all manner of retorts, she continued without a blink. "As I said, it's a dilemma. Regrettably we have no choice, as we've just heard." She looked pointedly at Contrea. "We'll make the announcement that the DeepStorm Questor mission will set off later this year, with the mention of fimans but we will make no mention of their superhuman development. We'll also have to explain the need for some seasoned humans going along – in key roles."

Her steely delivery won her a consensus on that, leaving Contrea to bide his time.

During the half hour break, UK Prime Minister Frank Morse, serving his term as EU Representative, conversed in the outer hall with Contrea and a visitor – Sven Hadder, "…we have little choice but to pool resources. Indications are that many areas will be affected."

I'd known Morse from school days. He'd been a steady, no-nonsense kind of kid who could always be relied on. Over time, I'd grown to respect this even more, seeing him now as a thoroughly upstanding statesman. On the social front, like DelMonte he was content with having a well enough proportioned physique rather than wasting time cosmetically with frivolous genetic enhancements.

"Prime Minister," Hadder's tone was unsettlingly dry, "when will it be too much for host countries to be putting up with increasing numbers of climate refugees?" His joyless stare was purpose driven.

Morse produced words sparingly, "We're a long way from anything that alarming," in the knowledge that EU refugees were pouring southwards through Edinburgh, Copenhagen and Kaunas. "The protocol agreed on, while admittedly not knowing how long this will last, is ultimately for all displaced persons to be repatriated." Satisfied at having said all there was to say, and earnestly wanting to move on, he glanced about. "You'll excuse me. I have to catch someone before we resume."

DelMonte, in conversation with Althorpe, stepped to one side for Morse to whisper in his ear. "Costa, we have a problem over there." They glanced in the direction of Hadder and Contrea, carefully relaying the impression of seeking someone beyond, before moving off in the opposite direction. Morse continued, "They make me uneasy."

DelMonte held nothing back from his close ally. "Uneasy?" A quick jerk of his head indicated that to be a gross understatement. "We have files that implicate those two in a tangle of political intrigues and assassinations."

Morse's intelligence was in sync. "Despots of another era," a reference relating to post World War II sovereign rulers, "a bankrupt and bloody one steeped in betrayal and injustice."

"Yeah, the world gone insane! That 'Arab Spring' was one trumpet call to end all that – with Arab Mediterranean countries and the EU at last coming to terms on religion, 'social societies', *and*

Palestine – and now, we've got these two jerks here with the sick hope that DeepStorm's trail of destruction will bankrupt the world yet again. Then, in they'll go."

"There's a huge risk of that actually coming about – and to them, the Questor task force," Morse was now alarmed, "our best chance to avert chaos, is a major hindrance to their achieving their aims."

"Absolutely. We're thinking sabotage. As you know, a number of suspicious incidents are under investigation." Morse had the classified reports – explosions in a Lunar ice mine, disruptions to ice tile deliveries bound for Questor vessels, a shuttle sabotaged en route to liner Lascaux and workers killed and maimed by a defective BoCracker on liner Avebury. He stopped walking and turned to face Morse. "That's the main reason for the navy escort. The Bering is the best we've got, anybody's got..."

"We can rely on Council members, can't we? China has turned out to be a super partner in European socio-economic development, and not the superpower threat we'd feared in the 2020s."

"Thankfully yes, among the best. And the marriages of Sino-Western corporations have been spectacular – especially in getting China to see beyond the feudalistic style conquering of territories – notably in resource rich Africa."

"Just in time, for by far the greatest challenge – of together developing the *infinitely* bigger Near Earth Territories."

Althorpe approached just as Jude Nade was leaving the pressroom. "Unsettled?" The admiral's face was compassionate, his eyes taking in the blue of hers. "With all that's going on in the World, I mean?"

"Yeah – it shows?"

"Just a little, to me." He noted the warm glow rise in her cheeks at his words.

Sure enough, she was continuously affected by the way this crusty dog addressed her and, though unaccustomed to showing her feelings in having to report objectively, Jude had increasingly been touched with pity and a growing sorrow for the World. In the face of those swelling feelings she welcomed the sense of ease and even safety this man brought to her whenever they met.

"Do you know why I'm here?" he was looking away from her eyes now, though noting the smooth sweep of her blond chignon.

With an indulgence he could barely allow himself, he imagined its fragrance, and stroking it, until it loosened.

"I haven't the foggiest." Although sensing his new and fragile feelings towards her, she also felt strangely shut out from him.

Althorpe was in a different kind of battle. He couldn't bear to become involved, only to deliver a blow or cause her any pain when it was time for him to leave

"There'll be an announcement, about a disturbance far upside," he read her expression for comprehension, also intent on *not* seeing his affections for her reflected there. "A Gwave is causing the DeepStorm phenomenon. They're sending a manned mission out to it."

The magnitude of that news flash hit home. "A Gwave? What the...? Where did that come from?" The implication was enormous. "And what..? It's your mission? You're going up to stop it somehow?" When he nodded, her faint smile faded.

"I'm totally unqualified..." he chuckled feebly, leaning closer, "clearly the wrong guy," resisting the urge to touch her cheek. "They'll see that and think better of sending me."

She sensed an embrace that did not happen. "Oh," her shoulders slumped under a weight of emotions – the scoop he'd handed her marred by visualising horrendous events to come, as well as her personal mix of fears for him, more vivid because of what had happened to her husband upside.

He was about to clasp her hand when visions of millions of kilometres of black space came and he pulled back, a slight tightening of his lips visible. "You know on the mission they'll mostly be young kids, like yours and mine. Except, instead of humans, they'll be a new space-breed – fimans."

"Hi, Madison..." Morse joined me as I reached the buffet table for coffee, "This storm. Your thing, right?" He hesitated then, catching sight of my silver tie clip with its image of a half-Moon. "You discovered it – and now what? You think you can beat it?"

My answer was straight on. "We have some idea of what is happening – and a lot of questions." I looked squarely at him. "It's early days yet."

"So true." He was equally face to face, with myself as the subject of the selection process he'd taken part in. UNNDC had deliberated hard on who'd head up the Questor mission. Some preferred a more experienced administrator. I was seen as too intimately involved scientifically, as well as too radical in my approach. And yet, in nominating me, Morse had backed DelMonte.

"There's a battle brewing, over the fimans," I offered, "and what happened to the AstBelt exofimans."

"It just needs to be handled carefully. In the 2030s they weren't actually genecrafting, just putting guys in cat suits. Right?"

"Ah ha, suits tougher than steel that flex and stiffen in tune with the bio-electrical pulses of the wearer's muscles. In fact the combination of super developed muscles, in that kit, made them almost cyborg strong." Sure, I gave a thought to Sashia, for her to fare better with her smart striders. "Unfortunately they were so mesmerised by how lucrative the mining tours were, they lost sight of how excessively long they'd been out in AstBelt. Before they knew it, ZeroG muscle attrition had done its work – it shortened their legs, as you know – while anyway, in their advanced state of osteoporosis, they could no longer stand in EarthG without their suits."

"Yeah, those mining administrators thought it wouldn't matter. They saw them fooling around, joking about being stunted gladiators clad in armour, and counted on everyone somehow adjusting to them looking different." Morse couldn't help but grimace. "No one did. Perhaps it was natural, after being ridiculed and shunned as freaks that they responded by becoming at best brutes and, at worst, callous. I understand some perceive them as psychopaths."

"The fimans aren't at all like that. They're regular people – all of them, fine human beings."

"Sure, that's the point," my good friend was earnest, and now steered the conversation towards my passion for going. "You're set on your *Cretaceous* hunch?" He was really only expecting confirmation from me, which he received in the slight lift of my jaw. "It hasn't got support – for all that DelMonte and I have tried. Everyone's resolute about you watching what DeepStorm does to planets out there," he was as if struggling to comprehend something. "Or, is there something else to this?"

Frustration bordering on anger I felt my eyes blaze. "When that thing gets here – the wave crest gets here – all hell will let lose! Mega tides will move oceans and whole continents. We might even see more – the stuff of our worst nightmares – quakes off the scale, tsunamis reaching far inland, supervolcanoes smothering continents!"

"And you can come up with answers? Answers that two centuries of palaeontology has not?" I felt he was trying to be constructive, my expression relaying hope in response as he continued, "You'll need a brilliant new approach to pull that off."

"Precisely," I smiled pointedly and purposely stroked my tie clip, "As prehistoric finds on the Moon and also in Antarctica show, I believe somewhere there's another way to look into the past." I eased up, regarding him tenuously in the hope of sharing the importance of this. "It's a long shot, but then we need clues wherever we can find them – and, just possibly, that's upside.

"You know, I said there's nothing to suggest there was a Gwave in the past. That's true. Except, by my computations, with the right precession and trajectory of a source – to generate a wave pattern in a plane that oscillates in and out of line with the Solar System's orbital plane – waves hitting the near side and then the far side of the Milky Way could have coincided with – and caused – each of the Earth's Mass Extinction events,"

I watched his blank expression, hardly expecting more. "Okay, forget about the maths," I let out a chuckle before turning gravely serious, "I'm saying it is possible for a series of DeepStorm waves to have hit Earth before."

"Christ!" His horror showed. "You mean this really could be a repeat of what happened millions of years ago – an annihilation of life on earth?"

"It doesn't prove it. We'd need the source for that. But, yes, it makes it plausible."

"Jaisus! And you said *waves*? There would be more to follow?"

"If I'm right, yes, trains of them! Each lasting a few million years, packed with millennia long waves, possibly." I wondered if he or anyone could imagine that, "Time enough for others to worry about the next ones." I added another short chuckle before returning to gravity. "This first wave is the toughest – there really is no time to spare."

"That's horrific! UNNDC knows about that?"

"They're reviewing my notes – and we are still figuring out the geometry." I gave him a cheery look, fingers pressed to his shoulder.

"Hey. One way or another, I won't let up on my hunches. I can't. I'll keep going at them."

He looked more pointedly at my Moon clip. "That anything to do with it?"

"Pretty incisive," I thought, and gave him a knowing nod.

Moving to the exit, Jude was also making contact with Jack, who was sitting at his desk. "They're sending a mission upside. It's okay. It's official – or will be later today."

"Good, that's great," he was grappling for the story in that... "What for?"

"Some Gwave is causing the DeepStorm disasters. They've got to find out why, using this special mission."

"Great!" he turned to an assistant, "Dig up all you can on Gwaves."

"A manned mission."

"Yeah? Sure, why not?" that excited him little.

"Upside," she got little more attention, having already said that, "Far upside." He raised his head. "Beyond Mars, or maybe even beyond AstBelt."

That got him to his feet. "They can't, the media'll dump on them. People can't go that far out!"

"They have a young new breed." How sensational this was only now began to dawn on Jude.

And there was Jack, at last seeing a real story from this mere weather girl. "*We'll* dump on them. Remember the exofiman debacle? A company tried to turn around its ailing robot mining operations in AstBelt with those guys. The operatives went as nuts as old gold prospectors. They became monstrous killers."

"These won't be the same." Jude was dismayed, sensing a negative pitch surfacing.

"Why? Sure it'll be the same," he was so excited he didn't even notice her crushed expression, "No, wait, the other channels will say as much. We can go one better."

"With what?" She bit her lower lip, concerned that he'd follow up with something tacky. She shunned the sensationalising of events through innuendo and suggestion, preferring to report facts and actual observation.

"Yeah, got it. It's great! They're announcing this, in Machu Picchu?"

"Yeah," the stretched out word conveyed her apprehension.

"So there's a corollary – it's fabulous! The headline – UN'S INCA-STYLE SACRIFICES TO THE STARS TO SAVE THE WORLD. Isn't it great?"

There it was, tacky – and totally insensitive to the dying and suffering, and to those, like Althorpe, about to risk their lives to try to save others. Jude shook her head, removed her glasses with the view of Jack, and wandered off, the cameraman observing her moistening eyes.

I was briefly on the dais again in the following session, lamentably to inform Council members of good news marred by disaster. "I am pleased to relay that contestants in the InviHundred series, organised for the final selection of our fimans, by far out performed top ranked human sportsmen, and combat trained forces, according to benchmarks set by the judges. For us this makes a resounding success. In fact the performance of a few individuals defied all conceivable expectations. The outcome is that we now have the quota of fimans we need.

"On a sad note, the last InviHundred event was disrupted by a tragic volcanic eruption. The venue, the volcanic island of Ni'moloka'i, was declared an off-limits nature reserve. It was not expected to erupt again so soon. That came without warning, causing loss of life – a human marshal, two organisers and even some fiman contestants." I bowed my head, said nothing more, and left the podium.

Morse took my place, allowing a moment of solemn reflection before resuming. "What befalls us now is to put the DeepStorm Questor report before members, which proposes the composition of the task force and in particular the contributions (as already agreed to in principle) of member states. The report is before you. Budgeting for this extremely long running mission, balancing cost against function, the essential public sector contributions are." He gestured to a screen that read –

UN

Home base   – UNNDC mission support, observatories, early
warning systems, disaster management

Territories   – UNNDC Chief Scientist, mission project control

USA, UNASUR

Home base   – NASA, AEB support

Territories   – Task force Commander

              – USS Bering (CCV-81), Sussex class battle-carrier
with displacement 3.32 cubic km and length 1.8 km, equipped with
BoBo and radiation protection systems, and a complement of –
- 120 Eurofighter T9 Twister tactical-shape-shift interceptors armed with lasers and cyber-dragnets
- 28 A16 Mamba attack craft armed with proton canons
- 10 B5 Komodo strategic launchers armed with thermonuclear missiles30 shuttles and 3 rescue terra-spheres
- 6,500 EarthG terraccommodated crew

UK, EU, Russia, Arab League, Canada, Australia

Home base   – ESA, Roscosmos, ASC, CSA ground support

Territories   – Avebury modified (Galahad) cruise liner
with displacement 2.77 cubic km and length 1.5 km, equipped with
BoBo and radiation protection systems, and a complement of –
- 15 shuttles and 2 mining terra-spheres
- 2,000 EarthG terraccommodated crew

China, India, Japan

Home base   – JAXA, CNSA, and ISRO ground support

Territories   – Lascaux modified (Galahad) cruise liner
with displacement 2.77 cubic km and length 1.5 km, equipped with
BoBo and radiation protection systems, and a complement of –
- 15 shuttles and 2 mining terra-spheres
- 2,000 EarthG terraccommodated crew

"The details are in the dossiers provided to you. The first task is to review potential mission leaders. Short-listed candidates are at the beginning of the document."

Those considered for the CEO appointment, Commanding officer of the Questor task force, were now individually presented to the meeting.

Connell Althorpe, that stalwart American, was called late in the session. He was proposed for recently serving as US Minister for

Defence, where in the face of fierce odds he'd demonstrated unerring strengths. He could be counted on to keep Questor objectives firmly in view, under any pressure.

After thanking the meeting for the honour of being put forward he went on to express, as he genuinely believed, that a younger, more agile executive would be better suited for such an important task. The UN Security Council selection committee were inclined to agree, preferring several high-ranking political candidates, all with military backgrounds. Defence headquarters from the Pentagon and White Hall to Brussels and Beijing, on the other hand, had backed higher-ranking military officers whom they saw as tougher meaner breeds.

However, in the course of the lengthy selection process, those candidates had one by one been drawn away to take up key military operations in the worsening theatres of engagement both terrestrially and upside. Candidates attending this session were all from further down the pick list. The overriding selection committee impression was that what mattered more for Questor, was the cadre of fimans. Taking the long view, they, in the end, would be in charge.

When votes were cast, it was close. Althorpe could be counted on to command the respect and loyalty of officers and crew. Being single also qualified him for extended service in space.

Having a member of his office aboard naturally pleased DelMonte.

Accepting his fate, Althorpe responded in good humour. "I am, indeed, honoured. Yet this might just be a case of misplaced accreditation. True, I do pronounce buoy as '*boy*' and not '*bu_y*' as most Americans do. But that hardly qualifies me as an international mariner..."

Later in the day, as members were leaving the hall, DelMonte found me waiting in the lobby, something in my manner telling him I anticipated bad news. Respectful of my scientific standing, he wasn't about to drag it out, "It's *no go*! The UN Security Council wants to minimise the risks of failure. Dinosaur hunts are out. The mission is to focus on what's in the path of this DeepStorm, and nothing more."

He would have discerned great disappointment in my eyes and, below that surface, the colour of fury. I could see this unsettled him, seeing as much in the person who was about to take charge of a mission costing billions.

I rebounded quickly, "It was a shot in the dark," and, smiling now, and fishing for something more reassuring to say, found, "They're right, of course. We'll be hard pressed in surveying and analysing planets. One thing's damn sure. We'll get results. And see what's to be done to contain the DeepStorm threat."

Striding away, my thoughts and admiration turned to Sashia for her courage and resolve – now my inspiration.

~*~

23

October 2067

Meanwhile, at the Flying Mountain base, Sashia was slumped on her bed, interred in the softness of a duvet, her leg in a fresh cast and propped on a pillow. Yet, for all that comfort, she had to wrestle to shut out the recent past and compose herself, before holoing Fayez.

The nightmares since leaving Ni'moloka'i held her in a vice. It was as if adrenaline remained high in her veins, keeping InviHundred memories all too vividly alive. A fog of swirling, changing images haunted her – her leg cast tearing, wounds stinging in saltwater, hands blistering on paddles or ropes in white water over lava.

She shook her head, concertedly focusing on the present, and attempted to adjust her appearance. Very carefully she angled the cam-optic to show only her head and shoulders and less of her bruised face and charred hair, so she would not have to explain too much. Finally, after allowing the distraction of the home entertainment to clear her head a little, she felt reasonably collected to holoe.

"Hi, Fayez here," he sounded sleepy.

"Hi there. Want a little company, a little dance?" she murmured, almost too softly for him to hear, she was trying so hard to conceal her fragile spirits.

"Starburst!" he hardly concealed his shock at seeing her condition. "Doesn't look like you're up to much. How are you? How'd you do?"

"Well," a haze of strained faces, Mei's and Guille's, clogged her thoughts, "it was something." Her words came slowly and she was now barely able to restrain the tears. Bryn's charred face, whipped by water, sent shivers down her spine again. She shook her head as if trying to empty it. "Extreme describes it," she blurted. "I'm here – at least."

He could not imagine half of what tortured her but just knew, staring into her exhausted, weepy eyes, that her pains were not just physical. He ached to reach out and cuddle her. But at least he could see his warmth reach her, watch her feed on it with a low, grateful smile. Their silent mutual connection meant everything, emotions running way too high for words.

For distraction from their intensity, Sashia directed his eyes to the ice storms and snowdrifts on the Sævrama Channel. Being aired were severe disruptions to Stockholm's infrastructure – traffic at a standstill, the port frozen over, refugee centres hopelessly overcrowded and streams of evacuees flowing in from the countryside.

"What a mess," Fayez shook his head sympathetically.

The next news item showed where school children had been buried in an avalanche. Rescuers were digging for survivors.

After the discovery that glaciers were advancing more rapidly than expected, bringing snowdrifts closer to remote towns, teams of specialists had been monitoring slopes with a range of trusted techniques – ultrasound scans, seismic surveys, ground penetrating radar, infrared imagery. The data enabled them to build avalanche simulations, with constantly broadcasting warnings about districts that needed to be evacuated. Tragically, this time, disaster struck too swiftly for local officials.

Rescuers on their way to an orphanage, after evacuating patients and their families at a mediresort, were now dragging out scores of crushed infants. Teams in yellow overalls moved about in stark contrast to the monochrome of broken walls, roofs and snow. Near an ambulance, a small naked foot and little blue trouser leg protruded from a stretcher cover. A child's body slung lifeless over the shoulder of a racing rescuer, jacket partially open, revealed a bloodied face set in golden hair that he covetously sheltered near to his heart.

Sashia's cheeks glistening, she quickly dabbed on a little face powder to conceal her distress.

"It's getting worse, isn't it Fayez?" The sight of children's bodies lingered on as if their ghosts could remain. She could take no more grief. Her concerns turned to her grandma, Magadan being on the same latitude as Stockholm, though she had seemed okay on holoe. With heavy heart, Sashia knew that the mission could not be more real, and her severe training never more meaningful than now.

"Yes," Fayez responded dejectedly, "there's no end to the bad news." Feeling powerless, to help even her, he gently tried to get her to switch off. "You must be exhausted. Why not have a hot soak and rest up. You know I understand. I am supportive – in whatever – if you believe your mission can make a difference."

"Yes, and yes I hope so. You don't mind?" Smiling at her, he shook his head affirmatively. "I'll be better later. Holoe in the night, okay?" She pressed her lips to his image as he closed the line.

In another week the long months of training ended in the briefest of graduation ceremonies, held in the Academy assembly hall. Removed of chairs, the scene was more reminiscent of an old military mess hall the day after a defeating skirmish. The InviHundred was just that in the mindset of survivors, now arriving in their slings and crutches and the deafness of Red Robin team members. Faces were grim, with the hollow eyes and damp cheeks of those whose bodies and minds had been stretched and pulled and yet endured. These beings were turned inside out and without adornment. Personal vanities, such as Mei's formerly glamorous nails, had been split and torn, and were all gone and forgotten.

No one had slept sufficiently. On top of everything, mounting tragedies on the Sævrama Channel were now a constant reminder of the possible or potential suffering of family, friends and loved ones. Many people were now jobless, displaced, homeless, even dead.

Tormented by their ordeal, one sleepless night Mei had confided in Sashia about the first time her life had been shattered by Ni'moloka'i exploding. Facing the truth of that, on the cliff face with the ill-fated Bryn, for Mei had finally brought that whole grisly chapter to a close.

Sashia's bombshell of the day was news that her hometown, Motyklejka, in Siberia, had been smothered by massive snowstorms. Mei and Guille comforted her by guessing that her grandma would have fled south accompanied by caring neighbours.

Vividly portrayed to all at the F-Academy was the real life and death threat that DeepStorm presented – and with that understanding, it would become their heavy burden, they as fimans, tested to destruction, if they should be judged as the right stuff to make a difference.

It was early morning when, mindful that the ceremony was scheduled for the afternoon followed by their immediate departure, I called Sashia and Mei to join me out on the snow. I'd found a quiet spot for them to update me on their progress. I began by enlightening Sashia, "Mei can hear okay, with the aid of a coms implant." I had decided, for us not to have Mei shouting all the time, that the imperatives of our work warranted fully activating her biombot. "Watch it, though. That function is strictly classified!"

"I can hear people close around me pretty well." Mei beamed. "Their audio output comes to me from FayWell."

"Hell! She could have done with that in the InviHundred!" Sashia protested on behalf of her friend. "But then," she winked at Mei, "you weren't doing that badly!"

"Anyway," Mei quickly dismissed a flashback of treating Guille in the woods, "they say stem cell treatment will get my normal hearing back. I'm starting it once we're underway."

Before nodding for them to proceed I wanted to include someone else, whom I'd already briefed. I gave Steve Nord his cue to join us on holoe from the UK. On his appearing, cool and confident as ever, I addressed all three.

"I believe you may have seen each other, in Hong Kong – and you met, briefly, in the InviHundred." That pleasantry dealt with, I dived right in, "Okay, you've got my notes, and with your ample qualifications I believe you'll catch on quickly enough, Steve. The girls have made some stunning progress in picturing what the *Cretaceous* world was about. An important avenue they've been exploring were the vast heathlands above tree lines and, in there, when birds came on the scene." At that, I looked to the girls to continue.

They all studied the snow scene, as Mei ordered, "FayWell, bring up the acrobatic raptors," and became quite self-conscious.

"How silly," FayWell muttered to Sashia, as she emerged in the snow as a tiny sparkling-white fairy with stardust-sprinkling wand, "saying that, with this stranger," when opening the last frames of their raptor scene.

"Who just happens to be Steve Nord – that irksome, bumptious Greenpeace activist!" added Mei as quietly.

"Hah!" Sashia, well past caring about the cocky dolphin protester, laughed at her friend's insecurities. "Yeah, you sounded like a circus act!" she muttered back flippantly,

"Thank you!" Mei managed a whisper, returning a cheeky grin before composing herself to say her bit, "When the earliest flyers, pterosaurs, graced *Triassic* and *Jurassic* skies they had reasonably average bones." She could neither sound nor feel relaxed in Nord's company, her old discomfort with peers resurfacing, especially in her present state. "As time went on they began to develop air cavities in thin walled bones, as well as holes in skulls – for the skeletal strength to be super agile. That's something to which we fimans can relate. We have that enhanced agility in common. The pterosaurs were joined, in *Early-Cretaceous* times, by theropod dinosaurs doing the same thing."

"But, in those ancient times, were they simply trying to be super agile? Or was there something else?" I prompted.

"They were adapting," Steve, as well versed in the fossil record, threw this in rather brusquely, "to changes in the physical world."

"Yes!" Mei retorted none too appreciatively, nerves still raw from the InviHundred. "Adapting to everything getting heavy, the air and weather getting heavy. Generation after generation, over tens of millions of years, they had to cope with an imperceptible creeping up of barometric pressures." Mei did not look his way, keeping her eyes keenly on the unfolding scene. "And, we've seen, as cloud began to settle more below the highlands, that the theropods up there protected themselves – from increasingly inclement elements – by developing lightweight downy feathers."

"Protection against wind-chill," undeterred, Steve was not totally oblivious to her pained look, "with which, by chance, they occasioned to experience lift – erm, according to your notes."

"And these little theropods, the cleaner dinosaurs," Sashia pointed to the mundussaurs, as she attempted a cheery note in their discourse, "were all about using that lift."

"With feathers like those of the crow-sized theropod glider archaeopteryx," Mei continued, a hint of a grin for her friend, but her brow nonetheless exposing her tension in not knowing how to cope with this man, "and a beak like that of its descendent confuciusornis. Our little mundussaurs, were now trickling downwards to the lowlands ahead of a much bigger movement that was to follow."

"Whoa!" I chortled, keen to move on but on a lighter note. "Back up a bit!" In just a short while they would be amongst thousands of fimans, many of them professional, and they all had to get on better than this, or life upside would be hell. "Are you saying, that all this adapting was down to Climate Change?"

"Well yes, but very subtly," Mei flashed me a smile, and another for Sashia. Still she looked tense. "It was a lot about cloud cover.

And gradients in weather systems that had long been gentle and ever so gradually got to be steeper. And, with that, winds and temperature differences that were picking up."

"And why was that?" I looked from her to Steve, and back to her again, to join them both in this.

"Over many millions of years, two main effects," Mei looked from me back to the snow scene, "were steadily pushing up atmospheric pressures – the Earth's rotation slowing and the receding Moon's tidal pull weakening. The Sun's rays warming also pushed up pressures and with pressures rising the temperature of evaporation rose, too – thinning out cloud cover."

"Other effects, notably the opening of the Southern Ocean and the glaciation of Antarctica," he followed her gaze, with a rather perfunctory attempt to empathise, "were also taking water vapour out of the atmosphere. Which, with the slowing down of continental plate movements, was not being replenished as much by volcanoes."

"Ah," I glared impatiently at both, but decided to ignore their prickliness for now, "very subtle Climate Change. Stronger winds. Clouds dispersing. Sounds like, Polar Warming was destined to end."

"That's about it – and, as aircrews know," Steve, who'd proved so tough in the InviHundred, glanced at Mei with few energy reserves left to weigh her up, "flight characteristics are incredibly sensitive to weather."

"That's the point. Look at this," she waved her hand at the entire scene. "It was like *we* have on a still wintry morning, with everywhere shrouded in mist. Conditions in the lowlands had long been moderate like that, with low pressure systems that were fairly predictable seasonally as well as at dusk and at high tide." She gave him a sideways glance before going full tilt into the subject. "But as skies cleared and cyclone systems got wetter and more turbulent for flight, and thermals gustier for soaring on, we now see that pterosaurs switched strategies to avoiding inclement conditions. They stayed low down – over coasts. And some used extraordinary head crests to fly by isobars.

"Raptors, on the other hand, had become hardened to the tempestuous conditions of bright and brisk heathlands. Their bones put them on a par for agility with pterosaurs, while feathers gave them super manoeuvrability. And – the clincher was a beak, formed of sheathes of horn, as strong as any jaw full of teeth, yet lighter than any for flight."

"Supremacy in the air," although at his endurance limit, Steve maintained his air of confidence, "that's what all this was about. The tipping point for pterosaurs was coming."

"There was something more," Sashia chirped in, about another of Mei's discovered scenes. "The tough heathlands – had made special nurturers of the mammals and raptors there. Its harsh conditions hardwired into their genes a fierce protectiveness, one that passed down and grew in all their descendants."

"Yes, we were amazed to see that," Mei sounded calmer and even, with a big point to make, a tad more assertive suddenly. "Anyway, as sunny areas grew, they were on the move. Look!" With another nod from her, FayWell was there. Except now she had the head and shoulders of *Makeda*, the black Queen of Sheba, on the body of a slick black panther – and adorning her hair of short tight curls, a crown of red gold was inset with emeralds and rubies. Her yellow slit eyes darted at Steve, and she snarled at him with earthquake intensity.

"FayWell?" Sashia whispered, half smiling at Mei's bemused look, and just before *Makeda's* claw touched the snow to refresh the image there.

They were now looking at aerial views of continents affected by the Deccan eruptions, pretty much as Vijay Singh had envisaged in Rajaspore Thermoport, at the *Close* of the *Late-Cretaceous* time. Mei was as amazed as when she and Sashia were compiling this visible pre-history, even tickled to see Steve's face light up, panning across wasteland devoid of dinosaur herds. Except, as Mei now commented, "With these next icegem sequences, which took place over very many millennia, we're seeing all-weather long-distance migrations – possibly among the first of their kind, to river deltas in Africa, South America and also Antarctralasia (breaking up into Patagonia, Antarctica and Australasia) – in a lowlands invasion, from highland lakes, by large flocks of aquatic birds!"

"We've identified them as the forerunners of ibises, flamingos and pelicans, wading for crustaceans and molluscs where pterosaurs had been dominant. Also, on stormy days out at sea, as seagulls do today, the pterosaurs headed over land but now met with fierce competition from the birds." Mei put her hand up, for FayWell to hold on one sequence, still analysing what they had. "Zoom in. Ah, yes, they were also making easy pickings of eggs and hatchlings in the nurseries of dinosaurs – dinosaurs downsized and now being further reduced in numbers, to endangered species levels. Other sequences have shown us ancient penguins and ratites active in the same ways in Antarctralasia."

She let FayWell move on to Ameurasian sequences, north of the Tethys Sea, Sashia carrying on to give her a break... "It was the same here, on rivers and along coasts. These aquatic birds were the forerunners of divers, grebes, cormorants, rails and sandpipers."

With the scenes gone from the snow, I put a summary to them. "Isobars, rather than isothermals, creep up over time – they always have, always will – right? Your pitch?" Each member of the group nodded, which was good because I wanted to draw out some synergy – inspire them to work as a team. "And with that we essentially have '*Climate Creep*' – it's a given – driving on evolution by Natural Selection, inexorably for complex organisms."

"Absolutely!" Mei was in no doubt. "The subtlest of changes in barometric pressures are apt to affect vascular activities. As can be seen in the strikingly different appearance of alpine versions of plants from those in the foothills. And, of course, it can be seen among us, in sufferers of weather migraine."

"Erm, but just supposing the *Cretaceous* conditions returned," Sashia remained curious. "Mightn't huge dinosaurs make a comeback? Evolve again, from birds?"

Steve shrugged, seemingly requited for now. "Impossible!" He shook his head emphatically. "Planets age. From birth to grave they age. Earth, too. And evolution has to fit right in with when the time is ripe, or miss the window of opportunity."

That afternoon, on schedule, the principal and staff gathered at one end of the assembly hall to oversee their painfully sombre graduation ceremony. Mei and Sashia shared the seriousness of Guille, who was reading his script on holoe.

"Everyone who has completed the course and succeeded in passing out is a winner – quite simply, *Best of Breed*," the Principal aimed, breaking their mood by his candid declaration. Nothing more was forthcoming, such as announcing who had won. The Red Robin trio actually wouldn't have wanted it any other way. "A select few, those who have excelled, will now join a special task force – some as reconneers, some taking up key crew appointments and others filling military ranks. Others who passed will join UNNDC, ISWA and various space agencies – notably NASA, ESA, JAXA, CSNA, ISRO, Roscosmos – which will be engaged in providing support from bases in the next phase of the Near Earth Territories. The rest of you will be highly sought after by private firms also setting up operations in the Territories. That's where the future is. A holoe message will notify all of you of your shuttle allocations. Once aboard you'll be informed which way you're headed.

"What I can say to you all is, you've reached a new plateau of personal achievement," the Principal's tone was appropriately solemn. "More than that, think about it. You tell me." He raised his voice, "Was it worth it?"

Stunned by his suggestion that overall endurance of what they had gone through could possibly be considered good in any way, by inference including the loss of colleagues, no one responded. Instead they looked around seeking some communal reaction, one voice that might speak up. All faces looked sombre.

Sashia thought of the kid's body slung over a rescuer's shoulder at the avalanche site, resolving to put her life at risk to save lives such as hers. She was sure Bryn would want that. And perhaps to achieve that would entail extreme engagement, to find whoever among them might succeed. After all, if all of what they'd been through was to bring off some kind of miracle then, but for the loss of colleagues, it had to have been worth all their misery. Similar thoughts surely ran through all their heads – each silently recognised that *yes* they'd become something of a new breed, and certainly none remained the kid they'd once been.

Smiles, tears and whispered words united them. "Sure." Their utterances rose to one strong defiant voice, the voice they'd hoped to find, not knowing it was inside each of them and the same – "Sure, we're strong! We've come through the worst. Strong enough. Ready. We're ready!"

"Go show 'em then," the Principal called, "Show 'em like you showed us. Goodbye – and good luck!"

Discussions immediately broke out on the prospect of going on the task force or being free. Sashia couldn't wait to holoe Fayez, half expecting to say she'd be rejoining him. She was, after all, by far the least qualified present. Mei, for instance, had even added ecologist and veterinarian to her qualifications.

"And the InviHundred? What of that? Who won?" a lone voice shouted, receiving no answer.

Speaking softly but high enough, Sashia commented only, "It made us," her teary eyes shifting focus from face to face. "All of us. It made what we've become." There was more to go for the Red Robins... they needed to acknowledge the biggest cost. Sashia's eyes engaged with those of Mei and Guille, and each knew what was in their hearts, their lips mouthing, "Bryn."

On his way out, followed by the instructors, the Principal veered to pass close by her. "Sashia," came his firm tone, like that of a reassuring physician, "Go conquer."

In the next moment bodies were milling in the icy cold, locating shuttles, hurriedly shouting goodbyes or quietly expressing regrets at parting.

The Red Robin trio were pleased to be on the same haul. Sitting beside Mei, Sashia holoed Fayez, "Guess what? We're done! We're heading out, right now!"

"What?" he was struggling for words, having wanted this day to come he was now taken by surprise. "Terrific, Starburst. Where will you land? I'll meet you." Her image came clearer, amazing him. "Hey. No scarf, in company? What happened?"

"Tell you, later," she smiled before reading the text stream at the bottom of her holoe. "They're giving me the info now. Oh no – no Fayez! I've been selected!"

The message from the F-Academy was brief. It read only "Congratulations Reconneer Sashia Dubchek."

Instantly a cloak of caution descended over their dashed hopes. "Erm, I'm with Mei. One hell of a trooper..."

"Do tell... Hi Mei," his voice was now teutronium heavy.

"Hi, Fayez. She's the real trooper..." Mei was being distracted by her own holoe. "Yow! Me too! We're both selected! We're reconneers!" Deep inside she suddenly lamented over not having someone like Fayez to share her own news.

Guille was making his way towards them, yelping and giving a thumbs up. "Yipes! I'm selected!"

The girls aimed thumbs up his way, Mei racing to text them. "We are three – the *Three Reconneers*! Congrats!"

Just then, Sashia felt a deep pang from seeing Fayez's crushed expression. "Seems we're among the lucky few." Everything was getting too complicated now.

She had recognised her own desire to help alleviate suffering everywhere. It burned in her. But so did her desire to be back at home with him. They'd not known when the training would end and when it did they'd hoped it meant their reunion. Now came the hammer blow. No one had prepared her for how this would feel, or how she should break it to him. She would not be coming home. "Fayez, I'm sorry, so sorry. This must all end sometime, God only knows when. Years maybe. Darling, don't wait for me? Not now. I'm sorry."

Sashia purposely blurred her cam-optic, but not before Fayez noticed the sheen of her eyes, the flush in her cheeks. "Hey. It's cool," he faltered. He'd seen her change through the months, seen her take up the challenge, integrate more deeply with the others, and loved and admired her the more for it. "You go see what they want."

Sashia stared at the misted holoe not knowing what to say, except to share more distress. "I heard yesterday that my grandma had to get out. She's gone south, but I don't know where. I'm so worried for her, Fayez." She was grateful seeing how he shared her concern.

"Oh, wait! There's another message. Huh, I'm booked on a shuttle to the Moon." She glanced at Mei and then Guille, who nodded. They were booked, too. "Leaving from ManusMax Spaceport, Papua New Guinea, in three days time. So soon...! But, oh," Sashia gave a pathetic little smile, and spoke with a squeaky voice, "I've a room at the Miandor hotel – and yes! I can have visitors. Will you come?"

"Yow! Is LTA light?" Fayez, in renewed euphoria was already shifting. "I'm on my way. See you there."

~*~

24

November 2067

Alighting aboard the battle-carrier Bering I was instantly gratified to see FayWell's playful form flowing through the beautiful battle grey of all the living columns, walls and ceilings. Punctuating the washed out shabby chic hue with just a few peach and ochre buds as highlights, her explicitly tight-fitting Barbarella-like costume was of dazzling gold and silver. These changes of hers were not exactly what we'd envisaged for uplifting the atmosphere in the ships – but it wasn't unwelcome either. Nor was the AI sliding provocatively up to me, with a soft cat-like voice, "Hi. Bad night?"

Bright as a pulsar to look at, though perhaps not so quick on the uptake where body language came in, she'd not figured on my being tired from worry. I wasn't up to idle chitchat. "Sort of."

"Everything alright?"

"Pestilent wee nymph," I levelled with her openly, rolling my eyes in mock despair. "The perfect little chat mate, impossible to hurt by ignoring or insulting, while the soul of discretion never hurting others."

"Mind how you go." FayWell remained courteous and alongside me, observing me staggering due to Earth weight all the way from the aft cargo bay to the Command Bridge at the bow of the ship. "You're adjusting from the shuttle's EcstasyG," came another pleasantly delivered but obvious line from her.

"Just tired. You know." And there was I, watching her watching me in the rest room mirror – or perhaps not, since her eyes were ever concealed. Still, all out in the open with her chatting away obtusely! Bizarre! Well, sort of. Except, after all, she was an AI. "No. You don't know, do you?" I offered, my turn to get chatty, "You won't know, either, how lucky fimans are, being spared our little discomforts."

Using a tiny laser-razor I removed some stubble on my chin, "The same goes for this." I twisted my neck, while stretching my back. "All the bothersome wee things that were sorted out, in their breed's billion dollar development programme." Yet, tucking my shirt into my trousers, I patted my trim tummy, assessed and appreciated my fine complexion and smoothed down my well-trimmed but plenteous hair. "Thank God scientists got control of this lot – and staying healthily active longer." However, on cleaning my teeth and nails I noted, "These still need sorting."

I needed that time alone to adjust and now felt pleasantly refreshed and more amenable when following FayWell to a wide mezzanine area. There, thankfully, a moving walkway transported me, without having to stagger, through the noisy construction work in interconnecting passageways and buildings.

With no doors in place yet, I was suddenly on the incredibly expansive Command Bridge. Suitably dimmed lighting gave the entire space a clean, soft feel, punctuated only by crystal-looking panes that slid out to display diagrams, controls and data. Mesmerised whilst also ungainly, when I turned to look in another direction, I saw a solitary uniformed officer looking at the Moon through the full width Bridge window. I'd no doubt about his rank. "Commander, I'm..."

The Admiral was instantly recognisable and when he turned there was no need to continue my sentence. He completed my introduction in the manner of a stiff businessman and certainly nobody's father image. And yet, he somehow seemed more approachable when eyeing the Moon on my tie clip. "Professor Mark Madison." He gave a dry smile, "FayWell did announce your arrival."

Understanding my awkward posture, he nodded towards a chair. "Please, take the weight off your feet." I smiled accord, preferring to half sit on a console than look up at him. "Anyhow this is what we've planned, you've planned. The two liners out there," he waved to the window, where Avebury and Lascaux lay so majestically, "and this battle-carrier. It's all here. Trillions worth."

That vista was certainly impressive and all spanking new, although the prospect of sharing months of executive solitude with this joyless apparition wasn't so uplifting. "I know," my manner, intuitively matching his, was also business-like. I didn't dare add how it was also daunting, now that the mission was truly upon us.

"There's a lot I have to go through with you." Naturally, as Chief Scientist leading the mission, I had orders to give. He smiled deferentially. "For instance, when we're far enough away for it not to matter, I'll instruct FayWell to set ship clocks to twenty-three-hour days. Including the Bering. Subject to your agreement of course?"

He regarded my raised eyebrow in silence, perchance gaining a glimmer of the Anglo-Saxon in me. "It's more natural to living things, and should improve everyone's endurance on the long space trek ahead." I omitted that that was typically a day in early Mesozoic times, which is what I wanted for the onboard parks. Of course, FayWell always kept Earth times too – also Ecstasy time and Mars times.

"As you say, in such matters." He attempted to change the subject. "We'll be joined by Dr Kaitlyn O'Malley, the three of us making up the Mission Board."

"Good. We've met, of course, for her wish list of medical facilities and staff training. Apart from her getting the latest and best available, everything for spiritual recuperation, medical hypnosis and such..."

"Going back to what you've planned," he cut to our imperatives, nodding towards to the liners. "What's the status on DeepStorm? Do we know any more on what we're faced with?"

"Some," I was cautious, wanting to take the measure of this man before opening up too much, "on what the wave crest is doing out there." I couldn't let on about our *Cretaceous* research, while still awaiting UNNDC clearance on that, but without saying too much I could simply elude to that time. "Looking ahead we consider huge tides to be a major risk, with abnormally large continental movements manifesting in unprecedented earth tremors and eruptions. Fallout from that, combined with abnormally low atmospheric pressures, could generate weather systems almost as weird as the dinosaurs had. Blankets of cloud bringing about Polar Warming as severe as in Cretaceous times."

The Commander clearly saw little in that. All I could do was to look him woefully in the eye before continuing, "Flowering plants, the mainstay of agriculture, will wither for lack of sunlight. That's what happened in 1815, known as the *Year Without a Summer*, when crop failures resulted from ash and steam from the Mount Tambora supervolcano eruption. Ecosystems are that sensitive."

"That's a worst case scenario?" The Commander was up with me now. "One of several doubtless?"

"Our situation could have been much worse, right now, without the progress made to bring Africa out of the dark ages and into prominence as a major breadbasket of the world. We'll have to see what losses we need to make up for, with growing-platforms out to sea, as has been considered. At least, with Polar Warming, the skies will be clearer there and the seas calmer than with present conditions…"

"Commander," FayWell butted in, officer-like, as was her remit, "the UN Security Council Summit has convened at Machu Picchu." Fed live to the craft, the images relayed were a double offering as the Sævrama Channel again appeared on a back wall of the conference hall.

Jude's subtitles scrolled over sky views. *"In a recent change in developments, skies everywhere are unusually overcast. There are also conspicuously large black clouds within the seas."* Satellite views of the Mediterranean, inset with underwater close-ups, showed lava outflows oozing away along the Euro-African continental divide. *"The scenes we've been seeing are horrific.*

"And now the fear is of major volcanoes, as happened when Krakatau erupted, altering global weather patterns. Hotspots all round the Pacific ring of fire seem to be abnormally active. It's the same through the Mediterranean Sea and the Arabian Peninsula, both remnants of the ancient Tethys Sea floor.

"More on that later. Just in – an earthquake of magnitude 6.8 on the Richter scale hit the outskirts of Cairo, Egypt, last night. Please note – the following scenes contain horrific and distressing images. They were captured by onlookers in the overhead thermoport."

On screen – digging equipment crawled through a veil of dust and collapsed buildings to drag aside girders and overturn fallen walls. Firemen lasered through concrete. Rescuers carried away the wounded and dying. Airborne craft glinted in the dim light of dawn. Thousands of people, sullied, dazed and fearing aftershocks, milled through toxic fumes in search of open ground. Noxious pools of black oil and brown oily seawater made surfaces underfoot slick.

Jude Nade's craft made a low-level swoop, before going to the planned rendezvous with ground operations. She was there to interview the grieving and bereaved in person. And soon her cameraman was relaying pitiful scenes of families huddled together in shock, and others consoling friends as best they could. A man climbed out from a window clutching a limp teenager. Others staggered through demolished doorways.

At the Summit the Sævrama dialogue was now not muted, for all to hear Jude Nade's on the spot broadcast. *"What we can see here are wrecked lives, with families torn or lost. They're struggling to hold on to life – in air that is stifling to breath. It's a tragedy on an unimaginable scale. Rescue operations began in earnest at first light, with meagre success so far in finding victims alive under all the rubble. All areas were instantly plunged into darkness and chaos, power supplies cut, shortly after midnight when disaster struck. The priority for now is getting people away to safety, and to where there are food, water and medical facilities."*

An ambulance edged its way through collapsing homes. Just ahead a rescue craft that had stopped to take a group on board, now sped off, an explosion shooting dust and smoke after it. Enveloped in the fug, a doctor and nurse were tending a baby in its mother's arms.

"Things are worsening by the hour. An aftershock brought floors and walls crashing down just an hour ago. The death toll is unknown, but expected to be in the many thousands. Over a million are believed to be displaced, missing or in danger. A massive rescue operation is underway to get them out of here."

Nade's craft was touching down when the screen image shook violently. Dead ahead, black oil shot into the air. To the right, water gushed over the ground. Further away, a three-story building crumpled and then sank into the muddy fluidised ground. The adjoining building did the same. Dead ahead again, another building collapsed in an oily pool. All three disappeared out of sight.

"My God what's happening? There's oil and water everywhere..."

The screen image shook again, accompanied by a bright flash and loud bang. Then it went blank.

There was an awful silence. No one spoke at the Summit. Phil, a reporter at the media station, cut in, putting a brave face on events, *"We've lost transmission from the delta."*

On the Bridge I caught the Commander's taut face, anxiety etched deeply there. At a previous Summit, I'd noticed a controlled interest between him and Nade. However, there was nothing I could say or do.

"We'll get back there just as soon as we have the team back on line." Phil's tone was low and reassuring. *"Meanwhile we have an*

expert on fossil fuels, on holoe – Andy Meadows, from HardRock Consulting. Welcome.

"The concern of all of us is for the people in the delta, and what they're suffering. But, Andy, while we're cut off, the loss of so much oil is bound to result in shortages." Aerial coverage of the vast scene replayed behind them. *"Would that, in turn, be cause for concern to people round the World? What is the state of reserves?"*

"The quick answer is, no. Storm chokes are designed to automatically shut in wells underground, to prevent further losses in events like this. And, while oil production from there is down, supplies can be made up from elsewhere."

"Yes, but there's a lot involved here. Proven oil reserves have dwindled steadily in recent decades and not been replaced by new finds in anything like the quantities that are needed. With that realisation, the UN was compelled to classify fossil fuel as a 'strategic resource'. And the World was finally forced to switch to alternative energy sources as well as product wrappings other than plastics."

"That's true – and that's happened. But an ever-increasing variety of materials are made from oil and gas, for which there's no alternative. What's the picture on worldwide reserves? Well, things were looking bleak until Arctic production increased recently, with new finds looking very promising. Now, of course, all eyes are on the vast oil concessions being awarded right across Antarctica."

At last a breathless reporter holoed from the delta, *"Phil, we lost our base station here. Luckily we got out. But we have no word from Jude. Wait... we have something."* His words were drowned in an immense roar. A thousand flames flared up. Satellite images revealed the delta ablaze. The reporter shouted, *"Phil, can you hear me?! I've found an alcove to shelter in!"*

"Go ahead. We can hear."

"It's pandemonium down here. The situation is unbearable. Everyone is racing to get out, relief operations too. We've got to go. Wreckage has been spotted. It might be Jude's vehicle – if that hasn't been engulfed in this inferno! Yes, we're getting an image! It's clear! There it is!"

Through the smoke a wrecked vehicle could be seen on the ground. The Sævrama insignia confirmed it as hers. *"I see movement! Someone's climbing out, and another... it's the pilot....*

and her! The second one is her! She looks okay. Her cameraman too! Jude, you hear me?"

"I'm okay, just dirteee!" Dry observation intact, but bruised, shaken, short of breath, Jude could hardly speak. Her unravelled hair clung lifelessly to her bright yellow rescue suit. Smeared in dust and oil, her face was blackened and ruddy. The Commander sat on the edge of his chair, silently watching her onscreen progress.

"Jude, are you really okay?" Jack was there, in her heads-up, genuinely anxious.

"Yeah, no problem," blood on her cheek and neck inferred some injury. "Let me do this." She clambered aboard a vehicle that had sped in and now instantly rose over the smoke.

"Okay, you're back on air!" Another vehicle arrived for the other reporter. Flames licked out, missing the descending craft, but then another flame jetted up. The vehicle was torched. It exploded. The reporter, who had run into the open to meet it, fell to his knees gasping for air amid the flames. All breaths were held for him as his body collapsed, lifeless, to the ground.

Wheezing and then involuntarily crying, Jude blurted out her commentary. *"This is unreal!"* She paused, to gain control and lowered her voice to present as professionally as possible. *"My friend is down there!"* As they gained height and the open sky she still struggled for composure, *"Hundreds of rescuers, thousands of men, women and children, consumed in toxic cloud! Can't see much now. What I was about to report, before that explosion, is that these scenes are occurring throughout the world now. The efforts of relief operations such as those below, are absolutely overwhelmed. Yet they keep going."* Her craft dipped back into smoke and sheared off again. *"We can't see a thing. We're having to climb away from all this."*

Phil, clearly disturbed by the loss of their crew, cut in again. *"So Andy, while Jude's off line, what's happening there? How could all that oil well up, over such a vast area? You said the wells would shut in."*

"I've had a call from my office, advising me on that. They say it's unprecedented for this to happen, considering all the safety measures that were implemented after the Gulf War oilfield fires last century. What they believe has happened, is that the quakes cracked open the reservoir's fault structure. If that's the case, oil is escaping

direct to the surface and not through the oil wells. There's absolutely nothing that can be done, except to evacuate the area immediately – as we've heard is happening. The situation is totally out of control."

"We're still off line back there. Coming back to what you said about reserves, will this change that view?"

"Oh most definitely. Those reserves are lost. There's no way to contain the outflow or the loss of pressure. It's too early as yet – petrologists will have to work out the numbers – but, at best, I'd expect these reservoirs to be relegated to secondary recovery oilfields. With substantially deferred reserves."

Phil had something to add, "Just in – the oil company says its digging wide channels along the north flank, most vitally to prevent the sea being polluted by the oil."

At the Summit the Sævrama audio was muted again so that work could continue. Addressing the assembly, Sustra Matri was subdued. "Before saying anything else, our heartfelt condolences go out to all those people in the delta – the injured, the bereaved, the brave souls trying their best to bring aid in as well as those reporting on events.

"This tragedy underlines what we're here for today. The entire World is now experiencing DeepStorm – and, at present, we're powerless to stop it. I'll hand over to Professor Madison, now on the Bering, to update us on the situation."

Regardless of whether I looked grave or not, which I'm sure I did, I cleared my throat and duly faced the optics FayWell rather formally directed me to. "First of all the Gwave crest, approaching Pluto's orbit, is roughly midway through the Kuiper Belt." I'd prepared to present this earlier, and already instructed FayWell to bring up the hologram of the Solar System I'd presented at previous Summits. "We've detected the pulling together of planetesimals in the Belt, much like seaweed in a wave on the ocean," I ran my hand round that part of the image, "and, as expected, collisions are nudging some of them outwards as bolides. There have been impacts on nearby bodies and others might go on to threaten Earth as NEOs.

"On Neptune's deep frozen moon Triton," FayWell refreshed the hologram, with an inset image of what I referred to, "there was a spectacular impact as well as an equally dazzling volcanic eruption. On Earth there's been an increase in shooting stars, small meteorites, with some hits on satellites as well as modest splashdowns in the seas. For decades now NASA has been keeping a watchful eye on NEOs of all sizes, including BoBos, after discovering many thousands in close proximity to Earth's orbit. They're on top of what's happening to those."

So much for space rocks. What was happening on the ground was another matter, as they'd just witnessed in Egypt. With due solemnity, I plunged to the point. "I cannot comment much on what we've just witnessed. That's something we'll all have to contemplate privately. Though I'd like to venture that we get our expert's view on the circumstances."

Steve Nord had already been contacted, FayWell now putting him on holoe. "As has been said, this is unprecedented. So not a lot can be offered until further studies are carried out." With uncharacteristic control, he kept his 'I warned you' aggression out of his tone. "There've been instances of drilling mud, also formation oil and water, bursting out of the drill casing. Whole rigs have sunk out of sight, in the surrounding fluidised area, as was spectacularly reported in the Gulf of Mexico decades ago. But there's never been anything on the scale we've just witnessed.

"What we're seeing is that continental plate activity – manifested in earthquakes, volcanic eruptions, landslides, tsunamis, and such – is generally up on past levels. To my mind, DeepStorm is almost certainly the cause."

"Thank you but," seeing he'd finished, my frown deepened in preparing to deliver a bombshell, "what's taken us completely by surprise, is that not all of the earthquakes being experienced are what we expect. Yes, they are all generated by colossal land deformation, subduction and abrasion within the 'lithosphere' [the Earths' solid crust and upper mantle beneath it]. And yes, that's the result of continental plates moving and colliding – which we've been closely monitoring across the globe. But not, it turns out, by the mechanism of continental drift alone. There's been no warning whatever of the severest disturbances of late, because they simply cannot be predicted. We suspect that quakes, big enough to reach the surface, are somehow being generated deeper down in the massive solid inner mantle or possibly even in Earth's inner core. In any case, we're dealing with a completely new geological phenomenon."

Those last words set the hall of dignitaries into a commotion. Saddened, I looked away from the Summit scene, to find the Commander looking relieved, undoubtedly over Jude Nade's escape.

Exhausted, dishevelled, yet composed, she was back on line and away from danger. Here words were subtitled. *"Reports have been coming in to us that at least one member state, and possibly two, have pulled their teams out of the UN aid effort here in Egypt. We have a newsflash on that. Yes, Nigeria and South Africa have both pulled out of the delta – and yes, of the whole Worldwide relief programme. As yet, we have no idea of the full implications of those actions..."*

~*~

25

November 2067

On arrival at the ManusMax Spaceport, in the Admiralty Islands, Papua New Guinea, Sashia and Mei jostled with the mêlée of guests on the tiled floor of the rather utilitarian Miandor hotel lobby. The crowd of excited fimans, with families and friends all trying to connect this way and that, had swamped the concierge and reception.

Sashia holoed Fayez in the hope of finding him, but heard that his flight had only just landed. Mei nonetheless beckoned Guille, over the heads filling the distance between them. To their relief he pressed through and lifted them onward. "At *last*! It's bloody well *over*!" Mei yelled, landing in front of an utterly bewildered receptionist. Their reflections in the mirror behind the lad, a trio of bandaged, gesticulating buffoons amidst a riotous assembly of war wounded in various states of relieved hilarity, had them in cross-legged laughter, with Sashia's crutch on the wobble worsening their condition.

Reaching her cheerful small room, furnished in Papua New Guinea style with floral duvet, drapes, and wall-mounted picture, Mei flung open interconnecting doors. Wasting no time, Sashia produced tumblers and dived into the fridge for mixes. "Time to celebrate!"

Mei quickly found whisky glasses, raising Sashia's eyebrows at this determined show of elegance. They toasted one another then, silently and slowly, looking deep into the other's eyes. But with barely a few sips taken wicked grins arrived and Mei pushed the unsuspecting Sashia onto a couch. Brandishing a pen, she attacked the virginal new leg cast, signing, *'What wriggly wormy wrecks we were, at sea in Ni'moloka'i!'* She burst out laughing then, filled with wonton school-girlish joy. "I've been dying to do that! That bloody fucking nightmare... island!"

Sashia's eyes flashed in retaliation. "Wriggly wormy wrecks? Hah! Me this!" Mei, bowled over by a cushion aimed at her head, instantly dived at the bed for missiles to hurl back. Sashia ducked. The fimans' drinks went flying as she hobbled to tackle her advancing assailant to the floor. Both down there, they realised Guille was standing in the doorway. With mischievous glances to one another they rose to expel him into the passageway under a barrage of pillows and cushions.

As they watched him their laughter trailed away. This was not their macho mate. Nonplussed, the fiman was waving sheepishly at a couple looking on down the corridor. Then he turned, very slowly, to collect up the pillows and cushions, his face very serious and unreadable.

"EEYAAH!" The burst of gusto came from nowhere. Guille slammed the pile and himself back into the room, to fight pillow-to-pillow with the girls. Moments later, pent up energies at last spent, they collapsed laughing in a big three-way hug.

Later, back in their respective rooms, Mei called out, "Hey, look at your screen! I've got appointments on mine!"

The messages were a stark reminder of their imminent departure.

RECONNEER MEDICAL: Time: 06:00 tomorrow. Venue: This room. Clinicians will dispense LN and 'LS' [Life Sign] patches to be applied to an area of skin of your choosing – for you to sign for things, like pressing your finger to a screen – and removed after 24 hours. It acts as an electronic fingerprint, taking on your DNA/ID at the molecular level. The applications will last six months.

CHECK-IN, Time: up to sixty hours from now and counting down. Venue: Your hotel foyer. Baggage allowance: 30Kg. Carefully select your clothing • more suitable clothing for space travel is available en route • what you leave behind will be stored for your return.

On hearing no reply from Sashia (in the shower) Mei flew to a case she'd had sent to the hotel to pull out and greet Twing with a mighty hug, delighted that bringing along such personal belongings was not only permitted but actually encouraged.

I called on her at that moment, glad to see her ever more relaxed. Instinctively she put Twing to one side, obviously to be formal with me. "Relax Reconneer." My holoed smile helped to put her at ease. "What do you reckon? Is this a view?"

The young scientist was clearly enthralled. "Oh, yes!" she whispered, seeing me on the Command Bridge of the Bering, with a big window onto the Moon behind me. "Stunning! Absolutely stunning!"

Not wanting to disrupt her break from trials or duty, I went straight to matters at hand, "I've been meaning to ask you about the InviHundred pictures you took, in Ni'moloka'i Park. But first, this is all about the first true birds... How many mutations did it take to arrive at the flight feather or the beak?"

"That's a trick question?" Shaking my head slowly, I watched her trying to answer. "Hmm! With random mutations, much like shot gun pellets mostly missing the mark, there'd have been a spread in variations mostly failing Natural Selection." I cocked my head to encourage more. "Well, okay, thousands? Millions?"

"And, have there been that number?"

"In the fossil record – or, in the icegems? No, no way. Just a relatively small variety of dromaeosaurids."

"So, if not random, what then? Not simply down to chance? More targeted than that?" I expected her nod and I left it at that for now. "Let's go back to your Ni'moloka'i pictures. They're stored in the mission's extensive data bank, which FayWell will help you to browse through. For the moment though, what was your impression of that environment?"

"Oh," Mei took a breath. "Well, where we started in it the forest was *Mid-Cretaceous* looking. But, as we progressed it turned out to be more *Late-Cretaceous* in appearance, which I eventually placed from the flora as more Chilean than Hawaiian. It was quite fascinating really, a strange concentration of exotic plants."

"You know, what happened there caught everyone unawares. There was no sign that the mountain was going to blow. Our instruments picked up nothing, until it was too late." I knew, I was putting nothing new to Mei. "Except you reported that the animals seemed to be spooked, before there were rumblings or geysers." Mei nodded. "Do you have any ideas about that? About why, or how, they sensed anything?"

"No, not a clue. Except, the birds seemed to be most alarmed. I suppose their agitation, also their commotion in flying off, might have unnerved the other animals?"

"Ah," I perked up, at that bit of news, "that's revealing." I watched for her to be with me on this, "The birds, huh? It's long been reported how animals flee ahead of impending catastrophes. There are records of that right through history. Not that anyone has ever come up with a specific ability of animals to do that – and I'm not sure that birds were ever singled out, especially, in that regard."

"Well, then, the birds might only have appeared to be more affected? Their commotion amplified by sheer numbers?"

"No. I think you've hit on something there. They, being dinosaurs after all, might throw some light on events back then," I ran my thoughts out to her, receiving back my reconneer's questioning looks. "You've seen in the icegems how the birds were thriving, and moving across continents to fill niches. It could just be that this sense kept them one step ahead of danger. Even navigating by it, regardless of surface conditions. If the other dinosaurs had it, and there's no telling that now," her eyes gratifyingly reflected her pleasure in our whole research, "they'd presumably have been stumped wherever their migrations were blocked by an impassable crossing.

"But my interest in that ability, if bird's have it, is to help us in detecting tremors that are too deep, below continental plates, for our instruments. All we've got to go by right now are seismic vibrations."

"What? You mean, in the mantle?"

I nodded, "Yes. We know that eruptions over hotspots, like under Ni'moloka'i, are caused by movements that far down. And we must find something to warn us of that. Anyway, something for you to think on."

"Hmm! Emperor penguins have a remarkable ability to find their way across Antarctica. Could there be a connection, possibly with them sensing tremors?"

"Ah, quite possibly. I'll anyway check with UNNDC about harnessing the gene, with a transductor, as a gravity sensor for mapping areas in low risk construction zoning." I had to smile, "You see why we'll always have to stay in touch with nature? To learn from it, as it evolves?" I waved goodbye and switched off.

Mei called home. "Hi mum? Is that you?" The holoe image was faint but she could just about make out her mother's face. "Terrible connection! How are you doing? How's So?"

"Mei! Hi, listen…"

"Is that you, So? Hi, how are you? I don't get to speak to you much!"

209

In her room Sashia fleetingly arranged her hair in a mirror, before calling ecstatically through the connecting doorway, "Fayez is here! I'm going to meet him downstairs."

The lift door opened to Fayez peering anxiously in, she standing there, scarf-less with crutch and cast, he wearing a scarf in a silly way, emulating her usual cover-up, and bearing three separate bunches of flowers. "Mine!" Sashia said, grabbing at them playfully and then grabbing him, "Mine!" and allowing him to sweep her up, his laughter now vibrating into her bare neck. Giggling joyfully, she pushed him back and jumped, sprightly as a leopard cub, to hold the lift door with one arm, and haul him in with the other. As the lift rose, seeing his reaction to her stunning scarf-less agility, she placed two fingers over his lips. "Don't ask, my love. Later... later."

Propelling Fayez to her room, she ensured the interconnecting doors were closed, also believing Mei would welcome some solitude. She would have to, anyway. Sashia wanted to be her man's lover, roused by him in every imaginable way. "Down to unfinished business," she whispered. Pheromones flew, garments flew, hungry for touch and scent.

"It's been so long," he moaned, "Slow. Let's make this last."

"Yeah? We can have slow... later."

Fayez, swimming in her embrace, melding with her body, their yearning driven and heightened by the longing of separation, was soon confused. Despite now finding themselves as one again, he felt as if in part she was also a stranger to him. It was her body – and yes, also her mind. He could not guess that she, too, was sensing changes in him. Their absorption with one another gradually dissolved such thoughts and fears. They lay side-by-side, comfortably meshed in one another's arms.

"Fayez?"

"Yeah."

"Do me a favour?"

"Sure."

"Let's take Mei and Guille out to dinner – especially Mei. We've been through so much together and this is our first crack at being civilised since I last saw you – besides, I want to show you off!" She knew from his smiling eyes that this was okay and was already donning a bathrobe and moving to knock on the connecting doors.

Mei was sitting at the holoe-optic, just as Sashia had seen her earlier, but now the girl's face was buried in her hands. She reached to gently touch her shoulder, and nodded towards the holoe by way of saying, "Who?"

"My brother, So!"

"How was it?"

"So, so!" Mei laughed, bringing on a bout of girlie giggling, another emanation of relief from tension.

"Come out to dinner? We'll make a group."

"No," Mei hid a grimace at the thought of meeting up with Fayez so soon. "You should be alone together! I'll be okay!"

"Then tomorrow?"

"I can't. So's picking me up," she saw Sashia's surprise, "I've got a pass. Something's up. My dad's had an accident!"

"That's terrible! That's it – settled. You're coming out. I'll have him to myself later … all night! I want Fayez to see I have a good friend to keep me company. I need you there for that. Put something pretty on. Who knows, but it's likely to be all work where we're headed."

"I'll call Guille?"

"Of course," Sashia turned away, smiling at her unexpectedly taking the initiative there.

In the art deco hotel brasserie the subdued lighting and delicate tones from a harp, delivered a gentle ambience. Sashia had selected a secluded table and arranged to have coms there for Guille to read subtitles of everything said, though his raised voice in conversation became a source of amusement for otherwise dour diners at tables further off.

They ignored the omnipresent Sævrama Channel, playing conspicuously in one corner of the room. Good, because I was on it, being interviewed by Jude Nade, and explaining how BoBo activity had intensified to the point of damaging communications satellites. If they'd paid attention, they'd have noticed that Guille's subtitles were a bit distorted.

In Fayez' company the reconneers had to be discrete about their exploits, which served Mei's reserve with him just fine. Although this could have been their chance, in gentle surroundings, to let go and perhaps delve into their shared deeper feelings, they soon found themselves laughing at some of their harrowing experiences – and even Bryn's expression when he slipped into that greenly unpleasant swamp.

Realising, by Fayez's bemused expression, that he was being unintentionally excluded, Sashia switched to telling Mei and Guille about the FDB bar, and asking him to update them on it. Listening to him, it was as if their weeks apart had narrowed to few, and she stiffened at the thought of again having to wrench herself from him.

For his part, Fayez was not insensitive to their abandon contrasting with the horrifying snippets they were releasing. Hurt, torture, grief were being unloaded without self-pity. There was something about them, something perhaps heroic, or something tragic, or both, that was also drawing the attention of other diners.

He held Sashia's hand firmly, trying to relay empathy with these fimans, and then he referred to Matri's speech at a UN Security Council Summit. "DeepStorm is what – catastrophic? It's going to be catastrophic?" The glum nods they gave him were quickly replaced by nonchalant shrugs. "Cities are at risk? Whole ecosystems too, like the Amazon rainforest? And, if that's lost, it can never be restored? Is that what you said in HK, Mei?"

"Sure!" Guille's voice came loud and clear, with a begrudging nod from Mei. "That's the size of it. What we'll lose in the world's rainforests will be most of the planet's biodiversity as well as an immeasurable storehouse of pharmaceutical knowledge and resources. Generations from now they'll lament only having documentaries and animated museums to remember it all by!"

"It's already a travesty," Mei inserted. "Our vast wildernesses? They only appear to be wild! And 'wild' stock? That's a joke! Anything big enough, farmers manage as livestock the same as domestic animals. And you think anything evolves *naturally* anymore? It can't, not even in the unpopulated taiga or Antarctica! Game reserves everywhere, all there for tourism, naturalists and consumption. All maintained from breeding stock. It's the same for the northern hemisphere forests and even for phytoplankton in the oceans. They're all industries now. Just lean, mean industries."

"It's Gaia under management – apart from the strategic wildernesses. Pure business, with no surplus, nothing in reserve," forester Guille freely exhibited his hatred of this, "and that makes our populations highly vulnerable, being reliant on that management."

"It's history repeating, on a massive scale. Every civilisation ancient and modern, that audaciously presumed to manage Gaia, failed into collapse," biologist Mei continued emphatically. "And DeepStorm looks set to make sure of that *or* – take us out of the equation and save Gaia."

"What Gaia gives, cannot be taken?" Sashia, the apprentice, came in. "That's what native American Indians have known and practiced for millennia, and what ancient Celtic Druids of Europe preached."

I regarded the trio with an inner glow, not only over the essence of what they had grasped but also from their synergy. Sure, they had the makings of a great team – but also one with such spirit. They were right on track, pointing to the impending collapse of cities and even states, possibly even the whole of civilisation.

The very huge poignancy of this collapse didn't escape me either. *Every creature as big or bigger than a chicken* was said to have perished in the *End-Cretaceous Mass Extinction*. "Is that the threat from our management of Gaia, now with DeepStorm?" I imagined them summing up.

The opportunity would come later, for me to go over all that. The grand vision for the Near Earth Territories was all along to preserve as much of the richness of nature, hundreds of millions of years in the making, as was possible. In short, to take across the new frontiers of space as much of Gaia as we could, in recognising that a future without it would be the bleakest and most pointless imaginable.

It was only then that Guille read in Mei's eyes another anxiety, this time over her father. But he also read there a greater composure than when he'd tended her wounds during the InviHundred. "You were really into the flora and fauna back there," he aired, aiming to lighten the subject, and reflecting that she'd been far more at one with their surroundings than any of them.

"Hmm, it's what I do. I love it." Mei found herself dwelling on the dimple sunk into his square cut chin, and the friendly ones that deepened in his cheeks when he grinned. She began to reflect on his love of forests, too. "It was beautiful – or part of it was. But, we were so preoccupied with getting through it." She surprised herself now, never thinking she could ever speak of Ni'moloka'i in this way, with anyone.

The atmosphere in the brasserie had altered and they felt it. People were looking across at the Sævrama channel and a view of the Yellow River overflowing uselessly makeshift banks. Lifeless muddied bodies, some misshapen by trauma, poured in the silted water, made crimson by the setting sun. Some, alive but held back in the flow by obstacles, were waving arms above the surface like puppets. All eyes watched the same images repeating over hundreds of ruddy kilometres, thousands of bodies flowing past. The source was a massive landslide in the Himalayas that had caused the great river to change course and flood thousands of kilometres of China's farmlands.

Jude had said DeepStorm was racking up disasters. Her reports were consistent.

Seeing the World in upheaval and despair, the gravity of their mission had again been underlined to them – and now also to Fayez. Between them all was an unspoken accord, it was in one another's eyes, in their silent forms.

Mei felt it for her family and particularly for her father, of whom she'd spoken so little on this night. "Things to be done," she thought, "Their own lives on hold."

The next morning Sashia overslept, woke feeling exhausted, and hurriedly prepared for her medical.

Eventually she opened her door to the medical team, to be greeted by a familiar face. "Tixa, you're a nurse?"

"Senior Nurse. Lucky you. How're you doing?"

"Fine. Fine."

"Good, let's see to your ankle." Tixa pulled off her striders and released the cast, guided by Sashia's hand to spare Mei's graffiti, and put that piece to one side. Then the nurse slipped Sashia's foot into a white tube, remarking, "You did incredibly well back there." The tube glowed with a white light, Tixa checking readings on her wristband. "As expected there're no breaks, just torn ligaments. The painkiller Mei administered still okay?"

"Just fine."

"Good. You know you were doubly lucky. She's highly qualified, among other things a fully qualified vet." Tixa sprayed on another cast, before checking Sashia's legs. "These okay?" the nurse

214

held her thin bones in astonishment. "This was so terribly tough on you." On receiving just a shrug, she continued with other checks.

With Sashia's medical over, the nurse went through to Mei. "I'm going to check your ears first." She probed with a pen-scope, "You're mending. Your friend Guille is okay, but he wasn't as exposed as you. *You* could have lost your hearing, permanently." She checked the scalds, happy with their appearance, and followed up with the medical before taking her leave, calling back, "Good luck, girls. Our thoughts are with you, you know."

Left to their own devices, Fayez and Sashia had no wish to leave their haven. "Hey, let's dance," Sashia invited playfully, throwing off the bedclothes.

He nodded, taking a music stick from his gold bracelet, "Try this. Something I composed, especially for you, a jazz symphony about your life – and ours. I tried for the unique essence of you, Sashia."

Slipping it into the entertainment centre she watched a diffused circle appear onscreen, but heard no sound. Sashia squinted at it uncomprehending, and then the image sharpened and she saw a full Moon framing her own face. Surrounding this, delicate shades emerged and strengthened to read 'The Girl in the Moon', and with that, a lone saxophone maintained a single far-off tone before breaking into pretty half-notes that fell on her ears like raindrops on a woodland's spring leaves. "The home you told me about, Sashia," Fayez prompted, "So it can always be with you.

"You're so, special, Sashia. Dance for me." Fayez sat enthralled as she slipped into classical movements and steps taught to her long ago when she was naturally fluid. Matching his musical strengths, she flowed into a dance of remembrance and uncertainties that she tried to make graceful. Then she had to alter pace to meet city sounds and a beat that stepped out and away. Laughing, she recognised the change as a parody of music reminiscent of the bars on Loc Hat Do. Where he'd made a living playing for crowds, rather than making this, his own kind of music. Still lightly laughing she whirled in a parody of seduction, moving about the room, then towards him, to stand hips face-level before twirling away and returning again.

"Listen, listen," he urged, "This next bit's us."

215

She held his hand amidst a tender hesitancy of tones that became an echo of playfulness from the childhood section, before slipping into a love song. And now he crooned this, along with the recorded singer –

> Sun tints her lips and sends beams through her hair,
> Sets stars in her eyes, lets the dawn kiss her skin
> Sets our lives in a spin. Makes my heart take her in....

Sashia was entranced, remembering now that difference she felt about him on their first meeting, their first night together. Now he was alone there, in HK, and in his solitude his musical talent was developing, along with his evolving artistic strengths and sensitivity.

The next evening Mei holoed Sashia. Her father had died of his injuries before she could reach his side. She'd worshipped him. She said she was managing, was in control, and was staying to help her brother So to console their mother.

The following night, their last, Mei's holoe showed visible distress. Sashia, with Fayez's blessing, tried to get a pass. Her request was denied. The mission was on a tight schedule, she was under orders and, besides, Mei was with family. Sashia took her chances and called Tixa, explaining about Mei. The medical team offered to look out for her, take her aboard with them, or otherwise some other medics would do it when ready to depart.

With nothing else she could do for Mei, and to put the doldrums behind them, Sashia made the most of her time with Fayez. After three days alone, the DO NOT DISTURB sign on the door, prompted room service to slip a note underneath. Fayez laughed relaying the message. "Room Service suggests they make our room up 'in the interest of hygiene'. Someone must have told them what a dirty little lady you are!"

Sashia threw a pillow that landed with fiman force in the centre of his chest. "Biff bang, thank you man," she retorted, tempting another pillow fight, in which he was increasingly aware of her enhanced physical strength. She won and won again despite his bulk.

Nonetheless, when their time to part came, Sashia admitted to him that she was the loser. Once more accompanying her to the gate for boarding, he held her tenderly there, and reaching fingertips to

Fayez's cheeks, Sashia took his tears and pressed them onto her lips before breaking free and walking on. At last, before rounding the security screens, she turned and gestured, as before, that she would holoe.

~*~

26

November 2067

The ManusMax Spaceport complex was operated by the 'ASC' [Australian Space Commission], under a long-term lease from Papua New Guinea. Resting at a porthole, to once again view bubble shaped vehicles rising up blue and amber laser beams, she was conscious of being joined by another passenger.

"First upside-elevator you've seen?" the voice by her was droll, while to her this whole scene smacked of déjà vu.

"What?" Turning, to the young man in jet-black-shot-with-red snaketex, her memories of him in HK and later in the InviHundred and then on holoe flashed through her mind. "Ah, Steve. Fancy seeing you here."

"We're headed up there," he pointed skyward, his Liverpool lilt also fresh in her acute memory, "ManusMax Thermoport, just…"

"One 120 kilometres above us. I know. Been somewhere like it." Eyes wide, she delighted in finishing his words. "You too?" she said, matter of fact, while begging an answer nonetheless and getting a nod, "En route to the Moon?"

"Now, yes. Before, nah," the fiman chuckled, "Before, I was just another day-tripping thrill seeker. One of the many who went to party, get married, join the thermo club!"

"Married? The thermo club? You've done those?" She eyed him a little coyly.

"No… and yes… Sure, it's magnificent! Nothing like it!"

As it happened, the two ended up on the same flight. And in their ascent after lift off, marvelling at sights with adrenaline pumping, Sashia's eyes were strangely wide. The strain of leading the Red Robin InviHundred team and then breaking through the pain barrier to endure more, were one thing. She'd got over them. But the vacuum created in leaving Fayez and even Mei – such an unexpectedly excruciating anticlimax – was more than she could bear. Now the excitement, the incredible rush of exertion she'd experienced, was flooding back. This time going up, she felt she would burst, and with the Earth falling beneath them she turned to the fiman. "Sin-bugs! This is so much more!" She paused. "By the way, I saw you before the InviHundred. A long while ago."

"Oh?" he responded, offering his hand to shake. Noticing a flame flicker in her brilliant silver-blue eyes, he found it firmly grasped – and tugged.

"Come on!" An electric charge stabbed from Sashia's eyes. The intense brinkman-like training, gambling with fate, dared her to glare challengingly into the very assertive eyes of this guy. "It'll be like diving through ice cream."

"Wha...?"

Unfastening her safety belt she climbed up and over the back of her seat, adrenaline fuelling her brain like octane. Closing up her suit she reached for a couple of chute packs, quickly clipping one on. The other she slapped into his hands, mischief in her eyes, "That's the equipment. If you've got the balls?"

He unbuckled and, climbing over, braced to force her back into her seat. He'd take control, stop her. But already covering her broad grin with a helmet, she reached for the exit door release. His eyes popped, conscious that he'd be expelled with the gust of depressurising air. With nothing else for it he stemmed his fury, closed up his suit, and donned his helmet just in time to be slammed into the freezing vacuum outside. Instantly, chute packs pressurised their suits.

Glancing back, they saw emergency systems trigger the door shut. Stunned passengers momentarily grapple with oxygen masks that dropped in front of them, which they let go of as the cabin quickly re-pressurised with hot air. She chuckled, relieved to see the utterly un-amused but unharmed expressions, while ecstatic at her impulse of skydiving from this great height.

The altimeter in his heads-up instrumentation read 33 kilometres. Rolling face down into a steep dive, arms to the side, he followed Sashia's lead Earthward. To his amazement all about was silence, no rush of air, and in the clear cloudless sky he even had no sense of speed. A few hundred-metres further down he caught up with her, levelling off before heading on down in tandem. Their pressurised suits stopped them from freezing and gave them air to breath. "You're nuts!" he railed into the helmet's coms, only to hear her laughing. To himself, he added, "A cosmic nutter. And a nymph. That's it. That's what you are. A ruddy *cosnymph*."

"Well, what would you expect? I'm Sashia Dubchek," she announced mischievously, "The white-water daredevil in the InviHundred? Remember?" It pained her even joking about it.

"Hah! Right! Maybe we could chat about that. Meaningfully! Before one or other of us plummets to our death?"

"Do we have to check our speed and angle of re-entry? To avoid burning up?"

"Huh! So much for your plan!" Such utter incompetence rattled him the more, "No. We're not speeding like rockets. More likely we'll freeze to death, if we don't get down quickly enough," in saying that, he was only getting back at her. But he had another concern. "You haven't a clue, have you, on where we'll land? If we stand any chance of being picked up? In the mountains of Papua New Guinea? Or, in the middle of the Pacific Ocean?" Their descent continued in stony silence, until he piped up, "Our trajectory will be coming up in our heads-up instrumentation. And then we'll see just how bad it is. Ah, not too bad, we're headed for the western Pacific. Just a few million square kilometres of rough seas, to find us in!"

Sashia was grinning in awe at the Earth beneath them, the blue of oceans, the green of islands, and white clouds, all brightly illuminated by the Sun's rays. And the two of them were flying over it all like shamans, surveying their worldly boundaries.

Mere minutes later the rush of air screeched at them, as they entered the troposphere. With bare minutes to spare, travelling fast, she made contact, "ManusMax Spaceport Tower, this is Sashia Dubchek and Steve Nord on approach. I can see the spaceport." Slowly banking, she veered over before diving steeply. Steve was certain she was hallucinating but had no option but to follow. She sensed that, calling to him, "Trust me." The tower was at a loss, not seeing any craft on their radar. But they matched their names, with two passengers that had gone missing from the upside-elevator. No one had had anything like this to deal with before, and no procedures for guiding the pair in.

"Sashia, take a moment to get our bearings. There's no spaceport or any other damn thing in sight!"

Conscious of his attitude before, generally ignoring everyone, she was comfortable returning the gesture now and continued unperturbed for a while longer. He swore under his breath at having to follow. They plummeted. She banked many times, correcting for wind shear. He followed her every move. A long way further down he at last saw ManusMax Spaceport. A little way further down she called it, "Okay. Let rip." They opened their chutes, making perfect landings. And were immediately greeted by waiting guards, swiftly apprehending them. "Oops," she managed, removing her helmet. His expression was a cross between a riled wolf and a bemused owl! Her antic was reckless. And yet they'd landed safely, on target. She had to help him out, pointing to her eyes, "Telescopic vision. Don't let on!" That wasn't it. She'd forced their deed on him. She knew that. "Sorry."

Standing mute in the enraged Adjutant's spacious yet functional looking office, the seriousness of their act was spelled out, "You have violated civil aviation regulations, jeopardised the lives of others, and used up valuable resources. Spaceport Authorities have contacted the police and are pressing charges for criminal negligence. Do you have anything to say?" The man looked each of them intently in the eye. This was Steve's chance to denounce responsibility for what happened, putting it all on Sashia. His selection for the mission was paramount, as his girl Carla was already up there. The miscreants exchanged glances, long seconds elapsing with nothing said, while he just threw his eyes skyward in resigned despair.

"Very well. You are here only as a formality. I have nothing to add that won't further waste my time. Good day!" The Adjutant's look was final, and dismissive. Watching the police march them away he holoed the Questor Commander, names and details in full view for him to see, saying he would send a detailed report. Meanwhile Commander Althorpe, with a predatory look in his steely eyes, contacted my office asking to access their files. I was duly notified of the request, and decided to see how this would be handled before getting involved myself. I released the files.

Moments later, in the white police van, the two accompanying officers received a call to stand to. They had to await further orders, which caused them to stop the vehicle and stare at each other as well as their charges. A short wait later, they received another call, "Blimey, seems like this is your lucky day."

"We taking the scenic tour then?" Sashia couldn't just sit there.

"Just watch it, right?"

Perplexed, the fimans nodded back agreeably while noticing that the van had taken a right angle turn. They were now heading straight for a launch dome. "We'll be sure nothing happens in this vehicle, eh?" the larger of the two escorts encouraged them aboard with his baton. And seating the pair well apart, they locked their safety belts.

"Look around. You've got all the seats to yourselves," the other police escort added dryly, "They can't risk anyone else travelling with you two, right?"

"You well connected then, or something? Celebrities perhaps?" the larger one shook his head. Then, leaning in on Sashia, he smiled slyly. "Eagle your middle name, huh? How was it anyway? Never heard of anyone doing that before."

"Nor have I!" Steve called back from the seat in front. With mellowed tone, he was reviewing the bizarre turn of events as well as how to relate to this firebug of a reconneer. Harebrained as her stunt was it seemed to have gone off perfectly, in every detail, right down to his being able to join Carla on the mission after all. To pull that off, without a hitch, was indeed a respectful caper and on the fly at that. He could hardly fault her.

"Me neither, that's why." Sashia leaned away from the man. "Just what I needed, it was fabulous! Why don't you two join us next time?" The officers laughed and took their leave, one with a mocking salute.

Soon airborne, the pair rode higher and higher. Until, back where their escapade had started, Steve looked apprehensively at Sashia. With a wicked wink, she merely motioned at their restraints and shrugged. Then, whiling the time in being pulled further up by mag-cable, Sashia had an urge to correct something with him. "You know, Mei is a good sort," she caught his blank expression, "Remember, my graduation ceremony? With you on holoe, as we reported to the Prof? Hello?" She was glad to see him pick up on that. "Well, she means well. It's just that, she's been through a hell of a lot." He just shrugged. "And remember when we met in the InviHundred? I said her hearing was impaired? And suggested you go over with her, some other time, what you said about the Armstrong Effect and geoshifts? She's highly specialised in that time on Earth, and would definitely want to hear about it."

"Sure. Why not? It's really mystifying what happened back then. Funnily, that's one area the oil companies have actually helped in. Their extensive archives, of drilling cores, have provided among the best insights into what was in those ancient seas."

Soon enough, the craft ascending through the floor of the ManusMax Thermoport and their safety belts releasing automatically, Sashia jumped out, and shrieked squeakily, "Yes! Great!" at the sheer relief of her battered body being light again.

She ran straight into the uniformed male AA greeting them. "Welcome to Ecstasy. Follow the yellow brick road to the transit hall, where a shuttle awaits you."

"Ecstasy? But that's on the Moon, where we're going," Sashia giggled, as much to get Steve out of his sour mood.

"Ah, Ecstasy. Indeed, that's really where you're headed," the attendant, obvious touches delighting him, followed up with the standard introduction, "It's an international Moon base, the grandest and first to be operative upside. Extraterrestrial Conurbation, as it was once called when names begged being made into acronyms. This one was XTC, hence the vernacular Ecstasy. Anyway you're in the Ecstasy *Service* now, not quite *in* Ecstasy you understand."

That really amused Sashia who looked at the bricks again.

"Ah yes," the attendant continued, "the road. We thought it a nice touch, suggestive of a make-believe world ahead of you. It's mainly for the benefit of day trippers." Following instructions on their coms they reached a gate in the transit hall where another male AA greeted them, "Hi. The shuttle is on schedule, departing in an hour. Other passengers will be joining. Meanwhile, please make yourselves comfortable." The pair moved lightly through a typical airline lounge, with tantalising shops they skirted around in anticipation of better ones in Ecstasy. They also paid little notice to the joyless looking crowd and instead went straight to the food hall.

Sashia excused herself to make a call, "Fayez, you there?"

"Hey Starburst. How about dropping over, check us out, up front and personal." His joviality was a thin disguise. "Know where you're heading yet?"

"Afraid not." She watched him closely. "Darling, static's terrible. Talk about us. You're very special to me, you know? Thank you for caring."

"Starburst. It should have been..." He cursed his inability to find the right words.

She became frightened. "You're talking as if we're in the past – don't do that. Wherever I'm going, we're what matters. It's hard for me too, you know. You're the best of my life, Fayez. I... I *love* you." The word was the best and the worst of it.

"When will you know how long this will take?" Fayez hedged, anxiety continuing.

Sashia cleared her throat, "They've only said it'll be a long assignment. Look, do something for me. Put me in a private part of yourself but make a door there – so we can re-open it. Yes? You have to help me out now... by letting go." She paused, her breath shallow. "You have to be without me. It's rotten. I can't explain. It's not simple."

She wanted so much to share with him the physical sensation of floating and the surprising glow she held within, and how complete she felt as a woman, despite her ordeals... and yet, as that woman, she was facing up to their physical differences in breeding, which might even prohibit them from having a child together. It wasn't just her disability that separated them. All these thoughts tore at her, yet she didn't know how to bring them up. Tears in her eyes and static in the holoe worked together to break up his face. "Can you hear me Fayez? Jumpin' Seamus! This line! Did you hear that?"

"...so, we're not talking weeks here," despite interference he saw her chin lift, "months then?" Her eyes glistened. "A year or so? Sashia, I'll wait, just so long as it's nothing else. Try to holoe as much as you can."

"I'll holoe and holoe, promise. But, it might become difficult." The static worsened. Her gut churned. "Promise me you'll fill your life, write your music. Promise me that?" The hologram distorted his bewildered expression. "Fayez?" Sashia called, "I'll tell you everything one day. Then it will all make sense. I promise..."

If she could, she'd have got to wherever they were heading right then. And dealt with the DeepStorm threat once and for all, so she could go home.

Downhearted she rejoined Steve seated at a bar, hoping he'd be over his hijack into a space-dive. But then she simply played with her food, too wound up about Fayez and despondent about the increasing distance from him. Prodding her dessert, an apple pie, she grinned at how lightly it bounced. In a fleeting thought she saw the difficulty of keeping food on forks and sipping drinks through spouts and she observed to no one, "Not Mei's style – too inelegant! Shit, it's just great though. My being so light!"

On an elevated screen the Sævrama Channel was showing animations of BoBos hitting communications satellites and explaining what was happening to them. Coverage then switched to a multi-story traffic intersection in Los Angeles, wrecked by tremors, with vehicles and passengers falling from severed sections of expressway. News segments rolled on, showing what was now shamefully becoming 'the usual harrowing scenes' all round the globe.

Another channel, another screen – a Red Cross craft had swooped to dive below tree lines out of sight. Bedraggled foot soldiers ran in disorder through undergrowth, stumbling and diving for cover. Treetops overhead, sliced by laser fire, toppled and crashed to the ground. A text stream ran, *"...Eastern Cambodia – Khmer Dragons are overrunning whole districts, press-ganging desperate refugees into their ranks."* The reporter shouted over the noise of nearby artillery, *"Government troops are under heavy fire. The order given, to pull out..."*

Sashia fumbled for words, trying to think of anything but that news. Instead she decided to clear the air with Steve. "How did you make out at the HK dolphin protest, by the way?"

Noting her moist eyes, his voice softened. In that moment, right then, reality hit them both. They'd left Earth. And this was far worse than being apart down there.

"Er, good. It was good PR – really good. We got more viewers and enquiries than at practically any other time."

"Yeah, but it wasn't wholly justified."

"Sure it was."

"It was such bullshit." Sashia checked herself, made a stop sign by holding her hands up, "Sorry, I'm sorry," before suddenly sobbing.

Steve half rose from his stool. His urge was to her, not as a prop but as a mate in fate – two new-breeds pitted against nothing they yet knew, in a totally new world. At least they shared that much. Instead, he looked at his drink, touched her arm and gave her space to compose herself.

Now she was blurting out her frustration over The Docks design. "Among the complexities, there was a pilot project – a waste disposal plant. Sceptics argued it would contaminate the area by turning out coral building blocks with traces of toxicity." Steve gave her a quizzical look. "It was rubbish." Sashia shrugged at the pun. "They're rendered safe," she laughed, "by the intense heat and pressure of the petrifying process – as Mei tells me."

He was ready to leave it at that, but she was quizzing him for his take. "Okay, about that." He was gentle. "For me, it was all about the dolphins. Just that."

Leaving it there, she grudgingly proceeded to the present. "At least it's clear cut what we'll be doing up here – and on the same side!" Sashia grinned.

"Yes, it's showing promise! Real promise!"

I knew from her notes how she still wondered about fitting in – with all those professionals. She so wanted *this* challenge, though – The Docks project having brought her a life-altering career taster. "I've got to do this. I'm *in* now, en route to join the mission. I can't blow it. The stakes, the lives of millions, make it so damned vital!"

"Okay, you guys," I cut in on their chat, with a pre-arranged party line holoe, "I know you've had little time for it, but I'm going to ask you to give me your latest results, right now. I've got other things to attend to and there's no better time."

"Where?" Sashia looked about.

"I've momentarily blacked-out all windows on one side of the port complex, so you can project scenes outside there." I sent them a plan showing the area I'd referred to and, as they walked to the place, I signalled for Mei to join in on holoe.

No sooner had Sashia called FayWell, than an apparition of the enigmatic and strong-willed Queen Elizabeth I of England floated before them in the black of space. With her distinctive crown, fine white-laced ruff and full-length red gown, she held her red head high. "FayWell?" Sashia exchanged surprised glances with Steve, before accepting that's who the apparition was. With the lightest of waves, from her regal hand, a forest scene materialised to one side of her.

Sashia took over from there. "This was in the *Mid-Cretaceous* Congo, Africa." In a wide and muddy river delta, a family of small marsupials scurried frantically from the undergrowth. After which the massive head and jaws of an allosauridae, not quite as big as the infamous tyrannosaurus – which was yet to evolve – descended to crunch the mother, while, with a foot claw, it nailed one of her young to the ground.

"That's not it. Not quite." Mei was still wary of Steve. "Look, there." Her hand pointed out large mats of vegetation choking a creek. One eyebrow raised to pointedly keep their attentions, she instructed AI Elizabeth I, "Zoom, there." Their new 'queen' refreshed the projection with another wave of her hand. "You see?" Some eggs were peeking through fronds. "And zoom there. Out at sea, on that raft. You see them?"

The raft was in a trail of vegetation flowing downstream, into the placid waters of the Atlantic. "Allosauridae hatchlings! See? They're probing through fronds for insects, lizards, caterpillars, slugs as well as dinosaur eggs."

"Wait. Go back, just there..." In all the searching for facts I wanted this replayed to dwell on the enchanting picture. In the incredible silence, small pterosaurs locked onto the slightest ripples and swooped to skim the water's surface with their long snouts. Tiny pterodactyls, of the same order, also swooped at small prey on the rafts. Larger ones swooped on hatchlings and small mammals. As quietly as I could, I expressed my own feelings... "So, so precious – seeing this from millions of years ago."

Smiling with delight – and winking at Elizabeth I for our fanciful AI to proceed – Mei presented an additional treat. "Zoom to the waterline. See, just under the surface!" Attached there, bigger than dinner plates, were the colourfully tinted shells of ammonites. Surrounding them, their squid-like tentacles were grasping at food.

The reconneer had even more. "Wait! Yes, there!" A very graceful dolphin-like snout prodded in the matting, before grabbing and prizing free a shell.

"Oh my, an ichthyosaur. That's... that's really beautiful." I was genuinely overwhelmed, reaching out as if to touch the creature, "These mats of vegetation are from flash floods?"

Mei nodded, "They were everywhere," while the clip panned to more scenes in that strange watery environment.

Also rummaging for morsels was a huge plesiosaur, which was not unlike a brachiosaur except with short tail and flippers. Further away they came upon a giant mosasaur, resembling something like a giant streamlined monitor lizard. "We've got scenes of these marine reptiles in the Indian and Southern Ocean too. It seems the mats drifted long distances, in the slow and predominantly calm ocean currents, before breaking apart.

"Also, the impression we have is that scenes like this might well have been common." Here were allosauridae hatchlings scampering up a beach in South America, their broken eggs still on the mats that had transported them there. "Even if landings like this happened only once in a decade or a century or even a thousand years. Either way it was effectively a land bridge for dinosaurs and pterosaurs, incubating in their eggs on the long journey. Mammal passengers were sure to have died of thirst."

After permitting a moment to absorb that magical atmosphere, I held up my hands, looking at them seriously. "Before we move on, we have to thrill at and indeed cherish these moments. I love it! However, a word of caution! Explore everything but try to avoid dead ends. This is wonderful research – but might it muddy the picture for UNNDC, as far as DeepStorm is concerned?"

"What? No!" Mei was horrified. "I'm sure it's relevant – somehow."

"And besides! This puts a whole new perspective on how fast or slow continental plates moved!" Steve's tone was noticeable for its switch from gruff to soft. "Rafting, on ocean currents, loosely connected the continents with species. So, for instance, India retained some connection with southern Africa, even though it was physically much further north than had been thought." He was dying for the chance to take on theories of continental drift and, so very unexpectedly, looked to Mei's qualifications for support. But he stopped there, seeing the stark truth in my eyes.

Sympathetic as I certainly was, I had to hold my ground. There was too little time. "We can't get side-tracked on geological theories." I watched Steve's disappointment mounting. "It's not what we're here for. Let's get through this." But I was thinking, "Ooh! Look how he's turning to Mei, against me on this. Good!" I let them simmer a bit. "Later, maybe, we can come back to this. For now concentrate on Natural Corrections and how the world coped, or failed to cope, with them. That's where we'll find analogies with today's events."

"And, if not?" Sashia had to ask, "If there are no more analogies, beyond what we've got so far?"

"Then, it's simple. We drop the investigations, immediately. Disband and redeploy you to something else." At that, I made to go… "For the record, you've opened up a very interesting argument for connecting the species of different continents and how that might influence thoughts on continental drift, but with little merit with regards to DeepStorm. Anyway thanks for the update. It was great." Mei was off, too.

Sashia's talks with Mei had sparked her interest in that period, spurred on by the very basic lectures she'd recently attended. Oddly, though he was infinitely more knowledgeable than herself, she appeared to be comfortable conversing on it with Steve, too. Her impression of him as super confident and cavalier, in stark contrast to Fayez's laid-back manner, had been swept aside by this empathetic stranger sitting next to her – or, perhaps her space-dive had levelled the ground for them.

Steve also appeared to feel an accord with this crazy space-diving girl. Just maybe, they could come up with something mad enough. For now, he just curved the conversation around to his pet grumble. "It wasn't my thing either, you know, coming out here. I had other stuff I was into."

"Yeah, tell me. Like trashing projects?" Sashia chided lightly.

"Hell no! Greenpeace just wanted my face there."

"Really? What then?"

"Wow! Where've you been?" He pulled his punch. "Hm. Not up with the media much, huh?" He stared at her, hoping to gain some vestige of recognition. "Oil? Stopping that whole messy business?" Gesturing to himself, he smiled encouragingly. "That's me, what I do. Or, did." Melancholia fell upon him. "All the damage that's been done to the natural world – the messed up countrysides and townships – that's what I wanted to stop, as well as all the strife and war that's been waged over it. Subverting whole cultures. Though it seems there was heaps of misinformation about the fighting for oil. Very misleading!"

"Phew, heavy. And you were winning?" He dropped his head, shaking it and shrugging. "Anyway. If I've got it right, from the media, it seems this mission might also be about that. In a BIG way safeguarding our environment." He looked up at her.

By the time they joined passengers boarding the shuttle, numbers had swelled to 50. On board, Steve eyed a sultry onscreen attendant. "Hi," the Marilyn Monroe tribute greeted, "I'm Sandy, your escort to Ecstasy." Lips pursing the AI winked... "I just love saying that."

"Coo!" remarked Sashia at his shoulder.

The cabin interior was roomy, with an appealingly large lounge that led to a well-appointed exercise area, with restrooms and sleeping cubicles quickly occupied by the other passengers. Sashia and Steve assumed they'd have been on rotation to work in Ecstasy.

"You'll notice there are only lounge and bar seats, no airline seats with safety belts. You'll also notice you're semi-weightlessness, so walking and sitting is much like in ManusMax Thermoport," Sandy pointed out. "You won't need to remain seated, as there's never any turbulence out here. There are arm restraints you can use though, to stop you drifting about and keep you on seats or bunks and such. Otherwise do move about freely, and help yourselves from the bar and canteen any time you fancy.

"We offer 3,000 entertainment channels, and at least one gives directions about what's on board to help you enjoy your flight. There's also a channel that explains what living in space is all about – for those of you who are new to the experience, including dangers to avoid, such as, prolonged exposure to weightlessness. It might seem silly, it being such fun, but long-term effects can be disastrous to your health.

"What's new are the four *swimmercisers*." She pointed to a transparent capsule. "I'll explain how to use them when you're ready. They're very popular. And it's highly recommended to exercise out here, including the next two days aboard this craft – to avoid being too legless when you get back to EarthG. Bicycles and rowing machines are also available."

Using the loo, Sashia was momentarily surprised by blasts of water and air that sloshed around, then ticklishly rinsed and dried her privates. There was much the same automation in the shower cubicle, where a mass of fine jets danced upon her skin before transforming into a stream that rippled over sinews and narrowed to jets that pounded around muscles. Then, naked in the softness of a fleecy bunk, Sashia slept dreamlessly.

On waking she sauntered to the breakfast bar, happily oblivious of the rest of the world, and just surfing through entertainment channels, and putting on earphones to hear Fayez's music. Not much later, she dozed off awhile, to wake again fully enervated and in the mood for play. On the look out for company, and finding no one up and about, she stopped at a swimmerciser, noting its size. "Hmm, big enough for two! No, not Steve! That one won't *ever* take a lead from me again! Alone again! Ho, ho, fetch the bikini."

"Hi there," Sandy's voice was soothing, "the swimmerciser is really easy – lay, breathe, start, move, stop. That's all there is to it. Basically – you get in, lying face down, head toward the control panel. Put on the mask for coms and breathing. Press the START button on the panel to close and fill with water. Press the MOVE arrows, up for faster, down for slower. And the flow," Sashia was at that point so distracted by Steve passing by, and waving in vain in his direction, that she missed the rest of the instructions, "will respond, either building or easing..."

With Steve now on the scene, others too possibly, she thought better of going in without her striders, just in her bikini. Instead she thought more elegantly for herself and had the legs join up to form a pearlised mermaid's tail. Inside alone, canopy closed and fingertip to the START button, she was soon submerged in a torrent of water that completely filled the capsule. A mild turbulence clouded her in bubbles. In this novelty Sashia was, as ever, only half listening to the guidance being given. The water soon cleared and, pressing the UP arrow, she could feel the current begin to mount. She was now swimming faster and faster, giggling inwardly, before releasing it.

"...breathe evenly, and swim as you would under water. When you're done press the STOP button. The cylinder will then empty and open the door. Otherwise, the session will stop automatically after forty-five minutes. Enjoy," Sandy, on seeing her swimming strongly, assumed this passenger had done it all before and left.

Soon bored with just swimming Sashia spied the ADVANCED button, which brought up a vividly illustrated menu of options. Surf Magic appealed. Whereupon the flow transformed into violent fluctuating turbulence, like being pounded by surf. She pressed FASTER. It became wild as Colorado white-water in a spring heat wave, except heavenly light and silky in its weightless caress – by design, with no teutronium flooring there – and sheer joy for her.

The girl was so totally absorbed she didn't feel her bikini top slip away. Steve threw himself onto a sofa, splitting his sides with laughter. For around twenty minutes, eying her trim form turning this way and that in there, he wagered to himself that the machine would time out before she'd ever tire. That's when he decided to project a baby mosasaur to slip around her tail. "Aaah!" she mouthed, spluttering and half choking! And that's when she realised her naked top.

Suddenly there was a deafeningly loud and violent *bang* and he and the other passengers were thrown off their seats. Stunned, he grasped at anything firm before twisting around to check on Sashia. She was doubled up with pain. Worried that she might be concussed by the percussion underwater, Steve pulled himself forward to reach her, fearing the craft would jolt again.

"Our apologies for that brush with a really small BoBo. All systems are okay," Sandy announced, "We're continuing on course. However, as a precaution, tomorrow we'll transfer you to another vessel being despatched from Ecstasy now." Passengers aimed for seats with restraints, alarmingly drawn to watching Sævrama's Jude Nade report on an incident in AstBelt. A large BoBo had punched a gaping hole in the hull of a freighter at anchor off an asteroid, before toppling a water tank and derailing three track mounted robotic excavators on the surface.

Another channel again featured the Los Angeles tremors, billing that as *the* major news item as more of the city's infrastructure was shaken and wrecked. The corporate headquarters of several major businesses lay in ruins, along with the homes of many rich and famous people. A throng of journalists had engulfed a mining magnate on the drive of her demolished home. Her bodyguards were cutting them short. A virtual world games star was also confronted, standing un-heroically in front of his totally trashed home. "*Hmmm,*" he said, feigning puzzlement, "*must have got up on the wrong world this morning!*"

Jude Nade grabbed most of their attention again – this time with a newsflash on some unaccountable disruptions to shuttle services, "*...so far three craft have been attacked. No one knows where these things have come from but they're adding to the chaos already being caused to communications by BoBos. There's no telling what they'll hit, presumably whatever they come across upside – satellites, craft, anything. Thankfully, no one's been hurt yet...*"

"There, we have a close up. My God! I can't believe this. It's a bat, with what seems to be solar wings!" The creature was life-like except very small, its body about the size of a golf ball. *"It's swooping at the hull of that craft! We can see the dents these things are making. One at least has even breached the outer skin. Huh, this one's got a beak. And, YUK! As it's pecking at the craft, what looks like golden threads are slithering off its back and tongue to go in there!"*

Steve saw the doubled up Sashia straighten, hold her head, and slowly reach for the STOP button. The canopy opened and the dazed girl clambered out gingerly and seeing him became vexed. "Trying to get even! Huh? That *thing* was one thing! But, playing with the flight controls!"

"Hardly!" he said firmly. "You okay?" Her nodded response was reassurance enough. Now he chuckled cheerfully and handed her a towel. "Put this on – you lost something."

"Hmm!" She grinned as she spoke, "So I saw!" and had her striders split again, for her to appear stepping down in smart jet-black boots.

"No complaints mind." He cut himself off by sombrely indicated there was a bat on the Sævrama channel. Sashia's jaw dropped in disbelief.

The rest of the journey was spoiled by that encounter with a BoBo, as well as the strange bat like thing. The two subjects dominated conversations, especially as the bats were purposely out to attack craft. Yet strangely there'd been no announcement, from any group claiming responsibility.

Sashia spent much of the time watching Jude Nade, on the Sævrama Channel, and with time to kill she lapsed into commiserating with her. The household figure, liked for her weather delivery as well as her charitable work, put things across in a personal caring way. Sadly, though, her brilliant industrialist husband had developed a strange neural condition some years back, before there were upside travel restrictions for humans, which had made him irascibly prone to outbursts. So many undiagnosed ailments had come out of those early excursions in space. He'd even been caught on camera two years back, leaving a ceremony in their vehicle, when he punched her with his stocky hand. Bruises to her cheek barely disguisable, in subsequent appearances. After that, simply accepting the emptiness of growing apart and not bringing herself to break up the family with two grown-up daughters, she'd taken heart in brightening people's days with good news about the weather. She'd buried her mind in that new career, in recent years giving out such good news it had become her hallmark. Though sadly, it was not what everyone was hearing from her of late.

Sashia was musing over that, when Steve wandered over with a coffee. "Deep in thought?" He knew, full well, she'd be concerned about the worsening situation. "We've done okay. Or rather you girls have, in uncovering stuff. Pity we haven't seen an actual extinction event, an eruption or whatever taking place, as the Prof wants. As if! Fat chance of catching that, in just these few stones! Right?"

"Yeah, well. We did catch allosauridae, rafted between continents. I thought that was neat."

"Sure, especially, and Mei would love this," he'd been thinking fervently on the matter, with some remorse about Mei fighting with him, "if those hatchlings re-established a line of allosauridae that had gone extinct in South America! Imagine! Extinction effectively defeated! Natural Selection defeated!"

"Yes, held in stasis!" I had to come in there, it was perfect timing. "Excuse my butting in. But that sounds as remarkably robust as the fused Jurassic continents, of Gondwanaland, only long after they'd broken up! How could it all have come to an end?"

"Er, you did say…" Sashia feigned flinching.

"Not to get side tracked!" I had no problem retracting what I'd said about rafting, now it had Steve better disposed to work with Mei, "I know! Well, okay, it seems I'll have to concede. The implications are incredible of *Chronic Natural Correction* having taken place, with extinctions ongoing for millions of years. Except we didn't see it, because rafting was repopulating everywhere!"

"Exactly! We've seen, in the stones, a lot of change creeping in. Some abrupt Natural Corrections too," Steve mulled things over, aloud, "and I suspect geoshifts were a major part of that." I imagined his growing rapport with Sashia had a lot to do with his softening attitude. "But, we're a long way off seeing the whole picture."

234

"Sure! FayWell, mark all this data to pass on to UNNDC." This was progress. But I suspected, it was just a hint of what DeepStorm had in store for us. We had to redouble our efforts. "What do you need?"

"More icegems," Sashia's response was immediate, "to cover more areas, and much more time."

"Okay," I left the room and reappeared bearing a wooden box, which I placed on a table, "These are all I've got. I've no idea when they'll cover. Or if they'll even help." I lifted the lid for them to see. The box was choc-a-block full of gems. "They'll be waiting for you, when you get to Ecstasy."

After transferring to the second vessel their Moon approach was perfect, with the entire orb on show. Sashia was relieved. She was also delighted to make out the beard, or comet-like tail, she'd seen growing on the Moon when a very small child. It had first appeared when the base was being established, just before she was born.

She now observed the wisp of mist close to, thrilling at it trailing off in the opposite direction to the Sun, and she followed the flow back to a crater overlooked by the Peak of Eternal Sunlight. There she zoomed in to see a very large 'lake' of ice, which she actually knew had been mined and put there as a protective shield against the hundreds of tiny bolides that used to bombard the surface daily. Now DeepStorm had significantly raised those stakes, especially the stakes of large BoBos testing the shield.

On their final approach, directly beneath the lowering craft, Sashia saw a slab of ice lift like a trap door. In the ensuing slow descent through the opening, they soon left direct sunlight behind.

Through their wide screen view she tried to estimate the length of the smooth-walled shaft, counting to some 15 metres before variations in lighting illuminated sights yet to be aired on Earth.

"Goodah. Oh Goodah," she whooped at Steve, seated beside her. He didn't listen. His black-shot-with-red-snaketex clad back was rigid, his expression frozen in wonder.

~*~

27

November 2067

Descent through the dome's gleaming blue-white ice roof opened up vistas that bore no resemblance to the Moon's crusty airless wasteland. Nor was Ecstasy like any city on Earth. As far as their eyes could see, architectural structures with their foundations in the dome itself, lowered with the fluidity and clarity of streaming crystal to some twenty-storeys down.

The city was like a cave of gigantic icicles, but the whole in no way a monotone. The colours of crowds and vehicles shifting within the vast rippled walls ensured the vista changed, like patterns in a remarkable kaleidoscope, a stunning effect that was constantly charged by over 75,000 inhabitants.

Within the top of a huge impressive glass icicle, disembarking travellers were ushered with their luggage onto gleaming translucent escalators that trailed down like so many sleek creepers. They descended through crystal floors alive with people and greenhouse plants bathed in diffused bright sunlight, and exited the city onto steppes resplendent with rambling parklands, lakes, paths and bridges to dwellings that spread out in all directions beneath the icicles.

At their hotel, Sashia and Steve simply dumped their bags in their rooms, all too eager to explore and meet with others. Directions took them through hanging gardens, rockeries and waterfalls, and past two full-length fairways that shape-shifted for golfers to play a variety of championship courses.

Further on they marvelled at watercourses that condition-shifted for sailing, canoeing, white-water rafting and even the gentler sport of fishing. And then came play areas that shape-shifted to accommodate squash, tennis, badminton, basketball, gymnastics and bowling. Under a canopy of gently rustling leaves, simulating fresh weather, Sashia caught at Steve's arm to point out riders trotting along on horseback. "Where are we, exactly?" she asked a passing stranger.

"The Park, in SnowVale," came the spirited reply of a man happily jogging on. To their relief people's spirits looked generally higher here, away from the woes on Earth.

Approaching another steppe, Steve surveyed bars and restaurants surrounding an ice rink at the base of a snow slope where skiers slalomed. In anticipation of meeting up with other reconneers, his gruffer manner crept back. "See any people dressed like me down there, Sashia?"

"Yes, funny you should say that," in their increased familiarity his change of tone could no longer faze her, "they look like rock-punk gipsies, all in black 'n red snaketex."

"See a girl, the same, hair shot with tortoise-shell highlights?"

"Yes."

"Great!" Steve's manner was hot custard and ice cream, tough-friendly again, as when they'd first met. "Let's go!"

At the café the girl swept towards him. Heading for a separate table, Sashia watched their embrace and then saw her thrust into his arms an ice-board, its blade glinting meanly. They looked well-suited, with the same easy throw-away style. "The latest!" The girl exclaimed, her accent definitely up-town girl. That and her shining grooming as well as the smart biker attire gave her a striking appearance. Steve was clearly delighted. The rest of the snaketex crowd gathered round, urging the pair to take to steep dunes carved in ice near the café.

"Carla Drew," with a flick of his wrist, he introduced each girl to the other, "Sashia Dubchek. Watch her, Sashia. Championship stuff!"

Picking up speed, blades rasping harshly on the ice, they shot up opposing slopes to resoundingly slam down past each other. Again, and again, they shot up and slammed down, laughing ecstatically to spur one another on, while swishing by just fingertips apart. Gaining momentum they rose higher and higher, until flying silently in the air they seemed to hang there, and then roll in slow motion, head over heels yet somehow managing to maintain eye contact at each roll. Movements over the ice were light, half their Earth weight, though a good bit heavier above Ecstasy's thick teutronium foundations than outside on the Moon's surface.

Finally, racing around the ice dunes, they sped faster and higher until they linked arms to twice twirl head over heels around each other in mid-air – a precision movement perfected in championships, now doubly spectacular in this setting. To the raucous applause of the snaketexs they sped, arms linked, and dropped to the ice, gaining a tear in Steve's legging and a graze on Carla's elbow, before bursting out laughing and laughing ecstatically for the sheer joy and exuberance of their sport – as well as being high on EcstasyG.

Among onlookers Captain Maurice Lane, Executive Officer of Lascaux, was sitting some way away alone. Among the sportspeople his black beard, fine wool white polo neck sweater and tailored trousers stood out. A swarthy, attractive Acadian, from West Point, he was passing the day taking in the scene – with long-legged Carla a light entertainment.

Flinging her arms around Steve's neck for an embrace, the black 'n red couple then headed back to the café, where Sashia, was preoccupied holoing. She barely acknowledged them, "...she's in a terrible state Fayez, naturally. Mei's tough though, she'll get through. In the InviHundred, hell-bytes! Well, she saved my life and she covered it up well when we met but she was very hurt and scalded."

Fayez could only know the half of what she was talking about but he sensed another change in her since their hotel meeting. "So, where have you got to Starburst?" he enquired lamely.

"Oh! Catch you later. I've got an incoming from Mei."

"Okay, bye," Fayez was determined to sign off first, before seeing her disappear on him.

"Bye my love, talk to you later," she offered softly, but quickly switched to Mei. "Hi! How's it going? How're you doing?"

"Oh, God, all the questions, endless questions! It's terrible. The police have gone, for now! It seems the other driver might be prosecuted for reckless driving. My mum's not okay but there's not a lot I can do. Not with having to leave so soon."

"Does she have anyone else there... your brother?" Sashia was concerned for her friend but also thinking of herself – feeling out of her element and vulnerable again and soon to be in the thick of academia and wishing her biologist mentor was there, too. That space jump of hers had probably been a desperate expression of what she now feared.

"Sure, So is here, so are an uncle and two aunts. They're very good. I know they'll look after her. I should be here though!" She paused to pick words from the muddle in her head, "Everything okay up there?"

"Yeah, you'll like it." Sashia yearned to share the thrill of the place but could not in her friend's period of grief. "He's here, in from London,," she pointed to Steve, "Well, erm, we shared the shuttle up. Insane! Have to tell you about it!"

"Yeah, sure," Mei's frown said it all about the prospect of being in his gruff company and, perhaps, there was a hint of jealousy, too, "Got to go... My mum's looking my way, needs my attention. I'll call later, okay?"

"Okay, later." Sashia was sad, in knowing Mei's eagerness to shoot up here – to be with her and our little group, but not others.

Knowing he was close enough to hear, Sashia slid nearer to coyly enquire of Steve. "Didn't we?"

"What?"

"Share the shuttle up."

"This is the nutter," he responded, smiling and murmuring to Carla. Clearly he had told her about the trip up. Carla nodded, full lips betraying a guarded smile.

"Hi, nice to meet you." Sashia was extra polite, anxious to squash any flippancy but also hugely impressed by this pair's exceptional skill and kindred daring. She glanced around the group. "Who's everybody? All shipmates?"

"Nah, the black 'n reds are friends, up from London for a few days. Seeing us off?" They all nodded back to Steve. "Except Carla, who's coming," he drew the girl into his side, lithe snake-like bodies intimate enough to flow in unison, "Aren't you sugar?"

Impressed anew at black 'n reds going to the expense of getting to the Moon just to see friends off, Sashia ordered a round of cocktails, choosing colours to suit. "Black 'n reds for the black 'n reds?" They nodded enthusiastically, while Carla signalled for a table to transmaterialise. She had already acquainted herself with this facility in Ecstasy, making tables dissolve and reappear as directed. Softening to the newcomer, she also helped Sashia scroll options in the carbonised surface and to sign for her order by pressing down with her LS.

"You're not originally from London, are you?" Sashia was sure of that but couldn't quite figure the accent.

"Pure New Englander – of Mayflower stock," Steve answered for his girl, who tended to deliberate before any conversation.

Ahead of the drinks, a tall distinguished-looking man approached Steve and Sashia. Though not now uniformed, nevertheless his authority was evident without an introduction. His voice sounded stern. "Reconneers, I'm Commander Connell Althorpe, and we're about to have the pleasure of each other's company, for some months to come. Would you join me, over there?" He pointed to a table nearby, but well out of earshot.

Face to face with the task force chief both reconneers shot up, "Sir!" to follow him. While Steve, sure of a reprimand, surprised himself in winking reassuringly at Sashia. This was where the geologist, in absolving her of her hare-brained space diving stunt, expected it to backfire on him. He prepared for them to get trounced.

"You caused me considerable difficulty, with people down there!" The Commander chewed out in his reference to authorities in Canberra, Australia, determined that their bracing for a lashing would make a mark on them.

Satisfied that they were sufficiently chastised, his next reference was obscurely aimed at their outstanding training records, "You had a point to make, with all the weird stuff that's been thrust on you. Maybe you reached bursting point – or some such thing." His look, particularly at Sashia, gave no opening for an answer. "It's done. That's that." Immediate affirmations, not excuses, were expected. When they nodded, the Commander cleared his throat, "Excellent! Not another word. Not from you, or anyone. Agreed?"

"Sir!" they snapped in unison, eager to comply. The Commander's raised eyebrow prompted a more positive response, "Yes, Sir!" they barked in earnest.

Steve, accustomed to tough talk from the oil industry, glanced with surprise at Sashia's more natural composure. "This girl's got nerves beyond belief," he noted just for himself.

"Good." His quizzical look almost seemed to invite something...

"More daring?" the thought flashed in and out of Sashia's head.

"Let's get on. As reconneers you're ready to stand by each other – and all other reconneers. Your pledge. That's the department of Professor Mark Madison, UNNDC Chief Scientist leading the mission. I expect rather more from you two, for your daring," he studied them both again, holding their attention and stopping short of telling them to act with restraint and sobriety, "and you, Sashia, for your keen eyesight, which I'll doubtless call on. Naturally I'll clear all of this with the Professor. Think you can handle that?"

"Sir!" they snapped out, but immediately added, "Yes, Sir!" Neither sure of her ground, nor the implications, Sashia nevertheless offered, "We appreciate your confidence in us. We won't let you down, Sir." Steve nodded sagely.

"Well, I assure you," he was stern again, watching them flinch in anticipation of some kind of whipping, "as fimans I expect nothing less of you. Just know that the confidence might come from me, but the responsibility you have will be to everyone else who *sails* with you." He paused, "Don't let them down!"

The Commander was interrupted by the sight of Jude Nade on a screen at the café entrance. She was presenting a Sævrama Channel report from Canada, where long lines of vehicles were making their way down remote valley roads. Royal Canadian Airforce planes were flying in relief supplies, landing or making parachute drops for the climate refugees. Scenes from the Andes came, all looking similar, but the subtitles indicated that the refugees' plight was worsening, with harassment on the increase, *"Relief operations, along treacherous highland roads, are hampered by renegade militia making off with sorely needed supplies. The same has been happening in Cambodia, where unrest has already fermented insurrection..."*

The Commander resumed, "DeepStorm has caught the World unawares, causing havoc with climates and terrains. If we don't do something, sharpish, our whole damn civilisation is going to come crashing down." He looked gravely at his new aides. "That's our mission – to find answers. We just might have to cut corners."

The pair collected their thoughts and, aware that all had been said, Sashia chipped in with a concern close to her heart, "Sir, we've been hearing about BoBos messing with communications – holoes, entertainment programmes and such." Her holoes with Fayez had been poor of late. "Will we be cut off?"

The Commander deliberated a little, "Well, possibly. Not that you should think that's the worst of your worries, because I assure you it's not. But, yes, BoStorms have intensified. Even though communications use miniaturised 'ice-cube' satellites, robustly built and clustered for redundancy, they are being knocked about.

"The smart cubes proliferate, in response to any being disabled, and cluster tightly or loosely in sync with ISWA reports on Cosmic Weather. But, as the situation worsens we're likely to lose that battle. So, yes, communications will deteriorate, hampering relief work even more."

He studied the backs of his hands. "As we move away from Earth, communications will in any case be frustrated by lengthy response times. At some point we'll be cut off, making it hard for our mission. Which is why it has to be manned. Also, it will make it impossible to keep in touch with those we've left behind, with their perils. Bear that in mind, with the others. It'll put everyone on edge."

The café scene froze, as a Sævrama newsbreak caught everyone's attention. In the States tens of thousands were seen fighting traffic jams in a city's outskirts, frantic to escape violent explosions in downtown districts. *This is horrific. A volcano is erupting out of nowhere, opening completely new vents in downtown Seattle, killing and injuring thousands.*"

A woman ran forward, grabbing up her small boy and nearly knocking the reporter over. People were running atop of cars, jumping from one to the next. Among them a pretty girl lost her footing and was trampled on the street where she fell. Suddenly a dense black pyroclastic cloud, a fiery flow of volcanic ash and gas, belched forward to incinerate and smother crowds. Racing on it headed straight for the reporter, whose voice rose. The cam shook. *"God! The people! Hundreds of thousands of people! The carnage of other eruptions round the globe, will be made the more poignant by the enormity of this tragedy..."* The screen went blank.

When the station came back on line, it broke a silence that no one would ever forget. Tears blurred eyes. There were no words. The Commander rose and simply stood there for a moment, looking around the café, grave and cold as a churchyard. Then, speaking up for all to hear, his voice gravelly, he expressed dark thoughts that would remain with him for a lifetime, "That thing out there, that DeepStorm menace, whatever, wherever, we'll find it. We'll find some way to thwart it. That, is *my* solemn pledge." He paused, as if to will his thoughts into Sashia and Steve's heads, before leaving as quietly and as unceremoniously as he had arrived.

The café crowd took a while to stir – and that's when Tixa shifted into their sphere, a mite too upbeat for everyone's mood. "Crumbs! You guys struck it big! That was the Commander, yes?" She laid a hand on Sashia's shoulder while looking at Steve, her smile sweetly encouraging them to share their news. "What did he want?" Her enthusiasm quickly evaporated seeing Steve and Sashia, fearful of the Commander's wrath, shaking their heads. What just went down was not open to discussion.

The drinks having arrived, they all raised their glasses in a glum toast, Steve saluting Tixa to show there was no bad feeling and Sashia saluting Carla to express that Steve's 'nutter' friend was harmless. Tixa's eyes flashed appreciatively, while Carla, hell-bent on DeepStorm not getting to them, murmured, "We must," as she swung around smiling determinedly and longingly at Steve, "ice-board some more! Fun, fun, fun, before we set sail!"

"You betcha." Still steely grim, Steve hugged her and they made to leave. "First, let's change our gear!" He winked cheekily. "Back in a bit you guys." Their friends forced away solemn grins and winked back knowingly.

The Commander was in time to meet and greet me, in a hanger-sized cargo bay reserved solely for shuttles serving the DeepStorm task force. I'd stayed on the Bering to check out progress with the ships, and had just arrived in Ecstasy. "Soon time, for your mission," he remarked candidly. The air about us was heavy with the whirring of robotic cranes, hoists and tractors, assisting in the inspection of crates and containers prior to transhipment to the vessels. He turned to face me, his executive tone resolute. "It's your mission. I'm the escort. I'll do everything in my power to see that you accomplish what you must do."

Everything was different now, the urgency more intense, since Seattle. I said and did nothing, but regarded him openly. That was enough, for him to shift on to other matters. "That reference Jude Nade made to Nigeria and South Africa. Intelligence sources have it that there's a connection with movements in Iran and Pakistan." He watched me, checking that I was getting the picture, "And DelMonte believes that somewhere, in all of that, there's a threat to our mission. Contrea and Hadder appear to be implicated. There's a lot more to that, lots more than DelMonte or Morse can make out right now.

"There's something else. Jude is worried that Morse might be headed for danger." None of this was welcome news, as we prepared to launch out into space. "He's scheduled a trip into Myanmar next week, after receiving intelligence tip-offs that insurrection is brewing there. He's trying to head it off, with peace talks. Failing which, he's ready to send a British led military mission of the EU and Australasia, to support government forces in the area.

"DelMonte says US forces are over committed across all fronts and can't back Morse up. China and India are similarly hard pressed. That's how bad things are." Althorpe's steely eyes betrayed his anger.

"So, that's why the military style training. We could have company," I stated this, rather than posing it as a question.

"Yes."

"Even for my reconneers," I reflected on the Special Forces exercises they'd been through.

"We mustn't be stopped." He observed me guardedly. "Most particularly, your reconneers mustn't."

I knew as much but shuddered nonetheless, lamenting that when it came to it they'd have to fight to the last. Best to switch to matters at hand. "It's a mess down on Earth." In stark contrast, spread out before us was SnowVale Park, tranquil and pretty under sunlight from the dome. "And this is galactically frustrating! BoStorms raging outside and we're in 'Ecstasy'! Literally! The safest damned place in the entire Solar System," my teeth clenched, "when we should be out there, getting on with this war!" I didn't look, didn't need to, to know his fists would be as tight as my own. "Is there anything else, that I should know?"

He shook his head, but then came an afterthought, "Just one thing... your plan of action." He was peering at me a little apprehensively. "For your research. It's not my business, but," he got straight to the point, "DelMonte said not to investigate the *Cretaceous* catastrophe. I overheard, in the Machu Picchu lobby." My hackles were bristling. "You going to leave it there?"

His jaw thrust forward as if in challenge for a fight. The whole subject was a political powder keg at UNNDC – and he was, after all, military. He had nothing whatever to do with the mission objectives, beyond seeing that we'd get wherever we were headed. I had to tread warily and stall, "Time! It's all about time to *prepare*," and gauge bringing him into my confidence, "...and the time to *go back to...*" His negative expression told me time was *against us*.

Enough, I reckoned, he was surely ready for my trust. "We have to get some history, of other times like this. If we're to have any chance of beating this phenomenon."

"I gathered."

"The dinosaurs, suffered an incredibly prolonged trauma while massively dying out. Whatever that was, it's certainly *not* dismissible as some chance accident never to happen again any time soon! More likely it's something we *must* learn about this planet, before it surfaces again. *And* why that's our task, is that I think *it's back* – with DeepStorm!"

His gravitas was worthy of an admiral facing a seemingly insurmountable battle scenario. "Your stance, firm then?"

"To go back in time. Yes, emphatically."

He watched me slew round and weigh up what his reaction would be. "Remember your English Admiral Horatio Nelson? Telescope to his blind eye, as he declared, 'I see no signal'?" He deliberately defied orders to discontinue the Napoleonic wars action at the Battle of Copenhagen, and went on to win." Certainly that victory was a highlight in British naval history – or all naval history. "Those reconneers, Sashia Dubchek and Steve Nord. They're defiant like that. Jumped out of an upside-elevator, from space. Had to haul their asses from a criminal negligence charge." He ended there, palms upturned and shrugging. It was up to me, after all, what I assigned my reconneers to do.

In that moment I felt a surge of strength in the knowledge that I was not wholly alone at board level. I couldn't thank him, overtly, for support not actually given but implied. I simply smiled courteously. "I'd better get going." I went to leave but then sensed we'd not 'done' on a personal level. "I think I'll join the others, get out of my skin for a bit. I believe they've gone to Exmorfs. You going?"

"Uh, no. Thanks. I have to confer with my executive officers on the route plan we'll log shortly with ISWA. First stop Mars, right?" I was nodding needlessly. Ultimately it would rest on him to take control in times of difficulty, summoning up the objectivity and authority to carry that through. For those reasons I supposed he had no wish to mingle socially and yet, for all his gruff military style, I also detected his desire to empathise with others. "You go ahead and mingle," he resumed a more relaxed tone. "Besides, there's a reporter I need to check in with." And there, I suppose was the nub of it – like most of us leaving Earth life was a wrench, in his case due to a woman he'd only recently met – and now could never be with. Most of us souls were so alone on that Questor mission.

Exmorfs – SnowVale's hive of bars, bistros and discos – attracted Questor officers, reconneers and ratings alike. Most young fimans contorted their light EcstasyG bodies there – as only they could, to the pounding life-size holoes of chart-topping groups and their seductive bioluminescent dancers. Lithe bodies seethed in tune with each wearer's passion, in the shimmering colours and patterns of organic sprayovers. A fusion of music, chat and laughter reverberated right through the maze of dimly lit chambers, corridors and cosy niches. The drink flowed and nowhere in those warrens of outrageous frivolity was anything said about missions or catastrophes or even missed hearts.

This place was away from the real world, where among the highlights was admiring one another's smart but inexpensively bought costume adornments. A 3-D snake tattoo, with flicking tongue, slithered into view at Carla's bare midriff. A gold and silver worm wriggled in a continuous loop through each of Tixa's earlobes. Tiny diamond-decked spiders crawled slowly about Sashia's hair. Miniscule icicles glistened from Steve's eyebrows.

FayWell was her usual straw blond self, wearing a metallic navy tube dress, though she remained discretely out of view. She had front row positions everywhere, much of the time seeing Carla comfortably wedged between Sashia and Steve, the three hollering to be heard, while Tixa, hovering nearby, hung on every word.

Meanwhile, Captain Lane seemed pleasantly surprised to catch glimpses of Carla, in a bar mirror through the crowd, nonchalantly touching her hair and peeking at him. Yet each time he tried to acknowledge her with a confident reassuring smile, she averted her eyes.

Much of the time Steve's remarkable body, even among the general perfection of fimans, performed exquisitely around the dance floors with Carla. He also drew out there Sashia, who in one dance shouted above the crowd about something that enthralled her, "Once there was beauty," she mused, looking up to the ceiling, on which she had projected a scene in calm water. An ichthyosaur was picking ammonites from under a raft. I saw, and immediately went to stop her, but saw that the crowd was too busy having fun to notice. Anyway, I was sure she wouldn't keep it there too long.

"Ah, yes, beau'ful – as you!" Steve wasn't really in the mood, but she pushed his elbow to deliver. "Hm, hungry for it?" He was enjoying the tease, smiling playfully as she delivered a dig to his ribs. "But then," he projected the image in place of hers – a scene of a choppy sea with broken up vegetation and no life attached to any raft at all. "All gone! The whole tranquil food chain – algae, rafting eggs, ammonites along with plesiosaurs, ichthyosaurs, mosasaurs and even ocean-going pterosaurs – all gone!"

"*Yeah! But*," she projected a raft with a nest on it, "See? Abelisaur eggs, in the Southern Ocean! Nasty, vicious carnivores, a little smaller than allosauridae, which – along with many other carnivorous theropods of that era – Mei reckons could have been related. And this," next there was a raft with hatchlings on it, "is a clutch of titanosaurs in the Indian Ocean, not dissimilar to brachiosaurs, which along with other sauropods they could have been related."

Her expression urged him on. "Patience. Well all right, maybe. If we had time, and more icegems, we could even establish 'raftways' that existed then. But, never mind that. Rafting was now finished!" He wagged a finger at her. "Approaching the *Close* of the *Late-Cretaceous*, that whole ocean environment was done and dusted. White caps in the Atlantic and," he broke into song, "nothing lives here anymore," and stopped, "Not on the surface, anymore."

"Vanishing land bridges between continents! What then?"

Steve whirled her around, enjoying the strange lightness of their bodies in their new atmosphere – gymnastics no problem on the Moon. Sashia laughed, moved close in front and, with a little jump, hands on his shoulders, rose until her hips came level with his eyes.

Then deftly she turned herself around him and landed up close at his back.

Pretty mouth in a feigned pout, she frowned. "Uh, yeah. We haven't got there yet, with the stones, right? Or, is this a trick question?" Steve was none too focused, in answering. She tilted her head. "What a right muck fuddle. Hmm, anyway, what next? No more interference with extinctions, I'd say. Not from rafting. Only teeny weeny lizards and airborne spiders maybe, not much more, got around from shore to shore."

"And this?" She referred to an aerial view of the Transantarctic Hills. "White caps up there! And winter ice along the coast."

Still clinging to him, her pretty jaw firm in challenge, he rose to it again. "Deflecting sunrays and desiccating the air. Wind chill, phew!" Steve repeated his song, "Nothing lives here anymore!" and peering through half closed eyelids, he grinned tauntingly, "Well almost."

"And, bigger hills in the Andes and Himalayas too."

"Yeah, yeah! Bigger weather all over and rougher seas."

"… and you said they were connected, the land and the sea?"

"Strange that, huh? More active seas, quieter continental plate movements – and vice versa. As if buffeting seas acted as a stress reliever for the continents."

"Strange too how such wisdom can sometimes come at times of letting lose," I thought, while enjoying how carefree this light spirit looked – free at last from physical pain. She rose and slipped down to land at his side.

Tixa swung by, observing the pair – and spotting Carla also close by flicked her head towards them to pull in her attention. Carla's immediate reaction, the more mature one, resenting the insinuation, was to shrug and dance away.

Tixa was unrelenting. Later finding Carla in the rest room, she wrinkled her nose mischievously. "Wow, she's *so* cool. Those leg thingies don't hold *her* back, do they? I suppose *here* they're hardly any impediment at all! Great dancer! So sexy!" Carla delivered only a cold look and walked out, set only on having fun and dancing. Aggravated by the continuingly obvious approval of Captain Lane, she drew him to the floor, prepared to douse his hot intentions. Nearing Steve and Sashia, she skilfully switched partners.

Into my third *Striker*, I was also unwinding. The cocktail was a vodka shot spiced with a branded stimulant. With my eye-patch of silver gauze and a parrot hologram nibbling at my ear – which called out *Nieces and Mates* to any who would speak to me – even I was dressed for fun. I was hungry and needed to feed on all that energy, to forget the bad Earth images and grief for just a few hours, as much for myself as for everyone who was looking to me as a role model. I couldn't be viewed as morose or let their courage down. So I drank a cocktail or two with them and occasionally allowed myself to be dragged to the dance floor by a few luscious young fimans.

After a while Tixa came to join me, undoubtedly disgruntled that Carla would not participate in her silly game. It was only then that I noticed she was high on drink or stimulant or both. Shortly after, she excused herself. "Enough! This place is *no fun*! Piss on them all!" She smiled a little inanely and peered at me, perhaps to remember who I was. "I see you tomorrow?"

"Me too," I reckoned, having made an appearance, I'd done my stint.

On our stroll home the girl attempted some sophistication, perhaps gaining an inkling of my role as a scientist. "Everything is coming together okay?" In truth, she was barely conscious of what she was saying or even that I might know who she was. "We will be going soon, yes?"

"Some of the finest and best medical facilities the World has to offer are being fitted out right now for our safety." Suspecting the girl to be not capable of more and might have meant well, I spoke kindly but firmly. "Hundreds of thousands of souls on Earth are screaming out for what will soon be in your hands."

She stopped short, "Oh, sorry," and only spoke again when we reached her door, which she unlocked and left ajar after walking in. "Would you like, a nightcap?"

"Thanks, but no." I was deliberately courteous. "Busy day ahead for me." Moving on I heard the automated door close and a light crash when hopefully she must have landed on the bed.

~*~

28

November 2067

A couple of days later Steve caught sight of Sashia and Mei at the ice rink. Sashia had met Mei on arrival, heard her news and of her uneventful trip up, and was recounting her own exploits, at that moment about being outrageous with Steve. The girls were laughing, their joy in reunion obvious, though also sombre over the loss of Mei's dad. Sashia chose not to tackle her directly on that. Instead, she touched the Buddha pendant hanging from her friend's necklace. "Love this."

"Yeah, saw it in a shop window and couldn't resist buying it." Mei's response was understandably joyless, regardless that she loved shopping. Naturally I felt for her and wanted to holoe in, but decided to catch them later. "I'll show you," Mei continued, "They have some incredible space gems."

Just when Steve was about to interrupt, Carla approached with their friends. "Our guys are bailing out. Going downside... back to Earth."

"Hey! All set?" He linked arms with two of them. "It was great you guys came to see us off. But, why not stay a little longer, 'till we leave?"

"Nah. This part of SnowVale is cordoned off, the cargo bay, too, just for you guys. We've been told to leave, so we might as well go back down now. Not that it's a bundle of joy down there. You know," the guy looked meaningfully at Steve, "You're in quarantine man!"

"One last drink then." Arm around Carla, Steve led them to the café. "But you did enjoy your week here?" With heavy hearts they bantered about meeting up again – when this was all over – and getting on with their lives as before. Sashia and Mei watched on, their own hearts heavy, but they too waved when the friends finally departed for the shuttle bay.

Sashia then received a holoe from Fayez. Though downbeat, about events down there, he was elated that his New York agent was 'over the moon' about 'The Girl in the Moon' symphony. He had to go there, contracts pending, a high note at last. In return, Sashia related some of her scene there, particularly with the task force Commander, and how that experience had made her feel like a professional. Sharing those successes, they were at once reassuring and loving with one another.

The following day – with all visitors and Ecstasy crowds gone – Questor fimans barely filled the bars and cafés at Exmorfs. They hung around, a little at a loss for what to do, the void amplifying how everyone felt inside. It took another couple of days for the atmosphere to pick up, slowly, as a steady stream of fimans arrived from all walks-of-life around the World. However, much of their talk was of the increase in nasty events down there and how distressing it was for those they'd left behind. Some admitted their relief at getting away. A call for a briefing, doubtless the prelude to going into action, must have made the blood flow discernably through their veins.

Sensing their hopes, the Commander seized his moment. "Ladies and gentlemen, humans and fimans, officers and reconneers," He pitched his voice for the clarity and depth of a bass church bell, "welcome, here in Ecstasy, to DeepStorm Questor.

"I am Commander Connell Althorpe. I have full charge of the mission's safety – your safety." In this kind of action, the crusty dog's eyes, now filled with energetic sparkle, told every headstrong postgraduate in the hall that he could be as mean as the next guy and fairer than all. "Where that's concerned, the buck stops with me. My task – to get you to where you'll kick some ass! Achieve your objectives," he scanned their faces, seeking gravity, "according to what will be set out by UNNDC Chief Scientist Professor Mark Madison – your boss." With a nod in my direction, he drew all attention to me.

Although impressed by his alpha wolf persona, I rather aimed to gather minds and hearts to me as a more accessible leader and sage. "You'll see three ships, on the screens." I felt I could breath again, finally back in my element. Free of delivering bitter pills of doom and destruction to politicians, I was beginning the organisation of meaningful scientific research. "They were to have been the start of the Near Earth Territories. The US navy Bering was to be the first Factory and Supply Ship, FASS1. Instead the vessel has been converted as our battle-carrier escort. Avebury and Lascaux were to be for timeshare owners and their tenants. Instead they will be our homes for the mission.

"Major refitting work for the ships is nearing completion. But, we're not waiting for that. We'll board just as soon as the exterior ice shields are in place and inside areas are liveable enough for us. It'll be rough, cramped and noisy while construction crews carry on with internal fitting works. But this," clips of the interior designs appeared on screens, "is how you'll be living when the fitters, all human, eventually disembark."

My words and the images were met with palpable amazement. It was the old level of resort-like comfort, only seen in movies, which knocked them out. Coming from crowded Earth, where 'home' was in such places as the public Lifestyle centres, they'd never experienced having a room let alone of any nice size or even permanency.

"The plan is to get underway by New Year's Day. We'll transfer to the ships in just a couple of weeks from now. By which time you'll all be up to speed with your tasks. After that, we'll have another two weeks aboard to get the ships fully operational.

"Okay, so why the rush? Where are we headed? And why all the superhuman training you've received? What's this all about? There's a single answer – DeepStorm. It's out there, threatening our World from deep space. That's where we're going. That's where we'll discover what's really going on. We must do this before it's too late for everyone downside.

"Once aboard the ships our AI, FayWell, will serve you in whatever way you need – to operate the vessels, carry out your scientific work and even to help with your personal wants and wellbeing. You'll find it strange at first because, in her role as a personal AI to all, and being the very intuitive, friendly and discrete AI she is – not to be confused with a physical AA – her holoe will appear 'virtually' everywhere. Remember she's there to serve you, as well as to protect this task force's objectives and wellness. So make full use of that, chat with her – and not just for work.

"Material from her super extensive library can come to you as a holoe or, if you want, direct to the biombot with which you're already equipped. They're switching on now. FayWell can elucidate further but, for now it's a nanobot video-cellphone, implanted directly to your cranial and optic nerves. You'll be impressed with the quality, far surpassing virtual reality. Now, we'll take a short break."

"Mine's active!" Mei perked up about that, explaining, "That's how they adjusted my coms, so that I can speak without blowing everyone's eardrums off."

After the break the Commander was again upbeat but stern. "We're now officially on the DeepStorm Questor mission. Everything divulged to you is classified. This includes what you've heard here today. Nothing can be repeated to anyone outside. From this point on, your external calls, all routed via FayWell, are being scanned and filtered for anything about the mission. She'll not repeat to me anything that's personal to you, but she will let me know of such indiscretions. So, be wise and very careful with what you say to family and friends.

"Thank you for your attention. And again, welcome and bon voyage to you all."

As everyone was leaving the hall, the Commander nodded at Sashia and Steve in a way that demanded they remain there. The pair instantly obeyed, already briefed on that first day in Ecstasy that he had them in his control. I also took his cue to remain there and watched him leave us.

Once alone, it was I who had words for this pair, "What the hell were you two playing at the other day in Exmorfs?" I was angry, though I'd enjoyed their 'show' and enthusiasm. Receiving and expecting, no answer I dived right in. "Your 'show' was notable – but, thank God no one else actually noticed it. Anyway, enough said. We've worked together, and made good progress with the icegems." It was certainly gratifying to see them cheer up at that mention. "You'll recall swearing not to divulge anything about them to others. I am, of course, holding you to that." I saw apprehension rise. "Well, here at Questor it's officially classified." They each returned worried looks. "Hence the ticking off I've just given you. What you did must never happen again. Agreed?" They were quick to reassure me of this, nodding several times.

"More than this, however, our work is unauthorised. This means you are not to continue with it!" They looked shaken to the core and even pitiful.

"You've got guts, I hear," I carried on, taking a bare second to digest their response. "What would you say, to shortening this war with nature?"

"The war on disaster?" Steve sounded hesitant, quandary fusing with his crushed state.

"On DeepStorm?" Sashia was as hesitantly anxious but more specific.

"Hmm," I tightened my lips stubbornly, "By *carrying on* with your work," whilst this blatant contradiction stunning them, "with a catch!" would tell what guts they truly had. It was gratifying to see them hold still, cheek muscles tight over gritted teeth. I had to chance it, declare my intentions openly as well as the dangers to them. "You'd risk prosecution for disobeying UNNDC orders – if you do carry on." They were with me, with poker faces. A blink, a sideways glance, betrayed the nervousness we shared that FayWell would be overhearing. I had to manage that, with the Commander too. I signalled for their responses with my hands.

There was an awkward silence. Steve would not be drawn to answer off the cuff.

"We have a choice?" Sashia stalled over what to say or think.

"You can walk away and have nothing more to do with this particular research," that was really hard to say, "but you know the stakes. Your last findings show that the planet can, and most likely will, be gripped by Chronic Natural Correction. This research is our only real chance of anticipating that…"

"I'm in," Sashia's face was graver than at any other time, but she didn't wait to hear more.

"Me too." Steve's response, almost impulsively reflecting Sashia's, was equally grave but positive.

"Okay, yes, you've got guts. Good, then you're my secret *Cretaceous Group*, the C-Group, along with Doctor Mei Sai Ling. I trust you're both fine with that? As senior biologist in the Questor task force, in charge of both of its parks, she is preparing to landscape areas for further in-depth study there – all of which will be invaluable for our work."

"Absolutely," said the certain Sashia. "I'll vouch for her." Steve only shrugged, but that was okay in terms of his mellowed attitude towards the biologist.

"I'll get with her, and go through this." The short nod I exchanged with the two was by way of a parting salute – and yes, a confirmed mark of respect.

Even though in the privacy of his own space, the Commander looked gruff. He was holoing the site office in Lascaux. "This is the Commander of DeepStorm Questor," he bellowed impatiently, "Who's the shift supervisor?"

A young man's voice nervously responded, "I am, Sir!"

"What's the status?"

"We're completing ice shields on the Bering. In another 10 days there'll just be internal work."

"And the liners?"

"Yes, the same there, too."

He cut the man off and called the construction company's office in Ecstasy. "Ecstasy anchorage, operations? This is the Commander of DeepStorm Questor. I want the shift manager."

"Certainly, Sir. He's just here."

"Brady here. Good day Commander. How can I help?"

"Your construction crews – could they relocate on board for the internal work, after ice shield tests are successfully completed, of course?"

"Live aboard? Sure. That's the idea once the protection of ice shields is in place, to cut down their exposure in shuttling back and forth."

"Good. And they could come with us? Any problem with that?"

"Ah," the man hesitated, "No, I guess not – if you're aiming to get away before they're finished. Depending on when they last had a spell of Earth weight. Of course, they'll get that on board, but it's regulations. They have to go downside at the end of each tour here. Management is strict on that, to comply with insurance policies."

"Okay. Check on that, will you? I'll get back to you."

The Commander then holoed me as I emerged from the hall. "What's to stop the launch date being brought forward?"

"Why? What's up?"

There was a moment's silence, in which I half regretted asking. He was brusque, addressing me with eyes undeniably afire. "It's time. Time to get out there, and kick ass!" He was chomping to take full Command.

255

"The moment we have the all clear on ice shield tests, it's planned for us to get farm staff aboard. We'll get some livestock loaded too," I thought aloud, as much as answering. "We've already started laying turf in the liners, but we have to get enough landscaping and planting done to get atmospheres breathable for everyone. HVAC units, operating in living areas, are a temporary measure with nothing like the capacity needed for large numbers. I'll have to check with Dr Mei Sai Ling, our Parks Manager."

I'd erred on the side of caution and now, sharing his urgency, spoke more reassuringly. "Anyhow, much of the terra-farming is scheduled for when we're underway, stocking the farms with upside breeds while we're in Mars anchorage. All considered, with no glitches, I'd say we could get underway a week early."

He made another call, this time to Sashia. "We're getting things moving. On my Command Bridge 07:00 hours. Steve, too."

"Sir, 07:00!"

Sashia went straight to Steve, sitting, at the café, manner languid and detached. She smiled nonetheless. "It's crunch time."

Something in her body language conveyed they were on orders to go somewhere. "Yeah?" He didn't ask where, sure she'd fill him in on the way, and he had no doubt that this reconneer was ready and able to take off – anywhere.

"Uhuh." She braced for him to be impressed. "We're summoned, to the Command Bridge of the battle-carrier." This would be their first ever visit to a ship in space – and this was the biggest of them all. "A shuttle's booked for us, leaving 05:00."

Sashia was ecstatic about the C-Group, feeling at last part of a team again and dying to tell Mei. However, she had to hold back, to let me inform her first. "Hi, want to show me where you got your Buddha pendant?" She had suggested they trot along to the shops, hoping to bring some cheer to Mei in her grief.

"Sure," Mei gave a pretence of enthusiasm.

They walked in silence, until Sashia began with, "It's surprisingly nice up here – don't you think?" Mei's shrug only relayed that there was a weight of other things on her mind. "Not the same as being at home of course." This wasn't productive either, getting no response.

"Hey, don't tell. But I'm falling about without my *Mr Right* – Fayez." Again her friend looked clean out of responses or humour.

As their day progressed, Sashia tried to just be there for her friend, though feeling there had to be something more she could do. It was just then that straw blond FayWell appeared, wearing a canary-yellow skirt and top, rippling over and through the plant-decked walls. "Nice people on the mission's medical staff are there for anything to do with wellbeing, and not just health. From what I've picked up, maybe you could do with chatting with Doctor O'Malley?"

"Who's that?" they both asked.

"She's the Senior Doctor for the mission, in charge of all health facilities – but she's also a very proficient counsellor."

Mei buckled, as if hurt as a wounded animal on the run. Sashia, on the other hand, leant towards the AI without hesitation and followed up with Mei. "I'll go with you?" Mei then quietly acquiesced and the pair set off in search of the doctor, with directions sent to their biombots by FayWell.

At the hospital the girls were 'blown away' not by Dr O'Malley's modest reception area, with its cream leather seating and light oak desk, but by the strangely stunning woman who darted out directly at Mei. Bald, frail looking, fair skinned, her pale green eyes rested gently on Mei's and then, in her crackling crisp white tunic she rapidly ushered the girl to a comfortable deep orange leather recliner in her consulting room. There she revealed dark shiny pinheads accentuating her spine, all the way down her bare neck to the base of her back. "Lie back, relax Mei," her voice was soothing and unmistakably an Irish brogue. Switching her attention, she ushered Sashia out. "You'll be her friend Sashia. She's in good hands now. Thanks for bringing her by." Sashia felt a little miffed, but was also grateful for the chance to holoe Fayez.

Mei, entranced by her host settling next to her, noticed how even her fair lips and eyelids were accentuated by having no eyebrows and not a scrap of makeup to hide or highlight anything. She looked so incredibly delicate that Mei imagined her needing help more than herself.

"So, it's not your health that's brought you here." The doctor wasn't asking. "You've had check-ups, which were fine."

"Sure, we all had medicals before arriving. I've got InviHundred injuries I'm recovering from. Fatigue too I guess. But otherwise I'm all right, physically. I'm just..."

"Quite. Not okay in yourself."

Mei stared aimlessly, "It's hard, so hard..." Tears swelled up.

O'Malley's tone softened, "What is?" Thin lips – a sign of deep passions in a woman – smiled as warmly as they were able. "Take it easy. You're not being charged for my time, so take as long as you want."

"Oh, I don't know – leaving I guess. Things are not good at home. My mum needs me. My brother So needs me. It couldn't be a worse time for me to be leaving, to be so far away."

Kaitlyn O'Malley gently stroked Mei's hair, and then pressed fingers into and around her shoulder blades. "Sure. Your mother and brother need you. And you imagine your friend Jacques needing you too, even though he left you. Your TuTu." The once popular endearment of couples TT, for True Troth, had somehow been twisted using the intimate French refrain *Tu* for *You* to become TuTu. Mei warmed to the massage. "Times like that are precious. Maybe you're right." Mei slipped into a sea of calm, feeling no compunction to speak. It was as if thoughts would find their own way. "Memories are tricksters, not always what they seem. The lives we know, and lose, are not always ours to save."

After the session Mei ambled back to her room in a comfortable daze, but soon imagined Sashia's words to Fayez. Their mission would not take months – but years, her friend would be saying. He must find a life without her after all. Mei's sadness returned, this time for Sashia.

When ready the C-Group invited me to join them by the watercourse in SnowVale Park. I took this opportunity to introduce Guille as a new group member. Once assembled, with little need for introductions, Sashia shifted into gear. "FayWell, project the latest Antarctica scene, please." Instantly, a mermaid with long flowing hair rippled the water as she swam into view. Swished at the surface, she presented an aerial view of the continent upon it.

"Mgoi, FayWell," Sashia thanked her in Cantonese, before getting a nod from Mei to introduce what they'd come up with. "We're at the *Close* of the *Late-Cretaceous* – actually the last million years or so. These images are of a largish herd braving shallow crossings to summer in Antarctica. It's a mix of antarctopeltae, medium-sized ankylosaurs," which, as big as a modern African elephant, were armoured herbivores with a huge club tail, "and massive titanosaurs." Sashia paused to watch the beasts hesitantly slip into the waters, their calls plaintive. "The waters of Drake Passage from Patagonia, as with the Tasman Sea from Australasia, were now treacherously deeper. See?" Fins cutting the choppy surface darted as victims, swept out further by fierce undertows, bucked helplessly. "That one," she waved for a close-up of a shark rocketing after a tarpon like fish, "is as long as the xiphactinus it's chasing, as well as the adult antarctopeltae – four or five metres!

"Added to this stress," the hunters breached and thrashed about their prey, whipping up the surface even more, "the season was off kilter! Listen to that howling wind – imagine the chill from it, brrr, with that pack ice!"

"They're magnificent, aren't they, those titanosaurs? And so *big*!" Mei was now beaming. "Though not as bulky, but as long as a blue whale, our biggest creature ever. Imagine that hulk on dry land – I mean the whale has buoyancy in water." To my relief she appeared to be too excited to be ill at ease with Steve, though perhaps also due to the return of Guille to be among them.

"Of course!" Steve dwelt on what Sashia had just said about the wind chill there, to apply his geological thinking to what the group had already learnt. "How weird is that? Warm fronts from a fresh Deccan eruption, steepened thermal gradients all over Africa and South America... which stirred up strong winds... and swept cold fronts over the very waters that were beginning to cut off Antarctica, the freezing Southern Ocean."

"Look!" As the killing scene unfolded, Mei continued to analyse and see so much more. "Those dinosaurs seem to be traumatised," she pointed to variously stressed individuals... I wonder, maybe, if the cold had combined with their migratory instincts, to press on, to disorientate them. They certainly look stuck out there! Wow! All that barking and yelping..."

"Not only did it stop lots of them getting across," Sashia moved the show to the far shore, "there were hardly any rafts beached over there now. And, anyway, it was also bleaker. Ice caps on the Transantarctic Hills were bigger."

259

"Nothing lives here anymore," Steve sang, contentedly enough, "Not much without feathers, anyway."

"Yeah, vast as that continent was, whatever was there or came there," though relaxing now, Mei was still avoiding eye contact with Steve, "was soon going to be there for good, summer and winter."

"Yow!" Steve shrugged at Mei's nuisance foibles, but he was impressed… very impressed. "What we've got here, in what we just watched with Antarctica being cut off, was just the biggest loss of territory – *half* of the great land mass of Antarctralasia through South America. That's on top of seeing in the previous session just about *everywhere* else sub-Tethys – clear across India, Africa and South America – radically transformed. "

It was a short session. But then, it served to get them more settled as a team – and to get Guille up to speed with how we worked. "Well, good." I really meant that. "You've now added to Climate Creep, another Natural Correction in the 'Southern-Ocean-Deccan-eruptions. Together, they amounted to hugely important catalysts for the Natural Selection of birds, over pterosaurs and non-avian dinosaurs. Well done."

~*~

Enlightenment

29

November 2067

Sashia and Steve were punctual the next morning, meeting at 04:30 at the cargo bay – and in time to see Mei already at work. Her friend, scanner in hand, was making box panels turn transparent to inspect the new shoots and saplings within. Judging by her cheery mood her night's sleep had been good. Except, when approaching Sashia, something seemed to be troubling her. "Did you mention anything to the doctor about Jacques?"

"Oh, I can't remember. I wouldn't think so. No. I only chatted briefly with her, on the way over. You heard. Why?"

"It was so strange, her referring to him – and as my TuTu." Mei realised that Sashia was missing something. "We only ever called each other that on our own, privately. No one knows about it." Mei looked confused. "And, she seemed to know I'd lost lives – more than one life. I'd not mentioned anything about that either."

"Well, I guess she'd have seen in your file about your dad and Bryn."

Accepting this possibility, yet knowing the mention of them had regurgitated images of Rad and Bryn, tearing at Mei's emotions, she felt as raw as when on the InviHundred. It was thoughts of her father and his words that saved the day, "Duty before self, always," she murmured, giving Sashia a backward glance. "I'm okay. Go. I've got more than I can handle right now – having to get this lot out there in a hurry," she looked at all the boxes, "and build up atmospheres for everyone so quickly." She waved at Sashia. "Go on. Go."

Mei also determined to connect with Carla Drew, her Chief Terra Engineer, to hear how irrigation equipment was coming along in Avebury and Lascaux parks. Her attention then switched to a heavily set but quietly spoken young zoologist now working closely with her. He was tending dairy cows. "Hi, Deymore. How're they? Producing okay?"

"Yeah, itching for cool hands! Nah, but really – a mild tranquiliser had them oblivious of a couple of small BoBos on the trip up. Never even saw the fun!" He led her further on, to where more boxes were stacked. "These chickens are popping out eggs again. Thankfully, we didn't have to tranquilise that lot!" he chuckled.

Mei was about to leave when she sensed someone watching her and turned to see a fair-haired guy leaning against boxes. She hadn't missed his attempt to hide his interest when seeing her look in his direction and approach. "Hi, do I know you?"

"Not exactly," the lad's composure melted, "I was so clumsy – nearly knocked you over – at the InviHundred gorge." Doubtless he wished she'd not remember the incident.

"Yeah? Really?" Her look was sympathetic, then she chuckled. "Oh, yeah, the gorge! Like I'm going to forget that. Sashia thought I needed rescuing from you."

"Yeah, my lot too. Sorry," he forced a smile, not knowing how she was taking him, "I didn't mean anything."

"I know," she smiled warmly, "Anyway, I'm Mei Sai Ling."

"Right, yes, I know," he pointed to his chest, "Torf Vland, trainee terra engineer. Carla Drew, my manager, asked me to check on installations. It seems," he made to excuse himself and catch the shuttle Sashia and Steve were boarding, "there's a rush to finish things."

"Ah," Mei was silently welcoming Torf and Deymore, two more colleagues whom she did not feel ruffled by. "Great, would you let me know too? I was going to ask that."

Aboard the shuttle, construction workers in bright leathery armour, sporting various company house colours, floated semi-weightless about Sashia and Steve, helping themselves to snacks and drinks.

The pair settled to watch in wonder as the dullness of the Moon turned silvery, and then it shrank behind them and three gleaming white cylinders with the surface texture of glaciers grew massively before them. Their first real sight of the task force ships was this magnificent spectacle of the gigantic cylinders, totally devoid of ports or windows or any other blemish, with mist trailing off for half their lengths. They just hung there, in space.

On approach, a *'Take your seats'* sign appeared and onscreen flight attendants checked that everyone did as told.

Steve and Sashia watched as the shuttle banked and rolled slowly in line with a green tracker beam while, dead ahead, a huge shutter flicked, open and shut, and suddenly they were in a vast hanger-like area, almost as big as that on Ecstasy, in the outer rim of one of the ships. The tiny shuttle settled on the floor and quite soon a flight attendant invited everyone to disembark.

The reconneers were so in awe at the scene outside that it was only as their legs buckled under them as they rose to leave their seats that they grimaced over the return of their Earth weight. Their fellow passengers, accustomed to shuffling a little awkwardly there, simply got on with it.

Alighting, they continued to negotiate their way clumsily, watching the construction workers disperse in all directions, before taking in even more disarray than in the Ecstasy cargo bay – scrap piled next to the arms of robotic fabrication benches, vehicles manoeuvring between boxes, tentacles writhing in all directions, slings and hoists gyrating all about.

Spotting a strange figure beckoning them through the chaos, Steve tugged at Sashia's sleeve to follow. They both soon twigged that the lusciously clad Barbarella, was in fact FayWell, there to lead them expertly through a mezzanine area and now calling out proudly, "Step right up! See the majestic Bering! Welcome, by the way." The pair exchanged amused looks as the fanciful AI's gold and silver image flowed through the lush plants that shaped the living walls.

Minutes later they were on the Command Bridge, stepping into an area that stopped them in their tracks. Wide, roomy, pristine, and with controls and displays appearing on demand, the Bridge had a massive window and there, framed full width and height, was the most compelling sight. The Questor liners Avebury and Lascaux were offset majestically against the Moon. Steve paid homage for them both, "Exquisite. So beautifully exquisite."

"It's a virtual window of course, not real, with the view constantly corrected for the ship's rotation, which would be too giddying! It's the only one of its size in the task force." The Commander was somewhere behind them and hardly veiling his pride in the ship, "Of course there's no question of even this window's view being as vivid as with your biombots, but so much more appealing to share. Aesthetically good, don't you think?" He knew he was right. Virtual windows were extremely desirable features in all the latest ships, as well as being therapeutically indispensable for the long haul with Questor.

They turned to greet him, just as something caught their eyes and apparently hit the window, though the impact made no sound. "Small BoBos. They can't hurt the window of course, it not being real." He was, at that moment, weighing up these slight fimans, who though not tough looking could take him apart piece by piece.

"So, Sir. It's got to have some awesome firepower." Steve now locking fingers to crack his knuckles, had wondered about warships in space. "This ship, I mean."

The Commander, fondling a small crucifix at the end of the fine necklace he wore about his neck, fixed on the reconneer's eyes. "With all the death and destruction going on down on Earth, you really have the appetite for this? You really want to see?" He dwelt on his own words. "Well of course you do. We have to be ready to defend ourselves. That's what much of your training has been about." His attention turned to the window. "FayWell, BoBos nine o'clock off bow."

The Barbarella-like babe, now affecting a stiff officer stance, reappeared on a living wall nearby. During a brief wait, when one by one several inset panels appeared along the bottom of the window, each with a BoBo in the centre, the Commander half turned to the reconneers. "Something about my having said 'nine o'clock off bow' – for onboard directions we use bow, amidships, stern and points of an analogue clock. FayWell makes corrections for our constant rotation. We're like hamsters in a treadmill, walking on the outer wall of the ship. Outside is under our feet. Our heads are pointing to the ship's centre. That rotation produces the gravity effect." The chief was clearly enjoying having the reconneers there to extol the ship's design.

"It all seems fairly nautical," Steve observed. "In fact, since we got here, everything seems to be that way."

"Yes, pretty much. It's a vast ocean out here, with navigation markers, anchorages and such. There are also attributes of an aircraft carrier, with fighters manned by flyers. However, mostly everything else has characteristics similar to vessels at sea, like it takes this ship 10 kilometres to come to a stop from full speed. The liners take much longer. Also there are ISWA rules of navigation, such as a ship on sunward tack has right of way.

"And just about nothing out here is particularly lightweight – doesn't need to be. As such, they'd fall and crash like BoBos in

Earth's atmosphere. Earth-atmosphere craft are for that, such as the upside-elevators you came up by. It's analogous to ships plying the seas, which never dive down like submarines.

"Anyway," he looked back to the window, calling out orders, "Select target. Zoom to half frame." One of the BoBos now half filled the inset panel. To one side were some details, including position and range, 0.03 mAU [milli-AU]. "Lock on. Are you watching? Fire." There was a faint flash, no sound, and the rock disappeared. "There, it's swatted. Vaporised!" His audience looked on, a little under-whelmed. "Oh, I know, no ringing in your ears. There wouldn't be, not in the vacuum of space. No searing laser bolt, either. The BoCracker's laser is safely concentrated at the tip of the conical beam you saw."

He moved around a navigation console. "Another thing, Commanders don't get to fire weapons. So I never fired that!" He winked at them, again fondling his crucifix. Steve and Sashia shared another thing – they just didn't know how to take this man.

"Okay," he gestured to the two liners. "Those are my charges. You'll be in the one on the left, Avebury." (I had already decided to keep the C-Group together there.)

He noticed how they slumped over the consoles. "You see, how bad it'll be when that Gwave crest reaches Earth?" He motioned to their wilting postures. "Gravity. You'll absolutely appreciate it out here. And how very sensitive living things are to it." The pair could certainly understand that, Sashia especially. "Prof Madison has got his task cut out trying to beat that thing. He can do with a couple that are screwball enough to maybe come up with some pretty off the wall answers."

He was now focusing intently on them, especially Sashia. Suddenly he let up. "So. I thought I'd give you two a chance to look around, before the hordes arrive. Go on over. Have a look at Avebury. Lascaux is identical."

The pair looked out at the ships. Construction craft of all shapes and sizes were milling around, swinging in and out of the pipe-like voids. With a flick of the Commander's head Barbarella set off, checking to see that the reconneers were following. Going via a storeroom, she invited each to take helmets with small rebreathers. Originally for scuba diving they had been greatly miniaturised. "You'll need these to breath in the void of Avebury, until the park there is operational and pressurised with fresh air. Just check they work okay." She paused to see them take hold. "The tank is light enough to sling over your back. That's it. You can talk normally, using your biombots. Okay, now put these on." The AI pointed to a rack of bulky silver-yellow spacesuits. "They're worn over clothing and will pressurise when you start out."

At the cargo bay she ushered them to a man standing by two open-top pods. "Jo will take over from here. Enjoy the trip."

Jo cut short anything that needed to be said. "You ridden one of these?" They shook their heads. "Maybe jet-skis?" Their eyes widened, causing him apprehension – but then, he shrugged, these weren't his machines. "Okay, but these 'Shwifts' are only the hottest racers out here – with the nitro propulsion and *all* they pack a hellish wallop." *All* referred to there being nothing to naturally slow them down in space. "Anyway, the throttle and such are the same. Reverse thrust comes from the same power unit!"

Jo read their expressions. These two were rearing to get out there. "Oh, what the heck," he muttered solely for himself, "these fimans, so full of gas, just have to light their farts and they're off. Phew, not half faceable though," he added, eyeing her figure. "What I could do with that tonight – out of my depth, but yippeee." He tapped the handlebars. "Plug in your suits for air, or you'll pass out quicker than shitting a chilli éclair with all the fun you'll be having. The rebreathers are for when you arrive." He pressed a switch with his foot. Plates swung up behind the Shwifts. Jo then looked over to where Barbarella had been, and was again.

Sashia paused for a moment, speaking quietly so as not to be overheard, "You know something that's struck me about FayWell? She never looks straight at us. I haven't seen her eyes, not once. Ever!"

Back on the Bridge, Barbarella was also addressing the Commander, "You sure about this? BoCrackers are trained around construction areas. These two will be out on their own and it's all new ground for them." She received a slow nod as he continued to watch Sashia and Steve on screen.

At the bay, Barbarella gave them a green light. "Okay. All Clear. There are no BoBos around, so go now. I've set the timer for twenty minutes, to give you just a bit of slack. It'll take you just ten to reach Avebury. Take any much longer than twenty-five and I'll commandeer your controls. You've got that much of a window. BoBos are a problem at the best of times out here. Now with DeepStorm it's worsened."

They jumped on, snapping their suits into the console before strapping in and firing up. Slender flames jutted out at the back. Through the film-thin transparent helmets they exchanged looks like kids with a wisp of a halo about to enjoy their first ice creams. Then, simultaneously throttling up, with a jolt that jerked their heads back they roared through the bay shutter laughing impulsively, Steve swinging out in a broad arc. "Hell! I've *got* to get one of these!"

Sashia looped over and back round before heading for Avebury, he right there with her. "You betcha!" The pair buzzed construction workers harnessed to the outside of the rotating hull, and went full length along the sunny outside of the ship before swinging out and around the far end.

Steve, reckoning she was about to trump him once more as she arced toward the end shutter, knew that wasn't going to happen, not a second time. Full throttle, he lunged ahead. So did she. Hurtling forward, their heads soon at the shutter, Sashia was ahead when she made a last minute loop and slipped onto his tail. Whooshing through to the inner void his helmet banged against the smart neoprene blades, momentarily disorientating him.

He glimpsed her broad grin as she slipped through suffering no knock at all. He wagged a finger at her, immediately having to weave and duck to narrowly avoid girders and stairways as he slipped between floors. They swung about sharply to dodge mulch disgorging from hoses, huge buckets and bundles of pipes swinging from cranes, wiring being pulled every which way, and masses of robots and workers zipping about their tasks. Ever so strangely, the only acoustic accompaniment in the whole airless spectacle, came from their voices.

Barbarella, taking in the chaotic spectacle, looked to the Commander on the Bridge for orders to shut them down. She caught his eye but received no word from him. He just grinned and shook his head, calmly watching the wild pair. Their reactions were split-second, firm, decisive and perfectly in sync with the ship's movement. Running full length through the tangled building site, dodging, weaving and laughing at one another, just big kids having a ball.

As they shot out from the far end, they again passed through a shutter, this time bending their heads low and letting their Shwifts take the blow. Just then, their timers signalled. They had to land. They were too locked in to care enough – they had to do just one more circuit. Half way through this, their controls went dead and their Shwifts headed straight for the shutter. Somehow, they passed through, landed and shut down.

Dismounting, catching his breath, Steve gave Sashia an accusing stare. Also breathless, she gave the same cocky shrug that had become his trademark. That got him. Shaking his head good-naturedly he conceded she had pulled off yet another good stunt at the first shutter. "Got to hand it to her," he mumbled, "This one has a real knack of getting the better of me. Or, rather, on the better side of me." Carla and mates excepted, most people wouldn't even guess he had one. And there they were, the two reconneers, unable to contain their elated laughter again.

The Commander on his Bridge also wore a broad grin, shaking his head at their having turned out as he'd expected. He admired their youth, healthy spunk, and Sashia's now unbridled spirit.

Just then Barbarella appeared on a thin metre high post, saying nothing about taking over their controls and demonstrating no reaction to their antics. "These posts are all along the walkways, at viewing stations throughout Forbes Park here. You can catch me just about anywhere."

"Anywhere? Actually FayWell, aren't you everywhere?" Sashia wondered at the AI's apparent omnipresence, "I mean, *literally* everywhere? In living walls, in plants in the park here…"

"Yes." As an AI would be, she saw no need for explanation and was not apologetic. "I'll be anywhere needed, in buildings and parks – as you say, anywhere there are plants."

"So, can I ask you to leave?"

"Uh, no. I can run and I can hide. But I can never actually leave."

"I bet you can see in the dark too."

"Yes, sure."

"Okay," Sashia liked her straight talk, "even when I'm on the loo?"

"Uh, yes. But your private suite is private. You can tell me to stay out."

270

"Oh good! In that case please, never ever come into my bathroom."

"Okay, noted."

"So, what's the deal with this thing?" Steve pointed to the shutter.

"Ah. The aperture is timed and sized to let very little air out when Avebury is fully operational and pressurised. The jet of expelling air would be strong then, except a percussion effect of the shutter will dampen that."

"Hm, I certainly got a bang!"

"It's still being calibrated, needs some further adjustment."

"And what triggers it so precisely, for those coming in?"

"Your LNs. Without them you'd have been zapped by the BoCrackers."

Sashia felt a nice warmth. Addressing the AI she turned to what looked like bright sunshine emanating from a cylinder above her. It ran full length along the centre of the ship. "What's with the simulated Sun? The light looks pretty real."

Barbarella responded dispassionately. "That's Axle. It radiates daylight." Her tone lifted as she carried on. "Within is TonicTime, an entertainment complex with bars, cafés, movies, disco, fitness centre and such. The difference is that there you'll get to do everything weightlessly, in ZeroG. While in the districts dotted around Rim," she motioned to where tower blocks stood inwards from the hull wall, their flat roofs decked with awnings and spas, "it's all very terrestrial. There you'll have Earth weight, EarthG. In between you'll experience a gradual shift from one weight to the other."

The Meadowvale platform Sashia and Steve were standing on was at the equator, half way between Rim and Axle, the rotational gravity there making them EcstasyG heavy. Rim was the ship hull's wall, where they were headed.

Steve was about to set off when Sashia, overawed, held him back. "This is incredible. Look how big it is!" Throughout the vast cavernous void, columns arced gracefully out from Axle in great spiral arms that tied it to Rim. And all along them were terraces the size of many football fields, with interconnecting paths and stairways all seemingly floating in relation to one another. Storey upon storey stretched out almost endlessly.

Barbarella elucidated further for them, as she would soon do for all newcomers. "You're seeing the whole structure undressed, end to end, and able to look all the way uphill from Rim to Axle. You won't have that view in a couple of weeks from now, when half of it is landscaped. As you go round now what you'll see being delivered, all bagged, are tons of turf and seeds, tens of thousands of cuttings and saplings, as well as several thousand full grown bushes and trees. What are missing, in the absence of air, are strong odours."

The AI allowed them time to savour the view. "The terraces above Rim are being worked into fields for grazing and harvesting. Cascading down them will be streams with lakes as well as wooded areas interspersed with orchards and vineyards. Landscapers are also working on nurseries and ornamental gardens between buildings at Rim. Leisure areas will have water features, barbeques, tennis courts as well as bridle, cycling and hiking paths. Also, Clarence Park, in Lascaux, will have a golf course. It's all going to be so amazingly beautiful!

"The whole of Forbes Park, the same with Clarence, is designed to be Earthly healthy in contrast to the surrealism of space. That's going to be great for you, don't you think, feeding your soul's senses with tangibly visual delights? I can't wait! Of course it's also perfect for filling malls with freshly grown produce and essential for flowing water to the districts and air to breath everywhere."

Surprised, the reconneers glanced at one another, Sashia whispering, "Did we just hear an AI waxing lyrical about scenery? Scenery! Is that possible even?" He shrugged, equally taken aback, but more comfortable with simply shaking the incident off. "Yeah, it's nothing. Anyhow. Let's go, check out TonicTime? Get really weightless!" Sashia was itching for more fun.

"Alright. Sure thing," he was game, too.

"The only quick way is by lift." Barbarella, winking knowingly, was pointing to a monorail signpost, "That'll get you to one in a jiffy! You're lucky. They're commissioning all the systems, so you can try them out."

Travelling through great views, in a rail car with big open windows, Sashia commented on the AI's use of words, "Jiffy? She said jiffy?" The girl just shook her head.

At TonicTime, becoming weightless, they took to floating and doing somersaults, pushing into each other and ricocheting off

furnishings. They also dived among workmen operating equipment.
Sashia was in stitches laughing at the real ecstasy of moving any way
she wanted, free at last from gravity. She didn't ever want to leave.

But, they did finally tire of play and after a while they floated
through a short passageway back to the park, where they pulled their
way to a viewing platform. An awning obscured the dimming light
of Axle, at the close of day, while construction lights were switching
off and workmen began to leave.

Steve and Sashia, still on an adrenaline high from their Shwift
run, and still in the mood for excitement, checked that there was no
one else about. Alone in that magical dusk, with small lights along
pathways and amid trees and bushes all the way down to the lit
buildings at Rim, they faced each other near a waterfall and pool and
fell into an intimacy electric with anticipation. He leaned in to her,
caressing her arm. She smiled without challenge, taking hold of his
hand, "Anyway. It seems we have a destiny together, bigger than
ourselves," while tapping at her helmet, "Back home, I have all the
TuTu I want."

Steve looked at her, puzzled by her words – and his own feelings.

~*~

30

December 2067

I heard from the Commander how things had gone on the Bering, impressed by the motivation he was striving for and that these best of breed reconneers didn't disappoint. We had absolutely no idea of the full potential any of them had. Observing the cool confidence of Sashia and Steve was a delight.

Nevertheless, my concern was our research. That's what I had to concentrate on – and I was becoming anxious. Thankfully, the C-Group notified me they were ready for another session.

Sashia was with Mei at the SnowVale Park watercourse and, though excited, she was nonetheless keen to wait for the others to arrive. She needed Guille's support to keep Mei buoyant. "The full C-Group is pitching up," she told me, and then Steve and Guille arrived. With no word spoken, she summoned FayWell, who swam forward as a mermaid, long blond hair billowing outward. Elegantly stroking it prompted intermittent *Mid-Cretaceous* cloud to waft across the water, revealing muddy currents that flowed into the otherwise clear Tethys Sea. The aerial view showed the Tethys flowing from Pacific to Pacific through the Gobi and Taklamakan basins, the Arabian Gulf, the Mediterranean Sea, and between the green and sandy shores of the Americas.

"See! This covers several seasons!" Sashia explained. As they watched, expansive blotches of white came and went where the United Kingdom and France would be.

When the clip ended, Sashia had to prod Mei into action. "Those coccolith blooms were falling to the sea floors throughout that epoch," Mei was not engaging well, "and compacting into whole hillsides of chalk. And now this…!" In place of the white blotches, yellow and orange ones came and went all over the Tethys Sea, but especially in the stagnant waters over the Arabian Gulf and up into Russia.

"Those algal blooms flowed with plankton and runoff water that was chock-full of organic matter," Steve was in his element, he could thunder ahead with this, but sensing Sashia's and also Guille's empathy for Mei, he mellowed. "Matter, like spores, pollen and also excrement from the rookeries of colossal dinosaur herds, all mixed into a deep orange-brown sludge. Buried deeper and deeper down, over the ages, it pressed into dark brown and then black kerogen. Under immense pressure and heat this eventually let off oil and gas."

As he spoke, *Late-Cretaceous* close-ups showed rainbow coloured tints on reef tops, beaches and dying mangrove trees. It was also visible on titanosaur eggs, laid in a South American river delta nursery. "You see..." he was sneering now, though not in an ugly way but, yes, in contempt of the whole fossil fuel industry, "even in *Cretaceous* times, what oil was responsible for! This mess!" And then a large oil slick, over a kilometre wide and several kilometres long, was oozing from the Western Interior Seaway straight into the Tethys Sea artery of global ocean currents. "That's oil released from where a rock structure, trapping it, had faulted open."

"Okay, an earthquake did that," I reasoned, "as we saw in Egypt recently?"

"Yeah, and us fools had to go and drill open hundreds of trillions of tons of the muck trapped down there!" Up he rose again, though less forcibly, that wildly impassioned oil protestor. "Then look! This is at the *Close* of the *Late-Cretaceous* time. Big oil slicks in the Gulf of Guinea, the Congo, the Taklamakan basin, Indonesia, and the Tasman Sea! Must've been a severe geoshift, for earthquakes to fracture reservoirs as widespread as that!"

"Hm, looks like a sizeable risk," visions of the recent Egyptian spill repeating, shook me, "with DeepStorm's tidal pull!"

"To get some perspective the worst man-made oil spill ever, early this century, in total poured half a million tonnes onto the Gulf of Mexico." Steve looked very grave now. "We're estimating that amount was dumped onto the *Cretaceous* globe every two months! Ongoing, of course, uncapped, for decades!"

"Happening again, that would be horrific." I was shocked, and yet relieved that we'd anticipated that possibility. "You, still up to sparring with oil giants? Alongside your Greenpeace buddies?" I fully expected him to smirk, which he did. "Well, it definitely bears checking out. I don't know how in the circumstances but, as soon as I can, I'll get you connected with UNNDC fossil fuel specialists."

Oddly, as the others left, FayWell hung around as a mermaid, bringing me a feeling of déjà vu. I remembered how strange she'd been when the group presented the first icegem findings. I was intrigued and only needed to give her a quizzical look, for her to begin spilling her AI mind. "Water. The Earth's mystique is water. That substance – temperature and barometric pressure constantly taking it in and out of ice, rivers, seas, air, cloud, living things and even the Earth's crust – is the planet's central heating. It defines the climate. Moves it on, *inexorably*." I liked this, simple and sound. "What those movements are can be computed only short range. Nothing more than that." That was it. FayWell stopped.

I was prepared to be apprehensive about her coming up with a new line of thinking, all her own, as she'd done before. Then I realised she wasn't spinning a line. She was talking facts. We could have fed her assumptions, but she was smart enough to know that was guesswork. In her precise thinking Climate Change over long periods of time was not so much a science, as an art.

In wanting to understand the insights about her life, and anyway get some rest from pain, Mei called Dr O'Malley and arranged to go there immediately. On arrival, however, the girl found the doctor rushing to leave her office. "I'm sorry, I have an emergency."

Realising Mei's concern, she invited Mei to, "Come, we can talk on the way." They raced along a corridor, literally dived through ambulance tail doors, felt them slam shut behind, and as they felt the vehicle rev to take off, quickly sat on benches either side of a stretcher, medical cords and wires hanging about them from the roof. The doctor conferred with a paramedic on readings and procedures, as they busily attended to the injured man lying there. She then called ahead for what was needed immediately on their arrival at the hospital. Then, it was time for Mei. "Right. One anxiety you have is saying goodbye to Jacques, your TuTu?"

"Yes, and…"

"And how do I know that."

"Right. I'd tried several times to contact him. And why do I get the feeling you already know all of that, and maybe a lot more about me."

"Okay, I do. And you want to know how."

"Yes, sure." To Mei it seemed important. It was possible she'd been in touch with some source or other, perhaps even the police about her dad.

"No I didn't hear it from anyone, not even the police." She held Mei's cheek, compassion in her eyes. "I'm *extremely* intuitive. I was born that way. Sometimes it's good – sometimes not so good. I have to live with it. It can help others. Okay?"

"Yes, I'm sorry. Certain things have been troubling me." By this, Mei didn't mean anything, but she was feeling her way towards help. "May I schedule another session?"

"Sure, call me." The vehicle stopped. "We're here and right now I have to concentrate on my patient." She swiftly moved out of the ambulance, intent on her job, but though she did not look back, she did add for Mei, "Don't worry about him, he's safe, and not hurting in any way." Instantly, doctor and patient were engulfed by paramedics and nurses.

Mei walked away, doubly perplexed, "What? Did she say Jacques is okay – and he's moved on? How could she possibly know that?"

Some hours later Dr O'Malley emerged from the operating theatre, her patient on a bed, a nurse at his side. "You okay?" Tixa got a nod from the doctor. "You did brilliantly, shot to pieces as he was."

"At least we got him through. They run such risks. Lasers can't stop all the grit and pebbles of BoStorms, from tearing into their suits and bodies like medieval grapeshot," the doctor looked at Tixa, her state one of distress, "hitting and ripping away flesh and bone."

Tixa knew she lamented the guys having to be out there. "There's no other way though." Both accepted that the robots needed close human direction and monitoring.

"Sure. Got to get the mission underway quickly." Keeping near the man being wheeled along the corridor, Dr O'Malley whispered, "This one's out of danger now."

Tixa tapped her shoulder reassuringly. "Thanks to you. We'll take it from here."

In a light, airy hospital room, with a view of glittering downtown Ecstasy, Tixa waited at the man's bedside when he stirred. "Hi there, you might not know it but you've had intensive care these last two days. I and the other girls have taken turns to hover around you and you haven't misbehaved once!" She beamed good-humouredly. "Anyway, how're you feeling?"

"Uh, what. Where am I? What's happening?" In his post-op state, the man's nerves were raw.

"Relax. Listen, you had an accident, but you're okay now." Tixa's voice swept over him, soft and soothing. "Remember, what you were doing?"

"I don't know. I, think I was on the ice shields outside of Lascaux, fitting some tiles. I remember pointing for another tile to be pulled forward... and, then..." his face showed horror, his eyes closed, "I can't remember after that..."

"You were hit by a BoStorm."

"Wha... but the lasers?"

"FayWell estimated there were more than a thousand tiny bolides. Nothing could have stopped it. It just hit the stern end, where your men were. Another crew brought you down."

"What about Murph and Draz?"

She shook her head regretfully, a shiver progressing down her spine as she thought of the report with its clips of dismembered bodies on the gleaming ice. "They wouldn't have felt a thing," she whispered trying not to alarm him even more. There was no way to cushion him against this news, all she could do was be there as he wept through bouts of grief and anxiety. His pulse rate gradually settled again as the medication she'd given took effect.

Quite some time passed before she had need to be beside him again. "How are you?"

His eyes rolled. He looked around him, speaking with a voice heavy as teutronium. "I don't feel anything."

"No, you won't. Doctor O'Malley has by-passed your nervous system, to make you comfortable. You'll get feeling back, soon enough. Meanwhile, you are in restraints to help your body to mend. Little by little we'll get you out of those and up-and-about exercising. For now, just take it easy, concentrate on getting better."

"Relax?" He turned his face away. "What's the damage?"

"Torn and broken ligaments, muscles and bones. You'll mend." He looked at her, expecting more. "You've lost one kidney, which we will replace as soon as your strength returns." He sensed more, gripped her hand. Tixa's throat felt dry. She swallowed. "One section of your spine is shattered. That's what the doctors will work on next." He stared at her in disbelief. "That's the whole picture.

There's nothing else. You're hurt and we're rebuilding you," she added positively. "As soon as you're fit enough we'll send you back down where your family can visit." The man looked dazed, bordering on traumatised. "You're a Hindu?" The man nodded. "Okay, let's talk about that…"

Just then Dr O'Malley arrived, alongside the Commander. "Hi, good to see you awake. How're you doing?" The man used his hands and head to suggest a shrug. "What the nurse has just told you is correct. On the spinal injury, I've been in contact with experts at Guys Hospital London. They're going to assist us remotely with a very successful nanobot stem cell treatment. Communications are deteriorating using conventional satellite links, so the Commander has organised a direct military link for this. You're getting very special interruption-free care, crucial as this is." The doctor gave him a reassuring smile and he warmed to this unfamiliar, slightly strange being.

The Commander also smiled reassuringly, while maintaining his solid stance of authority. "It must be an awful shock waking up to this hitting you square in the chest. There is no changing that this has happened, but you're in the very best of hands. As the good doctor says, you'll be okay."

Out in the corridor again, Commander and doctor fell into step, he observing her frail form, his body language demonstrating that he held her in high regard. Indeed, with all his heavy responsibilities, this was the one person with whom he could share his feelings. When next he spoke his tone was gentle and concerned. "We're getting injuries daily now, some fatal. We must find answers. I had to hasten the work. We must get out there."

Her nod was only of understanding, not the recrimination that could have come for speeding up the entire operation.

He patted her hand in recognition of her own burden. "You're doing marvellously. Will the man's spine work out?"

She shook her head. "He's human. We can give him synthetic nerves and work with stem cells. That will return most of his movements. Regrettably, that science is far from perfected as yet. He'll be able to get about – just not play tennis very well. At least he can have his life back, and possibly even reach a ripe old age."

The Commander was saddened nonetheless, for him and all those out there. "And you? How would you fare with such an injury?"

"As a fiman you mean?" Seeing him nod, she did not hesitate, having gone through such medical scenarios many times. "Well my spine would be horribly distorted and disfigured. My nerves excruciatingly stretched. But it's unlikely they'd be severed or shattered like this poor chap's. I'd survive, be rebuilt as new." She stopped to face the Commander. "Which is why, my dear Commander, with DeepStorm you, Professor Madison and the other humans must avoid going outside, if at all possible."

The fighting-man eyed this remarkably fragile-looking creature whom he knew to remarkably possess a superhuman body and mind. "Sure, that's why everyone else on this mission had to be fiman. It's just a pity they couldn't be trained up as construction workers and fitters in time. We simply couldn't wait." They walked on. "Anyway, for this guy, some spiritual healing is the order of the day? Is he getting that?"

"Sure, he's a Hindu. Tixa got him started on that the moment we left. She's sensitive and caring with people, just what it takes for battered nerves and confidences. She'll get his body rebuilding itself." Dr O'Malley visibly relaxed then. "Ah, he's coming round a bit. Yes, she's there and he's trying to smile. That's as well as can be expected."

"Good. Lucky to be in your good hands then." And then an idea came and he stopped again.

"You're thinking about Sashia," the doctor said.

"Right again. Would that nanobot stem cell treatment work for her?"

"That's tricky. It's been developed over decades, working with human patients," she wasn't totally negative, "with calcium bones. Fiman bones are different. But, I'm hoping to find a variation that'll work for her."

"Good, wonderful," he responded, squeezing her fine-boned shoulder.

The Commander holoed Lascaux site office. "Commander, DeepStorm Questor, here," he railed. "The shift supervisor there?"

"Sir!" the young man responded smartly.

"What's the status right now?"

"Just two days left to complete external work. We're now testing ice shields. Then there'll just be internal work."

"For all ships?"

"Yes, sir."

The Commander switched to calling the company's Ecstasy office. "Commander Althorpe here. Put the shift manager on."

"Good day Commander," Brady kept his response short, matching the Commander's military style.

"Your construction crews ready to relocate on board, and ship out with us?"

"Everything's checked out okay, with the insurance companies too. Once operational, the ships will be reclassified – Unrestricted EarthG Territories. Short rotation limits will no longer apply. Just a handful of the crew have personal reasons to return to Earth."

"Well done."

Next, he called me. "Ready to advance the launch date?"

"We're just waiting on the ice shield tests, before bedding things down. We'll be ready to get underway a week early, as agreed."

"Right. We'll get underway – just as soon as everything's loaded – 26th December."

"Right. Boxing Day."

~*~

31

December 2067

A week from Christmas, at crack of dawn, a magnificent spectacle unfolded. The doors in Ecstasy's huge ice roof opened to let a steady stream of shuttles pour out from the cargo bay. Like twenty fireflies in the black of space, they formed a big arc headed for the three gigantic white cylinders that gleamed in sunlight high above the Moon's surface.

The shuttles were headed for the Questor task force ships. The stream split, ten fireflies going to each liner, where one by one they slipped through the shutter at the equator.

Disembarking, the passengers faced a dazzling welcoming show – the lights of buildings at the hull wall, the faint light of dawn at the centre and seasonal tinsel with fairy lights adorning the landing platform.

They alighted on the polished wood deck in an atmosphere now built up sufficiently for them to breath unaided. And there they were, transfixed and pressing against the railings to wonder at the vast verdant chasm of the park before them. Fimans and humans alike gasped at the earthy freshness of morning dew on newly landscaped lawns and fields, and at cascading waters under wisps of mist, translucent in early morning light.

Judging the moment FayWell, in her usual guise of straw blond but wearing a white tee-shirt and skirt, greeted them from posts around the railing. "Hi there, landed well I see. No problems? Good, and of course you've got *all* your luggage? Anything left behind will go to a good cause – mine! Just kidding! What would I do with it? Ha, ha!" There were smiles all round, for this AI working the crowd. "Right, now. Feeling a little woozy? Hah, of course you are! That's the ships rotation. Take a moment to get used to that." They had all been prepped, so knew what to expect, though this show was jollying them along. She didn't wait. "Okay, that'll do! You're *not* feeling heavy? You soon will be! This is EcstasyG here, same as where you've been, but not where you're going!"

Sashia received a very brief call from the Commander, checking up on progress. "Welcome back – all going well?"

"Sir! Yes, all's well in Avebury." She couldn't leave it there, when this was so different to she and Steve going straight to Earth weight on the Bering. "It's like kid glove treatment for this lot." She bit her lip, expecting a ticking off for being cheeky.

"Ah, you noticed."

The crowd got started, with more advice from the faithful AI, "Take it easy in putting on weight going down!" The fimans soon noticed the effect. "Down there, where you're headed," FayWell continued with her directions, "Rim, is all EarthG. And, believe me, you'll be legless with having your old Earth weight back. I trust you've all been exercising in Ecstasy – as you'll be out of shape for it if you haven't."

Steve was there with Sashia, while Carla and Guille were busy elsewhere on landscaping works, and Mei on moving livestock. He laughed, nudging Sashia. "This does feel strange, almost like going up stairs rather than down."

"Hah! Tell me about it!" The pain of it, seemed to her to be more prolonged this way. "I'd just as soon have gone straight there, as we did in the Bering."

When the crowd did arrive at Rim, they likened the sensation they had to having climbed out of a pool waterlogged. FayWell had some choice words for them about that, "Tomorrow, expect to wake up feeling whacked. Like with jetlag!" In time you'll get used to the oddity of moving around here – and you'll be totally smitten by ZeroG! But, don't *ever* go overboard on it! I'll be monitoring your LNs, as a precaution, to advise you if you have!"

That's when FayWell surprised the moon-bugs off Sashia, with an aside to her, "Hm, imagine the scope! Cavorting semi-weightless in the lush rain free park – or frolicking weightless in TonicTime?" Sashia didn't know quite how to take this possible innuendo. Could the AI only mean getting relief for her legs on her own – or being raunchy with someone!

At the entrance to Soho, one of the districts at Rim, the duo were confronted by an oak door that liquefied and then solidified again when they'd passed through. "Wow!" They loved it, like kids, stepping out and back again a couple of times. FayWell chuckled, "Hah! You were also decontaminated." She caught their questioning looks. "I know, hydroponics would eliminate the need

283

for earth and the parks could be completely sterilised. I'll let you work that one out."

"No, explain." Sashia was not prepared to play her game.

"Good luck!"

That took them aback, Sashia half whispering, "Was I hearing things? Or did we just hear an AI speak her own mind and ignore our request?"

Steve wasn't having it. "The muck is out there for our health, right?"

"Right! For your immune systems, so you can go downside to terra firma again. *To live on the earth, is to live with the earth,*" she spoke the words like a jingle. "That's what Mei says, in her wisdom."

Stepping into the peachy cream ambience of a luxurious lounge area, they then jostled along mezzanines packed with baggage and people milling about along with fitters installing fitments and décor into shops and cafes. Everyone was staggering stodgily, dragging bags to their suites, some lending an ear to the dulcet accompaniment of a busker, euphorically lost in his tunes.

Finally, FayWell stopped them. "This is it, your lift. You're on the third floor here. You ready to go up?"

"Yeah, sure," Steve glanced at Sashia and shrugged.

"Sure," Sashia was in no hurry to see where she'd be holed up, after the platoon-like living she'd endured for months – and worse, on earth with just the club, before she met Fayez and they managed to get their small junk, which she'd treasured.

"Okay, we're there," the AI said, leading them to their respective suites. "Don't feel stuck with these by the way. You can swap with others if you want." Outside of Sashia's door she waved a hand towards the frame's right side. "Stand in front. That's it. The door knows your LN, as do other things of yours."

Sashia looked through the dematerialising door, tears welling up – at seeing a spacious studio apartment with a virtual window onto the Moon and a balcony overlooking the park! "I... I'm...Yes, this will do fine!" her voice quivered with joy.

"Do you feel suitably terraccommodated?" The AI was obviously enjoying this. "I can change the décor anytime."

At Steve's place, much the same, he got straight into getting the entertainment centre to know his style of music.

Later in the morning, Sashia was surprised by the sight of a punk figure standing at her door. Her instant assumption was that she had to correct the girl, who'd obviously been misdirected. But to her dismay FayWell interceded to explain that Sandra was a human fitter going part way, as the Commander had ordered. "Okay. It's okay." Sashia was resigned, allowing for their circumstances. Leaving behind the joy at having such quarters to herself, she rejoined the mezzanine crowd, where she delighted in finding that tables and chairs had already begun to spread out in front of un-furbished cafés.

Just then, Mei appeared and linked into her friend's arm. "Ley ho mah?"

"Jo san, gay ho ah. Settled in okay?"

"Well sort of. I have a roommate."

"Yeah, me too. Still, I've been thinking. FayWell said we could swap about so let's see if they'd like to share your place or mine? Whichever? Since we've got to share, let *us* do that."

"Sure! That'd be great!"

"Okay, settled. Fancy a drink?" Nudging Mei playfully, Sashia used her excellent sight to cut through the commotion and select a good place, finally drawing her friend along to a café a little way along the mezzanine.

There, Mei announced that she'd at last unpacked her case and pulled out Twing, her pet robot, whom she'd missed. They also chatted about exploring their new environment, surrounded by crowds rummaging in partly finished arcades where traders and window dressers were already window dressing with a variety of merchandise and services.

Their rippling conversation was interrupted when I appeared on screens everywhere. "I'd like the attention of all of you for a moment." I waited for total quiet. "We're finally moving towards a departure and I can see you're all settling in. FayWell will have greeted you all individually and helped you find your way around. Her design name is GHIS, but I won't bore you with that. She has free rein with domestic arrangements, and quite soon she'll seek a consensus on how you want the décors of open areas.

"Just remember what the reconneers among you are here for, which is to beat DeepStorm – so that we can all go home. So,

285

reconneers, first thing in the morning get stuck in – and the rest of you support them. Otherwise enjoy, have fun. This is your world."

Up early the next day, Sashia found herself negotiating her way through impromptu market stalls awash with wet fish, fruits and vegetables, juices, noodles, sizzling woks, roasting kebabs, boiling pasta, simmering vindaloo. She was knocked out by the feeling of being home, with everything so reminiscent of Causeway Bay, in Hong Kong. Everyone there also seemed happier, the fimans all looking more settled than when filled with arrival anxieties. Their revived spirits reflected on the humans, too. Most of them had slept on mezzanines, or similar anyway, knowing no other way than the likes of Hong Kong's Lifestyle centre.

Mei rolled up to join her friend for a breakfast bite. "It's all so familiar – so normal somehow." She waved to the produce about them. "What do you reckon my Hong Konger reconneer?" Just then she spied a favourite stimulant of hers, a safe trademark brand, and whooped. "Wow! My best pick-me-up!"

"Yeah, really!" Sashia's eyes feasted on the stalls, before turning the conversation to what she'd been musing over – the AI's asides of late. "That FayWell is so incredibly busy, don't you think?"

"Yes – and she's listening." Tixa popped up, waving a finger mockingly. "And so am I."

"Uh, that's okay." Mei wasn't perturbed. "She's discreet, never gets upset and is always ready to chat."

Tixa half whispered, "It's strange though. You never see her eyes."

I happened by, heard them and joined in. "Ah, you've noticed. Don't let that ruffle you," I shrugged. "That's how she is."

"You said her real name is GHIS." When curious, Tixa had a terrier's grip.

"FayWell is her nickname. Which seemingly came from someone calling her FlatWall, because of the way she appears." I gestured towards FayWell, now flat on a wall. "GHIS is short for *Galactic Human Intelligence Simulation*. It was never going to catch on."

Tixa looked at FayWell, talking to people all around them. "She's got so many different outfits, for everyone." A small pout of envy spread over her face. "And it's so incredible, her being able to manage all of Questor's myriad systems and converse with thousands of people, all at the same time!"

"Hmm! Unfathomably brainy, also she's good to look at and timelessly young. You couldn't hope for a nicer AI." That being enough trivia for me, I pulled the C-Group pair to one side and addressed Mei. "A thought for the day. The primary urge of living organisms is preservation?" I cocked my head. "Theirs – or their species?"

Mei's intrigue showed. "Ah! The selfish gene – and Natural Selection. Or, perhaps, something else besides?"

"Ah, but what?"

Mei ventured a notion. "Periods in time I've studied are consistent in one thing, they all advanced, complexly, in organisms. Gaia has advanced complexly."

"Good! Hold that thought!" I was inwardly smiling. "For now, concentrate on DeepStorm. Join me, in my suite, later – for an update?"

"Sure, we'll be there," the girls chanted, looking a little bemused. Not dwelling on it, they soon returned to converse with Tixa.

In time, Mei checked the time and rose, excusing herself. "I've got animals arriving."

Sashia rose too. "Okay, I fancy seeing the park – just love the smell of dung. Good for you, too, right?" She was half joking. "Anyway, it's all a bit crowded in here." She turned to Tixa, whose face dropped a bit. "See you later." Watching them go, Tixa shook her head.

Further along the mezzanine, Mei commented on the other girl's look of dejection. "Does she look put out, or what?"

"Oh? Well yeah, guess so. I think she'd have stuck with us," she looked sideways at Mei. "Tough, I'd like to have you to myself." She winked and slotted her arm through Mei's.

At Forbes Park, Sashia felt strangely invigorated. "There's, something… I smell something rich, earthy."

"Yeah, nice huh? It's countryside. Great odours. The richness is filtered out indoors. So coming out here is a therapeutic change, I think. And what's great is the flagrance varies all round the park."

They climbed up to the Meadowvale landing platform, Sashia feeling the relief of getting weight off her legs again with each step she took. Also admiring new shoots on plants, she realised how much effort Mei and the others had put into getting everything bedded in. "Oh," her shriek was sudden and piercing. "Is that, a cockroach?"

Mei grinned, "This *is* a *whole* ecosystem. Everything has its place out here, those included. *To live on the...*"

"I know, *To live on the earth, is to live with the earth*," Sashia sang out, recalling FayWell quoting this from Mei, "Wah! Too much reality!"

Deymore was at the platform, herding newly arrived cows to stretch their legs in a pasture. Mei, still smiling at having her quote recited to her, approached the lad. "Hi, they quiet?"

"Sure enough, not a bother." He amiably patted the neck of one cow. "As soon as it's dark I'll head them further down, let them feed on grain in the corral. You'd said to give all animals arriving a day there before moving them to the fields near Rim." As with the people, the animals needed to be where they could regain their Earth weight and stay at that level for their health.

"They'll get to stretch their legs every day, being herded to other pastures first thing in the morning and late afternoon." She led Sashia to the groves. "They'll love it," she assured, reaching to touch a branch. "What do you reckon? Just a month from now and we'll have juicy apples growing here."

"Delicious. Love it."

"Ah, you haven't seen the pièce de résistance." Mei moved on to the next terrace. "Just over there, look." Alone in a field, a magnificent grey mare tossed its mane and, spotting Mei, trotted towards the girls.

"She's a beaut alright." Sashia tickled the horse's nose and ruffled its mane, watching Mei on the other side hugging the animal around the neck.

"Come on, up!" Mei suggested, smiling.

"Bare back!"

Seeing her friend's dismay, Mei held the withers, jigged and then jumped, landing on the mare's broad back and sitting there, happier than ever. Sashia laughed fondly. "You're mad!"

They walked around the field, Sashia on foot, alongside her friend. "Mei, you're so organised, which is more than the rest of us can say." She looked up at the face high above her. "You get things done, despite everything. Have you heard any more?"

"No, I'll be calling as usual in a bit. I'm used to getting nowhere though, the transmissions are really bad now. It's hard to have a proper conversation."

"What about your brother? Doesn't he know anything?"

"No. Even when we can communicate, he doesn't say much. I really do better speaking with mum. What about you and Fayez?"

"Oh, we speak often enough, but it's the same, the reception's so poor. Imagine what it'll be like when we get further out."

Just then Deymore came up with an update, "They're all set, heading down okay."

"I saw. I'll come by again after I exercise Vireo here." Mei smiled seeing Sashia's quizzical look. "It is a girl's name, after a songbird of the Americas."

"I think I'll go and freshen up." Sashia could see Mei was keen for time with the mare and moments beyond work. "Fancy wandering over to TonicTime later? Make it a home-warming do tonight?"

"I'll see, maybe."

Sashia strolled with Deymore, whose talk about the animals revolved around his work with them and loving their company. Back at the landing platform she carried on, while he went to close a gate behind Torf, who was sauntering over to where Guille, with a robot, was connecting sections of pipe in a gully. At first, Torf said nothing. He just observed the work, until Guille noticed him. Then he spoke up, a little self-consciously, "You want a hand?"

Guille put him at ease, telling him about the job of increasing the water supply to the terrace so they could plant a scaled down forest. This was one of several enhancements envisaged to the basic irrigation and drainage scheme for the parks. Carla had handed down improvements ad lib to Guille, her innovative engineering assistant, who was becoming renowned for putting new ideas into practice.

I was also coming up with other plans for what to grow in the park.

On reaching Rim, Sashia made her way, highly dependent on support from her striders again, to my suite. The door, already informed of her arrival, immediately broke up into minuscule droplets that fell to a marble floor and reformed the instant she was through. "Hello," she called softly, expecting to enter a living space comparable to her own ultra-modern suite. It was not so. She stood, a look of delight spreading over her pert countenance, at the edge of a very large wooden floor that led out onto a wide balcony that overlooked the park. Another large window faced a majestic view over the Grand Canyon, where right then an eagle soared.

She was about to call out louder when, turning from the view, she saw me on a raised wooden floor where, surprised anew, she noticed my favourite old wooden desk – which I'd removed from my study to make room for the C-Group's work.

"Welcome!" I was pleased to see Sashia's visible approval of my accommodation. "Come." I led the way to the adjoining study, where, members of the C-Group were arranging equipment. "Now you can get down to things in earnest, no more moving around. This is your own place," I spoke with seriousness, but also enthusiasm, "Go to it all of you, let's complete this research."

In no time, left to it by me, they had the whole study festooned with screen images and movie clips. It had become an impressive array of evidence and hypotheses to come up with the all-elusive weapons of Mass Extinction. They'd arrived, settled in, and were ready for action in space!

Rejoining them later, I had to shout above the racket of fitters. "You've shown me what was happening in the southern hemisphere, and about the oil pollution. What's next?" By inference, I expected to learn of similar developments in Ameurasia – but, I was hardly prepared for what came next.

"A lot." Surprisingly, Steve was glancing sweetly at Mei, and then he winked, as if in reassurance, at Sashia. "That oil we saw, everywhere, at the *Close* of the *Late-Cretaceous*? I was right that a geoshift caused that." He motioned to a bank of screens and looked relieved when the fitters' noise abated momentarily. "See! Less than a millennium on, when the geoshift activity we'd seen had subsided, fresh oil slicks oozing out!

"And, the Atlantic!" He carried on as FayWell materialised – as Elizabeth I again – and waved regally to change the screen image. "It looked that much bigger, so we got FayWell to check it out. The ocean floor had widened and deepened!"

"It appears," Guille had helped in those observations, "the whole ocean basin had *wrinkled*!"

"There's more." Steve's excitement at such discoveries was surfacing. "A huge, upside-down, horseshoe-shape range, from Arizona up to Montana, across Beringia and down to the Gobi and Taklamakan basins in China," again a wave of Elizabeth I's hand refreshed the screen, "was breaking up."

"That was by far the biggest," Mei politely inserted, though again having to shout above the fitters' noises to finish her sentence, "as well as the oldest and richest of all dinosaur ranges."

"And look, there!" Sashia pointed to close-ups of choppy waves in the deepened Bering Strait. "Far more hadrosaurs than the comparably sized ankylosaurs, in the Antarctralasian event going on then!"

Some of the big herbivores waded bipedal with their duckbills nervously waving about, while others dropped to walk on all fours kangaroo fashion. "They barked their alarm, just the same, in those chilling shark-infested waters. Except there was a twist." Mei indicated tentacles flailing around one of the beasts. "In this grim scene, a giant octopus – as big as the mythical Kraken of pirate lore – was in their midst."

"Yeah," Sashia moved on relentlessly, "so reminiscent of wildebeest and zebra migrations today, in crossing crocodile infested waters of Tanzania and Kenya, East Africa. Except, all of these ancient straits ended up too treacherous to cross anymore."

"There's more – river courses had changed in the geoshift." Steve's eyes invited respect from Mei. "They'd been diverted when mountain ranges uplifted in the Himalayas and Rockies."

"Yes." Mei agreed, though still wary of him. Noise stopping again, she lowered her voice. "They no longer flowed to old deltas in the Gobi and Taklamakan basins. And, see – all those dinosaur herds. So stressed out! With the bird-like migratory instincts of the huge beasts, hardwired in them, they had no choice but to follow the same old river courses, to quench their huge thirsts. Except now they were severely emaciated after trekking along dried out riverbeds to reach high and dry rookeries.

"It was the same with the Western Interior Seaway deltas, in North America," Sashia edged in, aiming to give Mei a rest from her shyness tensions. "Although some rookeries there were also tinted with windblown oil!

"The same happened elsewhere in the world," Mei came in again, giving Sashia an affectionate look, "such as at the Eromanga Sea, inland in Australia,"

"And," Steve added, giving her a gentle look, "these scenes repeated again and again. There *is* only one explanation for such widespread changes." He changed tack, turning to address me, voice upbeat, though trying to conceal his jubilation at being proved right. "And that is, a *series* of prolonged geoshifts, as much as a decade long it would seem – and repeating millennia apart!"

He knew this was a Natural Correction to beat all. "Just a small deformation in global land levels, perhaps as little as half a metre or so, would have been all that it took each time." He glanced back at Mei as if to say, "Case closed," and then turned his attention solely on me. "That's got to change views on continental drift."

"Phew, the power released!" Guille, clearly astonished, had to raise his voice above the noise. "Like there was a bunch of supervolcano eruptions or asteroid hits around Earth? Imagine the earthquakes!"

I shuddered. "Those quakes doubtless registered above the Richter scale and drove tsunamis hundreds of metres high crashing round the globe! I've done some checking," I addressed Steve, "by far the largest volcanoes that ever erupted, or flowed across continents, were at 'hotspots' too remote or too big to have been from continental plate subduction. *And*, they were *all*, bar one, either in the tropics or in high latitudes."

"Hmm, sure," Steve's eyes shone with pleasure. "Geoshifts had wrinkled and buckled the crust in the tropics – as it did to the Atlantic – and stretched and torn it in high latitudes."

"But also, the hotspots had swung from being in the northern hemisphere pre-Jurassic," I coaxed him on, relieved again that the noise had abated, "to the southern hemisphere up to the *Late-Cretaceous*, and then back to the northern hemisphere again." I had more for him to ponder over, "And, they were fairly well distributed over time too."

"*Yes!*" Steve was at last getting on top of the issue, "You see! Geoshifts were just as big a force in shaping the planet, as continental drift was."

"Okay and, in studying them," I was going with his reasoning, "we should be able to predict the effects that DeepStorm's tidal pull will have?"

"Yes. And the geoshifts could have been triggered," Steve wasn't done yet. "There were a series of asteroid impacts – such as the Boltysh impact on Ukraine around the same time as the Chicxulub one, another in Manson Iowa was as big but earlier, and others in between might have landed in water. Each of those would have been far more disastrous by kicking off a geoshift, than in any other way."

"Hm, right. And if a DeepStorm had done all of that, with its tides flexing continents and NEOs crashing down," I was aligned with his logic, "to trigger a succession of geoshifts, that single cause would have been behind a very prolonged Mass Extinction! With rafting masking much of it."

I couldn't help but think further though. "Interesting, isn't it? The picture I now have is of forces building between grinding continental plates, right? And, before those all give, in a life extinguishing *super bang*, there's the flexing of strong tides and the buffeting of high seas to loosen it up – and they can still get stuck and build in places. So, very conveniently an asteroid whams in every now and again to shake it all loose? And just to make sure, Gwaves also come by with their super strong tides?" I was getting odd looks, questioning where this was leading. "It's pure magic! Evolution is driven on by nature's magic!"

That evening, drained by the effort of getting the mission underway, I took a very long, refreshing shower and planned to go out clubbing. When dressing, the Sævrama Channel got my attention. Jude was there, looking good, I thought, *"...protests have been taking place in numerous capital cities this week, with World leaders coming under increasing pressure to take control of events. Among them are action groups citing the impending meltdown of a nuclear plant or collapse of a large dam or some other major catastrophe happening as the result of an earthquake or an eruption..."*

Moments later I arrived at a TonicTime disco, with a parrot on my shoulder. I was enjoying the sensation of floating weightless before the receptionist, when I again honed in on the Sævrama Channel. Jude Nade was on air, *"One precautionary measure UNNDC has taken, in association with Spanish authorities, is the controlled detonation of the volcanic mountain range Cumbre Vieca in La Palma, Canary Islands. The UNNDC objective – the controlled collapse, of that water saturated range, to prevent a giant 650 metre high mega-tsunami racing across the Atlantic and wiping out the US east coast."*

The broadcast was interrupted by the Commander, who appeared on all screens. "I have something to convey to you as a family – for that is what we are, all family bound in the same cause. A theft has been reported of a silver Saint Christopher locket. I expect anyone, who knows anything about the thief, fence or recipient, to inform FayWell within the hour. All of those involved in this theft will be summarily dismissed from Questor. I'll say now, there will be zero tolerance for dishonesty aboard Questor vessels."

Somewhere behind me a girl quipped, "Oomph, such a stickler." But another stopped her dead. "What crap! Seems like we're in 'on-the-level city'," and for the girl and all around, she asserted, "What's wrong with that?" It was good to see the general and enthusiastic agreement.

Merry from wine I meandered through the boisterous crowd, bumping into various people doing the same, among them Captain Grossman, Executive Officer of Avebury, Captain DeGroet Executive Officer of the Bering and Captain Lane.

TonicTime discos had billed a number of famous pop artists and DJs, for the crowd to listen to live and interact with on life-size holoe. Popular too were poetry and book reading guests. I mingled and chatted. At one point I ran into Carla who, strange to see out of her usual black 'n reds, looked resplendently erotic covered in realistic looking feathers. "Hi there," I greeted. "How was your first day aboard? See you've been shopping."

For all her New England sophistication, Carla quite enjoyed being impulsively seductive, "Oh, yeah! Neat, floating in gorgeous feathers," with her costume as well as her now weightless full breasts. "This is the 'mostest'! This task force and everything in it!" Her eyes met mine. "Can't wait to get underway!"

"That bauble you're sporting is hardly an insignificant purchase either." I was holding her slightly dangerous flirtation at bay. An unabashed shopaholic, spoilt by a rich daddy and socialite mother, she was used to getting whatever – and whomsoever – she wanted, if only as a passing fancy or teasing exercise.

She fingered a Star Luna, fixed just above her cleavage, the one Sashia and Mei had admired in Ecstasy, her eyes twinkling with satisfaction. "I couldn't resist... and with the Commander making everywhere so safe, it's just such a pleasure to wear. Such an impressive task force."

I had no argument with that, and with life being for living. I patted her arm lightly. "Have fun." Before she could respond, I was happily on my way again.

Just then Tixa came upon Carla and was obviously stunned by her appearance. "Hi. Love your outfit, so sexy. Wow! That rock!" She was sweet as could be, bowled over by the Star Luna. "This is fantastic, isn't it? Floating freely, but not in water! Such a fun ship! Except for the drag of having to share suites."

"No drag," Carla felt no need to explain she'd doubled up with Steve. Shifting on into the throng, she came across Captain Lane. "So, you do leave your ship sometimes."

"Ah, bolide risks. Got to be a little crazy to be human up here," he wasn't hugely amusing. "You're on fair terms with the good scientist, the Prof, aren't you?" He was as tactless as an elephant shitting.

"Hallo to you too," she gave him a peck on the cheek. "Not in the mood, then?" Under dazzling, changing lights, Carla floated and spun slowly about him, fitting movements seductively to music. He did not respond with interest, however. "Has the Prof said anything, about where we're headed?"

"Oh, boring!" she gave him a push and melted back into the throng.

Across the crowd a bargirl, smiling cheerily, looked quite struck by Torf. Guille gently nudged him with his elbow, murmuring, "Getting somewhere?" Torf shrugged diffidently, but Guille persisted. "Hey! So, get in there!"

"Huh?" Torf turned to him, laughing. "Ah, Ah!"

"Ah, Ah? What's that?" Guille was perplexed. "Oh," he broke out laughing, "AA! She's an AA?"

"Yeah!" Torf's eyes were roaming.

"You're beaming," Guille noticed, and swung around, amazed. The one girl not with her back to them, who just then smiled, perhaps cautiously though, was Tixa.

Unassuming Torf had little else to say. "There, a smile." Guille shook his head, bemused that he could leave this at that.

Well away from them, in another crowded area, a girl who could only slur her words, was looking at their AI's elusive figure in the shadows. "Hiya FayWell. You well?"

"I well."

"There's a chant there somewhere," Sashia thought, thinking of Fayez and his composing and madly missing him. She looked on at the already high and merry crowd, not really feeling part of them, but nonetheless enjoying being weightless. She had downed drinks with no effect, except their effect had been to slow her down and relax her. In a while she stopped circulating, and held onto a bar. Looking around aimlessly she reflected morosely on Mei being alone too, alone with her home problems

Just when Sashia was planning to leave and reaching down to retrieve her bag, black and red trousers came in sight, right in front of her. Eyes wide, she slowly rose up and impulsively threw her arms around him. "Ah, Shteve."

"What? No pizzazz?" Her difficulty with words was obvious to him. "Not very inviting you know."

"I neither feel invitid nor invigor… invigr… invgrated" The girl managed to hold his face between her hands. "I was a BT, you know…" Her chuckle was infectious.

"A bacon and tomato on rye with mayo?" He gave her butt a firm slap, mockingly peering and teasing her, and added to himself, "Hmm, nice cherry sized tomatoes!"

Extricating herself, she elucidated, "No, schilly. A Blabby-Tabby," now trying to focus on his face. "Blab, blab, blab, just like a tabby." Easing back for emphasis, she continued. "Isht's true! A Blabby-Tabby!"

A rare smile, an approving smile, spread over his face, the face she was trying to see better. "Well, hell. When now you're Slabs the Blab, I reckon!" Earnest reconneer-to-reconneer respect was for

296

the head that sat squarely on those shoulders of hers. He murmured just for her, "If there's anyone I'd ride out there with, fight beside, it'd be this tough reconneer." He was now confused, observing a sudden sadness descend on her. "Hey? Where's that fearless thrill-seeking face?" He gently pulled her into nearer focus, brushing a tear aside, "What's this?"

"Oh. Tell you... shometime. Not now..." She smiled at him then and appeared to relax. "Look, dooo you mind ifff we go?" He shrugged indifferently. "To vhe park?"

He could see she was totally off the wall, and all that mattered to her was to be anywhere private, other than her suite. Sensing that need, he took charge, putting his arm around her waist and leading her away.

Outside they hung around the park enjoying the night ambience, under the awning they'd visited before, and he guided her by the hand to the edge of the lawn for them to gaze through the labyrinth of terraces, dressed in necklaces of path lights all the way down to the glimmering buildings of Rim.

"Come!" Hastily she took his hand... and made him jump with her over the railing, laughing hysterically – and as he rose, Steve suffered a flash of déjà vu. The terraces came and went, drifting past, she engaging him with excited smiles.

He sobered up quickly, concern growing over her antics. He grabbed a post just before, being less weightless, they would have been in for a hard fall. Slowly tumbling instead, he pulled her to a glade where a stream flowed and a meandering stairway was bordered by cascading waterfalls. Resting there, he looked down at the black waters glistening in the lamplight. "Peaceful, huh?"

Sashia put her arm round his waist and hung on to him. Inebriation and adrenaline were combining to sap and lift her energies simultaneously, making her drowsy yet boisterous. "Yez, reely beau'ful."

For a while they remained there, until he reflected, "I'm going to... spend quiet moments here, fishing." He was surprised by the incredulity this engendered in her and needed to explain. "Sure, you know, man's great meditation. You sit or lie, absorbed yet vacant. Reliving the electric charge of getting a bite and fighting a fish, while actually peacefully de-stressing. Catching anything is a bonus. Actually, most often it's a nice surprise."

She stared at the water. "There're fisheses in there?" She flopped back. "They'll all float out, and away. Jush like ush."

"Mei will be stocking it after she gets the other animals settled. There'll be orchids and other flowers too. Sounds very pretty, huh?" Her upturned face still begged an answer. "Uh, no. They won't float out. The streambed, underlined with teutronium, will keep water and everything flowing properly."

"Ah, poor Mei," Sashia was morose again.

Having none of this, he swung her around to face him, looked into her eyes and gently stroked her cheek. Then, dropping his head to one side and raising an eyebrow to query her mood, he smiled. No need for words.

Taking a breath, moistening and parting his lips, Steve very gently pressed them to her cheek, and held her there for a moment before lowering her head to his chest. After a good while, he caressed her back and shoulders, applying slight, soothing pressure to massage her ligaments, and he felt her relax in his arms. Slowly then, he ran his fingers down her back, massaging lightly as he went.

~*~

32

A day later, back at Rim, everyone awoke nursing heavy heads and had to wield heavy Earth-weight bodies out of bed. Legs felt as solid as tree trunks. It was to be the first of several really trying days for them, as they adjusted. Mei was up early to make her rounds of the Heather Farm buildings at the Rim end of Forbes Park. The yard, which opened onto pastures, was where the animals would spend much of their time with Earth-weight. She was checking in with her crew. Guille was there, checking out where Carla was planning to build a barn extension, before setting off uphill. Relieved to take a short break, Mei agreed to go with him to the bow of the ship just ahead of Axle. They floated there, erecting a platform and connecting cables to it.

That done, they went to Primrose Clinic, at the park's equator, where – after its opening in a day or so – patients would recuperate and benefit from being light-weighted. Guille had hot spring spas to check and she wanted to see how the plants were bedding down in low gravity. This was a truly therapeutic setting and – for now – they had it all to themselves. After disappearing for a while, he returned to find her labouring with a large potted plant and he rushed to help. At that moment, he knocked her arm and, embarrassed, held it gently, then noticing that her InviHundred scalds had gone. "No difficulties, your skin is all mended!"

"Sure, no problem." Nonetheless Mei looked perturbed. She was recalling the misery – and him there, so comforting.

"Your hearing is okay?"

"Yeah, same as you. Our biombots are a boon. We were a pair though, with that awful shouting and stupid expressions about everything anyone else said!" They laughed, comfortable with mocking themselves. "Anyway," he checked the time, "oughtn't we join the others for another report to Madison?"

When they reached her *Cretaceous* forest, Mei's eyes shone as she scanned the scene, breathing deeply. "So strange to think this idyllic setting replicates the world of giant dragons – dinosaurs! I imagine one over there, surrounded by flowers, like Ferdinand The Bull." She didn't need to look at him to know he was being attentive. "Professor Madison sees them as specimens, and he wants me to develop this area to study the physiologies of plants." She shrugged, "Of course I want that too, very much so." A frown, and shake of her head, suggested more. "I also want to create scenes, and see them grow as magnificently as only nature knows how." She realised that she wanted to talk with this man, as she'd not done since doing so with her dad and Rad, but, she could not relax.

The woodsman appreciated the verdancy, full well understanding her enthusiasm. "You're trying out some new nutrients and fertilisers?" He was guessing what lay behind the improvements, while also wanting to connect with her. "Is this research for the chemical companies that provide funding?"

"Sure. They're helping, as reported in the media… the same as at thermoports. But this is different – its' very special."

"You've got the conditions just right, barometric pressures (with the gravity) too? What if suddenly there'd been a lasting change in pressures?"

Puzzled, she pressed her lips together and raised her brow. This was not something she'd ever imagined happening. "Like somehow with a *big* geoshift? Well, that'd be weird, really weird, and definitely stressful for plants – and for animals too!"

Time passed, they still conversing, she explaining how other areas of the park were dedicated to life support as well as farm produce and much more. "But here the trees, creepers and groundcover, right down to mosses and lichens, are all the same as in the *Cretaceous*, or very nearly the same. Even the creepy crawlies are authentic. It's all to help us understand the icegem images better. Every bit counts."

Later that morning I joined Mei at the barn to check on the all-important progress in the park. I complimented her on getting atmospheres going quickly. Yet, on querying when the HVACs could be switched off, she rightly referred me to Carla, although adding that more trees, arriving over the next few days, would put the atmosphere recycling comfortably above required levels.

I'd already made a point to go over plans with Carla, including what I wanted for launching probes in GEM. It was all coming together beautifully, with Carla's crews also commissioning a ring of hot springs round the park equator – the shipboard central heating system – with Axle providing direct sunlight for the plants.

300

Casually resting a foot on a corral rail and relaxing, I was conscious of Mei doing likewise. The girl's care of all the animals was invaluable. I knew she appreciated that as much as she appreciated my taking time with her. However, she wondered at something. "Tell me, have you wandered up in the park yet?"

I shook my head a little forlornly. "Ah, if only – but I will, as soon as I've done my turn in TonicTime. I can't do too much of both, away from EarthG, otherwise FayWell will be on my case. You fimans are so lucky."

"Ah – the Commander too," Mei looked sorry.

"No matter. Well, I'd better be getting back. See you at the C-Group session."

We'd arranged to meet mid-day at the lake next to Primrose Clinic, just then being staffed and was also out of earshot of fitting works. Eager to follow on with their ancient scenes of chaos caused by geoshifts, the C-Group guys needed no prompting from me.

"It's staggering, yes?" Guille watched as FayWell swam underwater in her mermaid guise and, taking his cue, reached up to the surface to kick off a slides show. Commenting on the aerial views of the world that appeared, he began, "Continents and oceans, millennium upon millennium, on steroids restructuring! The climate too, all shaken up! With low pressure systems whisking up winds and high pressure systems clearing skies…"

"Big weather!" Sashia enthusiastically summed up the events, "Suddenly happening! When for ages it had all been so moderate."

"Nowhere frigid with continuous permafrost or ice sheets, though," Steve corrected her cheerfully. "Not yet."

"Yes, *they'd* had it so easy," Mei explained the implications of Sashia's summation, to living things. "Shaded by forest canopies and cloud cover, in the past big dinosaur herds simply had to keep moving through the lush acid-tolerant fern meadows of river basins, to let it all recover from their normal peeing and foraging! But that, of course, was all in a good cause – their humus and seed-rich excrement had been great in terraforming up and down continents!"

"But," Guille interposed, "this was all coming to an end. Look!" Broken up skies reflected on the ground." Slide after slide rolled over hills and valleys, where mists were being cleared, giving way to dappled sunlight and the shadows of lifting clouds.

"Now being sculpted was this patchwork vegetation," Mei drew their attention to a wooded fern meadow, which was all there once had been, whilst now it was strewn with grassy invasions from heathlands and also with brush and cactus. "Look, there!" A small hadrosaur herd by a lake, hooted and honked mating calls, surrounded on one side by a rock slope covered in heather and on the other by parched grassland. "They'd come this far, at the end of that long fern plain, and it was as far as these few would go now. A sign of the times, with the shrinking of old ranges matched by dinosaur herd numbers, even sizes, spiralling down in sync."

"Hah! Yeah! Where they no longer pooped," Guille was remembering the earlier information that morning, "ferns gave way to a much bigger spread of woody plants?"

"Yes! Incredible, huh?" Mei was clearly pleased about his interest. "The bigger weather of heathlands had brought about woodier ground cover, grasses and such, to stand up in the wind, heat and atmospheric pressure. That bigger weather was now down here, taking the hardier greenery much farther and wider than ever before."

"Greenery the dinosaurs had little stomach for!" Guille had taken in their preference for ferns over digesting the lignin in grasses.

"Right, a case of too much too soon! Too much change! Anyway it was the turn of birds flitting throughout the lands, as well as bees and ungulates too, to suddenly open up and paint the planet another kind of green – one more suited to them than dinosaurs."

"Exposed as everywhere now was," Steve grinned wickedly, "every little mite straying from cover was likely to be swooped on by eagle-eyed raptors!"

I presented them with a slow, grave clap. "Wow! There it came. Our modern world's tight symbiosis taking hold – and pushing out dinosaurs!"

"Those forests are like Gaia's organs," Guille romanticised lovingly about the scenes. "And those plains are her arteries, for migratory animals to course along as her lifeblood." He looked at Mei. "Imagine that, and in it all changing, Gaia was also being transformed – forever." Mei lowered her head to one side, regarding him, without a word.

I had in mind what I'd said previously, about nature's magic. "Hm, Gaia taking shape, an unstoppable force. Remember your thought Mei, about there being something bigger than the selfish gene and Natural Selection?" I nodded for her agreement. "Gaia?"

We had digressed. I drew them back to our quest. "To recap. Big weather was blowing away the clouds, clearing the skies – in effect taking away the extreme Polar Warming there had been, simply that and not the widespread warming or cooling we normally associate with Climate Change? With the heathlands invading further and further down hillsides, to encroach on the lowland domains of dinosaurs?"

"Actually, that outward growth of heathlands had been very erratic. We have also seen, millennia upon millennia, that the same dinosaur species were driven to extinction," Mei qualified his summation, "because of the life that kept rafting back in. In the end the heathlands did win out, rafting did end... and dinosaurs did fail."

"So, in terms of *now*, history could be repeating itself?" I got nods all round. "If DeepStorm's wave crest really could churn up our weather, swing us right back into cloud blanketing extreme Polar Warming – devastatingly for our agriculture – we still have a hell of a lot to work out in preparation for great changes arriving once again."

A couple of days later I called all reconneers to the Soho conference hall, with the Mission Board attending. I went straight to the point. "As the name DeepStorm Questor suggests, our primary objective is to explore the Gwave phenomenon." I paused to let them reflect on this. "We need to do this to prevent whole tracts of land from being destroyed on Earth and elsewhere. *We* cannot accept failing in that! Our little army will not! Your loved ones need us, that army to fight for them. Win we will." All eyes were on me. "Always remember you are handpicked reconneers, each and every one of you, the best of the best.

"We're already feeding data to UNNDC, with agencies across the globe eagerly awaiting more, to manage risks and to plan new protected environments like Ecstasy." I felt their tension ease somewhat as I continued. "We must deliver that data, fast. Get started right now – and keep me informed of your progress. Report your milestone achievements. Anything major, you must advise me immediately – day or night."

~*~

303

33

On Christmas Day, the last SnowVale passes were issued to Questor task force crews to attend a spectacular show organised by Ecstasy administrators. The ice rink was sprinkled with snow, and a huge, bauble bedecked Christmas tree stood tall to one side. Fairy laser lights sparkled and swirled everywhere. Christmas carols filled the air. For security reasons, the area was screened off from the public and the press, who packed the periphery of events. The Pope and Archbishop of Canterbury, Sustra Matri, Costa DelMonte and Frank Morse were among many dignitaries to join in on holoe, all adding their cheer and thanks to the valiant Questor task force, and wishing all crews God's speed in their quest – to find answers.

During the speeches, the Commander was making his way around the rink, deep in thought until he bumped into Kaitlyn O'Malley. "So Doctor, I suppose the cold is a seasonal touch?" Wrapped snugly in a pure white artic hare-like fur coat, her smile was cheerful as she reached to rub his gloved hands.

"Sure, the occasional change in climate." Her nose twitched in the way of a mischievous witch. "Good for everyone's demeanour! Ha-ha! Might be good for the plants, though – to kill off harmful parasites."

"How's the construction worker?"

"Dave? Oh, he's as good as he'll ever be. Gets about unaided, just not too nimbly. Look over there." There he was, the patient, walking freely on the far side of the rink. "I could have released him, but I gather you want him confined here on security grounds, until we all leave."

The Commander nodded. "He's enjoyed a liberal amount of mixing with our lot. I don't want the media to pump him for anything before we're away." He looked steadily at her. "Not long now, just to tomorrow."

"Hmm, Boxing Day."

"Yeah," he smiled somewhat mockingly, "as it happens. Not that this Yank wants to spoil your fun. It's just that we have a date with that crotchety old dame DeepStorm, who has no intention of waiting around."

"Stroppy old bitch! Time to burn her fucking britches!"

"Damned right!" He grinned, enjoying the banter despite what lay ahead. She knew, of course, her eyes on him, full of empathy. Her hand reached for his face and his eyes closed as if he was yielding to her touch. And she saw the woman in his thoughts, Jude Nade was there.

The Commander took control again. "Anyway, keep up the good work," he half whispered, leaning forward to most uncommonly peck her cheek with a kiss, and giving his two-finger victory salute before carrying on his way.

Quite soon he brushed past Sashia, wearing a red Father Christmas hat. She was on holoe to Fayez, also wearing that hat. Not wanting to disturb her he simply flashed a smile her way and moved on to hone up on the dinner arrangements.

Central to those was a superbly huge ice sculpture of a dragon hanging over the rink from the ice roof, with fluorescence deep within giving a blue and green glow along its body and red in the flames emanating from the mouth.

By evening, Christmas carols still in the air, the Dalai Lama and Hu Ma attending together on holoe – both, champions of caring societies – watched as the Ecstasy Christmas dinner ice sculptures lowered from a high trellised archway under the dragon, the entire scene now a son et lumière, highlighting silver clad chefs descending, as gold and silver fairies danced and a cook, cutting away the platform beneath, revealed a whole roasting oxen.

Further off, the Commander's enjoyment of the scene was evaporating. He had come upon a screen showing the Sævrama Channel, on which Jude Nade was presenting a retrospective on DeepStorm's trails of destruction and evacuations, with a text stream that read – • *Lost under snow and ice: Whole towns in northernmost Ameurasia* • *Essential services crippled: in many underlying areas and at high altitudes* • *Devastated by earthquakes and volcanic eruptions: Whole districts in the USA, the Mediterranean, Pakistan, Indonesia... Breaking News:: • displaced and homeless refugees: 23 million • Out of work: 234 million ...*

"*This is a catastrophic picture and interruptions to communications by Cosmic Weather certainly aren't helping. Authorities everywhere are struggling to cope with growing floods of refugees. Governments, facing drastic downturns in their own economies and resources, are being guided by the UN to help each other out – as best they can – with relief task forces and provisions. Meanwhile, they're also urged to reorganise and plan for replacing tent cities with new towns – wherever these could be deemed safe from DeepStorm. This is what everyone is hoping the DeepStorm Questor mission will find out.*

"Blighting all of this are the anarchists and insurgents, who are eating away at districts by intimidating and abducting refugees and their provisions while seeding despondency and despair through the DoomNet syndrome. Most notably Colombia and Myanmar are on the brink of civil war. Military movements on the ground are being monitored by the UN, as they are out at sea and, it has just been reported, even out in space."

I was nearby and couldn't help but notice the Commander's expression of empathy clearly focused on Jude. I imagined he would prefer to be somewhere nearer to there right now. I held back for a while longer before approaching him. "What's it going to take, huh?"

With weighted breath, he replied, "Ah, the zillion dollar question, hey, prof – only matched by, *'Is there time'?*"

"Time – exactly. It turns out, there is a pattern…" I had avoided facing him, but he now positioned himself to face me. "Gwaves hitting us on both sides of our Milky Way Galaxy, near and far." In giving him the picture I was keeping my voice down. "With a 68 million year interval, followed by a 118 million year one – this fits."

"Hell! You're sure?"

"I can't be categorical – not, that there actually was a Gwave in our past. There's no sign that there's ever been a binary system big enough or near enough to generate harmful Gwaves out here. It's just a possibility though – Black Holes and Dark Matter both have gravity, that's how they're detected, and it's conceivable there could be an as yet undetected system composed of one or other of those. Every one of the Mass Extinction events there's ever damned well been, fits the pattern I just mentioned. Including the dinosaur extinction."

"Which started when, your data, 68 million years or so ago?" My silence, said it all. "It's recurring *now* – DeepStorm wiped out the dinosaurs – and *it's back?*"

I came around to face him head on. "It certainly looks that way. The last event started 68 million years ago, and its effects went on for some three million years."

Soberly and stiffly he moved to where optics awaited his address to the gathering, the World – and Jude Nade. A smile being in order, he made poor work of it. *"This is a rather mixed moment – sad, in leaving those we'd most want to be with, daunting in what we might come up against and hopeful, in that we shall prevail. And prevail we shall, together. Above all, right now, we must also be joyous in this time of giving. A time we share with all mission members – just, as I've heard from you, we will share in your Muslim Eid, your Buddhist Wesak, your Hindu and Sikh Diwali, among other festivals. On these things I wish you, mission members of all persuasions, a Merry Christmas and every success – and to the World, God bless."*

The C-Group called later, very excited about something they *had* to show me. I found them outside, by the SnowVale Park watercourse, where they already had a theme projected on the water. "It's Chicxulub!" Sashia shouted in an ill-contained whisper.

The clip played. Immediately I saw a space-view of the Earth centred on the submerged Yucatan Peninsula. Just as I made out FayWell, now a mermaid, drifting beneath it, a bright object shot in from the east and, on smashing in, exploded with the size and brightness of a noonday Sun. A bright halo instantly radiated out to scorch and blast far into both Americas, followed by a wall of soot thousands of metres high – that buried all almost as far – and a tsunami that hit the coasts and raced up the Western Interior Seaway and down across Lake Maracaibo. Cloud was completely blown away in the whole wide vicinity and a dense brown-black pall formed in the stratosphere.

"Aaah!" Everyone gasped, reacting even though they'd seen individual images and clips in compiling this show. They were seeing the whole finished thing now.

"Colossal!" was all Sashia could croak out.

"As *big* as a hundred thousand Toba-sized supervolcanoes!" Guille was comparing the Chicxulub blast with one of the biggest eruptions ever. "Disruptions to weather patterns, from that 73 millennia old behemoth wreaked havoc on deciduous plants, lamentably hitting savannahs and meadows hard, globally."

"Riveting!" Steve stuck with the impact while the clip fast-forwarded, to show the blast's dense pall dusting heavily below it. Very slowly the jet stream carried the lot east over the Mediterranean region of the Tethys Sea, while easterly trade winds sluggishly took it to Hawaii. "Everywhere buried was the kill zone," he put in, "and that dark swirl at ground level, churning more soot westward into the Pacific, was an impact hypercane.

"And look!" Apart from bolts of lightning, just a few diffused glows could also be made out in all the murk. Yet Steve's tone betrayed none of his disappointment regarding how weak the ensuing Armstrong Effect was. "Eruptions in the Rockies and Andes! Pretty ineffectual perhaps, because it's come after the recent geoshifts you reckon? No, look there!" Excited, he pointed to another tsunami radiating from ground zero, and others that radiated out of Tethys as well as taiga and Antarctic regions. The oceans were also covered in raindrop like ripples. Several volcanoes erupted. "*See*, now you have it! A geoshift! Triggered by the impact!"

"And there! Oil!" Guille had spotted a huge slick, in the bull's eye of ground zero.

"And fresh seepages round the world..." Steve pointed to close-ups. "FayWell has estimated the amount at quadruple what we saw before."

The clips showed Tethys regions and elsewhere where coastlines, ocean reefs, shallow seas and river deltas, even reaching far into lowlands, were wasted by *oily tsunamis*.

"No one lives here anymore!" Steve sang softly, as they grimly listened and looked on at the devastation. "And see! Currents in the Pacific took the oil slick west to where tsunamis devastated the Gobi and Taklamakan deltas too."

"Wow! Yeah, not for a very, very, long while!" Guille agreed.

"Oily winds battered places far inland too, with violent storms and monsoons. See?" Mei might have been shocked, but she also looked ecstatic that her gut instincts had not been too wrong. "That's strange, though..." She scanned around the scenes, "I don't see any dinosaurs – not one, anywhere. Of course we've just about seen that marine reptiles and pretty well all pterosaurs went extinct earlier, with the end of rafting and with competition from the heath-lands. But, had all the dinosaurs gone, too?"

"We don't have views everywhere," Sashia offered, "but it seems to me everything in and around ground zero was trashed…"

"No, she's questioning if they weren't there at all. The thing is, there's never been any sign of dinosaurs right at the moment of the impact," Steve enlightened her, but he could hardly believe the real effect of the asteroid impact they were witnessing. "Though everywhere in the kill zone was buried under fallout," he reflected hard, "not a single dinosaur fossil has ever come out of those layers. Not one. It's as if, as we're seeing now, there weren't any to be buried."

"Okay, no fossils. *But* absence of fossil evidence is not evidence that they were not there. A cardinal rule of palaeontology," Mei smiled, reluctantly sensing a synergy in their thinking.

"Just as the absence of any view of them, limited as our icegem coverage is," he leaned in, "is also not evidence of their absence.

"Anyway, if they were somewhere in this," Mei couldn't resist some smugness, "ironically the biggest deltas, where the rookeries of large herds would have been, was where much of the oil doing the damage had formed."

"Hah! Which means," Guille loved this, "they were done for, in their own poo-poo!"

"It was all the same for millennia afterwards," Steve also grinned as the clips again fast-forwarded, "with no fossils and no icegem sightings of dinosaurs. But then, in the dearth of volcanic soot, rain and landslides, following this geoshift, nothing much would've been buried anyway."

"And if any had survived," Sashia was relieved at Mei seeming to thaw a little with Steve, "see? Chaos everywhere. Well outside of ground zero flowering heath-lands had died back under a persistent haze."

"As well as from drought and a critical dip in carbon emissions," Steve expounded. "All the results of volcanic inactivity. Possibly there were traces of iridium in that haze," he mused, "from the asteroid itself. Although, possibly too, from oil reservoirs somewhere that contained meteorite deposits…"

"Some small groups had survived many millennia later?" Sashia set before them some old fossil reports. "Bits from hadrosaurs and ceratopsians, as well as running dromaeosaurus, were found in the hills of Montana and Mongolia, and iguanodons in the Pyrenees."

"Well," Mei regarded her fondly, "It's never been resolved whether those fossils were "reworked" geologically, as some have argued. They could have been disturbed somehow and reburied in later layers."

"So, there's nothing we've got that can tell us there were *or* were not any dinosaurs anywhere at the time of the Chicxulub impact. Or, anywhere after it either," Guille tried to crystallise their findings. "So, what? Shallow seas were purged of marine invertebrates, but everything else that went extinct did so *before* the impact? And whatever might have survived went extinct some while after?"

"Yep, we already witnessed the extinction of reptiles – caused by Chronic Natural Correction. This view, now, is the outright purging of all coastlines along with all lowland habitats – by a *catastrophic* Natural Correction," Mei gave Steve a sideways glance, "except, anything on when the end did finally come about for reptiles."

"Well, this changes all previously held views on the great *End-Cretaceous*. Certainly mine!" Steve, was clearly astonished. "That impact, the Manson impact and the Deccan eruptions too, however massive each was, played a part but *none* were the end in itself. I guess we'll never see the end, whether before or after the impact, because anyway, the end was when there was nothing left *to* see."

"Okay, it happened sometime then," surprisingly Mei looked upon Steve less acrimoniously.

"That's life!" I was emphatic. "We're done here." I'd been taken up in all of this, as intrigued as they were. I could hardly conceal my dread over what we'd witnessed, but I had to call a halt now. We had gone as far as we could in our aim to anticipate the effects of DeepStorm, with insights from the ancient past. There was a lot to sort through before compiling our report to UNNDC.

I had to decide how best to put this to them, seeing that the research was also unauthorised. I had to ensure that none of the findings would be disregarded. Looking at these guys I saw the same sentiment expressed in their faces.

"By the way," I held them back for one more thought, addressing Mei in particular. "Did you think any more on evolution? On the selfish gene and Natural Selection – and about the magic of Gaia?"

"Yes," Mei sounded cautious. She obviously wanted to broach something else. "I think we're beginning to see patterns, with ever more complex life forms that built on one another. And Natural

Corrections kicked them on again whenever they stalled. That was the magic." I studied her, letting her paint the picture in her head. "The vast forest-terraforming world of dinosaur giants, gave birth to a fringe world of birds and, in suddenly fragmenting, was only vast for the birds. One world gave birth to the next, before fading away…"

"Okay, good. A succession of worlds," I coaxed, "each time getting more what – more intelligent?"

"Er…" Mei's gaze was distant, as if seeking inspiration, "More Gaia. It's about Gaia, maturing…"

"Terrific! Yes," I had so looked forward to this moment, "Gaia transforming from one form to another, like egg to caterpillar to chrysalis to a butterfly?

"We've seen snippets of when she took to the air," Mei was recalling those icegem images in a fond way. "Before that, there was the period when she went from sea to land. And after this, she's taking to space – with us. It's almost as if she's meant to be going somewhere…"

"Great! So, where to – and what's next?" Blank expressions faced me. All I could do was offer them a relaxed smile.

~*~

34

All Boxing Day intense activities on the Command Bridge of the Bering were nonetheless calm and business-like. Ship's officers, aided by FayWell smartly attired in a white uniform though still with hair flowing over her eyes, called out system checks for their Captains and the Commander to hear:

From Lascaux, "...ship's crew – CHECK..."
From Avebury, "...fire and safety systems – CHECK..."
From Avebury, "...provisions – CHECK..."

All three ships were busier than bee hives. FayWell, overtly fastidious now, kept track of literally all LNs – whether belonging to the task force or contractors or even visitors – to account for absolutely everybody's and everything's due presence and wellness.

Even with FayWell's thoroughness regulations required that all staying, going ashore or coming aboard, had to be double-checked with the full involvement of ship crews – for anything that might have been missed. In the event of unseen eventualities, regardless of systems, *they* had to have intimate knowledge of the state of their vessel. There'd be no turning back for anything once underway.

Dr O'Malley had holoe reports on all medical provisions and facilities, likewise military officers on their ordnance, and ship's engineers on their systems.

I was on the Bridge, having taken a shuttle across from Avebury, receiving reports from Carla on life support systems and from Mei on the liner parks.

The Bering Navigation Officer was in communication with ISWA and Ecstasy Navigation Control for updates on shuttle and shipping movements.

Meanwhile, contractors were updating their Moon offices about returning plant and crews.

The Commander stood impressively on the Bridge, while subtly vigilant over all and, taking in the entire scene on translucent panes, his execs were undoubtedly borrowing from his strength. Through the large window were the huge gleaming white liners, with shuttles and construction equipment busily coming in and out and robots roaming over ice shields for anything left behind. Overall, this vast vista was resplendent, with the grey Moon behind larger than life, and the blue Earth and amber Sun to either side.

In that magical moment, the strength came to me to release our *Cretaceous* discoveries and, with all haste, pass on to UNNDC what risks we had gleaned regarding DeepStorm – even though I fully acknowledged the risk of my being sanctioned over the unauthorised work – and possibly even sacked on the very point of departure. "On the other hand, might they even terminate the mission if this information is enough to go by?" I wondered. I had to admit that, not having expected to be in this position with results this early on, I simply hadn't been prepared to go to them yet. "It's so niggling," I reasoned, "not having their support, and not being able to fully enjoy sharing this news. At the very least," I considered, "they should concede how right it was to look for and find answers from the past." For all my deliberations, I knew I had no choice but to go ahead – for the greater good of mankind.

And for my reconneers' sakes, for them not to be seen as accomplices, in my report I gave credit to their involvement only up to the time of joining Questor upside – and not after.

The body of my report covered the threats and measures to deal with risk, much of which I'd already gone over in Security Council Summits, with our new discoveries foremost in prominence. I also outlined what we'd be monitoring in our outward journey, and how that data would be streamed back to other space agencies engaged in the 'ERASE' [Earth Risk Assessment Search and Evaluation] initiative. The pun there was never lost on audiences. Erase what – risks or mankind?

My executive summary concentrated on the risks to major cities and provinces, as well as to life sustaining ecologies – of a series of major geoshifts setting up rumbles in the Earth's mantle and triggering worldwide tremors, tsunamis, eruptions and oil slicks.

Primary recommendations of mine, all aimed at mitigating risks, were to – intensify agriculture in tropical and sub-tropical zones, prioritise Construction Exclusion Zoning in geologically unstable areas and, most vitally, build a worldwide capability to deal with and even avert *oil slicks* on the oceans.

Officers continued their preparations and one by one control screens on the bridge of each vessel displayed ALL CHECKED AND CLEAR.

FayWell reported, "Commander, Questor is clear to GO. Clear to get underway."

"Captains, RAISE ANCHOR. TURN ONTO TRAJECTORY," the Commander ordered, voice low and even.

Immediately a bank of screens switched to news channels featuring the big event of the task force moving out. Quickly joining the scene, flotillas of small silver craft appeared, braving a chance encounter with a BoBo to afford passengers and media alike front row seats at the ceremonious send off. Several well-known reporters were present, with Jude Nade providing Sævrama Channel voice-overs from a location on Earth.

The Commander looked intermittently at his Captains, Jude Nade, O'Malley and I, all of us conscious of the long months this first leg to Mars would take. After which we'd be long gone in black space. The gut instinct I had was that it could quite possibly be much longer – much, much longer.

Anchor systems deactivated, the vessels very slowly began to turn onto their trajectory. All that remained was for Mei, gallantly assisted by Guille, to arrive. They'd reported leaving Ecstasy with a construction barge full of livestock, because that was the only transport available to them. FayWell had computed a two-hour path, authorised by the Bering Navigation Officer, for them to meet the lumbering task force as it picked up speed.

Sævrama Channel coverage showed all three Questor vessels turning, their distinctive comet-like tails trailing out the same as from Ecstasy's ice roof, and dwarfing the myriad craft dotted about us. Jude spoke over the scene, her voice upbeat and yet concealing emotions with a barely perceptible quiver, *"This is truly magnificent – so reminiscent of explorers that once set sail to cross the uncharted waters of the Atlantic. Just the same, these intrepid explorers will be going the furthest that mankind has ever ventured. They'll be setting the way for all who follow. Our hearts and prayers go with them. Our hopes for us all ride with them."*

Control screens on all three bridges, duplicated on the Command Bridge, instantly displayed LOCKED ON TRAJECTORY.

A moment of expectation followed, the Commander poised to give the order Full Speed Ahead. That's when it appeared – a large black cloud against the Moon! Immediately turning, like a swarm, it first headed for the departing shuttles and then, splitting, also made for the flotillas. Close ups showed small bats, tens of thousands of them, flitting about craft and lighting up in a sparkler-like tangle as they were blasted by BoCrackers.

Immediately mayday calls came from two shuttles, one with a navigation malfunction and the other with a cabin pressure fault, while construction workers aboard also screamed for help on their coms. Just moments before this, they'd been homeward bound, via Ecstasy, relieved that the long months of dangerous work on Questor ships was finally over. A craft full of reporters covering the event careered off course, and abruptly stopped while all aboard agitatedly relayed to their media stations what was happening. A contractor's crane veered wildly, the operator unable to jump free, and crashed into Lascaux in a cloud of pulverised ice. The wreckage cartwheeled over and over, breaking up while gouging across the surface. A robotic pump raced past, impaled by bats, and crashed resoundingly above the Bridge.

"BATTLE STATIONS," the Commander ordered his execs, calmly. They knew the drill. It was the same on all three vessels, the view from their bridges instantly showing the automatic fire of their BoCrackers. The sound of boots running reverberated everywhere.

"ENGAGE ENEMY." In a flash the Strategic Planning Officer had authorised the long range targeting of bats, under the command of the Gunnery Officer and Squadron Officer, using profiles provided by FayWell.

The dazzling fireworks display, bursting out explosively, reflected on the gleaming ice hulls of all three gigantic ships. The same show was on news channels throughout Questor, with feed coming in live from crew and reporters in the thick of it. A cacophony of whooping and other jubilant yells accompanied the spectacle.

"Rescue One SCRAMBLE. Rescue Two SCRAMBLE," the First Officer ordered instantly.

Dr O'Malley's paramedics were already racing, all the way through the throng to the cargo bay, to board the box-shaped craft.

"Fighters SCRAMBLE," the Squadron Officer ordered. Onscreen he detailed two Eurofighter T9 Twisters to give escort, another three to engage the enemy and all others to be on standby.

The Bering Navigation Officer took full charge of ISWA civilian operations, overriding Ecstasy Navigation Control, "This is Bering Control. Moon flight space is now a military no-fly zone," he ordered, "Repeat, Moon flight space is now a military no-fly zone. All civilian craft are to instantly clear the area and make for the nearest landing port."

"This is Ecstasy Control. On what authority are you acting?" Ecstasy Navigation Control was also on a separate line, seeking orders from ISWA.

"This is the Questor task force Commander. With immediate effect I am assuming full jurisdiction over Ecstasy anchorage around the Moon," stony grave and fighting mad, his clenched knuckles white, the Commander's spirit had quickly carried through the Bridge and to all military personnel throughout the Questor ships.

With deadly composure he then took in the whole chain of orders that ensued, with FayWell emulating his calm manner in relaying all necessary information. To his annoyance, some media reporters objected to the no-fly order. Their irate editors also got on line. The bats were a major event and well under control following the immense show of firepower coming from the task force. The Commander stood firm.

"This is Ecstasy Navigation Control. Commander, we have your authority confirmed by ISWA headquarters. You have full control." At the same time, the Commander received UNRO confirmation of ISWA compliance.

Ice in my veins, I could only stare in awe and admiration at the man's steady, iron-fisted control and I took note to never intercede wherever military matters were concerned. Assured of that strength, my concern was rather for our civilian fimans who I could see had stopped work. Quite sensibly they were gathering in the relative safety of mezzanines in Lascaux and Avebury. A few military personnel were running to leave and get to the Bering. Sashia was with a dumbfounded crowd, in Soho, where they watched the commentaries of departing reporters on screens all about them. Steve was with Carla at Heather Farm.

The operators of civilian craft had no option but to follow orders, insurance policies and craft licences at stake. Craft furthest off picked their way through the mess, of bats and fireworks, and headed for Ecstasy. Others, close by, headed for the nearest task force landing bay. Examinations of the craft showed where an acid suspension of nanobot bugs, from the bats, had targeted cabling and wiring.

Questor rescue units made straight to the occupants of stricken shuttles to get them out, while reporters amongst them obstinately stuck to presenting to the World. Meanwhile guns of the five Twisters despatched out there, joined in blazing away at the bats.

Finally, "Show over!" some reporters reflected dejectedly, on landing.

At that moment I was alerted to a holoe message from UNNDC, "We've noted your prognoses. Needless to say we have to keep the geoshift threat under wraps, from the media, until we get the right slant on how to proceed. They'd make banner headlines of it, and the Questor mission, getting it all off kilter and feed on that for weeks." To my relief, for now, they'd omitted any mention of the work, and so the findings not being authorised. Possibly, the magnitude of what we'd opened up prevented any comeback. As it were, maybe we were at 'PNR' [the Point of No Return]?

Other messages came in, all classified. "We recognise Steve Nord's valuable work in the past with us," the Greenpeace representative enthused, "And the threat of oil slicks on the scale mentioned is horrendous. The Questor research on that is sterling stuff. Especially in highlighting just how fragile seismically active areas are. Oil companies have to identify those as a matter of urgency and get out of there."

"The Exxon representative concurred, adding, "We are reviewing to pull out of the North Sea, with capping all remaining wells. We will review our Arctic strategies with Rosneft."

"We are revisiting our Alaskan and other Arctic strategies," the BP representative vouched.

"We need more time to confer with specialists," the Shell representative was cautious.

"Unidentified craft. Sixty in total," FayWell reported in a matter of fact way, as insets of a tight formation of gleaming black stealth fighters appeared in the Bridge window. "Distance 1,000 kilometres, closing fast. Barely discernable, only now picked up by instruments."

With hardly a pause they were suddenly out there and closing fast with the reforming bat swarms, again drawing massive task force fire. Behind that shield the 'Mantas', as they were quickly dubbed, smashed with lasers and guns blazing through the mêlée of civilian craft. High intensity laser bolts ripped through metal. A shuttle, crippled by a searing bolt, immediately came to rest. A contractor's cement barge was hit by a hail of shells and exploded. A patrol vessel careered out of control, reporters within screaming for rescue, among them a Sævrama Channel cameraman, "...are you getting this?" trying desperately to contact Jude. Other craft veered out of the line of fire, desperately trying to head for safety.

The First Officer approached the Commander about whether to block media channels aboard their vessels. Considering this carefully, the Commander decided against it, reasoning that it would be better for those aboard to see what was going on rather than imagine the worst.

Coolly assessing the situation, the Strategic Planning Officer reported to the Commander that civilian craft had merely been in the way of the enemy's real objectives. "They're targeting the liners, Avebury and Lascaux."

On this advisement the Navigation Officer countermanded his previous order. "All civilian craft not close to a Questor landing port, disregard the earlier directive! Repeat, disregard the earlier directive! You are to head straight for Ecstasy! Repeat, head straight for Ecstasy!"

All the while, eating up the distance to their targets, all sixty shielded Mantas ceaselessly strafed the liner surfaces which merely sent up clouds of vaporised ice. Flying over, those pilots were amazed and dismayed to see the hulls they'd expected to rip apart merely heavily pock marked. They'd had no more effect on those thick hulls than medieval canon hitting glaciers.

And then, far off, the formation could be seen looping around undaunted, tactics and weaponry reconfigured, to make another pass.

Throughout the liners, I could see personnel watching screens faces betraying fear, most muffling their ears against the pounding sounds of lasers and shells on the hull walls.

In the Soho mezzanine crowd Sashia looked up to see Steve arrive accompanied by Carla. "Who'd have thought?" he managed his old cocky manner, to lift her spirits, "Overwhelming send off, eh?"

"Hmm, someone in a strop about us leaving?" Sashia got a rousing cheer.

"Some guys just can't handle rejection!" Carla added darkly, to Steve's and Sashia's amusement.

"FULL RESPONSE," the Commander ordered full out battle. And, on a direct line, sought orders from UNRO, "I formally request a state of hostilities applies." Among other things his request meant a suspension of peacetime military conventions regarding the use of weapons – and it was immediately approved. "All weapons to full strength," he ordered.

"Reconfigure BoCrackers to laser bolts," the Gunnery Officer ordered FayWell. "FIRE AT WILL," he ordered his gunners to shoot canon manually when FayWell was having difficulty in tying down Manta profiles to target automatically.

"Fighters SCRAMBLE," the Squadron Officer ordered and, because the Commander wanted nothing left to chance, he also detailed superior numbers, eighty Eurofighter T9 Twisters, to attack with full strength lasers.

The enemy was now swarming from afar, close-up glimpses revealing bloodshot eyes. Doubtless they were incensed that their shield was now being ripped apart by heavy fire as well as how futile their own incessant blazing had been. The battle-carrier had opened fire with a barrage of lasers, large calibre guns and missiles. The remaining civilian craft and rescue vehicles also hastened to get clear and, with those, all news coverage faded away.

The two Twister escorts broke off, to reform tightly with the other three. Wherewith the pilots glanced resolutely at one another, giving a fiman three finger wave, before turning. Before them were clouds of ice, from hits on the liners, and beyond that the cloud of the enemy speeding and blazing forward.

The Twisters shot forward, not with malice but intent to protect Avebury and Lascaux. Distance to targets vanishing, they could see FayWell's difficulty in profiling them. "It's not just that they're shielded! The Mantas are shape-shifting their stealth design, like squid," the lead pilot reported, "Their skins are flowing silk-like, constantly changing colour while thinning and puffing out randomly, so that they have no fixed appearance."

"We can see that now," FayWell sounded coldly pensive. "They're also shifting their friendly-fire algorithms in line with ours, as quickly as I'm making changes. Their AI is doing that." This meant we couldn't even target them electronically.

"Can you locate it?" The Strategic Planning Officer was thinking along the line of disabling their support network.

"No. I don't see," FayWell concentrated hard and warily, "but sense her, looking at me." That said something about the other AI's gender, if not her power. I just wondered at all of that though, FayWell talking about *sensing* another AI who was *looking* at her! What was all this? Where did it come from in FayWell?

With the advanced line of Mantas nearly upon them, the Twisters rolled and looped to attack along their flank, dogfight fashion. Going in firing they immediately scored two hits, through the thinning mist of bats, but didn't wait to see them disintegrate in flashes. Another enemy crashed to the surface of the Moon. "Eeyaah! Come and get it you bastards!" The Twisters sped on with pent up rage, brewed up by DeepStorm and now these unprovoked attacks, and only now revealing itself. Officers on the Bridge looked on iron-faced, at those hopelessly outnumbered few.

The enemy pilots' eyes were hard and unflinching, not buying the distraction of dogfights. Instead, they concentrated on breaking the liner hulls with wave after wave of missiles, which, hit by BoCrackers, succeeded in raising a curtain of explosions a kilometre or so out.

None of that could be heard in Avebury. But, just then, there was a terrifying explosion followed by the sound of ice cracking! A missile had hit them! The noise reverberated in the heads of fimans as much as in mezzanine walls. Steve, fire in his eyes while conscious of everyone shuddering, clasped Carla's hand, "What they need out there are ice-board champions..."

"To kick ass!" Carla finished off with a yell, squeezing his hand and glaring as defiantly.

Reporters nearing Ecstasy had to zoom in to get a view of the explosion, which was barely discernable through the shroud of fire and mist surrounding the liner.

"DEPLOY cyber-dragnets," the Squadron Officer ordered. The Twisters looped back, dragging the electromagnetic force field of charged particles three kilometres across and, lasers blazing, swept across the enemy cloud. Behind them they left a trail of bats, and a couple of Mantas, shut down with immobilised control systems.

The enemy formation carried on unperturbed and instead, streaming over Avebury, the pilots encouraged at seeing the crater on the surface. They immediately looped back intent on releasing missiles closer to, with several Mantas perishing in the intensified curtain of fire. It was hit and miss. FayWell, even using infrared through the remaining bats, was still having difficulty in profiling them. Nevertheless, those brave Twister pilots were now spotting them for the battle-carrier gunners, changing the odds, but, regrettably, not before another missile hit Avebury and yet another hit Lascaux.

The enemy pilots were sure to have sensed that shift in odds – and now saw it worsen as Twisters streaked out in force from the Bering. Yet, still encouraged, they spread out to loop and fire at will. Some took on the five intrepid Twisters in their midst, sending one careering off in flames.

Then, out of nowhere, a shower of BoBos streaming through at treble their speeds smashed into a Manta, took out a bunch of bats and fatally crippled a Twister. The Mantas carried on undeterred and took out a third Twister, while the others persisted with targeting the liners and stoking the curtain of fire there.

The arriving Twisters formed up quickly, with fiman waves for their lost mates, before attacking the Mantas and forcing them into dogfights. "ENGAGE AquaScabbards." The lead pilot had decided on using the navy's prized weapon. The canon fired a continuous shaft of charged-water-shards at speeds designed to rip into hulls and screens, tearing apart wherever it froze and disrupting controls, or even killing with the charge. The tactical advantage of that ordinance was that it was easily replaced in space, huge quantities were stored in bulk and small quantities used in firing. It was effectively in limitless supply.

Suddenly the whole of Ecstasy anchorage erupted in battle with a mishmash of craft, bright laser bolts, gleaming shards and missiles!

With so much firepower concentrated on them Manta casualties soon mounted – flying past out of control with torn skins, or shattered windscreens, or draped in bolts of electricity, or trailing smoke. They were taking intolerably heavy losses, their numbers soon reduced by a third against the Bering's loss of just six fighters.

Even so, the intensity of the fight didn't lessen until the enemy saw, through clouds of ice and smoke, where pockmarks on the surface of the liners were healing. The holes, even the craters they'd managed to make at great cost, were automatically filling with water and freezing as good as new.

Their situation was hopeless, overwhelmingly outgunned and getting nowhere. They had to have known, right from the start, even with the element of surprise they had, what a gamble attacking so close to the massive battle-carrier was. Now, on seeing their efforts so easily dashed, they finally lost their appetite for the fight. Despondency setting in, they broke and ran.

Regardless, two Mantas defiantly changed tactics, concentrating their fire on one Meadowvale shutter of Avebury. Lasers downed one craft on approach, while the other, with a lucky hit, triggered the shutter fully open. It came in firing randomly into the park and succeeded in scattering cattle, sheep and free-range chickens. Torf ran out, "You want our livestock, you shit?" grabbing what came to hand – a high-pressure jet for cleaning surfaces, which he trained on the Manta's nose, "Take that!" Deymore, grabbed a quick-action rivet gun and dashed forward, firing repeatedly. The Manta banked, crashing through terraces, still training its fire on them. Laser bolts and bullets tore up turf, fencing and trees. A bull crumpled in a heap. Sheep were mown down into mounds of wool. The two defenders fell to the ground, not looking so brave, strafing occurring all about them and yet, yes they were inwardly preparing themselves for more, before the fighter's nose brushed overhead. They rolled over to see it smash into a rock waterfall with an explosive *bang*, both yelling their joy and raising fists.

The enemy routed, Sashia was surprised when the Commander called her. "Report on the Command Bridge. Immediately. FayWell, arrange a Shwift – and watch out for BoBos for her." Sashia leaped up and willing her strider heels flat amazed Carla and Steve with running off so fast, to the cargo bay, where she immediately flew onto a waiting Shwift and sped straight at the shutter. She'd no doubt whatever that it'd open and that she'd cross the void between ships unharmed. Pumping her striders on the

Bering, she arrived on the Bridge to find FayWell bringing up images on a pane.

The AI was peering into space with an advanced optical telescope. The Commander, in full control yet coaxing too, motioned for Sashia to do the same. "This lot have come from somewhere nearby – a carrier of theirs. They're not up from Earth, having strictly an upside design and not an Earth-atmosphere one."

Just then FayWell located two unidentified objects. And, on enlarging the indiscernibly grainy images, those on the Bridge could see they were medium to large stealth warships. An officer put the likelihood of them waiting in ambush at medium to high. Meanwhile Sashia spotted a tiny pimple on the edge of the Moon, which FayWell enlarged to reveal the nose of something big just peeking out from the dark side.

Just then the Strategic Planning Officer drew the Commander's attention to the enemy Mantas. "They're not leaving. They're headed for Ecstasy." The Moon base only had light defences and reinforcements could not arrive from Earth at such short notice. The Commander conferred with UNRO chiefs. The order received was to delay the Questor launch and draw the enemy, to spare Ecstasy. On the Commander's authority the Squadron Officer gave the order Twisters RE-ENGAGE. They were to take the dogfight the opposite way around the Moon, away from the big ship skulking over the horizon. The Twisters complied, repeatedly engaging and breaking away in the prescribed direction.

Despite now being outnumbered two to one, the enemy did not run but fought on. "They're following too readily. That's what they wanted," the Strategic Planning Officer observed dryly. "They want to draw our Twisters out. They can't hurt the liners, so they'll cause as much damage to our ordnance, the fighters, as they can."

"Yes, they'd no intention of attacking Ecstasy. That was a ruse," the Commander concurred.

"And our ruse, with the dogfight, is to reconnoitre that big ship round the Moon?" the Strategic Planning Officer only sought confirmation in the light of events. The Commander, standing firm, was confirmation enough, and the Squadron Officer immediately detailed two Twisters to break off and make the recce.

"The no-fly zone is temporarily lifted," the Navigation Officer ordered. With the threat of enemy fighters gone, this was an opportunity to get everyone back to where they should be. "*All* civilian personnel, craft and equipment are to head immediately for Ecstasy."

Naturally enough there were no dissenters, with everyone simply too eager to get to where they might leave for Earth. Nine injured were in that complement. In subsequent checks, twenty-one civilians were reported killed and twelve missing. As the flotilla of civilian craft headed out, Mei and Guille were signalling aboard their barge that they were en route to Questor. In confirming all movements, Ecstasy Navigation Control also confirmed that of the barge.

"Recce accomplished," the Squadron Officer reported.

"What is it?" the Strategic Planning Officer enquired.

"A battle-carrier," came the reply from the lead pilot.

"Just one?" the Strategic Planning Officer queried.

"Yes, just one."

"Right. Order the men home," the Commander was aware of casualties, with six more Twisters lost to space and also the Moon's surface. The enemy tally overall was thirty-two downed, just over half their number. Even so, the Strategic Planning Officer knew the enemy would persist with the dogfight and bring the action right back to Ecstasy anchorage.

"The no-fly zone is reinstated," the Navigation Officer ordered. The civilian flotilla had made good progress but Mei and Guille were slower. He'd have ordered them back, except it was too late. They were beyond PNR. Additionally, with the last of the civilian craft already in Ecstasy and the ice doors shut firmly, Ecstasy was secured as tightly and as impregnably as any fortress.

In that moment Duardo Contrea was on the Rio thermoport, over Rio de Janeiro. "Get Admiral Nodus, for me!" he bellowed at an officer.

Some minutes passed before the holoe of the man appeared, "Buenos dias, your diablo muchacho at your service!" Nodus maintained his best droll manner, putting on a Latino inflection, his voice rasping as usual, "Wanna obliterate some enemies?"

"Timing! Timing is everything! The Questor task force is moving out!" Contrea railed, voice dolefully flat, having no time for anything other than solid objectives, "They're getting away!"

"Do eagles have…"

"I know, I know, do they have talons!" the man's patience had been horribly stunted since birth. "What's that about?"

"You want to tell me, not to let them get far! And, am I ready?" He well knew that his tease was wasted on this tiresomely bullish dullard. "So no worry, no worry, as eagles have talons, yes, I am ready."

"Hell! Okay, see that?" The man was ready to badger him on tactics but, for now, directed him to see where Mei and Guille were positioned.

"How can I not?" Nodus was well aware. "That pair are out there on their own. Ripe for the picking! You want hostages? I'll get a boudoir ready for her – and me." His look was lascivious.

"Get them! We'll have them, at least, to show for this debacle!"

For over an hour the plucky duo kept coming, I watched helplessly through the Bridge window. Agonising for them, Sashia called Steve and Carla still with him. Moments later he holoed her back. "Meet me! The cargo bay – now!" Swiftly he left Carla, who had to stay – with her overall responsibility for the parks.

For all the times she'd bettered Steve with her stunts, now Sashia just knew he had a far stronger side. This would be its platform. Already his unwavering tone commanded the way she had to follow. She had shot out of the Bridge, heels still flat, and run hell bent along the corridors, FayWell rippling along through the plants following their every move and gaining clearance for them every step of the way, and more importantly seeing it in the Commander's eyes.

I was taken aback and filled with apprehension and despair, even as he shook his head for me to stand down and not stop them. Combat was thankfully out, where I was concerned, that being strictly the Commander's department.

In cargo bays of separate ships, Bering and Avebury, the duo equipped themselves with high calibre lasers before jumping onto Shwifts and shooting through shutters to meet in space. By the time they reached the barge a dogfight was raging all about. They had no time to dock safely amid the bullets and laser bolts tearing up the deck. Slamming their Shwifts there they returned fire while grabbing for a hold on anything to keep from floating away. Just then a Manta, weapons firing, swooped in, heading straight for Mei in the pilothouse. She and Steve dived to either side and with good aim, at the same moment Mei instinctively swung the barge sharply around, saw their lasers hit home and the Manta explode in a ball of flames. "Hallo guys," the immensely cheery Mei greeted them. "Glad you got the invite. But what took you so long – fancying yourselves up, heh? About time you got here."

Still firing one handed while grabbing handrails and chains fastened on the deck, the duo began to crawl to her, Sashia responding, "Damn rush hour traffic!"

"Chickens are below. Hope you like your eggs scrambled!" Mei threw back.

As Guille sprang out to help Steve, the two of them swinging an A-frame around to smash into another Manta, the pilothouse exploded in flames. Sashia stopped firing and, quickly stepping against a post, had her striders shoot her sternward. Another blast sent her hurtling back, as she caught a fleeting sight of Mei. Frantically she rose and raced to the smouldering house to find her friend crumpled up under a console, unconscious, her suit burnt and torn. With no time to check her out, Sashia bumped her up and over her own shoulder and, firing with one hand, crawled away from the billowing smoke. "Eugh," she wheezed, "You see? Hellish traffic!" Staring around at the chaos surrounding them, she received no answer

Steve and Guille were prying open the deck to take over the barge controls. All three were now numbed and appalled at the sight of Mei's body, lying limp and motionless where Sashia had lain her.

They were now close enough to Avebury for Guille to steer in a beeline for the Rim shutter. Soon enough the barge slipped through and was immediately sprayed by fire extinguishers.

Paramedics took Mei on an ambulance buggy, Sashia and Guille with them. Steve remained to show the now recovered, and anxiously concerned, Deymore and Torf where the animals were in the hold of the barge.

"Fighters DISENGAGE," the Squadron Officer ordered. "RETURN TO BASE."

"All vessels LOCK DOWN," the Commander ordered with finality after the last of the Twisters had returned to the Bering. The battle-carrier and liners closed and locked all shutters. Now the invaders were left out there alone, shut out of Ecstasy and the Questor task force. Grave as ever, the Commander turned to his officers, "Now we complete the task."

"Damn right. The big ship is a battle-carrier. So, we'll deny these Mantas a safe landing by eliminating it?" The Strategic Planning Officer received a nod from the Commander. "We'll bring the liners to protect them?" He gained another nod.

"Captains, set trajectory the same as the fighters took around the Moon," the Commander ordered, "TURN ONTO TRAJECTORY." And then he added, by way of explanation, "We'll sneak up on the enemy battle-carrier, just out of range of their guns."

LOCKED ON TRAJECTORY was swiftly displayed on control screens on all three vessels.

"FULL SPEED AHEAD," he ordered.

Control screens refreshed to display, ALL SYSTEMS ARE GO. QUESTOR TASK FORCE UNDERWAY. QUESTOR VESSELS MAKING WAY, ON COURSE AND GAINING SPEED.

It was not the ceremonious occasion it was slated to be. No media. No well wishers. Instead we moved forward replete with malice – driven to it.

~*~

35

The trip from the cargo bay to Soho Clinic was short. Sashia and Guille were dropped off in the visitors' lounge en route to the operating theatre. Dr O'Malley was there and prepped to work on the badly injured girl.

In the waiting lounge the couple waited and waited, Guille visibly sharing Sashia's exhausting concern for Mei. Some while later, Steve and Carla arrived. Still later, Tixa came out to break the news that Mei was in a coma and to guide them to her room. They all stayed to take turns to speak to the motionless girl, all hoping to reach her mind and bring her around.

Dr O'Malley came by, but could only say that the state of certain functions in her brain and nervous system had proved indeterminable. While MRI scans of other vital organs looked fine, she had received severe burns, all now treated. Her friends would simply have to wait patiently for her to rally.

They determinedly organised shifts, Carla taking the first while the others were being medically checked and treated before cleaning up and receiving fresh clothing.

When Sashia's shift came, she tried to connect with Mei about the parks, what they were doing, and how important their achievements were. For all her efforts, "See, Mei, I've brought Twing for you," she received no response, not even a movement behind the girl's eyelids all of which began to break Sashia's spirit. Crumpling, she sank to the floor, her head resting on the edge of Mei's bed.

"When you feel..." FayWell drifted slowly in from the shadows, her sentence unfinished. The AI, straw blond hair casually flowing over a pale yellow tube dress, said and did nothing more at first, and although Sashia could not see her veiled eyes, she somehow knew FayWell was just looking. It was so unlike her. When she spoke at last, there was a breath, gentle as a summer breeze, caressing Sashia's hair, "...the *power* you feel with is what I feel."

"What?" She could not grasp what this meant. Lacking the energy to even think about it, Sashia simply stayed put, though still welcoming some comfort. "You really wouldn't want these feelings, this hurt. Believe me," her words weren't fully out when her lips quivered and along came uncontrollable sobs.

"I am facts." Though still soft, the AI's tone was now resigned, "knowing things, the whole World of things, and computing things as in driving this whole task force." Sashia now detected a wistful edge creeping in. "Yet, what I hear most from everyone are not facts. It's about others, about others thinking about them, and about fitting in." Sashia peered closely with her keen eyesight and, for the very first time, not only saw one of the AI's 'eyes' but a hint of a tear and compassion there. With a start, she seemed to see her own reflection! "And, it's about hidden meanings and perceptions. Illusions."

"Ah. You'd not be far wrong in surmising that's what being human is all about!" At other times, Sashia would have laughed but now she felt oddly grateful for the AI's words, whether meant to relieve her misery, or not, she'd no idea. But, the words sounded quite caring, as caring as this electronic marvel could be. "Okay. But right now, this is about Mei. Super confident Mei who's had so much joy robbed from her and anyway hasn't been and still isn't all that secure with others." Sashia, paused, "She's my friend, FayWell. I'm scared to lose her."

Outside the room Tixa was rubbing tears from her face. She was in the middle of imploring Dr O'Malley not to tell Sashia just how critical Mei's condition was, recognising that this would demolish her already exhausted state

Suddenly their conversation ended. They rushed in to check Mei. Her life signs had stopped. Fleet of foot, they whisked her off to the operating theatre before Sashia had time to even summon her thoughts.

"I am discreet, as everyone knows," FayWell made her presence known again, delicate as a snowflake. "So you're not hearing this from me." Sashia's heart was pounding. She simply could not believe all that was happening, and least of all this conversation. "Mei's not been an illusion. She's been true in her thoughts about you and everyone." Apparently crest fallen, the AI spirited herself away, leaving Sashia amazed as well as full of gratitude for the sensitivity shown towards her friend and indeed herself.

In the theatre they fought to resuscitate the injured girl, also using non-invasive electromagnetic brain stimulation and other tools such as using nanobots to target neurons with sonic pulses. None worked. Mei's life signs remained flat.

Tixa was too upset to tell the others. The doctor broke it to Sashia, who collapsed. Steve and Guille came as quickly as they could, Guille turning his head along the way to conceal tears. He looked very lost and alone.

Tixa, needing to be practical in the face of sorrow, began to move the body, but Dr O'Malley told her kindly that she'd done enough. Someone else would now do what had to be done.

The reconneers began to turn away but Sashia begged them to wait. She had remembered something important. Running she retrieved Twing from the ward, clutching him to her chest and whispered, "I promise, I will never let *you* go." Pressing his heavy hand gently on her shoulder, Guille drew her to the exit.

Once alone, the doctor quickly introduced oxygen enriched XO blood to Mei's body. Then, guided by a live radiological scan of the heart, she inserted nodes straight into the still organ, kick started, and set up a continuous infusion. Late in the night, with Mei set up and covered up, the doctor drove the buggy through the mezzanine and out to Forbes Park and onward to the still empty Primrose Clinic.

There the doctor laid the girl on a shallow ledge of a hot spring, and resting her head on a cushion, she left Mei comfortably there, while she went to gather herbs.

Among other innovations in the parks, especially genecrafted plants provided medications in prescribed concentrations. Conveniently located around Rim, for general use, were willow trees with aspirin in the sap and tiny spatulas for people to dip in and sip. There were sweet violet flowers containing antiseptic in their petals conveniently to rub onto wounds, and there was wild honey, also with enhanced antiseptic properties to smear on cuts.

FayWell, ever readily to hand, was the first source of information they'd all refer to for what to use. Failing that, they'd check with a doctor. This self-service culture, apart from being extremely economical, was highly therapeutic, for it added to everyone's feeling of self.

O'Malley made haste, soon to return to her patient, immediately caressing Mei's brow. She did not speak but used thought, "You know you can hear me. I can hear you. But if you cannot speak, you can blink to acknowledge me."

Dr O'Malley's telepathy was a gift she hardly comprehended or relied on. In everyday chat, as FayWell had expressed, it was hard enough for anyone to know what was really being said, let alone thought. Was she really hearing thoughts – right now? Or was it her imagination, or simply her thinking wishfully? She'd brought Mei there, discreetly, not wanting to raise anyone's hopes in vain. Perhaps she was doing that to herself. She'd not shown her feelings until now, not feeling a part of anyone's group.

The hours passed before the doctor allowed herself to accept the inevitable. She gazed on the sweet lifeless face that living had scarred, as it had done the spirit of this woman not long from childhood. The doctor held her close then, and stroked her hair before letting her limp body slip from her.

And indeed, so many tears cascaded down Dr O'Malley's cheeks that they rippled the still water.

~*~

36

As we approached the far side of the Moon, through the window execs on the Command Bridge could see that the enemy carrier had already retreated, in fact, it was heading out so fast that its Mantas were struggling to get back to it. At one point we were sure of seeing two vessels skulking in the distance, but then we were back to seeing just the same very large one again. That mother ship appeared to advance but never came closer.

"Maybe it just got bigger," the Strategic Planning Officer mused. Then, it disappeared.

"Set trajectory to Ecstasy anchorage. TURN ONTO TRAJECTORY," the Commander ordered. His brief was to defend Ecstasy and the Questor task force, not engage the enemy.

Some hours later the control screen displayed, NO ENEMY SIGHTED.

"STAND DOWN BATTLE STATIONS," the Commander ordered, "FULL SPEED AHEAD."

Without hesitation he conferred with UNRO chiefs. The decision made was to order up rapid replacements of military ordnance before proceeding, and meanwhile anchor off Ecstasy. Structural repairs would be made en route. If the enemy had intended to delay our departure they had succeeded in some small measure – only by three days. Also, for the first time since hostilities began, the Commander convened the Mission Board to appraise us on those developments.

What I felt about developments over the past few days was overwhelmingly that the Bering would ensure our safety in doing whatever we had to do out in space. Out there, our reconneers would continue to engineer solutions to DeepStorm's wrath. It was early days yet but my confidence in everyone was on the up. They'd all performed excellently. And the Commander had proved himself more solid than any Earth rock.

It was with heavy hearts that the Mission Board met to hear the Commander's update and for the essential purpose of conferring on our route. We were headed for Mars, where the stocking of the parks would still be completed – despite the tragic loss of Mei – and where all human fitters would disembark. There was no need for Dr O'Malley to announce the fate of the biologist, the Commander and I already having learnt that she'd passed away. "I think," the doctor's voice was so weak it was hard to hear, "a minute's silence would be appropriate."

"We might then guard our own thoughts privately," I added, feeling the Commander's agreement.

As to the military business at hand, the Commander was brief. On other matters, our course objectives were already known to him and to Dr O'Malley. They were also fully aware that getting out there was where all our efforts would be concentrated over the next few months. Beyond this, all information was strictly on a need-to-know basis. Our destination was so highly classified that only I, DelMonte, Matri and my UNNDC chief, had that intelligence. Those were our orders.

As to my report to UNNDC, the Commander was aware only of my classified despatch without being privy to the content. So that, merely out of courtesy, I now confided to him, and naturally to Dr O'Malley, that we'd succeeded – with Mei's invaluable lead technically – in correlating the worst *Cretaceous* occurrences with what might now have transpired with DeepStorm. And, that we were working on solutions for that, at least. We were on the right track. His only response, which he put firmly but sincerely, was, "It's your mission." I guess he had returned the confidence I'd shown in him.

At that point Dr O'Malley looked askance at a screen view of the whole task force, seeing all three ships, and she invited our view, "Our transport?" I shrugged and nodded, to which she shook her head and almost whispered, "Our destination!" The Commander took her seriously but was bemused. I was less in doubt.

I was then alerted to Steve's holoe message to UNNDC, painstakingly drafted by the two of us. Excusing myself, intent on leaving the room, the Commander and the doctor left instead.

Steve was not aware that, in UNNDC's eyes, he was speaking merely as a specialist now and not as someone intricately involved. "Steve Nord here. I have to correct perceptions about our oil findings. Oil reservoirs are indeed fragile. But the *natural* seepages we're talking about are of an order of magnitude far greater than anything there's been with accidents, in oilfield exploration and in production. The BP oil spill of 2010, in the Gulf of Mexico, was miniscule by comparison. The latest one, recently in Egypt, although also small, will give some idea of how devastatingly uncontrollable natural ruptures will be.

"I know this isn't what you'd all expect to hear," Steve swallowed hard, "and certainly not from myself, as a Greenpeace activist." What he and I had fought tooth and nail over went so against everything he stood for – and yet he also kept coming around to the same inescapable answer, "It's not oil *operators* that have to *get out*. It's all the *oil* that has to *get out*.

"To stop DeepStorm from ripping open rock formations, and unleashing millions of tons of oil onto our land and oceans, we have to do a pre-emptive clean up job. We *must empty* all reservoirs – drill them all out – immediately, and responsibly!"

During our delay, all task force check procedures had been updated, so that, late in the evening of the third day, control screens displayed, ALL CHECKED AND CLEAR.   FayWell, attired in her white uniform, reported smartly, "Commander, Questor is clear to get underway."

"Captains, RAISE ANCHOR. TURN ONTO TRAJECTORY," came the Commander's order.

Control screens immediately displayed, LOCKED ON TRAJECTORY.

Whereupon he ordered, "FULL SPEED AHEAD." The no-fly zone was still in force for Ecstasy anchorage, so there was no send-off flotilla.

"We're on our way," exuding full confidence, the man in absolute control of the moment went on the air to all in the Questor task force. "You can view the Moon and Earth slipping behind us now." The vessels were oriented sideways to the Sun, for the ice shields to give optimum protection from charged particles in the solar wind and to collect that fuel for propulsion.

I was later alerted to answers conveyed by UNNDC. "So you're saying, carry on in Alaska?" The Greenpeace representative was guarded and sought to make that message absolutely clear. He'd meanwhile conferred on coms with colleagues, to reach a rapid consensus from the reports received. Their concern always was for the greater good of the planet – and nature spoiling it with black oil could not be allowed to happen.

"Nothing is proven.   Nevertheless there are prospects of very large reservoirs offshore Antarctica," the Shell representative was more direct. "Are you advocating that exploration and production commence there?"

With the task force slowly building speed, my attention was then drawn to a UN news flash, *"...the Questor mission is heading out now. They will study, from wherever they go, everything that's happening to our Solar System with DeepStorm..."*

The Sævrama Channel showed the ships, their broad comet-tails trailing off. Jude Nade spoke earnestly and sounded a little choked, *"Come back safely."*

The Commander went on the air again, this time publicly, to Ecstasy as well as to the whole of the UN. No one, anywhere, was doing anything that could be left in order to watch intently the man who was taking the Near Earth Territories away. As for him, his mind was split two ways – the one focused on the space ahead, the other resting on the image of a certain reporter so far back now.

"The DeepStorm Questor mission is on its way," he intoned. Those in Ecstasy, we salute you and thank you for your kind hospitality. Those at the UN, and peoples of the World, we are committed to finding answers and will not let you down."

He addressed the First Officer next, a broad smile on his and then all our faces, *"Time to catch the wind."*

The ships spread out, each ejecting a faint jet from the bow that shot out five kilometres, like a lizard's tongue. One by one, these splashed outwards in all directions to form a translucent dish eight km across, at first limp but soon filled out. The spectacle filled the big window on the Bridge, dazzling everyone.

Jude gave a commentary on that. *"Transmaterialising parasails."* There was hesitant excitement in her voice, *"The light display, there, is much the same as the northern lights. Charged particles are interacting with the sail membranes to create those brilliant arches and streams. The sparkler effect is where tiny bolides are splashing through."*

This was the first time the sails had ever been deployed on ships this large. It was the first show of its kind.

The First Officer switched the big window's view, now seeing ahead of the parasail. "We have optics on the other side," he explained.

While everyone watched, spellbound, I retreated to give UNNDC our parting message from Ecstasy anchorage. "In our view – with no way of knowing with any certainty where geoshifts will trigger quakes – oil exploration and production, to authorised earthquake proof storage above or below ground, must be licensed and even encouraged – *with immediate effect* – and as a matter of *urgency*.

"To be clear, this most vitally includes Areas of Outstanding Natural Beauty (AONBs), UNESCO World Heritage List sites and Nature Reserves worldwide. And, yes, this includes the whole of Antarctica. And, accordingly, the UN must put into International Law and hold all parties accountable – that, *overriding international and national statutes in particular addressing employment opportunity,* the very highest internationally recognised skill levels and standards of safety for life and environment, must at all times be engaged in the exploration and production, without exception, of all hazardous products such as fossil fuels."

I expected no response as we set sail on the outward tack of our journey in space. And certainly there had been no hint of a reprimand coming my way for the unauthorised research I'd instigated. "Strange," I thought, "not even a comment on my conduct. And nothing more on our objectives..." My mind wandered, "As if that's superfluous to our simply being out there, a Territory of fiman travellers in deep space..." And it struck me then that we would be akin to those ancient creatures, drifting away on rafts from mighty troubles towards we knew not what...

Oblivious of that gravitas, but most fittingly at this time, there was an auspicious comment from the Ecstasy Corporation Chief Executive. *"That is one spectacular exit. Well done. From all of us here we wish all of you who sail in our defence, God speed. Our hopes and prayers go with you on this most noble of missions. Thank you."*

King William also relayed a brief message, speaking as a fellow in arms as much as head of the Commonwealth of Nations, Queen Catherine radiant in support at his side, *"Know that we are with you, all of us in the World are, to do what only you can bravely do. God speed."*

The UN also responded, Sustra Matri speaking. *"A beautiful sight. Magnificent. Seek, find, discover, our most valiant fellows, bring an end to our terrible ordeals. Our earnest prayers are to welcome you back to an Earth of everlasting peace and happiness."*

"The no-fly zone is removed," Bering's Navigation Officer reported.

"Thank you," Ecstasy Navigation Control acknowledged. "God speed."

~*~

Geological Timescales

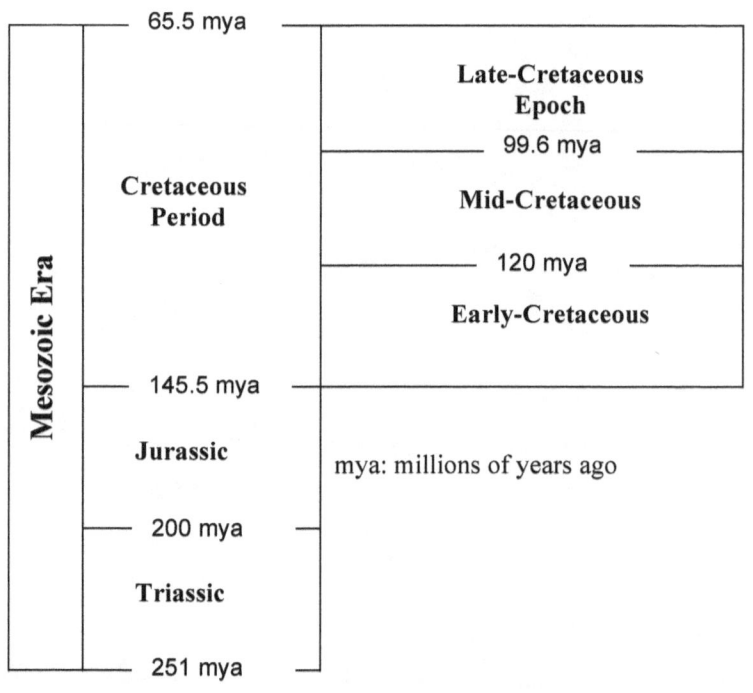

Glossary

(Author's terms or usage in DeepStorm OutTack)
(Conversion: 1km = 0.6214 miles, 1m = 3.281 ft)
Terms : * Copyright © 2012 by George S Boughton/DeepStorm Novels
in *italic* relate to the Cretaceous/other prehistoric periods

AA | Artificial Attendant – an AI engaged in hospitality e.g. waitress, receptionist, store cashier, guide, flight attendant, physio (p110...)

Abelisaur | bipedal theropod dinosaur, carnivore, like T-Rex – in Patagonia (southern South America) part of Antarctralasia, over 7m long (p247)

AEB | Brazilian Space Agency – a civilian authority (p182)

AI | Artificial Intelligence – a neurocomputer with human-like appearance, interfacing with humans, and logic to operate equipment/systems (p10...)

Allosauridae | bipedal theropod dinosaur, carnivore, like T-Rex – allosaurus approx 8.5m long (p227, 228, 234, 247)

Ameurasia | geographical area joining (by varying land bridges) North America, Europe and Asia – separated from the Southern Hemisphere (including India) by the Tethys Sea (p61...)

Ammonite | free-swimming / free-floating marine invertebrate mollusc (shellfish) related to squid & octopus – up to 2m in diameter (p227, 247)

Ankylosaur | armoured quadruped dinosaur, herbivore, the largest having a huge bony tail club – over 6m long & as tall as an average thoroughbred horse 1.6m to the withers/shoulder blades (p259, 291)

Antarctopeltae | medium-sized ankylosaur of Antarctralasia – approx 4m long (p259)

Antarctralasia | geographical area joining Antarctica, Australasia and Patagonia (at various times, connected with the rest of South America) (p118...)

AquaScabbard | canon that fired a continuous shaft of charged-water-shards – which would freeze &, at speeds designed for it, tear into & rip open hulls, screens & controls with also maiming/killing crew (p321)

Arabian Gulf | the continuation of the Tethys Sea between the Taklamakan basin & the Mediterranean Sea (p274)

Archaeopteryx | an early raven-sized gliding dromaeosaurid (p149, 189)

Armstrong Effect * | the treatment of the Caribbean continental plate, with the Yucatan Peninsula (Mexico) just by it, as a keystone at the apex of the North American and South American plates – in the asteroid impact that blasted out the Chicxulub crater and, by triggering a geoshift, caused worldwide devastation (p162, 222, 308)

ASC | Australian Space Commission – a government agency (p182, 218)

ASEAN | Association of Southeast Asian Nations (Brunei Darussalam, Cambodia, Indonesia, Laos, Malaysia, Burma/Myanmar, Philippines,

Singapore, Thailand, Vietnam) – 2010 population 600 million, GDP $1.8 trillion (p64)

AstBelt | Asteroid Belt – an extremely thinly distributed collection of asteroids surrounding the orbit of Mars with half the overall mass in just 4 of these (Ceres, 4 Vesta, 2 Pallas, and 10 Hygiea) (p33…)

Asteroid | see Bolides & AstBelt

AU | Astronomical Unit – measured as the mean distance (roughly) from Sun to Earth (p62, see also KAU & mAU)

Aurora borealis | display of light, best seen in polar regions, naturally caused by the collision of energetic charged particles with atoms high up in the thermosphere (p110)

Avebury | one of two terraformed spaceliners in the DeepStorm Questor task force – complement: 2,000 young fimans (just a few human executive officers – execs) (p70…)

Axle | ZeroG core section of spaceliner Avebury – housing: shipboard systems, propulsion, parasails, HVAC, water tanks, TonicTime (p271…)

Bering | terraformed US Navy battle-carrier, escort for the DeepStorm Questor task force – complement: 6,500 young fimans (just a few human executive officers) & ordnance of guns, fighting craft, missiles (p87…)

Beringia | ice free land bridge between Alaska and Siberia – approx 1,600 km wide (p144, 291)

Biombot | bionic communications nanobot (cellphone) implant (p7…)

Birds | the Cretaceous world the Questor reconneers revealed was important in large part because of the birds (p5, 8, 37, 105, 132, 140-2, 145, 147, 149, 159, 164, 188, 191-2, 208-9, 260, 291, 302, 311, & see Mundussaur)

BoBo | name of ISWA pilots for a boulder-bolide – as small as a coconut & as big as a van (p29…)

BoCracker | BoBo laser defence system – firing a conical beam focused on the target (p71…)

Bolides | general term for hazardous objects in space – e.g. meteoroids, comets, asteroids, planetesimals & even manmade space junk (p21…)

BoStorm | shower of BoBos (p63, 83, 241, 244, 277, 278)

Boxing Day | the day after Christmas (now a holiday) in UK, Australia & New Zealand – origin: possibly from post-Roman times when servants received a boxed gift the day after Christmas (p1, 281, 304, 312)

Brachiosaur | quadruped long necked sauropod dinosaur, herbivore – up to 26 m long & browsing up to 9 m off the ground (p146, 147, 227, 247)

Brazil | Federative Republic of Brazil – a sovereign state, 2010 population 191 million, GDP $2.0 trillion (p27, 29)

Britain | (p34 & see UK)

Caribbean Sea | continuation, with the Gulf of Mexico, of the Tethys Sea floor between the Atlantic Ocean and the Pacific Ocean

Ceratopsian | horned, beaked and neck frilled quadruped dinosaur, herbivore – up to 9m long (p21, 144, 147, 309)

Chicxulub crater | depression blasted out by an asteroid 65.5 million years ago in the submerged Yucatan Peninsula, Mexico (p82, 88, 111, 117, 162, 293, 307, 310)

China | People's Republic of China – a sovereign state, (22 provinces, 5 autonomous regions, 4 directly administered municipalities, 2 highly autonomous special administrative regions) 2010 population 1.3 billion, GDP $5.9 trillion (p1, 6, 32, 34, 40, 57, 60, 64, 92, 108, 110, 113, 115, 144, 176, 182, 214, 244, 291)

Chronic Natural Correction | prolonged condition of one or more recurring Natural Corrections (p234, 254, 310)

Clarence Park | terraces landscaped for recreation & cultivated for terra-farming in spaceliner Lascaux (p272)

Climate Change | change in weather patterns of significantly long duration (p10...)

Climate Creep | subtle but sustained change in climate manifested over millions of years by the Earth aging and the Moon receding (p192, 260)

CME | Coronal Mass Ejection – a huge burst of gas and electromagnetic radiation several hours long shot from the Sun which can deform the Earth's magnetosphere & cause it to release terawatts of power – endangering near Earth facilities & power grids on the ground (p63)

CNSA | China National Space Agency – a government agency (p108, 182)

Coms | communications (p72...)

Continental drift | in theory the movement of continental plates relative to each other, widely considered to be a gradual process (notwithstanding flood basalt eruptions, supervolcanoes & geoshifts) of separation, crashing, and subduction (p204, 228, 229, 292)

Coldhouse climate | see Icehouse Climate

Command Bridge | the Commander's bridge (**Bridge** in short) aboard the Bering (p196...)

Commonwealth of Nations (or the **Commonwealth**) | an expanding intergovernmental organisation of sovereign states (of the former British Empire with others added e.g. Mozambique and Rwanda) that accept English for Commonwealth communication and cooperate to promote democracy, human rights, good governance, the rule of law, individual liberty, egalitarianism, free trade, multilateralism, and world peace – 2005 population 2.1 billion, 2009 GDP $9.8 trillion (p34, 60, 336)

Construction Exclusion Zone | area of land where construction for human occupation/work is prohibited for reasons of personal safety (p1, 57, 313)

Confuciusornis | crow-sized dromaeosaurid, closer to microraptor than archaeopteryx, with a beak (p189)

Cosmic Weather | conditions in space such as BoStorms and CMEs, monitored by ISWA (p242, 305)

Cretaceous | geological period in time (see Geological Timescales) – from the Latin "creta" for chalk, the period is particularly associated with when the chalk hills of England & France were created (p9... & see Late-Cretaceous)

CSA | Canadian Space Agency – a government agency (p182)

Cybsilorg | AI with neurocomputer logic, crafted into the siliceous tissue of plants, that grows and propagates in ways of its own choosing (p118)

Deccan Traps | 2 km high plateau covering much of Western India – created by intermittent flood basalt eruptions over an 8 million year period straddling the close of the Late-Cretaceous epoch (p16, 111, 113, 117, 132, 191, 259, 260, 310)

DeepStorm | an interstellar Gwave phenomenon threatening Earth (p61...)

DeepStorm OutTack * | book title – the work of fiction in a novel exploring the sciences of: humankind's migrations to space, escalating natural disasters on Earth & parallels with the extinction of dinosaurs

DeepStorm Questor * | mission task force – manned primarily by fimans assigned to researching DeepStorm close-to in interplanetary space (p137)

Dinosaur | terrestrial archosaurian reptile with limbs held erect beneath the body – including birds but excluding other reptiles e.g. crocodiles, turtles, ichthyosaurs, mosasaurs, plesiosaurs, pterosaurs (p1...)

D-Notice | Disclosure Notice or gag rule (p19, 172)

DoomNet Syndrome | malaise in social networking at risk of critically dispiriting netizens & incapacitating communities (p103, 139, 173, 306)

Dromaeosaurus / Dromaeosaurid | flightless running bird-like theropod dinosaur – with wings, jaw of teeth, long bony tail, grasping hands, sickle-shaped claw on each hind-foot, generally wolf sized but some as tall as a man (p144, 148, 208, 309)

EarthG | Earth gravity – the pull of gravity experienced on Earth (p24)

Ecstasy | the first manned territory on the Moon – developed as a collection of colonies of UN member states working in partnership with one another, with the aim of exploring and exploiting resources for upside construction as well as for studies of the universe (p32)

EcstasyG | Ecstasy gravity – the pull of gravity experienced in Ecstasy facilities, made possible using teutronium flooring, half that of EarthG and the standard for all territories and transport upside (except just selectively in the Near Earth Territories) (p69, 196, 238, 246, 271, 282)

ERASE | Earth Risk Assessment Search and Evaluation – a key initiative in combating the effects of DeepStorm (p313)

ESA | European Space Agency – an intergovernmental organisation of the EU headquartered in Paris (p62, 84, 85, 91, 111, 182, 193)

EU | European Union – expanding economic & political union of supra-Mediterranean/Saharan sovereign states, 2010 population 500 million, GDP $16 trillion (p31/60)

Exmorfs | entertainment venue with bars, bistros and discos in SnowVale Park (p245, 256, 251, 253)

Exofiman | humans with an exo (external) skeletal suit, adapted for space operations of long duration (p138, 158, 174, 178, 180)

Fern meadows | the Cretaceous world the Questor reconneers revealed was important in large part because of the fern meadows (p119, 131, 301-2, 307)

Fimans | new breed of hominini, produced in a programme of genecrafting humans for living in space (p47...)

Flood basalt eruption | gigantic eruption or series of eruptions of hotspot basaltic magma (e.g. Deccan Traps eruptions, India) – which occurred at random (rather than gradual) intervals of enhanced activity in the Earth's crust (and in the mantle too possibly) (p16 & see Continental Drift, Deccan Traps, Hotspot)

Forbes Park | terraces landscaped for recreation & cultivated for terra-farming in spaceliner Avebury (p270...)

Gaia | the Earth's living biosphere seen as an individual entity (p5, 7, 39, 46, 118, 212, 213, 287, 302, 303, 310, 311)

Galahad | design of spaceliners developed for the Near Earth Territories (p19, 29, 69, 86, 87, 182)

Galileo | global navigation satellite system of EU-ESA (p128)

GAM | Great AstBelt-Mars divide – area of space between the orbits of Mars and the Asteroid Belt (p65)

GEM | Great Earth-Mars divide – area of space between the orbits of Earth and Mars (p65, 300)

Genecraft | genetically modify a being/organism (p47, 52, 137, 138, 178, 330)

Geoshift * | phenomenon of accelerated continental drift, in which the Earth shape-shifts to accommodate its decaying rotation – endangering regions on Earth with quakes, tsunamis & eruptions (p162, 163, 222, 234, 275, 290-3, 300-1, 308-9, 313, 317, 336)

Global Warming | Climate Change in which the average temperature of the Earth's atmosphere & oceans rises – in so doing it raises sea levels by melting ice sheets (whether from natural or human activity disrupting the oxygen, carbon, water and greenhouse cycles of nature & Gaia) risking a de-terraforming of the planet with extreme weather (p90, 131)

GLONASS | Global Orbiting Navigation Satellite System – Russian Space Forces rival to GPS (p128)

Gobi basin | continuation, in northern and north-western China and southern Mongolia, of the Tethys Sea between the Pacific Ocean and the Taklamakan basin (p144, 274, 291, 308). **Gobi Desert** – is today where the Gobi basin once was (p115)

GPS | Global Positioning System – of USA's Department of Defence (p128)

Gravitational-wave | see Gwave (p61)

Gravity sensor | the means to detect & define gravity contours (p209)

Greenpeace | international non-governmental environmental organization coordinated from Amsterdam, Netherlands, with the goal to "ensure the ability of the Earth to nurture life in all its diversity" and focusing on

Global Warming, deforestation, over fishing, commercial whaling and anti-nuclear issues (p34-5, 38, 41, 48, 162, 188, 229, 275, 317, 334)

Ground zero | area on the ground in the immediate proximity of a calamitous occurrence (p161, 308-9)

Gulf of Mexico | continuation, with the Caribbean Sea, of the Tethys Sea floor between the Atlantic Ocean and the Pacific Ocean (p204, 275, 333)

Gwave | gravitational-wave (or pulsing gravity) predicted by Einstein to emanate from giant stellar entities twirling about each other (p61)

Hadrosaur | duckbilled bipedal ornithopod dinosaur, herbivore – also walked on all fours, kangaroo fashion, in Ameurasia (p144, 291, 302, 309)

Heads-up (display / instrumentation) | display of instrumentation, maps, persons etc, in optical aids such as glasses or visors but also with implants such as biombots (p35, 77, 125, 172, 202, 219-20)

Heather Farm | farm with buildings at Rim end of Forbes Park, in spaceliner Avebury (p299, 316)

Heathland | the Cretaceous world the Questor reconneers revealed was important in large part because of the heathlands (p118-9, 131, 140, 144, 149, 188, 190-1, 302-3, 308-9, 316)

Holoe | videophone hologram communication or to make such (p27...)

Hong Kong SAR (HK) | Hong Kong Special Administrative Region of China – the region's charter of full autonomy was extended indefinitely beyond the original expiry date of 2047, in line with new charters for China's upside colonies (p25...)

Hotspot | volcanic magma chamber, either too remote (e.g. the Galapagos and Hawaiian Islands chains) or too big (e.g. Iceland) to have been produced by the subduction forces of continental drift – by far the largest (e.g. Deccan Traps flood basalt eruptions) to explode or flood across continents, were all either in the tropics or in high latitudes (just outside the tropics, were southwest USA and Karoo South Africa) and swung from being in the northern hemisphere pre-Jurassic to southern hemisphere up to the Late-Cretaceous and then back to northern hemisphere again (p131, 199, 209, 292)

HVAC | heating ventilation and air conditioning (p72, 256, 300)

ice age | colloquial term for glacials, including the Last Glacial Maximum, within the overall Ice Age (p47, 61-2)

Ice Age | time ongoing to this day, from 2.6 million years ago, when an Icehouse Climate has prevailed (p90, 136, 140)

Icehouse Climate | prevailing Ice Age climate, with (as now) fluxes in the average temperature of atmosphere and oceans as well as with polar and alpine ice sheets (p60, 141)

Icegem | gemstone with images frozen in time (p122, 130, 133, 144, 191, 208-9, 235, 247, 253, 275, 300, 309-11)

Ichthyosaur | dolphin like marine reptile – fed on invertebrates & small reptiles & gave birth to live young, up to 4m long (p227, 247)

Iguanodon | bipedal (partly quadruped) dinosaur, herbivore – with large thumb spike, about 10m long (p144, 147-8, 309)

India | Republic of India – a sovereign state, 2010 population 1.2 billion, GDP \$1.6 trillion (p16, 57, 60, 80, 108, 110-5, 120, 182, 228, 244, 247, 260)

InviHundred | extreme event, in which 25 four-man teams competed to race on foot across mountainous terrain (p102…)

ISRO | Indian Space Research Organisation – a government body (p108, 182, 193)

ISWA | International Spaceways Authority – with jurisdiction for the safety of all craft movements upside (p28-9, 58, 108, 193, 242, 245, 266, 312, 316)

JAXA | Japan Aerospace Exploration Agency – a national agency (p182, 193)

KAU | Kilo-AU – 1,000 Astronomical Units (p63)

Kerogen | dark brown / black substance which under immense pressure and heat (buried deep down over the ages) lets off oil and gas – origin: deep orange-brown sludge mixed from matter like spores, pollen & excrement from the rookeries of colossal dinosaur herds (p91, 275)

Kuiper Belt | similar to but hugely bigger than AstBelt – extends from Neptune's orbit (30AU from the Sun) to approx 55AU (p63, 81, 136, 203)

Lascaux | one of two terraformed spaceliners in the DeepStorm Questor task force – complement: 2,000 young fimans (just a few human executive officers – execs) (p69…)

Late-Cretaceous | last epoch in the Cretaceous period (see Geological Timescales) (p6, 88, 112, 119, 132, 140, 142, 144-5, 161, 191, 208, 247, 258, 275, 290, 292)

Leo | terraformed spaceport permanently in orbit around Mars – serving as the rest and recuperation destination for operatives and settlers in MarsG as well as for space travellers (p109)

Lithosphere | the Earths' solid crust and upper mantle beneath it (p204)

Little Ice Age | cold spell in the Icehouse Climate, that took place in the Northern Hemisphere during the sixteenth to nineteenth centuries – contributing to that, the eruption of Mount Tambora (Indonesia) brought about the Year Without a Summer (1815) (p43, 135-6, 172)

LN | LifeNote – health monitoring device that emits: life signs, location, ID/DNA-ID and automatic health check history, for fimans a molecular level implant powered by a transductor, for inventories an imprint powered by tidal pull (on/near Earth) (p95, 160, 168, 207, 271, 283-4, 312)

LS | Life Sign – patch worn on the body for biometric authentication when the person signs for goods and services (p207, 239)

LTA | Lighter-Than-Air – relating to materials in a branch of graphene nanotube technology used in the construction of thermoports, upside-elevators and Earth-atmosphere-craft (p83, 158, 195)

Mag-cable | magnetic cable that an upside-elevator rides partway up & down, between ground spaceport & thermoport (p90, 108, 110, 222)

Manta | an upside fighter craft of the enemy (p318-327, 332)

MarsG | Mars gravity – the pull of gravity experienced on Mars, just over one-third that of EarthG (p109)

Mass Extinction | extinction (i.e. ceasing to exist) of a high proportion of species or families of species – just 5 such extinction events are recognised as having occurred on Earth – End Ordovician, Late Devonian, End Permian, End Triassic, End Cretaceous (p9, 17, 88, 100, 111, 117, 179, 213, 290, 293, 306)

mAU | milli-AU – 1/1,000[th] Astronomical Unit (p267)

Meadowvale | landing platform with EcstasyG at the equator of Forbes Park, in spaceliner Avebury (p271...)

Mediterranean Sea | the continuation of the Tethys Sea floor between the Arabian Gulf and the Atlantic Ocean (p199, 274)

Mesozoic | geological era (see Geological Timescales) of which the Cretaceous period was the last (p164, 198)

Microgravity | see ZeroG (p6, 29, 110, 115, 139)

Microraptor | small, four-winged dromaeosaurid dinosaur – with asymmetrical flight feathers (p148)

Mid-Cretaceous | the middle epoch in the Cretaceous period (see Geological Timescales) (p9, 36, 118-9, 130, 140, 208, 226, 274)

Milky Way Galaxy | barred spiral galaxy of hundreds of billions of stars – our Solar System is 2/3 of the way out from the centre (p62, 82, 179, 306)

MoonG | Moon gravity – the pull of gravity experienced on the Moon, one-sixth that of EarthG (p20)

Mosasaur | marine reptile with body more streamlined than modern monitor lizards – lived in warm shallow seas, gave birth to live young, dieted on seabirds & fish, & fought with sharks, up to 17m long (p5, 228, 232, 247)

MRI | Magnetic Resonance Imaging – widely used in imaging inside people in hospitals & objects in research (p328)

Mundussaur | sparrow sized microraptor dromaeosaurid – with feathered arms & legs, identified by Questor reconneers as cleaner flyers (as opposed to cleaner fish) & forerunners of birds (p149, 189)

Nanobot | robot with microscopic scale components – widely used in medical procedures & in advanced classified weaponry (p7, 53, 118, 137, 252, 279-80, 317, 329)

NASA | National Aeronautics and Space Administration – an executive branch agency of the USA government (p62, 85, 111, 131, 182, 193, 204)

Natural Correction | occurrence so powerfully abrupt in redefining the landscape of organisms, as to override Natural Selection (p37, 113, 117, 133, 163, 228, 234, 254, 260, 292, 310 & see Chronic Natural Selection)

Natural Selection | term and concept of English naturalist Charles Darwin (UK) – basically the suiting of organisms to environments, in the strength of characteristics (passed on genetically), over those of competitors (p6, 8-9, 37, 112, 117, 192, 208, 234, 260, 287, 303, 310)

Near Earth Territories * | purpose-built facilities terraformed for generations of fimans to take up permanent residence upside – initially anchored in close proximity to Earth (p6, 19, 25-6, 29, 40, 44-6, 56, 60, 65, 69-70, 86-7, 109, 138, 174, 176, 182, 193, 213, 251, 281, 335)

NEO | Near-Earth Object – any object on a path or orbit closer than 1.3 AU to Earth's orbit (p28-30, 45, 61, 63, 81, 88, 117, 141, 203-4, 293)

Northern lights | see aurora borealis (p29, 335)

Nursery | nesting ground of reptiles, including dinosaurs (p132, 147, 192, 272, 275 see also rookery)

Obliquity | tilt in a planet's rotation (p63, 81, 113)

Oort Cloud | cloud of billions of comets believed to surround the Solar System – starting at 50 KAU (almost a light year) from the Sun (a quarter of the distance to the nearest star) (p62-3)

Oviraptor | small theropod dinosaur – with feathery down, long clawed arms, & hatched its young bird-like (p148)

Paleo | prehistoric (e.g. p6 paleogeography, p7 paleobotanical, p11 paleoclimatology, p14 paleo-marine, p22 paleobiogeography)

Phytolith | mineral secretion of plants (p119)

Plesiosaur | aquatic carnivorous reptile with 4 flippers – most varieties with long neck & short tail, & spent most of the time in water, averaging from 3 to 20m long (p5, 227, 247)

PNR | Point of No Return (p136, 317, 324)

Polar regions | from the North Pole south to the timberline in Ameurasia, and all of Antarctralasia (p130, 162)

Polar Warming | Climate Change in which the temperature of the Earth's atmosphere and oceans rises at the poles and, as with Global Warming, raises sea levels by melting ice sheets there – but risking a de-terraforming of the planet (for crops) with extremes of both cloud cover and calm (p131, 190, 198-9, 303)

Primrose Clinic | clinic with EcstasyG at the equator of Forbes Park, in spaceliner Avebury (p299, 301, 330)

Pterodactyl | by the popular name (correctly pterodactylus) a relatively small pterosaur – with wingspan of about 1.5 m (p227)

Pterosaur | flying reptile with jaw and wings of skin membrane – quadruped on the ground, with varieties that mostly had teeth, no fur and were largely ocean going (p5, 147-9, 188-91, 227-8, 247, 260, 308)

Rafts | the Cretaceous world the Questor reconneers revealed was important in large part because of the mats of vegetation/rafts on the oceans (p227, 234, 247-8, 259, 293, 303, 308, 336)

Raptor | Present day – a naturalist's term for a bird of prey

Raptor | Prehistoric – informal for a dinosaur of the family dromaeosauridae (while in films short for velacoraptor) (p11, 17, 126, 148)

Ratite | flightless running bird (p140, 192)

Reconneer | fiman trained as a reconnoitring scientist (p54...)

Redundancy | inbuilt backup to a system or operation in the event of component/constituent failure (p86, 241)

Rim | hull wall EarthG area of spaceliner Avebury (p271... also 45, 265)

Rookery **(rookeries)** | see *nursery* (p274, 291-2, 309)

Roscosmos | Russian Federal Space Agency – a government agency (p182, 193)

Russia (Russian) | A sovereign state (83 federal subjects) – 2010 population 143 million, GDP $1.5 trillion (24, 34, 90, 182, 274)

Sævrama (and Sævrama Channel) * | media channel covering the wild world, increasingly natural events & especially DeepStorm (p32...)

Sauropod | any of several long-necked long-tailed quadruped (four-legged) (plant-eating) dinosaurs, herbivore – with a tiny head and massive body, which included brachiosaurs and titanosaurs (p247)

Shwift * | like jet-skis to look at, these were the fastest racers yet deployed in space (p268, 270, 273, 322, 325)

Silverworm | imprint on the brain's temporal lobe for enhancing the acuity of sight as well as short-term memory (p53, 93, 122, 125, 133)

Sinornithosaurus | small dromaeosaurid with bird-like shoulders for flapping (p148)

SnowVale Park | areas landscaped for recreation and cultivated for terra-farming in the Ecstasy Moon base (p236, 244, 250, 258, 274, 304, 307)

Soho | one of the districts at Rim, in spaceliner Avebury (p283, 303, 316, 319)

Soho Clinic | an EarthG clinic at Rim, in spaceliner Avebury (p328)

Solar System | the Sun orbited by four inner rocky planets (Mercury, Venus, Earth and Mars) and outer planets (Jupiter, Saturn, Uranus and Neptune) (p62, 106, 136, 174, 179, 203, 244, 335)

Spaceport | ground facility for launching and landing Earth-atmosphere craft (p39, 65, 77, 83-4, 90, 108-9, 195, 206, 218, 220, 221)

SPS | Space Positioning System – extension to GPS, GLONASS, Galileo - (p128, 170)

Subduction | process in continental drift by which a continental plate forces a colliding one to sink under it, into the Earth's mantle, and in that zone the heat of friction fuels localised volcanic activity (p204, 292)

Supervolcano | volcano with a volume of ejecta greater than 1,000 cubic kilometres, which occurs when a hotspot builds up magma in impassable rock formations until it bursts through super explosively – known examples : Yellowstone, and Vales Caldera USA, Lake Toba Indonesia, Taupo New Zealand and Aira Caldera Japan (p5, 21, 63, 83, 143, 161, 179, 198, 292, 307) a

Taklamakan basin | continuation, in China, of the Tethys Sea between the Gobi basin and the Arabian Gulf (p144, 274, 275, 291, 308). **Taklamakan Desert** – is today where the Taklamakan basin once was (p115)

Terra Engineer | engineer qualified in the science of terraforming (p263-4)

Terraccommodate | to provide terraformed conditions/housing (p86-7, 138, 182, 284)

Terra-farming | activity of farming on terraformed land (p256)

Terraform | make an environment/land habitable for Earth life forms (p6…)

Terra-sphere | self-contained terraformed habitat (p8, 39, 65, 83, 138, 182)

Tethys Sea | body of water that separated Ameurasia in the Northern Hemisphere from the Southern Hemisphere including India – flowing from Pacific to Pacific through the Gobi basin, Taklamakan basin, Arabian Gulf, Mediterranean Sea, Caribbean Sea and Gulf of Mexico (p91, 115, 120, 144, 161, 192, 199, 274-5, 308)

Teutronium | high gravity neutron material used in the construction of floorings to simulate EcstasyG everywhere upside (except selectively in the Near Earth Territories) (p51, 69, 110, 194, 231, 237, 278, 298)

Thermoport | high altitude floating spaceport located 120 km up in the thermosphere, over a ground spaceport – constructed of LTA graphene nanotubes (p83, 86, 90, 108, 110, 138, 191, 199, 218, 223, 300, 324)

Theropod | primarily a dinosaur carnivore with long legs, short forearms and massive head – included tyrannosaurs, abelisaurs, dromaeosaurs and allosauridae (p144-5, 189, 247)

Titanosaur | quadruped long necked sauropod dinosaur, herbivore – up to 30m long (p247, 259, 275)

TonicTime | ZeroG entertainment complex with bars, cafés, movies, disco, fitness centre and such, located in spaceliner Avebury at Axle (p271…)

Transantarctic Hills | the highlands when the Transantarctic Mountain Range began to uplift (p131, 248, 259)

Transantarctic Mountain Range | mountain range stretching from the Ross Sea to the Weddell Sea the entire length of Antarctica, 3,500 km – which uplifted beginning around 65 million years ago (p90, 163)

Transductor | implant in the body that cyborg fashion taps the body's electrochemical energy to energise devices there (p51, 95, 125, 209)

Transmaterialise materialising of objects on command, if desired with transferring them from one place to another (p239, 335)

Twister | short for Eurofighter T9 Twister – an upside fighter craft on the battle-carrier Bering (p182, 316-327)

Tyrannosaur (T-Rex) | bipedal theropod dinosaur, carnivore – with massive skull balanced by long heavy tail, very small forearms, and a coat of down/proto-feathers – related to dromaeosaurs, T-Rex up to 12.8m long (p144, 227)

UK | United Kingdom of Great Britain & Northern Ireland – a sovereign state (comprising England, Northern Ireland, Scotland, Wales), with EU & Commonwealth of Nations memberships, 2010 population 63 million, GDP $2.3 trillion (p19, 34, 39, 56, 60, 90, 158, 175, 182, 188, 244-5, 274)

UN F-Academy | college specialised in training and assessing fimans for their roles upside (p33, 36, 47, 74, 78, 102-3, 123, 128, 187, 194)

UN Peacekeeping HQ | arm of the UN charged with undertaking peacekeeping operations (p30)

UN Security Council | principal organ of the UN charged with the maintenance of international peace & security – by charter requiring the passing of resolutions by permanent and non-permanent members to establish peacekeeping operations, impose international sanctions and take military action (p6, 19, 29-30, 43, 57, 60, 80, 85, 134, 172, 183, 199, 313)

UNASUR | Union of South American Nations – an intergovernmental union of sovereign states (Argentina, Bolivia, Brazil, Chile, Colombia, Ecuador, Guyana, Paraguay, Peru, Suriname, Uruguay, Venezuela) (p64, 139, 182)

UNNDC | UN Natural Defences Committee – a permanent agency of the UN charged with anticipating the events and mitigating the effects of natural disasters Worldwide with DeepStorm – primarily in the areas of early warning systems, Construction Exclusion Zones, rapid evacuation, aid and temporary shelter, and reconstruction (p29...)

UNSDO | UN Strategy Development Organisation – a permanent agency of the UN Security Council (p6, 19, 29, 85-6)

UNRO | UN Rapprochement Organisation (successor in the same role as NATO) – the organisation coordinates the engagement of armed forces, of Security Council members (p29, 44, 50, 158, 316, 319, 323, 332)

Upside | the old World War II expression fighter pilots used for action off the ground, now referring to anywhere up in space (off Earth), including thermoports (p6...)

Upside Elevator Corporation (USEC) | worldwide transport network of LTA upside-elevators connecting ground spaceports with thermoports (p90, 108, 110, 218, 220, 245, 267)

USA | United States of America – a sovereign state (50 states + 1 federal district), 2010 population 312 million, GDP $14.6 trillion (p1, 43, 56, 59-60, 85, 87, 90, 174, 182, 244, 251, 294, 305)

Velacoraptor | bipedal feathered dromaeosaurid theropod dinosaur, carnivore – with long stiffened tail and enlarged sickle-shaped claw on each hind-foot, up to 2m long (p11)

Western Interior Seaway | body of water that inundated various areas in the central latitudes of North America and at different stages connected to one or both of the Gulf of Mexico and the shallow Arctic Ocean (p162, 275, 291, 307)

WHO | World Health Organisation – public health arm of the UN (p37, 141)

WOMB | World Organisation for Maintaining the Biosphere – an agency of the UN (p9, 37, 43, 58)

World | the Earth and colonies in space (p28...)

Xo-type blood refined plasma (p137)

ZeroG | zero gravity or microgravity (p29, 100, 138, 174, 178, 271, 283)

Other 2013-14 GBP Publications   (See full reviews/interviews at www.gbpublishing.org)

isbn 9780957672864

Sci-Fi and sex on a trip to die for

Driven by future technology a round-the-world trip transports Ruth and Pearce to unspoken secret fantasies until...

Nothing and no one can be trusted. As readers follow their descent deeper into danger and dementia, they must address the snarled demand: "Entertain me!"

Science fiction has never been this sexy or fun – or scary.

Imagine an adult-only Hitchhiker's Guide to the Galaxy...

Seafaring
The Full Story

isbn 9780957672826

Times Literary Supplement: "*His book is genuine sea salt...warm colours of Mr Shoesmith's pictures accord well with the romantic story*" of days before steamships

John O'London Weekly: "*An excellent book*"

Lloyds List & Shipping Gazette: "*one of the best books on life at sea that have been published for many a day*"

The Spectator: "*recalls emotions* [on sea-life] *that have fleeted from the minds of most*"

The Traveller's Gazette, Thomas Cook: "*All will read the pages of 'Seafaring' with unalloyed pleasure*"

Blue Peter Journal, AT Stewart Commander Royal Navy: "*This book is stamped with the personality of a thorough seaman, the sea-breezes [and chanties] stir in its pages*"

isbn 9780957297050

A world where nothing is as it seems

ForeWord Reviews Book Of The Year 2013 Finalist, Horror Category

Vitina Molgaard, Horror Novel Reviews: This story "*needs to be read to even begin to grasp Ritchie's vision*" His "*alternate worlds... may throw you for an entertaining loop.*"

Rebbie Reviews: House of Pigs will "*horrify you with some really gritty and gory events... I love the imagery and the pace.*"